SUTTON

J.R. Moehringer, winner of the Pulitzer Prize for feature writing in 2000, is a former national correspondent for the *Los Angeles Times*. Author of the bestselling memoir, *The Tender Bar*, he is also the co-author of *Open* by Andre Agassi.

ALSO BY J.R. MOEHRINGER

The Tender Bar
Open

SUTTON

J.R. MOEHRINGER

———

blue door

Blue Door
An imprint of HarperCollins*Publishers*
77–85 Fulham Palace Road,
Hammersmith, London W6 8JB

This paperback edition 2013
1

First published in the USA by Hyperion 2012

Page 11: *On the Road* by Jack Kerouac, Penguin Classics
Pages 11, 208, 316, 357, 366: "Francesca" by Ezra Pound, from *Personae*, copyright © 1926 by Ezra
Pound, © Estate of Ezra Pound. Reprinted by permission of New Directions Publishing Corp. and
Faber and Faber, Ltd.
Page 129: From *Complete Poems of Hart Crane* by Hart Crane, edited by Marc Simon. Copyright 1933,
1958, 1966 by Liveright Publishing Corporation. Copyright © 1986 by Marc Simon. Used by
permission of Liveright Publishing Corporation.
Page 141: From *Soldiers' Pay* by William Faulkner. Copyright 1954 by William Faulkner. Copyright
1926 by Boni & Liveright, Inc. Used by permission of Liveright Publishing Corporation.
Page 197: © Bertolt Brecht, Ralph Manheim and John Willett, *Threepenny Opera* and Methuen Drama,
an imprint of Bloomsbury Publishing Plc.

ISBN: 978-0-00-748993-0

Printed and bound in Great Britain by
Clays Ltd, St Ives plc

Find out more about HarperCollins and the environment at
www.harpercollins.co.uk/green

For Roger and Sloan Barnett,
with love and gratitude

After spending half his life in prison, off and on, Willie Sutton was set free for good on Christmas Eve, 1969. His sudden emergence from Attica Correctional Facility sparked a media frenzy. Newspapers, magazines, television networks, talk shows—everyone wanted an interview with the most elusive and prolific bank robber in American history.

Sutton granted only one. He spent the entire next day with one newspaper reporter and one still photographer, driving around New York City, visiting the scenes of his most famous heists and other points of interest in his remarkable life.

The resulting article, however, was strangely cursory, with several errors—or lies—and few real revelations.

Sadly, Sutton and the reporter and the photographer are all gone, so what happened among them that Christmas, and what happened to Sutton during the preceding sixty-eight years, is anyone's guess.

This book is my guess.

But it's also my wish.

I have said it thrice: What I tell you three times is true.

—LEWIS CARROLL,
THE HUNTING OF THE SNARK

PART ONE

Thus in the beginning all the world was America . . . for no such thing as money was anywhere known.

JOHN LOCKE, *SECOND TREATISE OF GOVERNMENT*

ONE

HE'S WRITING WHEN THEY COME FOR HIM.

He's sitting at his metal desk, bent over a yellow legal pad, talking to himself, and to her—as always, to her. So he doesn't notice them standing at his door. Until they run their batons along the bars.

He looks up, adjusts his large scuffed eyeglasses, the bridge mended many times with Scotch tape. Two guards, side by side, the left one fat and soft and pale, as if made from Crisco, the right one tall and scrawny and with a birthmark like a penny on his right cheek.

Left Guard hitches up his belt. On your feet, Sutton. Admin wants you.

Sutton stands.

Right Guard points his baton. What the? You crying, Sutton?

No sir.

Don't you lie to me, Sutton. I can see you been crying.

Sutton touches his cheek. His fingers come away wet. I didn't know I was crying sir.

Right Guard waves his baton at the legal pad. What's that?

Nothing sir.

He asked you what is it, Left Guard says.

Sutton feels his bum leg starting to buckle. He grits his teeth at the pain. My novel sir.

They look around his book-filled cell. He follows their eyes. It's never good when the guards look around your cell. They can always find something if they have a mind to. They scowl at the books along the floor, the books along the metal cabinet, the books along the cold-water basin. Sutton's is the only cell at Attica filled with copies of Dante, Plato, Shakespeare, Freud. No, they confiscated his Freud. Prisoners aren't allowed to have psychology books. The warden thinks they'll try to hypnotize each other.

Right Guard smirks. He gives Left Guard a nudge—get ready. Novel, eh? What's it about?

Just—you know. Life sir.

What the hell does an old jailbird know about life?

Sutton shrugs. That's true sir. But what does anyone know?

WORD IS LEAKING OUT. BY NOON A DOZEN PRINT REPORTERS have already arrived and they're huddled at the front entrance, stomping their feet, blowing on their hands. One of them says he just heard—snow on the way. Lots of it. Nine inches at least.

They all groan.

Too cold to snow, says the veteran in the group, an old wire service warhorse in suspenders and black orthopedic shoes. He's been with UPI since the Scopes trial. He blows a gob of spit onto the frozen ground and scowls up at the clouds, then at the main guard tower, which looks to some like the new Sleeping Beauty's Castle in Disneyland.

Too cold to stand out *here*, says the reporter from the *New York Post*. He mumbles something disparaging about the warden, who's refused three times to let the media inside the prison. The reporters could be drinking hot coffee right now. They could be using the phones, making last-minute plans for Christmas. Instead the warden is trying to prove some kind of point. Why, they all ask, why?

Because the warden's a prick, says the reporter from *Time*, that's why.

The reporter from *Look* holds his thumb and forefinger an

inch apart. Give a bureaucrat this much power, he says, and watch out. Stand back.

Not just bureaucrats, says the reporter from *The New York Times*. All bosses eventually become fascists. Human nature.

The reporters trade horror stories about their bosses, their editors, the miserable dimwits who gave them this god-awful assignment. There's a brand-new journalistic term, appropriated just this year from the war in Asia, frequently applied to assignments like this, assignments where you wait with the herd, usually outdoors, exposed to the elements, knowing full well you're not going to get anything good, certainly not anything the rest of the herd won't get. The term is *clusterfuck*. Every reporter gets caught in a clusterfuck now and then, it's part of the job, but a clusterfuck on Christmas Eve? Outside Attica Correctional Facility? Not cool, says the reporter from the *Village Voice*. Not cool.

The reporters feel especially hostile toward that boss of all bosses, Governor Nelson Rockefeller. He of the Buddy Holly glasses and the chronic indecision. Governor Hamlet, says the reporter from UPI, smirking at the walls. Is he going to do this thing or not?

He yells at Sleeping Beauty's Castle: Shit or get off the pot, Nelson! Defecate or abdicate!

The reporters nod, grumble, nod. Like the prisoners on the other side of this thirty-foot wall, they grow restless. The prisoners want out, the reporters want in, and both groups blame the Man. Cold, tired, angry, ostracized by society, both groups are close to rioting. Both fail to notice the beautiful moon slowly rising above the prison.

It's full.

THE GUARDS LEAD SUTTON FROM HIS CELL IN D BLOCK through a barred door, down a tunnel and into Attica's central checkpoint—what prisoners call Times Square—which leads to all cell blocks and offices. From Times Square the guards take Sutton down to the deputy warden's office. It's the second time this month that Sutton has been called before the dep. Last week it was to learn that his parole request was denied—a devastating blow. Sutton and his lawyers had been so very confident. They'd won support from prominent judges, discovered loopholes in his convictions, collected letters from doctors vouching that Sutton was close to death. But the three-man parole board simply said no.

The dep is seated at his desk. He doesn't bother looking up. Hello, Willie.

Hello sir.

Looks like we're a go for liftoff.

Sir?

The dep waves a hand over the papers strewn across his desk. These are your walking papers. You're being let out.

Sutton blinks, massages his leg. Let—*out*? By who sir?

The dep looks up, sighs. Head of corrections. Or Rockefeller. Or both. Albany hasn't decided how they want to sell this. The governor, being an ex-banker, isn't sure he wants to put his name on it. But the head of corrections doesn't want to overrule the parole board. Either way it looks like they're letting you walk.

Walk sir? Why sir?

Fuck if I know. Fuck if I care.

When sir?

Tonight. If the phone will stop ringing and reporters will stop hounding me to let them turn my prison into their private rec room. If I can get these goddamn forms filled out.

Sutton stares at the dep. Then at the guards. Are they joking? They look serious.

The dep turns back to his papers. Godspeed, Willie.

The guards walk Sutton down to the prison tailor. Every man released from a New York State prison gets a release suit, a tradition that goes back at least a century. The last time Sutton got measured for a release suit, Calvin Coolidge was president.

Sutton stands before the tailor's three-way mirror. A shock. He hasn't stood before many mirrors in recent years and he can't believe what he sees. That's his round face, that's his slicked gray hair, that's his hated nose—too big, too broad, with different-size nostrils—and that's the same large red bump on his eyelid, mentioned in every police report and FBI flyer since shortly after World War I. But that's not him—it can't be. Sutton has always prided himself on projecting a certain swagger, even in handcuffs. He's always managed to look dapper, suave, even in prison grays. Now, sixty-eight years old, he sees in the three-way mirror that all the swagger, all the dapper and suave are gone. He's a baggy-eyed stick figure. He looks like Felix the Cat. Even the pencil-thin mustache, once a source of pride, looks like the cartoon cat's whiskers.

The tailor stands beside Sutton, wearing a green tape measure around his neck. An old Italian from the Bronx, with two front teeth the size of thimbles, he shakes a handful of buttons and coins in his pocket as he talks.

So they're letting you out, Willie.

Looks like.

How long you been here?

Seventeen years.

How long since you had a new suit of clothes?

Oh. Twenty years. In the old days, when I was flush, I'd get all my suits custom-made. Silk shirts too. D'Andrea Brothers.

He still remembers the address: 587 Fifth Avenue. And the phone number. Murray Hill 5-5332.

Sure, Tailor says, D'Andrea, they did beautiful work. I still got one of their tuxes. Step up on the block.

Sutton steps up, grunts. A suit, he says. Jesus, I thought the next thing I'd be measured for would be a shroud.

I don't do shrouds, Tailor says. No one gets to see your work.

Sutton frowns at the three reflected Tailors. It's not enough to do nice work? People have to see it?

Tailor spreads his tape measure across Sutton's shoulders, down his arm. Show me an artist, he says, who doesn't want praise.

Sutton nods. I used to feel that way about my bank jobs.

Tailor looks at the triptych of reflected Suttons, winks at the middle one. He stretches the tape measure down Sutton's bum leg. Inseam thirty, he announces. Jacket thirty-eight short.

I was a forty reg when I came in this joint. I ought to sue.

Tailor laughs softly, coughs. What color you want, Willie?

Anything but gray.

Black then. I'm glad they're letting you out, Willie. You've paid your debt.

Forgive us our debts, Willie says, as we forgive our debtors.

Tailor crosses himself.

That from your novel? Right Guard asks.

Sutton and Tailor look at each other.

Tailor points a finger gun at Sutton. Merry Christmas, Willie.

Same to you, friend.

Sutton points a finger gun at Tailor, cocks the thumb hammer. Bang.

THE REPORTERS TALK ABOUT SEX AND MONEY AND CURRENT events. Altamont, that freaky concert where those four drugged-out hippies died—who's to blame? Mick Jagger? The Hells Angels? Then they gossip about their more successful colleagues, starting with Norman Mailer. Not only is Mailer running for mayor of New York, but he just got one million dollars to write a book about the moon landing. Mailer—the guy writes history as fiction, fiction as history, and inserts himself into all of it. He plays by his own rules while his rule-bound colleagues get sent to Attica to freeze their balls off. Fuck Mailer, they all agree.

And fuck the moon.

They blow on their hands, pull up their collars, make bets about whether or not the warden will ever be publicly exposed as a cross-dresser. Also, they bet on which will happen first—Sutton walks or Sutton croaks. The reporter from the *New York Post* says he hears Sutton's not just knocking at death's door, he's ringing the bell, wiping his feet on the welcome mat. The reporter from *Newsday* says the artery in Sutton's leg is clogged beyond repair—a doctor who plays racquetball with the reporter's brother-in-law told him so. The reporter from *Look* says he heard from a cop friend in the Bronx that Sutton still has loot stashed all over the city. Prison officials are going to free Sutton and then the cops are going to follow him to the money.

That's one way to solve the budget crisis, says the reporter from the Albany *Times Union*.

The reporters share what they know about Sutton, pass around facts and stories like cold provisions that will have to get them through the night. What they haven't read, or seen on TV, they've heard from their parents and grandparents and great-grandparents. Sutton is the first multigeneration bank robber in history, the first ever to build a lengthy career—it spans four decades. In his heyday Sutton was the face of American crime, one of a handful of men to make the leap from public enemy to folk hero. Smarter than Machine Gun Kelly, saner than Pretty Boy Floyd, more likable than Legs Diamond, more peaceable than Dutch Schultz, more romantic than Bonnie and Clyde, Sutton saw bank robbery as high art and went about it with an artist's single-minded zeal. He believed in study, planning, hard work. And yet he was also creative, an innovator, and like the greatest artists he proved to be a tenacious survivor. He escaped three maximum-security prisons, eluded cops and FBI agents for years. He was Henry Ford by way of John Dillinger—with dashes of Houdini and Picasso and Rasputin. The reporters know all about Sutton's stylish clothes, his impish smile, his love of good books, the glint of devilment in his bright blue eyes, so blue that the FBI once described them in bulletins as *azure*. It's the rare bank robber who moves the FBI to such lyricism.

What the reporters don't know, what they and most Americans have always wanted to know, is whether or not Sutton, who was celebrated for being nonviolent, had anything to do with the brutal gangland murder of Arnold Schuster. A fresh-faced twenty-four-year-old from Brooklyn, a baseball-loving veteran of the Coast Guard, Schuster caught the wrong subway one afternoon and found himself face-to-face with Sutton, the most wanted man in America at the time. Three weeks later Schuster was dead, and his unsolved murder might be the most tantalizing cold case in New York City history. It's definitely the most tantalizing part of the Sutton legend.

THE GUARDS MARCH SUTTON BACK TO ADMIN. A CLERK CUTS him two checks. One for $146, salary for seventeen years at various prison jobs, minus taxes. Another for $40, the cost of a bus ticket to Manhattan. Every released prisoner gets bus fare to Manhattan. Sutton takes the checks—this is really happening. His heart begins to throb. His leg too. They're throbbing at each other, like the male and female leads in an Italian opera.

The guards march him back to his cell. You got fifteen minutes, they tell him, handing him a shopping bag.

He stands in the middle of the cell, his eight-by-six home for the last seventeen years. Is it possible that he won't sleep here tonight? That he'll sleep in a soft bed with clean sheets and a real pillow and no demented souls above and below him howling and cursing and pleading with impotence and fury? The sound of men in cages—nothing can compare. He sets the shopping bag on the desk and carefully packs the manuscript of his novel. Then the spiral notebooks from his creative writing classes. Then his copies of Dante, Shakespeare, Plato. Then Kerouac. *Prison is where you promise yourself the right to live.* A line that saved Sutton on many long nights. Then the dictionary of quotations, which contains the most famous line ever spoken by America's most famous bank robber, Willie Sutton, a.k.a. Slick Willie, a.k.a. Willie the Actor.

Carefully, tenderly, he packs the Ezra Pound. *Now you will come out of a confusion of people.* And the Tennyson. *Come into the garden, Maud, I am here at the gate alone.* He says the lines under his breath. His eyes mist. They always do. Finally he packs the yellow legal pad, the one on which he was writing when the guards came for him. Not his novel, which he recently finished, but a suicide note, the one he began composing an hour after the parole board's rejection. So often, he thinks, that's how it happens. Death stands at your door, hitches up its pants, points its baton at you—then hands you a pardon.

Once Sutton's cell is packed, the dep lets him make a few phone calls. First he dials his lawyer, Katherine. She's incoherent with joy.

We did it, Willie. We *did* it!

How did we do it, Katherine?

They got tired of fighting us. It's Christmas, Willie, and they were just tired. It was easier to give up.

I know how they felt, Katherine.

And the newspapers certainly helped, Willie. The newspapers were on your side.

Which is why Katherine's cut a deal with one of the biggest newspapers. She mentions which one, but Sutton's mind is racing, the name doesn't register. The newspaper is going to whisk Sutton aboard its private plane to Manhattan, put him up at a hotel, and in exchange he'll give them his exclusive story.

Unfortunately, Katherine adds, that means you'll have to spend Christmas Day with a reporter instead of family. Is that okay?

Sutton thinks of his family. He hasn't spoken to them in years. He thinks of reporters—he hasn't spoken to them *ever*. He doesn't like reporters. Still, this is no time to make waves.

That'll be fine, Katherine.

Now, do you know anyone who can pick you up outside the prison and drive you to the airport?

I'll find someone.

He hangs up, dials Donald, who answers on the tenth ring.

Donald? It's Willie.

Who's this?

Willie. What are you doing?

Oh. Hey. Drinking a beer, getting ready to watch *The Flying Nun*.

Listen. It seems they're letting me out tonight.

They're letting *you* out, or you're letting *yourself* out?

It's legit, Donald. They're opening the door.

Hell freezing over?

I don't know. But the devil's definitely wearing a sweater. Can you pick me up at the front gate?

Near the Sleeping Beauty thing?

Yeah.

Of course.

Sutton asks Donald if he can bring him a few items.

Anything, Donald says. Name it.

A TV VAN FROM BUFFALO ROARS UP TO THE GATE. A TV reporter jumps out, fusses with his microphone. He's wearing a two-hundred-dollar suit, a camel-hair topcoat, gray leather gloves, silver cuff links. The print reporters elbow each other. Cuff links—have you ever?

The TV reporter strolls up to the print reporters and wishes everyone a Merry Christmas. Same to you, they mumble. Then silence.

Silent Night, the TV reporter says.

No one laughs.

The reporter from *Newsweek* asks the TV reporter if he read Pete Hamill in this morning's *Post*. Hamill's eloquent apologia for Sutton, his plea for Sutton's release, addressed as a letter to the governor, might be the reason they're all here. Hamill urged Rockefeller to be fair. *If Willie Sutton had been a GE board member or a former water commissioner, instead of the son of an Irish blacksmith, he would be on the street now.*

The TV reporter stiffens. He knows the print guys think he doesn't read—can't read. Yeah, he says, I thought Hamill nailed it. Especially his line about banks. *There are some of us today, looking at the mortgage interest rates, who feel that it is the banks that are sticking us up.* And I got a lump in my throat at that bit about Sutton reuniting with a lost love. *Willie Sutton should be able to sit and watch the ducks in Prospect Park one more time, or go to Nathan's for a hot dog, or call up some old girl for a drink.*

This sets off a debate. Does Sutton actually deserve to be free? He's a thug, says the *Newsday* reporter—why all the adulation?

Because he's a god in parts of Brooklyn, says the *Post* reporter. Just look at this crowd.

There are now more than two dozen reporters and another two dozen civilians—crime buffs, police radio monitors, curiosity seekers. Freaks. Ghouls.

But again, says the *Newsday* reporter, I ask you—why?

Because Sutton robbed *banks*, the TV reporter says, and who the hell has a kind word to say for *banks*? They should not only let him out, they should give him the key to the city.

What I don't get, says the *Look* reporter, is why Rockefeller, a former banker, would let out a bank robber.

Rockefeller needs the Irish vote, says the *Times Union* reporter.

You can't get reelected in New York without the Irish vote and Sutton's like Jimmy Walker and Michael Collins and a couple Kennedys in one big Mulligan stew.

He's a fuckin thug, says the *Newsday* reporter, who may be drunk.

The TV reporter scoffs. Under his arm he's carrying last week's *Life* magazine, with Charles Manson on the cover. He holds up the magazine: Manson glares at them.

Compared to this guy, the TV reporter says, and the Hells Angels, and the soldiers who slaughtered all those innocent people at My Lai—Willie Sutton is a pussycat.

Yeah, says the *Newsday* reporter, he's a real pacifist. He's the Gandhi of Gangsters.

All those banks, the TV reporter says, all those prisons, and the guy never fired a single shot. He never hurt a fly.

The *Newsday* reporter gets in the TV reporter's face. What about Arnold Schuster? he says.

Aw, the TV reporter says, Sutton had nothing to do with Schuster.

Says who?

Says me.

And who the fuck are you?

I'll tell you who I'm not. I'm not some burned-out hack.

The *Times* reporter jumps between them. You two *cannot* get in a fistfight about whether or not someone is nonviolent—on Christmas Eve.

Why not?

Because if you do I'll have to write about it.

The talk swings back to the warden. Doesn't he realize that the temperature is now close to zero? Oh you bet he realizes. He's loving this. He's on some kind of power trip. Everybody these days is on a power trip. Mailer, Nixon, Manson, the Zodiac Killer, the cops—it's 1969, man, Year of the Power Trip. The warden's probably watching them right now on his closed-circuit TV, sipping a brandy and laughing his fat ass off. It's not enough that they have to be part of this massive clusterfuck, but they also have to be the dupes and patsies of some crypto–fascist macho dick?

You're all welcome to sit in my truck, the TV reporter says. It's warm. We've got TV. *The Flying Nun* is on.

Groans.

SUTTON LIES ON HIS BUNK, WAITING. AT SEVEN O'CLOCK Right Guard appears at the door.

Sorry, Sutton. It's not happening.

Sir?

Left Guard appears behind Right Guard. New orders just came down from the dep, he says—no go.

No go—why?

Why *what*?

Why *sir*?

Right Guard shrugs. Some kind of beef between Rockefeller and the parole department. They can't agree who's going to take responsibility, or how the press release should be worded.

So I'm not—?

No.

Sutton looks at the walls, the bars. His wrists. The purple veins, bubbled and wormy. He should've done it when he had the chance.

Right Guard starts laughing. Left Guard too. Just kidding, Sutton. On your feet.

They unlock the door, lead him down to the tailor. He strips out of his prison grays, puts on a crisp new white shirt, a new blue tie, a new black suit with a two-button front. He pulls on the new black socks, slips on the new black wingtips. He turns to the mirror. *Now* he can see the old swagger.

He faces Tailor. How do I look?

Tailor jiggles his coins and buttons, gives a thumbs-up.

Sutton turns to the guards. Nothing.

Right Guard alone leads Sutton through Times Square, then past Admin and toward the front entrance. God it's cold. Sutton cradles his shopping bag of belongings and ignores the cramping and burning and sizzling pain in his leg. A plastic tube is holding open the artery and he can feel it getting ready to collapse like a paper straw.

You need an operation, the doctor said after the insertion of the tube two years ago.

If I wait on the operation, will I lose the leg, Doc?

No, Willie, you won't lose the leg—you'll die.

But Sutton waited. He didn't want some prison doctor opening him up. He wouldn't trust a prison doctor to open a checking account. Now it seems he made the right call. He might be able to have the operation at a real hospital, and pay for it with the proceeds of his novel. Provided someone will publish it. Provided there's still time. Provided he lives through this night, this moment. Tomorrow.

Right Guard leads Sutton around a metal detector, around a sign-in table, and to a black metal door. Right Guard unlocks it. Sutton steps forward. He looks back at Right Guard, who's belittled and beaten him for the last seventeen years. Right Guard has censored Sutton's letters, confiscated his books, denied his requests for soap and pens and toilet paper, slapped him when he forgot to put a *sir* at the end of a sentence. Right Guard braces himself—this is the moment prisoners like to get things off their chests. But Sutton smiles as if something inside him is opening like a flower. Merry Christmas kid.

Right Guard's head snaps back. He waits a beat. Two. Yeah, Merry Christmas, Willie. Good luck to you.

It's shortly before eight o'clock.

Right Guard pushes open the door and out walks Willie Sutton.

A PHOTOGRAPHER FROM *LIFE* SHOUTS, HERE HE IS! THREE dozen reporters converge. The freaks and ghouls push in. TV cameras veer toward Sutton's face. Lights, brighter than prison searchlights, hit his azure eyes.

How's it feel to be free, Willie?

Do you think you'll ever rob another bank, Willie?

What do you have to say to Arnold Schuster's family?

Sutton points to the full moon. Look, he says.

Three dozen reporters and two dozen civilians and one arch-criminal look up at the night sky. The first time Sutton has seen the moon, face-to-face, in seventeen years—it takes his breath.

Look, he says again. *Look* at this beautiful clear night God has made for Willie.

Now, beyond the crush of reporters Sutton sees a man with pumpkin-colored hair and stubborn orange freckles leaning against a red 1967 Pontiac GTO. Sutton waves, Donald hurries over. They shake hands. Donald shoves aside several reporters, leads Sutton to the GTO. When Sutton is settled into the passenger seat, Donald slams the door and shoves another reporter, just for fun. He runs around the car, jumps behind the wheel, mashes the gas pedal. Away they go, sending up a wave of wet mud and snow and salt. It sprays the reporter from *Newsday*. His face, his chest, his shirt, his overcoat. He looks down at his clothes, then up at his colleagues:

Like I said—a thug.

SUTTON DOESN'T SPEAK. DONALD LETS HIM NOT SPEAK. Donald knows. Donald walked out of Attica nine months ago. They both stare at the icy road and the frozen woods and Sutton tries to sort his thoughts. After a few miles he asks if Donald was able to get that thing they discussed on the phone.

Yes, Willie.

Is she alive?

Don't know. But I found her last known address.

Donald hands over a white envelope. Sutton holds it like a chalice. His mind starts to go. Back to Brooklyn. Back to Coney Island. Back to 1919. Not yet, he tells himself, not yet. He shuts off his mind, something he's gotten good at over the years. Too good, one prison shrink told him.

He slides the envelope into the breast pocket of his new suit. Twenty years since he's had a breast pocket. It was always his favorite pocket, the one where he kept the good stuff. Engagement rings, enameled cigarette cases, leather billfolds from Abercrombie. Guns.

Donald asks who she is and why Sutton needs her address.

I shouldn't tell you, Donald.

We got no secrets between us, Willie.

We've got nothing but secrets between us, Donald.

Yeah. That's true, Willie.

Sutton looks at Donald and remembers why Donald was in the joint. A month after Donald lost his job on a fishing boat, two weeks after Donald's wife left him, a man in a bar said Donald looked beat. Donald, thinking the man was insulting him, threw a punch, and the man made the mistake of returning fire. Donald, a former college wrestler, put the man in a choke-hold, broke his neck.

Sutton turns on the radio. He looks for news, can't find any. He leaves it on a music station. The music is moody, sprightly— different.

What is this, Donald?

The Beatles.

So this is the Beatles.

They say nothing for miles. They listen to Lennon. The lyrics remind Sutton of Ezra Pound. He pats the shopping bag on his lap.

Donald downshifts the GTO, turns to Willie. Does the name in the envelope have anything at all to do with—you know who?

Sutton looks at Donald. Who?

You know. Schuster?

No. Of course not. Jesus, Donald, what makes you ask that?

I don't know. Just a feeling.

No, Donald. No.

Sutton puts a hand in his breast pocket. Thinks. Well, he says, I guess maybe it does—in a roundabout way. All roads eventually lead to Schuster, right, Donald?

Donald nods. Drives. You look good, Willie Boy.

They say I'm dying.

Bullshit. You'll never fuckin die.

Yeah. Right.

You couldn't die if you wanted to.

Hm. You have no idea how true that is.

Donald lights two cigarettes, hands one to Sutton. How about a drink? Do you have time before your flight?

What an interesting idea. A ball of Jameson, as my Daddo used to say.

Donald pulls off the highway and parks outside a low-down roadhouse. Sprigs of holly and Christmas lights strung over the bar. Sutton hasn't seen Christmas lights since his beloved Dodgers were in Brooklyn. He hasn't seen any lights other than the prison's eye-scalding fluorescents and the bare sixty-watt bulb in his cell.

Look, Donald. *Lights.* You know you've been in hell when a string of colored bulbs over a crummy bar looks more beautiful than Luna Park.

Donald jerks his head toward the bartender, a young blonde

girl wearing a tight paisley blouse and a miniskirt. Speaking of beautiful, Donald says.

Sutton stares. They didn't have miniskirts when I went away, he says quietly, respectfully.

You've come back to a different world, Willie.

Donald orders a Schlitz. Sutton asks for Jameson. The first sip is bliss. The second is a right cross. Sutton swallows the rest in one searing gulp and slaps the bar and asks for another.

The TV above the bar is showing the news.

Our top story tonight. Willie the Actor Sutton, the most prolific bank robber in American history, has been released from Attica Correctional Facility. In a surprise move by Governor Nelson Rockefeller . . .

Sutton stares into the grain of the bar top, thinking: Nelson Rockefeller, son of John D. Rockefeller Jr., grandson of John D. Rockefeller Sr., close friend of— Not yet, he tells himself.

He reaches into his breast pocket, touches the envelope.

Now Sutton's face appears on the screen. His former face. An old mug shot. No one along the bar recognizes him. Sutton gives Donald a sly smile, a wink. They don't know me, Donald. I can't remember the last time I was in a room full of people who didn't know me. Feels nice.

Donald orders another round. Then another.

I hope you have money, Sutton says. I only have two checks from Governor Rockefeller.

Which will probably fuckin bounce, Donald says, slurring.

Say, Donald—want to see a trick?

Always.

Sutton limps down the bar. He limps back. Ta da.

Donald blinks. I don't think I get it.

I walked from here to there without a hack hassling me. Without a con messing with me. Ten feet—two more feet than the length of my fuckin cell, Donald. And I didn't have to call anyone *sir* before or after. Have you ever seen anything so marvelous?

Donald laughs.

Ah Donald—to be free. Actually *free*. There's no way to describe it to someone who hasn't been in the joint.

Everyone should have to do time, Donald says, smothering a belch, so they could know.

Time. Willie looks at the clock over the bar. Shit, Donald, we better go.

Donald drives them weavingly along icy back roads. Twice they go skidding onto the shoulder. A third time they almost hit a snowbank.

You okay to drive, Donald?

Fuck no, Willie, what gave you that idea?

Sutton grips the dashboard. He stares in the distance at the lights of Buffalo. He recalls that speedboats used to run booze down here from Canada. This whole area, he says, was run by Polish gangs back in the twenties.

Donald snorts. Polish gangsters—what'd they do, stick people up and hand over *their* wallets?

They'd have cut the tongue out of your head for saying that. The Poles made us Micks look like choirboys. And the Polish cops were the cruelest of all.

Shocking, Donald says with dripping sarcasm.

Did you know President Grover Cleveland was the executioner up here?

Is that so?

It was Cleveland's job to knot the noose around the prisoner's neck, drop him through the gallows floor.

A job's a job, Donald says.

They called him the Hangman of Buffalo. Then his face wound up on the thousand-dollar bill.

Still reading your American history, I see, Willie.

They arrive at the private airfield. They're met by a young man with a square head and a deep dimple in his square chin. The reporter presumably. He shakes Sutton's hand and says his name, but Sutton is drunker than Donald and doesn't catch it.

Pleasure to meet you kid.

Same here, Mr. Sutton.

Reporter has thick brown hair, deep black eyes and a gleaming Pepsodent smile. Beneath each smooth cheek a pat of red glows like an ember, maybe from the cold, more likely from good health. Even more enviable is Reporter's nose. Thin and straight as a shiv.

It's a very short flight, he tells Sutton. Are you all set?

Sutton looks at the low clouds, the plane. He looks at Reporter. Then Donald.

Mr. Sutton?

Well kid. You see. This is actually my first time on an airplane.

Oh. *Oh*. Well. It's perfectly safe. But if you'd rather leave in the morning.

Nah. The sooner I get to New York the better. So long, Donald.

Merry Christmas, Willie.

The plane has four seats. Two in the front, two in the back. Reporter straps Sutton into one of the backseats, then sits up front next to the pilot. A few snowflakes fall as they taxi down the runway. They come to a full stop and the pilot talks into the radio and the radio crackles back with numbers and codes and Sutton suddenly remembers the first time he rode in a car. Which was stolen. Well, bought with stolen money. Which Sutton stole. He was almost eighteen and steering that new car down the road felt like flying. Now, fifty years later, he's going to fly *through the air*. He feels a painful pressure building below his heart. This is not safe. He reads every day in the paper about another plane scattered in pieces on some mountaintop, in some field or lake. Gravity is no joke. Gravity is one of the few laws he's never broken. He'd rather be in Donald's GTO right now, fishtailing on icy back roads. Maybe he can pay Donald to drive him to New York. Maybe he'll take the bus. Fuck, he'll walk. But first he needs to get out of this plane. He claws at his seat belt.

The engine gives a high piercing whine and the plane rears back like a horse and goes screaming down the runway. Sutton thinks of the astronauts. He thinks of Lindbergh. He thinks of the bald man in the red long johns who used to get shot from a cannon at Coney Island. He closes his eyes and says a prayer and clutches his shopping bag. When he opens his eyes again the full moon is right outside his window, Jackie Gleasoning him.

Within forty minutes they make out the lights of Manhattan. Then the Statue of Liberty glowing green and gold out in the harbor. Sutton presses his face against the window. One-armed goddess. She's waving to him, beckoning him. Calling him home.

The plane tilts sideways and swoops toward LaGuardia. The landing is smooth. As they slow and taxi toward the terminal Reporter turns to check on Sutton. You okay, Mr. Sutton?

Let's go again kid.

Reporter smiles.

They walk side by side across the wet, foggy tarmac to a waiting car. Sutton thinks of Bogart and Claude Rains. He's been told he looks a little like Bogart. Reporter is talking. Mr. Sutton? Did you hear? I assume your lawyer explained all about tomorrow?

Yeah kid.

Reporter checks his watch. Actually, I should say today. It's one in the morning.

Is it? Sutton says. Time has lost all meaning. Not that it ever had any.

You know that your lawyer has agreed to give us exclusive rights to your story. And you know that we're hoping to visit your old stomping grounds, the scenes of your, um. Crimes.

Where are we staying tonight?

The Plaza.

Wake up in Attica, go to bed at the Plaza. Fuckin America.

But, Mr. Sutton, after we check in, I need to ask you, please, order room service, anything you like, but do not leave the hotel.

Sutton looks at Reporter. The kid's not yet twenty-five, Sutton guesses, but he's dressed like an old codger. Fur-collared trench coat, dark brown suit, cashmere scarf, cap-toed brown lace-ups. He's dressed, Sutton thinks, like a damn banker.

My editors, Mr. Sutton. They're determined that we have you to ourselves the first day. That means we can't have anyone quoting you or shooting your picture. So we can't let anyone know where you are.

In other words, kid, I'm your prisoner.

Reporter gives a nervous laugh. Oh no, I wouldn't say that.

But I'm in your custody.

Just for one day, Mr. Sutton.

TWO

DAYLIGHT FILLS THE SUITE.

Sutton sits in a wingback chair, watching the other wingback chair and the king-size bed come into view. He hasn't slept. It's been five hours since he and Reporter checked in and he's nodded off a few times in this chair but that's all. He lights a cigarette, the last one in the pack. Good thing he ordered two more packs from room service. Good thing they had his brand. He can't smoke anything but Chesterfields. He always, *always* had a footlocker of Chesterfields in his cell. He washes down the smoke with the ice-cold champagne he also ordered. He puts the cigarette in his mouth and holds the white envelope to the daylight. He still hasn't opened it. He won't let himself until he's ready, until the time is right, even though that means he might not live to open it.

His body is doing everything the doctor warned him it would do in the final stages. The vise feeling in the small of his back. The toes and legs going numb. Claudication, the doctor called it. At first you'll have trouble walking, Willie. Then you'll simply stop.

Stop what, Doc?

Stop everything, Willie—you'll just *stop*.

So he's going to die today. Within a few hours, maybe before noon, certainly before darkness falls. He knows it in the same way he used to know things in the old days, the way he used to know if a guy was right or a rat. He's given death the slip a hundred times, but not today. He invited death in with that suicide note. Once you let death in, it doesn't always leave.

He turns the envelope slowly, shakes it like a match he's trying to extinguish. He sees the one sheet of loose-leaf inside, covered in Donald's scrawl. He sees Bess's name, or thinks he does. It wouldn't be the first time he's seen Bess when she wasn't there. Has she already heard about his release? He pictures Bess standing before him. Conjures her. It's easier to conjure her in a suite at the Plaza than in a cell at Attica. Ah Bess, he whispers. I can't die before I see you, my heart's darling. I can't.

A faint knock makes him jump. He slips the white envelope into his breast pocket, hobbles to the door.

Reporter. His dark brown hair is wet, neatly parted, and his face, freshly scrubbed, is pink and white. From the neck up he's the color of Neapolitan ice cream. He's wearing another banker suit and the same fur-collared trench coat. In one hand he's carrying a big lawyerly briefcase, in the other a paper box filled with bagels and coffee.

Morning, Mr. Sutton.

Merry Christmas kid.

Were you on the phone?

No.

I thought I heard voices.

Nah.

Reporter smiles. His teeth look twice as Pepsodenty. Good, he says.

Sutton still can't remember Reporter's name, or which newspaper he works for, and it feels too late to ask. He also doesn't care. He steps aside. Reporter walks to a desk by the window, sets down the paper box.

I got cream, sugar, I didn't know how you take it.

Sutton shuts the door, follows Reporter into the suite. Are we not going down to the restaurant kid?

Sorry, Mr. Sutton, the restaurant is much too public. You're a very famous man this morning.

I've been famous all my life kid.

But today, Mr. Sutton, you're the *most* famous man in New York. Producers, directors, screenwriters, ghostwriters, publishers, they're all staking out my newspaper. Word is out that we've got you. Merv Griffin phoned the city desk twice this morning. Johnny Carson's people left four messages at my home. We can't take a chance of someone in the restaurant spotting you. I can just see some waiter phoning the *Times* and saying: For fifty bucks I'll tell you where Willie Sutton is having breakfast. My editor would skin me alive.

Now at least Sutton knows Reporter doesn't work for the *Times*.

Reporter clicks open his briefcase, removes a stack of newspapers. He holds one before Sutton. On the front page is Sutton's face. Above it is a Man-Walks-on-Moon-size headline: SANTA SPRINGS WILLIE SUTTON.

Sutton takes the newspaper, holds it at arm's length, frowns. Santa, he says. Jesus, I'll never understand all the good press that guy gets. A chubby second-story man. What, breaking and entering isn't against the law if you wear a red velvet suit?

He looks to Reporter for confirmation. Reporter shrugs. I'm Jewish, Mr. Sutton.

Oh.

Sutton can hear it in Reporter's voice, the kid is waiting for him to say, Call me Willie. It's on the tip of Sutton's tongue, but he can't. He likes the deference. Feels good. Sutton doesn't remember the last time someone, besides a judge, called him Mr. Sutton. He returns to the wingback chair. Reporter, carrying his paper cup of coffee, sits in the other wingback, peels off the plastic lid, takes a sip. Now he leans forward eagerly. So, Mr. Sutton—how does it feel to be famous?

I don't think you heard me kid. I've been famous all my life.

Arguably you've been infamous.

That seems like splitting hairs.

What I'm saying is, you're *a living legend*.

Please kid.

You're an icon.

Nah.

Oh yes, Mr. Sutton. That's why my editors are so keen for this story. In the page one meeting yesterday, a senior editor said you've achieved a kind of mythic status.

Sutton opens his eyes wide. Boy, you newspapermen love myths, don't you?

Pardon?

Selling myths, that's what you fellas do. The front page, the sports page, the financial pages—all myths.

Well, I don't think—

I used to buy in too. When I was a kid. I used to lap it all up. Not just newspapers either—comic books, Horatio Alger, the Bible, the whole American Dream. That's what got me so mixed up in the first place. Fuckin myths.

I think maybe I haven't had enough coffee.

Try some champagne.

No. Thank you. Mr. Sutton, all I'm saying is, America loves a bank robber.

Really. America has a funny way of showing it. I've spent half my life locked up.

Take your famous line. There's a reason that line has become part of the culture.

Sutton stubs out his cigarette, shoots two plumes of smoke through his nostrils. Because the nostrils are different sizes, the plumes are different sizes. It's always bothered Sutton.

Which line is that kid?

You know.

Sutton makes his face a blank. He can't help having fun with this kid.

Mr. Sutton, surely you remember. When you were asked why you robbed banks? You said: *That's where the money was.*

Right, right. I remember now. Except I never said it.

Reporter's face falls.

One of your colleagues invented that line kid. Put my name to it.

Oh no.

Like I said. Myths. All my life, if reporters weren't making me out to be worse than I am, they were making me out to be better.

Wow. That makes me embarrassed for my profession.

We all pay for the sins of our colleagues.

Well, Mr. Sutton, rest assured, I won't be putting any words in your mouth today.

Sutton cocks his head. How old are you kid?

Me? I'll be twenty-three in February.

Young.

I guess. Relatively.

If Willie's such a hot ticket, like you say, how come your bosses sent a cub to be my chaperone?

Um.

You draw this assignment because you're Jewish? No one else in the city room wanted to work Christmas?

Reporter sighs. I won't lie to you, Mr. Sutton. That might be the case.

Sutton gives Reporter a long slow once-over. He misjudged this kid. Reporter isn't a Boy Scout, Sutton decides. He's an Eagle Scout. And an altar boy. Or whatever the Jewish equivalent might be.

Reporter looks at his watch. Speaking of the assignment, Mr. Sutton. We should probably get going.

Sutton stands, checks his breast pocket. He pulls out the white envelope, puts it back. Then he pulls out a tourist map of New York City—he had the front desk send it up with the Chesterfields and the champagne. He's marked it with red numbers, red lines and arrows. He hands it to Reporter.

What's this, Mr. Sutton?

You said you wanted the nickel tour of my life. There it is. I mapped it all out.

All these places?

Yeah. And they're numbered. Chronological order.

So these are the scenes of all your crimes?

And other key events. All the crossroads of my life.

Reporter moves his finger from number to number. Crossroads, he says. I see.

Problem?

No, no. It's just. It looks as if we double back several times. Maybe there's a more direct route?

We have to do it in chronological order. Or else the story won't make sense.

To whom?

You. Me. Whoever. I can't tell you about Bess before I tell you about Eddie. I can't tell you about Mrs. Adams before I tell you about Bess.

Who?

See what I mean?

Right. No. But, Mr. Sutton, I just don't know if we'll have time for all of this.

It's all of this or none of this.

Reporter laughs, but it sounds like a sob. The thing is, Mr. Sutton, your lawyer. Made a deal with my newspaper.

That was her deal. This is Willie's deal.

Reporter takes a sip of coffee. Sutton watches him hunch deep into his fur-collared trench coat, thinking out his next move. Fear and anxiety are written in big crayoned letters across the pink-and-white face.

Take it easy kid. We don't have to get out of the car at each stop and have a picnic. Some of them we can just cruise by. So Willie can eyeball the place. Get the lay of the land.

But my editors, Mr. Sutton. My editors make the rules and—

Sutton grunts. Not for me they don't. Look, kid, this isn't a negotiation. If my map doesn't work for you, no sweat, we'll just go our separate ways. I'm more than happy to stay in this nice room, read a book, order a club sandwich.

Checkout is at noon.

I checked out early from three escape-proof prisons, I think I can figure out how to swing a late checkout at one cream puff hotel.

But—

Maybe I'll even make a few phone calls. Is the *Times* listed?

Reporter takes another sip of coffee, blanches as if it's straight scotch. Mr. Sutton, it's just that this, your *map*, appears to be more *story* than we can accommodate.

Why not wait to hear the story before you say that?

Also, if we could just go to certain places first. Like the scene of Arnold Schuster's murder.

Sure, and once you've got me at the Schuster scene, you don't need me anymore, and then I don't get my ride to all the other places. I know how you newspaper guys operate.

Mr. Sutton, I wouldn't do that, you can trust me.

Trust you? Kid don't make me laugh. It hurts my leg when I laugh. Schuster comes last. End of story. Are you in or out?

But Mr. Sutton—

In or *out* kid.

Sutton's voice is suddenly an octave deeper. With a serrated edge. The change stuns Reporter, who puts a finger on the dimple in his chin and presses several times, as if it's an emergency button.

Sutton takes a hard step toward Reporter. He concentrates on assuming an at-ease posture while also conveying an air of total control. He used to do this with bank managers. Especially the ones who claimed not to remember the combination to the safe.

You seem smart for a cub, kid, so let's not bullshit each other.

Let's put our cards on the table. We both know you only want a story. Sure, it's an important story for you, your career, your newspaper, whatever, but it's still just a story. Next week you'll be on to the next story and next month you won't even remember Willie. What I'm after is *my* story, the only story that counts with me. Think about it. I'm free. *Free*—for the first time in seventeen years. Naturally I want to go back, retrace my steps, see where it all went sideways, and I need to do it my way, which is the only way I know how to do things. And I need to do it right now, kid, because I don't know how much time I've got left. My leg, which is thoroughly rat-fucked, tells me not much. You can be my wheelman or not. It's your call. But you need to decide. Now.

I won't be your wheelman.

Fine. No hard feelings.

We're meeting a shooter. He'll be driving.

A what?

A photog. Sorry—photographer. In fact he's probably downstairs by now.

So you're in?

You give me no choice, Mr. Sutton.

Say it.

Say what?

Say you're in.

Why?

In the old days, before I'd go on a job with a guy, I always needed to hear him say he was in. So there'd be no misunderstandings later.

Reporter takes a gulp of coffee. Mr. Sutton, is this really—

Say it.

I'm in, I'm in.

SUTTON STEPS ON THE ELEVATOR, CURSING UNDER HIS BREATH. Why did he stay up all night? Why did he drink all that whiskey with Donald? And all that champagne this morning? And what the hell is wrong with this elevator? He was already feeling unsteady on his feet, but this sudden free fall to the lobby, like a space capsule plunging to earth, is giving him vertigo. In the old days elevators were manageably, comfortably slow. Like people.

With a ping and a thud the elevator lands. The doors clatter open. Reporter, not noticing Sutton's pained expression, looks left and right, making sure no other reporters are lurking behind the lobby's palm trees. He takes Sutton by the elbow and guides him past the front desk and past the concierge and through the revolving door. There, directly in front of the Plaza, stands a 1968 burnt sienna Dodge Polara, smoke gushing like tap water from its tailpipe.

This your car kid?

No. It's one of the newspaper's radio cars.

Looks like a cop car.

It's a converted cop car, actually.

Reporter opens the passenger door. He and Sutton look in. A large man sits behind the wheel. He's roughly Reporter's age, twenty something, but he wears a fringed buckskin jacket that makes him look like a five-year-old playing cowboys and Indians. No, with his shoulder-length hair and Fu Manchu mustache he looks like a grown man pretending to be a five-year-old playing cowboys and Indians. Under the buckskin jacket he's wearing a ski sweater, and around his neck a knitted scarf the colors of a barber pole, all of which spoil whatever Western look he was going for. He smiles. Bad teeth. Nice smile, but bad teeth. The exact opposite of Reporter's teeth. And they're as big as they are bad. His eyes are big too, and flaming red, like cherry Life Savers. Sutton would kill for a Life Saver right now.

Mr. Sutton, Reporter says. I'd like you to meet the best shooter at the paper. The *best*.

Reporter says the photographer's name but Sutton doesn't

catch it. Merry Christmas, Sutton says, reaching into the car and shaking Photographer's hand.

Back at you, brother.

Sutton climbs into the backseat, which is covered with stuff. A cloth purse. A leather camera bag. A pink bakery box. A stack of newspapers and magazines, including last week's *Life*. Manson glares at Sutton. Sutton flips Manson over.

Maybe you'd be more comfortable up front, Reporter says.

Nah, Sutton says. I always ride in the rumble.

Reporter smiles. Okay, Mr. Sutton. I'm happy to ride shotgun.

Sutton shakes his head. *Riding shotgun*—civilians use the term so blithely. He's actually driven countless times with men riding shotgun, holding shotguns. There was nothing blithe about it.

Photographer squints at Sutton in the rearview. Hey, Willie, man, I've just got to say, it's a trip to meet you, brother. I mean, Willie the Actor—holy shit, this is like meeting Dillinger.

Ah well, Sutton says, Dillinger killed people, so.

Or Jesse James.

Again—killed.

Or Al Capone.

A pattern seems to be developing, Sutton mumbles.

I *asked* for this assignment, Photographer says.

Did you kid?

Even though it was Christmas. I told my old lady, I said, baby, it's *Willie the Actor*. This guy's been fighting the Man for decades.

Well, I don't know about the Man.

You fought the law, brother.

Okay.

You were an antihero before they invented the word.

Antihero?

Hell yes, man. This is the Age of the Antihero. I don't have to tell you, Willie, times are hard, people are fed up. Prices are soaring, taxes are sky high, millions are hungry, angry. Injustice.

Inequality. The War on Poverty is a joke, the war in Vietnam is illegal, the Great Society is a sham.

Same old same old, Sutton says.

Yes and no, Photographer says. Same shit, but people aren't taking it anymore. People are in the streets, brother. Chicago, Newark, Detroit. We haven't seen this kind of civil unrest in a long long time. So people are crazy about anyone who fights the power—and wins. That's you, Willie. Have you *seen* today's front pages, brother?

It's a nonstarter, Reporter whispers to Photographer. I already went down this road.

Photographer is undaunted. Just the other night, he says, I was telling my old lady all about you—

You know *all about* Willie?

Sure. And you know what she said? She said, This cat sounds like a real-life Robin Hood.

Well, Robin Hood *was* real life, but anyway. She sounds lovely.

Oh, I'm a lucky guy, Willie. My old lady, she's a teacher up in the Bronx. Studying to be a masseuse. She's changed my life. Really raised my consciousness. You know how the right woman can do that.

Your consciousness?

Yeah. She knows all about the trigger points in the body. She's really opened me up. Artistically. Emotionally. Sexually.

Photographer starts to giggle. Sutton stares at the Life Saver eyes framed in the rearview—Photographer is stoned. Reporter is staring too, clearly thinking the same thing.

Trigger points, Sutton says.

Yeah. She's studying the same techniques they used on Kennedy. For his back. I got a bad back—this line of work, it comes with the territory—so every night she works out my knots. Her hands are magic. I'm kind of obsessed with her, in case you couldn't tell. Her hands. Her hair. Her face. Her ass. God, her ass. I shouldn't say that though. She's a feminist. She's teaching me not to objectify women.

You had to be taught not to object to women?

Objectify.

Oh.

Reporter clears his throat. Loudly. Okay then, he says, shutting his door, spreading Sutton's map across the Polara's dashboard. Mr. Sutton has kindly drawn us a map, places he wants to show us today. He insists that we visit them all. In chronological order.

Photographer sees all the red numbers. Thirteen, four—

Really?

Really.

Photographer drops his voice. When do we get to, you know? Schuster?

Last.

Photographer drops his voice lower. What gives?

It's his way, Reporter whispers, or no way.

Sutton bows his head, tries not to smile.

Photographer throws up his hands as if Reporter is robbing him. Hey man, that's cool. It's Willie da Actor—he's da boss, right? Willie da Actor don't take orders from nobody.

Reporter pulls the radio from the dash. City Desk? Come in, City Desk.

The radio squawks: Are you guys garble leaving the static garble Plaza?

Ten four.

Photographer puts the car into drive and they lurch forward, toward Fifth Avenue, cruising slowly past the former sites of two banks Sutton hit in 1931.

Traffic is light. It's seven o'clock Christmas morning, the temperature is twelve degrees, so only a few people are on the street. They turn onto Fifty-Seventh. Sutton sees three young men walking, debating something intensely. Two of them wear denim jackets, the third wears a leather duster. They all have long shaggy manes.

When exactly, Sutton says, did everybody get together and decide to stop getting haircuts?

Reporter and Photographer look at each other, laugh.

Sutton sees an old man rooting in a trash can. He sees another old man pushing a shopping cart full of brooms. He sees a woman—youngish, pretty—having a heated argument. With a mannequin in a store window.

Reporter peers into the backseat. Was the homeless problem bad before you went to prison, Mr. Sutton?

Nah. Because we didn't call them homeless. We called them beggars. Then bums. I should know. When I was your age, I was one.

Hey Willie, Photographer says, if you're hungry, man, I bought donuts. In that box on the seat.

Sutton opens the pink box. An assortment. Glazed, sugar, jelly, crullers. Thanks kid.

Help yourself. I bought enough for everybody.

Maybe later.

Donuts are my weakness.

You'd have loved Capone.

Why's that?

Al used to hand out donuts to the poor during the Depression. He was the first gangster who gave any thought to public relations.

Is that so?

That was the rap against him anyway, that it was all for show. I met him once at a nightclub, asked him about it. He said he didn't give a shit about PR. He just didn't like seeing people go hungry.

Sutton feels a burst of pain in his leg. It flies up his side, lands just behind his eyeballs. He lets his head fall back. Eventually he's going to have to ask these boys to stop at a drugstore. Or a hospital.

So, Photographer says. Willie, my brother—how does it feel to be free?

Sutton lifts his head. Like a dream, he says.

I'll *bet*.

Photographer waits for Sutton to elaborate. Sutton doesn't.

And how did you spend your first night of freedom?

Sutton exhales. You know. Thinking.

Photographer guffaws. He looks at Reporter. No reaction. Then back at Sutton's reflection. *Thinking?*

Yeah.

Thinking?

That's right.

You didn't get enough time in prison to *think*?

In the joint, kid, thinking is the one thing you can't let yourself do.

Photographer lights a cigarette. Sutton notices: Newport Menthol. Figures.

Willie, Photographer says, if I was in prison for seventeen years, and they let me out, thinking is the last thing I'd do.

I have no trouble believing that.

Reporter starts to laugh, pretends it's a cough.

Photographer squints at Sutton in the rearview, runs two fingers down the stems of his Fu Manchu.

Sutton sees signs for the tunnel. In a few minutes they'll be in Brooklyn. Jesus—Brooklyn again. His heart beats faster. They pass a movie theater. They all look at the marquee. TELL THEM WILLIE BOY IS HERE. Reporter and Photographer shake their heads.

What a coincidence, Photographer says.

Of all the films to open this week, Reporter says. I'll have to work that into my story.

Sutton watches the marquee until it's out of sight. Who plays Willie Boy? he asks.

Robert Blake, Photographer says. I saw the coming attractions. It's a Western. About a guy who kills his girlfriend's father in self-defense, then goes on the run. There's a huge manhunt for him, the largest in the history of the West—it's based on a true story. Supposedly.

They pass the corner of Broadway and Battery Place.

Canyon of Heroes, Reporter shouts over his shoulder. Seems like, this year, we've had a ticker-tape parade along here every other week. The Jets, of course. The Mets. The astronauts.

Isn't it telling, Sutton says. When someone's a hero, they shower him with little pieces of the stock market.

Photographer laughs. You're singing my song, Willie.

Sutton sees some ticker tape still in the gutters. He sees another bum, this one curled in the fetal position. Bums lying in ticker tape, he says. They should put that on a postage stamp.

I covered every one of those parades, Photographer says. Got beaucoup shots of Neil Armstrong. Cool guy. You'd think a guy that just walked on the moon would be stuck up. He's not. He's really—you know.

Down to earth, Sutton says.

Yeah.

Sutton waits. One, two. Photographer slaps the wheel. I just got that, he says. Good one.

Everyone praises Armstrong and Aldrin, Sutton says. But the real hero on that moon shot was the third guy, Mike Collins, the Irishman in the backseat.

Actually, Reporter says, Collins was born in Rome.

Photographer gawks at Sutton. Collins? He didn't even set foot on the moon.

Exactly. Collins was in the space capsule all alone. While his partners were down there collecting rocks, Collins was manning the wheel. Twenty-six times he circled the moon—solo. Imagine? He was completely out of radio contact. Couldn't talk to his partners. Couldn't talk to NASA. He was cut off from every living soul in the universe. If he panicked, if he fucked up, if he pushed the wrong button, he'd strand Armstrong and Aldrin. Or if they did something wrong, if their lunar car broke down, if they couldn't restart the thing, if they couldn't blast off and reconnect with Collins forty-five miles above the moon, he'd have to head back to earth *all by himself*. Leave his partners to die. Slowly running out of air. While watching earth in the distance. It was such a real possibility, Collins returning to earth *by himself*, that Nixon wrote up a speech to the nation. Collins—now that's one stone-cold wheelman. That's the guy you want sitting at the wheel of a gassed-up Ford while you're inside a bank.

Reporter looks searchingly in the backseat. Seems like you've given this a lot of thought, Mr. Sutton.

In the joint I read everything I could get my hands on about the moon shot. The hacks even let us watch it on TV—in the middle of the day. A rare privilege. They put a set in D Yard. It was the first time I didn't see black guys and white guys fighting over the TV. Everybody wanted to watch the moon landing. I think some of you people on the outside might have taken the whole thing for granted. But in the joint we couldn't get enough of it.

Why's that?

Because the moon shot is mankind's ultimate escape. And because the astronauts were in one-sixth gravity. In the joint you feel like gravity is six times stronger.

The car windows are fogging. Sutton wipes the window to his right and looks at the sky. He thinks of the astronauts returning from the moon—250,000 miles. Attica is at least that far away. He lights a Chesterfield. Some nerve, he thinks, identifying with astronauts. But he can't help it. Maybe it's that setup in a space capsule—two in front, one in back, like every getaway car he's ever ridden in. Also, he'd never say it out loud, not if you hung him up by his thumbs, but he sees himself as a hero. If he's not, why are these boys chauffeuring him through the Canyon of Heroes?

Canyon of Antiheroes.

What's that, Mr. Sutton?

Nothing. Did you boys know, after the three astronauts returned, Collins got a letter from the only man who understood how completely alone he'd been? Charles Lindbergh.

Is that true?

They enter the tunnel, drive slowly under the river. The cab of the Polara goes dark, except for the dash and Sutton's glowing cigarette. Sutton closes his eyes. This river. So full of memories. And evidence. Guns, knives, costumes, license plates from getaway cars. He used to hammer the plates into tiny squares the size of matchbooks before dropping them in the water. And former associates—this river was the last thing they saw. Or felt.

We're here, Reporter says.

Sutton opens his eyes. Did he doze off? Must have—his cigarette is out. He looks through the fogged windows. A lifeless corner. Alien, lunar. This can't be it. He looks at the street sign. Gold Street. This is it.

You committed a crime here, Mr. Sutton?

Sort of. I was born here.

He wasn't born, Daddo always said—he escaped. Two months early, umbilical cord noosed around his neck, he should have died. But somehow, on June 30, 1901, William Francis Sutton Jr. emerged. Now, emerging from the Polara, he steps gingerly onto the curb. The Actor has landed, he says under his breath.

Down the street he goes, dragging his bad leg. Reporter, jumping out of the Polara, flipping open his notebook, follows. Mr. Sutton, is your family—um—still?

Nah. Everyone's a fine dust. Wait, that's not true, I have a sister in Florida.

Sutton looks around. He turns in a full circle. It's all different. Even the light is different. Who would have thought something so basic, so elemental as light could change so much? But Brooklyn sixty years ago, with its elevated tracks, its ubiquitous clotheslines, was a world of dense and various shadows, and the light by contrast was always blinding.

No more.

At least the air tastes familiar. Like a dishrag soaked in river water. The energy feels the same too. Which may be why Sutton now hears voices. There were so many voices back then, all talking at once. Everyone was always calling to you, yelling at you, hollering down from a fire escape or terrace—and they all sounded angry. There was no such thing as conversation. Life was one long argument. Which nobody ever won.

Reporter and Photographer stand before Sutton, concerned looks on their faces. He sees them talking to him but he can't hear. They're drowned out by the voices. Old voices, loud voices, dead voices. Now he hears the trolleys. Night and day that cease-less rattling is what makes Brooklyn *Brooklyn*. Let's take the rattler to Coney Island, Eddie always says. Of course Eddie is long gone, and there is no rattling, so what is Sutton hearing? He puts a hand over his mouth. What's happening? Is it the champagne? Is it the leg—a clot rattling toward his brain? Is that why he now hears his brothers taunting him, Mother calling from the upstairs window?

Mr. Sutton, you okay?

Sutton closes his eyes, lifts his face to the sky.

Mr. Sutton?

Coming, Mother.

Mr. *Sutton?*

THREE

CHICKENS, HORSES, PIGS, GOATS, DOGS, THEY ALL WALK down the middle of Gold Street, which isn't a street but a dirt path. The city sometimes sprinkles the street with oil to keep the dust down. But that just makes it an oily dirt path.

Neighborhood boys are glad the street is dirt. Gold Street got its name because pirates buried treasure beneath it long ago, and on summer days the boys like to dig for doubloons.

There. A narrow wooden house, three stories tall, like all the others on Gold Street, except for the chimney, which tilts leeward. Willie lives there with Father, Mother, two older brothers, one older sister, and his white-haired grandfather, Daddo. The house is painted a cheerful yellow, but that's misleading. It's not a happy place. It's always too hot, too cold, too small. There's no running water, no bathroom, and a heavy gloom hangs in the tiny rooms and narrow halls since the death of Willie's baby sister, Agnes. Meningitis. Or so the Suttons think. They don't know. There was no doctor, no hospital. Hospitals are for Rockefellers.

Seven years old, Willie sits in the kitchen watching Mother, grief-sick, at the washbasin. A small woman, wide in the hips, with wispy red hair and bleary eyes, she scrubs a piece of clothing that used to be white and never will be again. She uses a powdered detergent that smells to Willie of ripe pears and vanilla.

The name of the detergent, Fels, is everywhere—newspapers, billboards, placards in the trolley cars. Children, skipping rope, chant the Fels advertising slogan to keep rhythm. *Fels—gets out—that tattle—tale gray!* Meaning, without Fels, your gray collar and underpants will tell on you. Judas clothes—the idea terrifies little Willie. And yet Mother's constant scrubbing makes no sense. A noble effort, but a waste of time, since the second you step outside, splat. The streets are filled with mud and shit, tar and soot, dust and oil.

And dead horses. They keel over from the heat, fall down from the cold, collapse from disease or neglect. Every week there's another one lying in the gutter. If the horse belongs to a gypsy or ragpicker, it's left where it falls. Over time it swells like a balloon, until it explodes. A sound like a cannon. Then it gives off an eye-watering stench, bringing flies, rats. Sometimes the New York City Street Cleaning Department sends a crew. Just as often the city doesn't bother. The city treats this nub of northern Brooklyn, this wasteland between the two bridges, as a separate city, a separate nation, which it is. Some call it Vinegar Hill. Most call it Irish Town.

Everyone in Irish Town is Irish. Everyone. Most are new Irish. Their hobnailed boots and slanted tweed caps are still caked with the dust of Limerick or Dublin or Cork. Mother and Father were born in Ireland, as was Daddo, but they all came to Irish Town years ago, which gives them a certain status in the neighborhood.

The other thing that gives them status is Father's job. Most fathers in Irish Town don't work, and those who do drink up their wages, but Father is a blacksmith, a skilled artisan, and every Saturday he dutifully, proudly places his weekly twelve dollars on the outstretched apron of Mother. Twelve dollars. Never more, but never less.

Willie sees Father as a fantastic collection of nevers. Never misses a day of work, never touches liquor, never swears or raises a hand in anger to his wife and kids. He also never shows affection, never speaks. A word here, a word there. If that. His silence, which gives him an aura, feels connected to his work. After eleven hours of hammering and pounding and swatting the hardest thing in the world—what's to say?

Often Willie goes with Father to the shop, a wooden shed on a big lot that smells of manure and fire. Willie watches Father, streaming with sweat, slamming his giant hammer again and again on a piece of glowing orange. With every slam, every metallic clank, Father looks—not happy, but clearer of mind. Willie feels clearer too. Other fathers are drunk, on the dole, but not his. Father isn't God, but he's godlike. Willie's first hero, first mystery, Father is also his first love.

Willie thinks he'd like to be a blacksmith when he grows up. He learns that when you make a piece of metal longer, you *draw* it, and when you make it shorter, you *upset* it. He learns to pump the bellows, make the flames in the hearth swell. Father holds up a hand, signaling *careful*, not too much. Every other week another blacksmith shop burns to the ground. Then the smith is out of work and the family is on the street. That's the fear, the thing that keeps Father hammering, Mother scrubbing. One bad turn—fire, illness, injury, bank panic—and the curb is your pillow.

If Father never speaks, Daddo never stops. Daddo sits in a rocking chair by the parlor window, the one with the curtains made from potato sacks, delivering an eternal monologue. He doesn't care that Willie is the only one listening. Or doesn't know. A few years before Willie was born, Daddo was working in a warehouse and a jet of acid spurted into his eyes. The world went dim. The hard part, he always says, was losing his job. Now all he does, all he can do, is sit around and blether.

Most often he talks about politics, stuff that goes over Willie's head. But sometimes he tells larky stories to make his youngest grandson giggle. Stories about mermaids and witches—and little men. To hear Daddo tell it, the Old Country is overrun with them.

What do the little men do, Daddo?

They steal, Willie Boy.

Steal what?

Sheep, pigs, gold, whatever they can lay their grubby little mitts on. Ah but no one holds it against the lads. They're just full of mischief. Bad little actors.

Do you remember the exact spot where you were born, Mr. Sutton?
    Sutton points to a tan brick building, some kind of community center. Tell them Willie Boy was—here.
    Was it a happy childhood, Mr. Sutton?
    Yeah. Sure.
    Photographer shoots Sutton in close-up, the Brooklyn-Queens Expressway behind his head. The expressway was built while Sutton was in prison. God what a monstrosity, Sutton says. I didn't think they could make Brooklyn uglier. I underestimated them.
    Cool, Photographer says. Yeah, brother, right there. That's tomorrow's front page.

Willie's two older brothers despise him. For as long as he can remember it's been true, a changeless fact of life. The sun rises over Williamsburg, sets over Fulton Ferry, and his brothers wish he were dead.

    Is it because he's the baby? Is it because he's William *Junior*? Is it because he spends so much time with Father at the shop? Willie doesn't know. Whatever the reason—rivalry, jealousy, evil—the brothers are so united against him, they pose such a seamless two-headed menace, that Willie can't tell them apart. Or doesn't bother. He thinks of them simply as Big and Bigger.

    Willie, eight, is playing jacks on the sidewalk with his friends. From nowhere Big Brother and Bigger Brother appear. Willie looks up. Both brothers hold egg creams. The sun is bracketed by their giant heads.

    So feckin small, Big Brother says, glaring down at Willie.

    Yeah, Bigger Brother says, snickering. Feckin runt.

    Willie's friends run away. Willie stares at his jacks and his little red ball. His brothers move a step closer, looming over him like trees. Trees that hate.

It's embarrassin, Bigger Brother says, bein known as your brother.

Put some meat on your bones, Big Brother says. And quit bein such a sissy.

Okay, Willie says. I will.

The brothers laugh. What happened to your friends, Willie Boy? You scared them.

The brothers pour the egg creams over Willie's head and walk away. You scared them, they say, imitating Willie's thin voice.

Another time they make fun of Willie's big nose. Another time, the red bump on his eyelid. They always make sure to tease him in the streets, away from any grown-ups. They're as sly as they are heartless. They remind Willie of the wolves in one of his storybooks.

When Willie is nine his brothers stop him on his way home from school. They stand directly in his path, their arms folded. Something about their faces, their body language, lets Willie know this time will be different. He knows that he'll always remember the high blue of the sky, the purple weeds in the vacant lot on his left, the pattern of the cracks in the sidewalk as Big Brother knocks him to the ground.

Willie writhes on the sidewalk, looking up. Big Brother smirks at Bigger Brother. What are we gonna do with him?

What can we do, Brother? We're stuck with him.

Didn't we tell you to quit bein such a sissy, Big Brother says to Willie.

Willie lies on his back, eyes filling with tears. I'm not.

Is it liars you're callin us?

No.

Don't you want us to tell you when you're doin somethin wrong?

Yeah.

That's what big brothers are for aint it?

No. I mean yeah.

Then.

I wasn't. Being a sissy. I promise I wasn't.

He's callin us liars, Big Brother says to Bigger Brother.

Grab him.

Big Brother jumps on Willie, grabs his arms.

Hey, Willie says. Come on now. Stop.

Big Brother lifts Willie off the sidewalk. He puts a knee in Willie's back, forces him to stand straight. Then Bigger Brother punches Willie in the mouth. Okay, Willie tells himself, that was bad, that was terrible, but at least it's over.

Then Bigger Brother punches Willie in the nose.

Willie crumples. His nose is broken.

He hugs the sidewalk, watches his blood mix with the dirt and turn to a brown paste. When he's sure that his brothers have gone, he staggers to his feet. The sidewalk whirls like a carousel as he stumbles home.

Mother, turning from the sink, puts her hands to her cheeks. What happened!

Nothing, he says. Some kids in the park.

He was born knowing the sacred code of Irish Town. Never tattle.

Mother guides him to a chair, presses a hot cloth on his mouth, touches his nose. He howls. She puts him on the sofa, leans over him. This shirt—I'll never get these stains out! He sees his brothers behind her, hovering, glaring. They're not impressed that he didn't tattle. They're incensed. He's deprived them of another justification for hating him.

The sidewalk whirls like a carousel. Sutton staggers. He reaches into his breast pocket for the white envelope. Tell Bess I didn't, I couldn't—

What's that, Mr. Sutton?

Tell Bess—

A stoop. Six feet away. Sutton lurches toward it. His leg locks up. He realizes too late that he's not going to make it.

Willie, Photographer says, everything cool, brother?

Sutton pitches forward.

Oh shit—Mr. Sutton!

It varies widely, for no apparent reason. Sometimes the brothers simply knock Willie's books out of his hands, call him a name. Other times they stuff him headfirst into an ash barrel. Other times they scratch, punch, draw blood.

They pretend there are offenses. Crimes. They stage little mock trials. One brother holds Willie while the other states the charge. Showing Disrespect. Being Weak. Kissing Up to Father. Then they debate. Should we punish him? Should we let him go? They make Willie plead his case. One day Willie tells them to just get it over with. The waiting is the real torture. Big Brother shrugs, sets his feet, rotates his hips to maximize the power. A straight right to Willie's midsection, the punch lands with a surprisingly loud *whump*. Willie feels all the wind rush from him, like the bellows in Father's shop. He drops to his knees.

When Willie is ten he tries to fight back. Bad idea. The beatings escalate. The brothers get Willie on the ground, kick their hard shoes into his kidneys, ribs, groin. One time they kick him so hard in the back of the head that he suffers nosebleeds for a week. Another time they twist his head until he passes out.

His parents don't know. They don't want to know. Father, after a twelve-hour day, can't think about anything but supper and bed. Even if he knew, he wouldn't say anything. Boys are boys. Willie used to admire Father's silence. Now he resents it. He no longer thinks Father a hero. He goes one last time to Father's shop, sees it all differently. With every unthinking swing of the hammer, with every metallic clank, Willie vows never to be like Father, though he fears that in some inescapable way he'll always be just like him. He suspects himself of the same capacity for boundless silence.

And Mother? She sees nothing but her own grief. Three years after Agnes's death she still wears black, still broods over the Bible, reading aloud, interrogating Jesus. Or else she simply sits with the Bible open in her lap, staring and murmuring into space. It's a house of sadness and muteness and blindness, and yet it's Willie's only refuge, the only place his brothers won't attack, because there are witnesses. So Willie clings to the kitchen table, doing his homework, using the rest of the family as unwitting bodyguards, while his brothers glide through the rooms, watching, waiting.

Their chance comes when Father is at work, Mother is paying the iceman, Older Sister is studying with a friend. Big Brother pounces first. He takes Willie's schoolbook, tears out the pages. Bigger Brother stuffs the pages into Willie's mouth. Stop, Willie tries to say, stop, please, stop. But he has a mouthful of paper.

Ten feet away Daddo stares above their heads. Here now, what's happening?

Reporter catches Sutton just before he hits the ground. Photographer rushes to Sutton's other side. Together they guide Sutton to the stoop.

Willie, Photographer says. What is it, man?

Mr. Sutton, Reporter says, you're shaking.

They ease Sutton onto the stoop. Reporter takes off his trench coat, wraps it around Sutton's shoulders.

Thanks kid. Thanks.

Photographer offers Sutton his barber pole scarf. Sutton shakes his head, pulls the fur collar of Reporter's trench coat around his neck. He sits quietly, trying to catch his breath, clear his head. Reporter and Photographer loom over him.

After a few minutes Sutton looks up at Reporter. Do you have siblings?

No. Only child.

Sutton nods, looks at Photographer. You?

Three older brothers.

Were you picked on?

All the time, brother. Toughened me up.

Sutton stares into space.

You, Mr. Sutton?

I had an older sister, two older brothers.

Did they pick on you?

Nah. I was a tough little monkey.

Somehow he does well in school. He earns all A's, one B. He doesn't want to show his report card to anyone, but the school requires a parent's signature. He cringes as Mother hugs him, as Father gives a proud nod in front of the whole family. He sees his brothers fuming, conspiring. He knows what's coming.

Three days later they catch him coming out of a candy store. He manages to escape, runs home, but the house is empty. His brothers burst through the door right behind him, tackle him, hold him down, drag him into the foyer. He sees what they have in mind. No, he begs. No no no, not that.

They push him into the closet. It's pitch dark. No, he begs, please. They lock him in. I can't breathe, he says, let me out! He rattles the knob, pleading. He pounds the door until his knuckles and nailbeds bleed. Not this, anything but this. He scratches until a fingernail comes clean off.

He weeps. He chokes. He buries his face in the dirty coats and scarves that smell like his family, that bear the distinctive Fels-cabbage-potatoes-wool scent of the Sutton Clan, and he prays for death. Ten years old, he asks God to take him.

Hours later the door opens. Mother.

Jesus Mary and Joseph, what do you think you're doing?

Mr. Sutton, do you feel up to continuing?

Yeah. I think so.

*Reporter helps Sutton to his feet, guides him to the Polara.
Photographer walks a few paces behind. Sutton eases into the
backseat, lifts his bad leg in after him. Reporter gently shuts the door.
Photographer gets behind the wheel, looks at Sutton in the rearview.
How about a donut, Willie?*

God no kid.

I think I'll have one. Could you pass them forward?

Sutton hands the pink box across the seat.

*Photographer picks a Bavarian cream, passes the box back.
Reporter gets in, turns up the heater. The only sounds are the
heater blowing, the radio crackling, Photographer smacking his
lips.*

*Now Reporter unfolds Sutton's map, leans toward Photographer.
They whisper. Sutton can't hear them over the heater and radio,
but he imagines what they're saying.*

What are we gonna do with him?

What can we do, brother? We're stuck with him.

FOUR

WILLIE COMES HOME TO FIND MOTHER IN THE PARLOR, reading the Bible to Daddo. His brothers are out. For the moment they're someone else's problem. With a sigh of relief Willie pulls a chair next to Mother, rests his head on her shoulder. The Fels smell. It makes him feel safe and sad at the same time.

The late fall of 1911.

Mother skips back and forth from Old Testament to New, slapping at the crinkly pages, murmuring, demanding an answer. The answer. Each pause gives Daddo a chance to tap his cane and offer commentary on the sublime wisdom of Jesus. Now she lands on Genesis, the story of Joseph and his brothers. Willie's mind floats on the lilt of her voice, the soughing of the potato sack curtains. *And when they saw him afar off, even before he came near unto them, they conspired against him to slay him. And they said one to another, Behold, this dreamer cometh. Come now therefore, and let us slay him, and cast him into some pit, and we will say, Some evil beast hath devoured him: and we shall see what will become of his dreams.*

Willie lifts his head from Mother's shoulder.

And it came to pass, when Joseph was come unto his brethren, that they stript Joseph out of his coat, his coat of many colours that was on him; And they took him, and cast him into a pit: and the pit was empty, there was no water in it.

Willie puts his hands over his face, shakes with sobs. Mother stops reading. Daddo tilts his head. The boy, he says, is moved by the Holy Spirit.

Maybe he'll be a priest, Mother says.

The next day she pulls him from P.S. 5 and enrolls him at St. Ann's.

Photographer is peeking in the rearview, driving fast. Peeking faster, driving faster. Reporter, trying to make notes, can't keep his pen steady. He turns to Photographer. Why are you driving like someone is chasing us?

Because someone is chasing us.

Reporter looks out the back window, sees a TV news van riding their bumper. How the hell did they find us?

We haven't exactly been inconspicuous. Maybe somebody witnessed a certain bank robber fainting in the middle of the street . . . ?

Photographer mashes the gas, runs a red light. He spins the wheel to the left, swerves to avoid a double-parked truck. Sutton, tossed around the backseat like a sock in a dryer, tastes this morning's champagne, last night's whiskey. He realizes that he hasn't eaten solid food since yesterday's lunch at Attica—beef stew. Now he tastes that too. He puts a hand on his stomach, knows what's coming. He tries to roll down a window. Stuck. Or locked. Converted cop car. He looks around. On the seat beside him are Photographer's camera bag and cloth purse. He opens the camera bag. Expensive lenses. He opens the cloth purse. Notebooks, paperbacks, The Autobiography of Malcolm X, *Norman Mailer's* The Armies of the Night, *a plastic baggie full of joints—and a billfold. Sutton touches the billfold.*

He sees the pink box of donuts. He lifts the lid, feels the contents of his stomach gathering on the launchpad. He shuts his eyes, swallows, gradually fights back the rising wave of nausea.

Photographer makes a hard right, steers toward the curb. The Polara fishtails. Squealing brakes, shrieking tires. They screech to a stop. The smell of scorched Firestone fills the car. Reporter kneels on the front seat, looks out the back. They're gone, he says to Photographer. Nice job.

I guess it pays to watch Mod Squad, *Photographer says.*

They sit for a moment, all three of them breathing hard. Even the Polara is panting. Now Photographer eases back into traffic. Tell me again—what's our next stop?

Corner of Sands and Gold. Right, Mr. Sutton?

Sutton grunts.

Sands and Gold? Christ, that's a block from where we just were.

Sorry. Mr. Sutton's map is kind of tough to read.

I was hitting the champagne pretty hard when I made it, Sutton says.

The Polara hits a pothole. Sutton's head hits the roof, his ass hits the seat.

You don't need to drive like a maniac anymore, Reporter says.

It's not me, Photographer says, it's these roads. And I think this Polara is shot.

Willie is shot, Sutton rasps.

The Polara hits another pothole.

One-sixth gravity, Sutton mumbles.

We're almost there, Mr. Sutton. You okay?

Just realized something kid.

What's that, Mr. Sutton?

I'm in the back of a radio car without handcuffs. I think that's part of what's got me on my heels this morning. That's why I don't feel like myself. I feel—naked.

Handcuffs?

We used to call them bracelets. The neighbors would say, Did you hear, they dragged poor Eddie Wilson away in bracelets?

Sutton holds up his wrists, stares at them from different angles. The purple veins, bubbled and wormy.

Photographer grins at Sutton in the rearview. If you want handcuffs, brother, we can get you some handcuffs.

* * *

Two classmates at St. Ann's become Willie's friends. William Happy Johnston and Edward Buster Wilson. That's how newspapers will most often refer to them. Everyone in Irish Town knows, Willie is the smart one, Happy is the handsome one, Eddie is the dangerous one. Everyone in Irish Town knows, you better watch your step around Eddie Wilson.

He used to be such a sweet kid, Irish Towners say. Then his aunt and uncle took ill. The lung sickness. They had to move in with Eddie's family—it was either that or a pesthouse. In no time their doctor bills wiped out Eddie's family. This was just after the Panic of 1907, the country spiraling into a Depression. Irish Town passed the hat, saved Eddie's family from being put on the street, but Eddie felt more embarrassed than relieved. Next, Eddie's old man lost his job as a driller. Again the neighborhood passed the hat, again Eddie cringed. Finally Eddie's mother got the lung sickness, and there was no money left for a doctor. She and Eddie were especially close, neighbors whispered at the funeral.

Overnight, everyone agrees, Eddie changed. His royal blue eyes turned stormy. His eyebrows drew together into a permanent V. He looked wounded all the time, ready to fight. When the Italians started to encroach on Irish Town, Eddie decided it was his job to hold them off. He was forever muttering about *them Eye-ties, them fuckin Dagos*. Every other week he was in another hellish battle.

The first time they meet, Willie sees only Eddie's courage, not his pain. Something about Eddie reminds Willie of polished, martial steel. Also, he seems equally loyal and lethal. And Eddie sees Willie through the same rosy lens. Assuming Willie's many bruises are from street brawls, not his brothers, Eddie grants Willie his deepest respect. Willie, in need of a friend, doesn't set Eddie straight.

Happy never had to earn Eddie's respect. They've been friends since birth. Their families live across the street from each other, their fathers are thick. That's why Happy is always laughing at

Eddie's bad temper, because he remembers the old Eddie. To Willie, laughing at Eddie seems like asking for trouble, like the lion tamers at the street circus putting their heads between those pink dripping jaws. But Eddie never snaps at Happy. Happy is so *happy*, so damn good looking, it's hard to be mad at him.

Some say Happy was born happy. Others say he's happy about the way he looks. Unbearably handsome. Unfairly handsome. Most agree that some percentage of his constant cheerfulness is traceable to his family's nest egg. The Johnstons aren't rich, but they're among the few Irish Towners who don't live on the rusty razor's edge. Happy's father got hit by a trolley years ago and the family won a settlement. Moreover, they were smart enough not to put their windfall in a bank, hundreds of which have gone bust.

Daddo asks Willie about his new friends. He's heard Happy's voice from the street. He says Happy sounds handsome.

He is, Willie says. He has black hair and black eyes and the girls in school all love him.

Daddo chuckles. Bless him. What I wouldn't give. And the Wilson boy?

Yellow hair. Blue eyes. He gets in fights. And steals sometimes.

Be careful, Willie Boy. Sounds like he has a bit of the Old Nick in him.

The what?

The devil.

Willie doesn't understand what Daddo means. Until an older boy down the block, Billy Doyle, gets pinched. Housebreaking, shoplifting, something minor. What makes it major, what makes it the talk of Irish Town, is that Billy has given up the names of his confederates. The cops beat the names out of Billy, but that's no excuse. Not in Irish Town.

Right after the cops turn Billy loose, he sits on his stoop, his jaw broken, his left eye purple and running with pus, a rotted plum. He's a pitiable sight, but people walk past all day long as if he's not there. Even mothers pushing prams give him the standard Irish Town treatment for rats. Silence.

Eddie, who grew up with Billy's brothers, and likes him, watches from up the street for hours. After a while he can't take it anymore. He crosses, walks up to Billy, asks how he's feeling.

Not so good, Eddie.

Eddie leans in, puts an arm on Billy's shoulder, tells him to hang in there.

Billy looks up, smiles.

Eddie spits in his eye.

Weeks later Billy Doyle drinks iodine. There is no funeral.

Sutton sees a family walking along the street, dressed for church. Dad, Mom, two little boys. Father and sons are wearing identical suits. In the old days, Sutton says, his voice weak, the worst thing you could be was a Judas.

Reporter glances into the backseat. Are you referring, by any chance, to Arnold Schuster?

No.

That whole ratting thing, that whole Code of Brooklyn—where does that come from?

Sutton taps his chest. From in here kid. The deepest part. When I was ten years old the cops found a man lying in the middle of our street, a baling hook in his chest. He was a stevedore, got crossways with some of the boys on the waterfront. As the cops took him to the hospital they asked who did this to him. He told the cops to go fuck themselves. Those were his last words—imagine? Three days later the whole fuckin neighborhood turned out for his funeral, including the guys who offed him. There was talk of petitioning the city to name a street after him.

All because he didn't name the guys who murdered him?

People are clannish, Sutton says. We didn't become human a million years ago until we hopped out of trees and split into clans.

You betray someone in your clan, you open the door to the end of the world.

But the people who murdered him were in his clan? Didn't they betray him?

Ratting is a hundred times worse than murder.

It all sounds kind of—barbaric, Reporter says. It sounds like people making life harder than it needs to be.

No one is making anything kid. It's just how human beings are built. Two thousand years later, why do we know the name of Judas and not the soldier who nailed Christ to the cross?

In 1913 Willie's brothers move out. One gets a job at a factory in West Virginia, the other joins the Army. They give Willie one ferocious goodbye beating in the shadow of St. Ann's, but Willie doesn't feel it. Knowing they'll be gone in a few days, knowing they won't be part of his world anymore, makes the blows bounce off. *But the Lord was with Joseph, and shewed him mercy, and gave him favour in the sight of the keeper of the prison.* Watching Big Brother and Bigger Brother saunter away, Willie picks up his hat, licks the blood from his lip, laughs.

Sutton kneels on the cobblestones at Sands and Gold. He looks as if he's about to propose to Photographer and Reporter.

Mr. Sutton—what are you doing?

St. Ann's, my grammar school, used to be right here.

A gust of wind sends a few loose newspaper pages fluttering like birds. Sutton pats the cobblestones. These are the same cobblestones I walked on as a kid, he says in a half whisper. Time—the subtle thief of youth.

What? Who's a thief?

Time. Some dead fuckin poet said that. Father Flynn quoted it all the time. Made us memorize it. He probably stood right there, where you two are standing, saying that line, which is pure horseshit.

Time is a thief, but he's not subtle. He's a thug. And youth is a little old lady walking through the park with a pocketbook full of cash. You want to avoid being like youth? You want to keep time from robbing you? Hold on for dear life, boys. When time tries to snatch something from you, just grab tighter. Don't let go. That's what memory is. Not letting go. Saying fuck you to time.

Photographer puts a Newport between his lips. Uh—Willie?

Sutton looks up. Yeah kid.

Willie, this isn't really working for me—creatively? You, at the site of your former school? It's static, brother.

Static.

Yeah. Also, you're kind of freaking us out.

Why kid?

Well. You're talking to yourself, for starters. And you're not making sense. Compared to you, most of the cats I met at Woodstock were acting straight.

Sorry kid. I'm just. Remembering.

Reporter steps forward. Mr. Sutton, maybe you could tell us some of what you're remembering? Share something about your early life? Your childhood?

I don't remember much.

But you just said—

Okay, Sutton says. Let's go. Stop Number Three—Hudson Street.

Photographer helps Sutton to his feet. Willie, can you at least tell us the point of Stop Number Two?

Youth.

Youth?

Yeah. Youth.

What about youth, Willie?

She's just fuckin asking for it.

There are no ball fields in Irish Town. No playgrounds, no gyms, no rec centers. So the neighborhood boys all gather at the Hudson Street slaughterhouse. In their short pants and vests, their collarless shirts and ragged shoes, they hang around the loading docks, mooching hooves and feet, heckling the animals on their way to die.

None of the boys respects the slaughterhouse like Eddie. None but Eddie roots for the butchers. If there were trading cards of butchers, Eddie would collect them. He cheers when the butchers slit a pig's throat, laughs when they stab a cow in the eye or lop off a sheep's head. He gazes worshipfully when they dip a mug into the raw blood at their feet and slurp it down for nourishment.

In 1914, however, Eddie sees something at the slaughterhouse that haunts him. One black castrated male sheep leads all the other sheep up the ramp to the killing door. At the last minute the black sheep does a shifty little sidestep, saving himself.

What's with that sheep there? Eddie asks.

That's the Judas sheep, a butcher says. It's actually a goat that looks like a sheep.

Sutty, get a load of this fuckin sheep. Look how he double-crosses his buddies.

He's just a sheep, Ed. Or a goat.

Eddie punches his palm. Nah, nah, that rat knows what he's doin.

A few nights later Eddie rousts Willie and Happy from their beds and drags them down to the slaughterhouse. He jimmies the lock on the door to the loading dock and leads them into the filthy pens where the river barges unload the animals. In a far corner they find the black Judas sheep lying on its side. The sleep of the innocent, Eddie says, grabbing a board and giving the sheep a whack on the head. Blood goes everywhere. It spurts into Willie's eyes and sprays the front of Happy's white shirt. The sheep scrambles to its feet and tries to run. Eddie chases. Come here, you. He swings the board like a baseball bat, hits the sheep on the backside. Where you think you're going? He gives the sheep another whack, and another. When the sheep is down, Eddie leaps on it, puts a tourniquet around the fleecy neck. Happy holds the kicking legs while Eddie slowly tightens.

Sutty, grab that board, give him one.

No.

Willie could never hurt a defenseless animal. Even an animal that rats out other animals. Besides, the sight of Eddie and Happy holding down the Judas sheep reminds Willie of his brothers. *I seek my brethren: tell me, I pray thee, where they feed their flocks.* Willie keeps his distance, though he doesn't look away. He can't. He watches Eddie and Happy torment the sheep, watches Eddie pull out a knife and stab it and stab it until the frantic *baaa* becomes a pathetic *ba*. Eddie and Happy are his best friends, but maybe he didn't know them until now. Maybe he'll never know them. He watches them laugh at the sheep's lacquered black eyes going white, then pearly gray. He closes his own eyes. Tattletale gray.

Sutton paces up and down Hudson Street. He inhales deeply through his nose. Wet hide, offal, blood. Smell that, boys? Somehow that stench didn't bother us as kids.

I don't smell anything, Photographer says to Reporter.

Sutton points to his feet. Daddo said Eddie had the devil in him—I found out on this spot what that meant. Eddie's first kill.

Now we're talking, Photographer says, pushing Reporter out of the way, shooting as Sutton points to the ground.

Reporter sets down his briefcase, clicks it open, pulls out a stack of files.

What are those? Sutton asks.

The newspaper's Willie Sutton files. Some of them anyway. There's an entire drawer devoted to you, Mr. Sutton. You mentioned your grandfather. I saw him in one of these files. Was he the actor?

No. The actor was my father's father. Back in Ireland. They say he knew most of Shakespeare by heart. I'm talking about my mother's father.

Photographer keeps shooting. But who got killed here, brother?

A sheep, Sutton says.

Photographer stops, lowers his camera. A what?

There was a slaughterhouse here. I used to come with my best friends, Eddie and Happy. One night they killed a sheep. Or a goat pretending to be a sheep.

Why?

It ratted on the other sheep.

Photographer rests his camera on his hip. The sheep ratted, he says to Reporter. You hearing this?

Mr. Sutton, you mentioned Eddie. Do you mean Edward Buster Wilson? With whom you were arrested in 1923?

Yeah.

In this one clip, the judge said you were like outlaws in the Old West.

Nah, the judge said that about me and another guy. But it was sure true of me and Eddie.

Reporter flips open a file. Okay. Here we go—Sutton and Wilson. Unlawful entry, armed robbery.

Sounds about right, Sutton says.

And Happy—now, Mr. Sutton, is that William Happy Johnston? With whom you were arrested in 1919?

The same.

Burglary. Larceny.

Good old Happy.

Kidnapping. Wait—kidnapping?

You had to be there, Sutton says. You had to know Happy. Not that anybody really knew Happy. Not that anybody fuckin knows anybody.

Who did you and Happy kidnap?

Chronological order kid.

FIVE

AS WILLIE LISTENS FROM THE HALL, FATHER AND MOTHER sit up all night, a gas lamp between them, going over the family account book. Mother asks, What will we do? Father says nothing. But it's the way he says nothing.

First it was those newfangled bicycles everywhere, now it's these accursed motorcars. Not long ago people said the motorcar was a fad. Now everyone agrees it's here to stay. Newspapers are filled with ads for the latest, shiniest models. New roads are going in all over the city. The fire department has already switched to horseless hose trucks. All of which means hard times for blacksmiths.

The summer of 1914. Despite his troubles at home, despite running the streets with Eddie and Happy, Willie manages to graduate from grammar school at the top of his class. There's no thought of high school, however. The day after he gets his diploma he gets his working papers. His mother's dream of him in priest robes gets shelved. His own dreams are never mentioned. He needs to get a job, needs to help his family stay afloat.

But it's hard times for more than just blacksmiths. America is mired in a Depression, the second of Willie's young life. Willie applies at the riverside factories, the downtown offices, the dry goods stores and clothing shops and lunch counters. He's bright, presentable, many people know and admire Father. But Willie has no experience, no skills, and for every available job he's competing with hundreds. He reads in the newspapers that crowds of unemployed are surging through Manhattan, demanding work. Other cities too. In Chicago the crowds are so unruly, cops fire on them.

Daddo asks Willie to read him the newspapers. Strikes, riots, unrest—after half an hour Daddo asks him to stop. He mutters into the potato sack curtains:

Feckin world is ending.

To save money the Suttons quit Irish Town, move to a smaller apartment near Prospect Park. They have so little, the move takes only one trip in a horse-drawn van. Then Father lays off his apprentice. Despite slower business, despite an arthritic back and aching shoulders, Father now puts in longer hours, which aggravates his back and shoulders. Mother talks to Daddo about what they'll do when Father can't get out of bed in the morning. They'll be on the street.

Father asks Willie to join him at the shop. Big Brother, thrown out of the Army, is helping too. I don't think I'm cut out for blacksmithing, Willie says. Father looks at Willie, hard, not with anger, but bewilderment. As if Willie is a stranger. I know the feeling, Willie wants to say.

After a day of shapeouts, interviews, submitting applications that will never be read, Willie runs back to the old neighborhood. Eddie and Happy can't find jobs either. The boys seek relief from the rising temperatures and their receding futures in the East River. To get in a few clean strokes they have to push away inner tubes, lettuce heads, orange rinds, mattresses. They also have to dodge garbage scows, tugboats, barges, corpses—the river claims a new victim every week. And yet the boys don't mind. No matter how slimy, or fishy, or deadly, the river is sacred. The one place they feel welcome. In their element.

The boys often dare each other to touch the sludgy bottom. More than once they nearly drown in the attempt. It's a foolish game, like pearl diving with no hope of a pearl, but each is afraid to admit he's afraid. Then Eddie ups the ante, suggests a race across. Perched like seagulls atop the warped pilings of an abandoned pier, they look through the summer haze at the skyline.

What if we cramp up, Happy says.

What if, Eddie says with a sneer.

The mermaids will save us, Willie mumbles.

Mermaids? Happy says.

My Daddo says every body of water has a mermaid or two.

Our only hope of getting laid, Eddie says.

Speak for yourself, Happy says.

Willie shrugs. What the hell have we got to lose?

Our lives, Happy mumbles.

Like I said.

They dive. Tracing the shadow of the Brooklyn Bridge they reach Manhattan in twenty-six minutes. Eddie is first, followed by Happy, then Willie. Willie would have been first, but he slowed halfway and briefly toyed with the idea of letting go, sinking forever to the bottom. They stand on the dock, dripping, gasping, laughing with pride.

Now comes the problem of getting back. Eddie wants to swim. Willie and Happy roll their eyes. We're walking, Ed.

Willie's first time on the Brooklyn Bridge. Those cables, those Gothic brick arches—beautiful. Daddo says men died building this bridge. The arches are their headstones. Willie thinks they died for a good cause. Daddo also says this bridge, when first opened, terrified people. It was too big, no one thought it would stay up. Barnum had to walk a herd of elephants across to prove that it was safe. Part of Willie is still terrified. Not by the size, but the height. He doesn't like heights. It's not a fear of falling so much as a queasiness at seeing the world from above. Especially Manhattan. The big city is intimidating enough across the river. From up here it's too much. Too magical, too desirable, too mythically beautiful, like the women in *Photoplay*. He wants it. He hates it. He longs to conquer it, capture it, keep it all to himself. He'd like to burn it to the ground.

The bird's-eye view of Irish Town is still more unsettling. From the apex of the bridge it looks slummier, meaner. Willie scans the chimneys, the ledges, the grimed windows and mudded streets. Even if you leave, you never escape.

We should take the BQE, Photographer says.

No, Reporter says, stay on surface streets.

Why?

Buildings, stores, statues—there's stuff on the streets that might jog Mr. Sutton's memory.

While Reporter and Photographer debate the best route to their next stop, Thirteenth Street, Sutton rests his eyes. He feels the car stop short. He opens his eyes. Red light.

He rolls his head to the right. Tumbledown stores, each one new, unfamiliar. Is this really Brooklyn? It might as well be Bangkok. Where there used to be a bar and grill, there's now a record store. Where there used to be a record store, there's now a clothing store. How many nights, lying in his cell, did Sutton mentally walk the old Brooklyn? Now it's gone, all gone. The old neighborhoods were just cardboard sets and paper scenery, which someone casually struck and carted off. Then again, one thing never changes. None of these stores looks to be hiring.

What's that, Mr. Sutton?

Nothing.

Sutton sees an electronics store. Dozens of TVs in the front window. Stop the car, stop the car.

Photographer looks left, right. We are stopped. We're at a red light, Willie.

Sutton opens the door. The sidewalk is covered with patches of frozen snow. He steps carefully toward the electronics store. On every TV it's—Willie Sutton. Last night. Walking out of Attica.

But it's also not him. It's Father. And Mother. He hadn't realized how much his face has come to look like them both.

Sutton presses his nose against the window, cups his hands around his eyes. On a few screens closer to the window is President Nixon. A recent news conference.

Reporter walks up.

Did you ever notice, kid, how much presidents act like wardens?

I can't say as I have, Mr. Sutton.

Trust me. They do.

Have you ever voted, Mr. Sutton?

Every time I took down a bank I was voting.

Reporter writes this in his notebook.

Tell you one thing, Sutton says. I'd love to have voted against President Shifty Eyes here. Fuckin criminal.

Reporter laughs. I'm no Nixon fan, Mr. Sutton—but a criminal?

Doesn't he remind you of anybody kid?

No. Should he?

The eyes. Look at the eyes.

Reporter moves closer to the window, looks at Nixon, then back at Sutton. Back at Nixon. Now that you mention it, he says.

I wouldn't trust either of us as far as I could throw us, Sutton says. Did you know that Nixon, when he worked on Wall Street, lived in the same apartment building as Governor Rockefeller?

I'm not really a Rockefeller fan.

Join the club.

Personally, I liked Romney. Then, after he dropped out, I rooted for Reagan. I was hoping he'd win the nomination.

Reagan? God help us.

What's wrong with Ronald Reagan?

An actor running the world? Get a grip.

When the river is too cold for swimming, the boys take their fishing poles to Red Hook. They buy tomato sandwiches wrapped in oil paper, two cents apiece, and sit on the rocks along The Narrows, dangling their lines in the slimy water. Even with no jobs, they can at least contribute something to their families if they catch a striper or two.

One day, the fish not biting, Eddie paces the rocks. Whole fuckin thin is rigged, he says.

What thing, Ed?

The *whole* thin.

Behind him a tug plows through the silver-green water, a barge glides toward Manhattan. A three-masted schooner heads for Staten Island. The sky is a chaotic web of wires and smoke-stacks, steeples and office towers. Eddie gives it all the evil eye. Then the middle finger.

Eddie's always been angry, but lately his anger has been deeper, edgier. Willie blames himself. Willie took Eddie to the library, persuaded him to get a library card. Now Eddie has books to support his darkest suspicions. Jack London, Upton Sinclair, Peter Kropotkin, Karl Marx, they all tell Eddie that he's not paranoid, the world really is against him.

Some fuckin system, he says. Every ten or fifteen years it crashes. Aint no system, that's the problem. It's every man for his-fuckin-self. The Crash of '93? My old man saw people standin in the middle of the street bawlin like babies. Wiped out. Ruined. But did those bankers get pinched? Nah—they got richer. Oh the government promised it wouldn't happen again. Well it happened again didn't it fellas? In '07. And '11. And when them banks fell apart, when the market did a swan dive, didn't them bankers walk away scot-free again?

Willie and Happy nod.

I'm not saying the man who shot McKinley was right in his head, I only say I understand what drove him to it.

Get yourself pinched talking like that, Ed.

Eddie wings a rock at the water. *Blunth*—a sound like a fat man gulping. We're on the losin team, boys. We're Irish *blunth* and broke *blunth* and that makes us double fucked. Just how the rich want it. You can't be on the top if there aint no one on the *blunth* bottom.

How come you're the only one talking about this stuff? Happy says.

I aint the only one, Happy. Read a goddamn book, willya?

Happy frowns. If he reads he won't be happy.

Of all the evil rich, Eddie thinks the evilest by far are the Rockefellers. He scans the horizon as if there might be a Rockefeller out there for him to peg with a rock. He's obsessed with Ludlow. Last year J.D. Rockefeller Jr. sent a team of sluggers to put down the mine strike there, and the sluggers massacred seventy-five unarmed men, women, children. If anyone else did that, Eddie often says, he'd get the chair.

Tell you what I'd like to do, Eddie grumbles, winging a rock at a seagull. I'd like to go uptown right now and find Old Man Rockefeller's mansion.

What would you do, Ed?

Heh heh. Remember that Judas sheep?

Photographer circles Grand Army Plaza, swings right on Thirteenth Street. He pulls over, double-parks. It's gone, Sutton says, touching the window. Fuck—I knew stuff would be gone. But everything?

What's gone, Willie?

The apartment house where we moved in 1915. At least the apartment house next door is still standing. That one right there, that gives you an idea what ours looked like.

He points to a five-story brownstone, streaked with soot and bird shit.

That's where I saw my parents grow old before their time, worrying about money. That's where I watched the lines on their faces get deeper, watched their hair turn white. That's where I learned that life is all about money. And love. And lack thereof.

That's it, Mr. Sutton?

Anyone who tells you different is a fuckin liar. Money. Love. There's not a problem that isn't caused by one or the other. And there's not a problem that can't be solved by one or the other.

That seems kind of reductive, Mr. Sutton.

Money and Love kid. Nothing else matters. Because those are the only two things that make us forget about death. For a few minutes anyhow.

Trees line the curb. They nod and bow as if they remember Sutton. As if beseeching him to get out of the car. My best friends were Eddie Wilson and Happy Johnston, Sutton says softly.

Photographer yanks a loose fringe off his buckskin jacket. You mentioned that.

What was Happy like? Reporter asks.

Broads loved him.

Hence the name, Photographer says, starting up the car, pulling away. Where to next?

Remsen Street, Reporter says.

Happy had the blackest hair you ever saw, Sutton says. Like he was dipped in coal. He had one of those chin asses like yours kid. A smile like yours too. Big white teeth. Like a movie star. Before there were movie stars.

And Eddie?

Strange case. Blond, real All-American looking, but he never felt like an American. He felt like America didn't want him. Fuck, he was right, America didn't. America didn't want any of us, and you haven't felt unwanted until America doesn't want you. I loved Eddie, but he was one rough sombitch. You did not want to get on his wrong side. I thought he'd be a prizefighter. After they banned him from the slaughterhouse, he hung out in gyms. Then the gyms banned him. He wouldn't stop fighting after the bell. And if you crossed him in the streets, Jesus, if you did not show proper

respect, God help you. He'd give you an Irish haircut quick as look
at you.

Irish what?

A swat to the back of the head with a lead pipe wrapped in
newspaper.

Their luck changes in the fall of 1916. Eddie lands a construction
job at one of the new office towers going up, and Happy's uncle
arranges jobs for Happy and Willie as gophers at a bank. Title
Guaranty.

The bank job will require new clothes. Willie and Happy find
a haberdasher on Court Street willing to extend them credit.
They each buy two suits—two sack coats, two pairs of trousers,
two matching vests, two silk cravats, cuff buttons, spats. Walking
to work his first day Willie stops before a store window. He
doesn't recognize himself. He's delighted not to recognize himself.
He hopes he never recognizes himself again.

Better yet, his coworkers don't recognize him. They seem not
to know that he's Irish. They treat him with courtesy and kindness.

Weeks fly by. Months. Willie loses himself in his work. He
finds the whole enterprise of the bank exhilarating. After the
Crash of 1893, the Panic of 1907, the smaller panic of 1911, the
Depression of 1914, New York is rebuilding. Office towers are
being erected, bridges are being laced across the rivers, tunnels
are being laid underneath, and cash for all this epic growth
comes from banks, which means Willie is engaged in a grand
endeavor. He's part of society, included in its mission, vested in
its purposes—at last. He sleeps deeper, wakes more refreshed.
Putting on his spats each morning he feels a giddy sense of relief
that Eddie was wrong. The whole thing isn't rigged.

They pull up to the former home of Title Guaranty, a Romanesque
Revival building on Remsen Street. Sutton looks at the arched

third-floor windows where he used to sit with Happy and the other gophers. In one window someone has taped a sign. NIXON/AGNEW. *This is where I had my first job, Sutton says. A bank robber whose first job was in a bank—imagine?*

Photographer shoots the building. He turns the camera, dials the lens, this way, that. Sutton shifts his gaze from the building to Photographer.

You like your work, Sutton says. Don't you kid?

Photographer stops, gives a half turn. Yeah, he says over his shoulder. I do, Willie. I dig it. How can you tell?

I can always tell when a man likes his work. What year were you born kid?

Nineteen forty-three.

Hm. Eventful year for me. Shit, they were all eventful. Where were you born?

Roslyn, Long Island.

You go to college?

Yeah.

Which one?

I went to Princeton, Photographer says sheepishly.

No kidding? Good school. I took a walk around the campus one morning. What did you study?

History. I was going to be a professor, an academic, but sophomore year my parents made the fatal mistake of buying me a camera for Christmas. That was all she wrote. The only thing I cared about from then on was taking pictures. I wanted to capture *history instead of reading* about *it.*

I'll bet your folks were thrilled.

Oh yeah. My father didn't speak to me for about three months.

What do you like so much about taking pictures?

You say life's all about Money and Love? I say it's all about experiences.

Is that so?

And this camera helps me have all different kinds of experiences. This Leica gets me through locked doors, past police tape, over walls, barbed wire, barricades. It shows me the world, brother. Helps me bear witness.

Witness. Is that so.

Also, Willie, I dig telling the truth. Words can be twisted but a photo never lies.

Sutton laughs.

What's funny? Photographer says.

Nothing. Except—that's pure horseshit kid. I can't think of anything that lies more than a photo. In fact every photo is a dirty stinking lie because it's a frozen moment—and time can't be frozen. Some of the biggest lies I've ever run across have been photos. Some of them were of me.

Photographer faces straight ahead, a slightly miffed look on his face. Willie, he says, all I know is, this camera took me to the bloodbath in Hue City. Tet Offensive—those aren't just words in a book to me. It took me to Mexico City to see Tommie Smith and John Carlos raise their fists. It took me to Memphis to see the chaos and the coverup after they shot King. No other way I would've gotten to see all those things. This camera lets me see, brother.

Sutton looks at Reporter. How about you kid?

How about me?

Did you always want to be a reporter?

Yes.

How come?

I'm a yeshiva student from the Bronx—in what other job would I get to spend the day with America's greatest bank robber?

FBI agent.

I don't like guns.

Me neither.

I admit, Mr. Sutton, some days I don't love this job. No one reads anymore.

I do nothing but read.

You're the exception. TV is going to make us all extinct. Also, a newsroom isn't exactly the happiest place on earth. It's sort of a snake pit. Politics, backstabbing, jealousy.

That's one nice thing about crooks, Sutton says. No professional jealousy. A crook reads about another crook making off with millions, he's happy for the guy. Crooks root for each other.

Except when they kill each other.

True.

Tell him about editors, Photographer says to Reporter.

What about them? Sutton says.

They can be a real pain in the ass, Reporter says into his lap.

Sutton lights a Chesterfield. What about your editor? In what way is he a pain in the ass?

He says I have a face that begs to be lied to.

Ouch. And what did he say when he sent you off to spend the day with Willie?

Photographer laughs, looks out his window. Reporter looks out his.

Go on kid. You can tell me.

My editor said I had three jobs today, Mr. Sutton. Get you on the record about Arnold Schuster. Don't let another reporter or photographer near you. And don't lose you.

Sutton blows a cloud of smoke over Reporter's head. Then you're fucked kid.

Why?

You've already lost me. I'm back in 1917.

Willie standing in the vault. It's larger than his bedroom on Thirteenth Street, and it's filled, floor to ceiling, with money. He gazes at the tightly wrapped bills, the strongboxes of gold coins, the racks of gleaming silver. He inhales—better than a candy store. He never realized how much he loved money. He couldn't afford to realize.

He loads a wheeled cart with cash and coins, slowly rolls the cart along the cages, filling the tellers' drawers. He feels all-powerful, a Brooklyn King Solomon dispensing gifts from his mine. Before returning the cart he cradles a brick of fifties. With this one brick he could buy a shiny new motorcar, a house for his parents. He could book a cabin on the next liner sailing to France. He slides one fifty out of the pack, holds it to the light. That dashing portrait of Ulysses Grant, those green curlicues in the corners, those silver-blue letters: *Will Pay to the Bearer On Demand*. Who knew the fifty was such a work of art? They should hang one in a museum. He slides the bill carefully back into the pack, sets the pack back in its place on the shelf.

Evenings, after work, Willie sits on a bench in the park and reads Horatio Alger novels, devours them one after another. They're all the same—the hero rises from nothing to become rich, loved, respected—and that's exactly what Willie loves about them. The predictability of the plot, the inevitability of the hero's ascent, provides a kind of comfort. It reaffirms Willie's faith.

Sometimes Alger's hero starts as a gopher at a bank.

Pedophile, Sutton says.

Photographer is trying to get the City Desk on the radio. Yeah, he says, yeah yeah, that's right, we're leaving Remsen Street, headed to Sands Street, near the Navy Yard.

Goddamn perv, Sutton says.

Photographer lowers the radio, turns. You say something, Willie?

Sutton slides forward, leans across the seat. Horatio Alger.

What about him?

He'd cruise these streets looking for homeless kids. They were everywhere back then, sleeping under stairs, bridges. Street Arabs they were called. Alger would bring them home, interview them for his books, then molest them. Now he's synonymous with the American Dream. Imagine?

Malcolm X says there is no American Dream, Willie. Just an American nightmare.

Nah, that's not true. There's an American Dream. The trick is not waking up.

After six months at Title Guaranty, Willie is summoned to the manager's office.

Sutton, your work is exemplary. You are diligent, you are conscientious, never tardy or sick. Everyone at this bank says you are a fine young man, and I can only agree. Keep this up, my boy, keep on this path, and you are sure to go places.

A month later Willie is laid off. Happy too. The manager, red-faced, blames the war in Europe. Trading has collapsed, the world's economy is teetering—everyone is cutting back. Especially banks. Into a hatbox Willie folds his sack coats and matching trousers and vests, his cravats and cuff buttons and spats, then sets the box on the shelf of Mother's closet.

He buys five newspapers and a grease pencil and sits in the park. On the same bench where he used to read Alger novels he now combs the wants. He then walks the length of Brooklyn, filling out forms, handing in applications. He applies for bank jobs, clerk jobs, salesman jobs. He holds his nose when applying for salesman jobs. The idea of tricking someone into buying something they don't need, and can't afford, makes him sick.

At the start of each day Willie meets Happy and Eddie at Pete's Awful Coffee. Eddie's been laid off too. The builders of the office tower ran out of cash. Whole fuckin thin is rigged, Eddie mutters into his coffee cup. No one at the counter disagrees. No one dares.

Then, just around the start of the 1917 baseball season, on his way to meet Eddie and Happy, Willie spots a newsboy from half a block away, waving the extra. That one word, big and black and shiny as the badge on the newsboy's shirt—WAR. Willie hands the newsboy a penny, runs to the coffee shop. Breathless, he spreads the newspaper across the counter and tells Eddie and Happy this is it, their big chance, they should all enlist. They're only sixteen, but hell, maybe they can get fake birth certificates. Maybe they can go to Canada, sign up there. It's war, it's nasty, but Jesus—it's something.

Count me out, Eddie says, shoving his cup away. This is Rockefeller's war. And his butt boy, J. P. Morgan. I aint takin a bullet for them robber barons. Don't you realize we're already *in* a war, Sutty? Us against them?

I'm surprised, Willie says. I really am, Ed. I thought you'd jump at the chance to kill a few Dagos. Unless maybe you're afraid those Dagos might get the best of you.

Happy laughs. Eddie grabs Willie's shirtfront and loads up a punch, then shakes his head and eases himself back onto his stool.

Sutty the Patriot, Happy says. Don't you worry, Sutty. You're feeling patriotic? There'll be plenty of ways to do your part. My old man says every war brings a boom. Sit tight. We'll soon be in clover.

Within weeks it's true. New York is humming, a hive of activity, and the boys land jobs in a factory making machine guns. The pay is thirty-five a week, nearly four times what Willie and Happy were making at Title Guaranty. Willie is able to give his parents room and board and a little more. He watches them count and recount the money, sees the strain of the last few years falling away.

And still he has something left over for a bit of fun. Every other night he goes with Eddie and Happy to Coney Island. How did he live so long without this enchanted place? The music, the lights—the laughter. It's at Coney Island that Willie first realizes: no one in the Sutton household ever laughs.

Best of all he loves the food. He's been raised on wilted cabbage and thin stews, now he has access to a sultan's feast. Stepping off the trolley he can smell the roasted pigs, the grilled clams coated with butter, the spring chickens, the filet chateaubriands, the pickled walnuts, the Roman punches, and he realizes—he's been hungry for sixteen years.

No delicacy at Coney Island is so exotic, so addictive, as the recently invented Nathan's Famous. It's also called a hot dog. Slicked with mustard, slotted into a billfold of soft white bread, it makes Willie moan with pleasure. Happy can eat five, Eddie can eat seven. There's no limit to how many Willie can put away.

After gorging themselves, and washing it all down with a few steins of beer, the boys stroll the Boardwalk, trying to catch the eyes of pretty girls. But pretty girls are the one delicacy they can't have. In 1917 and 1918 pretty girls want soldiers. Even Happy can't compete with those smart uniforms, those white sailor hats.

Before catching a rattler home Eddie insists that they swing by the Amazing Incubator, the new warming oven for babies that come out half cooked. Eddie likes to press his face to the glass door, wave at the seven or eight newborns on the other side. Look, Sutty, they're so damn *tiny*. They're like little hot dogs.

Don't eat one by accident, Happy says.

Eddie yells through the glass door. Welcome to earth, suckers. The whole thin's rigged.

SIX

THERE ARE HUNDREDS SPRINKLED THROUGHOUT THE CITY, but Happy says only two are worth a damn. One under the Brooklyn Bridge, the other on Sands Street, just outside the Navy Yard. Happy prefers the one on Sands. The girls aren't necessarily prettier, he says. Just more obliging. They work ten-hour shifts, taking on three customers an hour, and more when the fleet is in. He relates this with the admiration and wonder of a staunch capitalist describing Henry Ford's new assembly line.

Around the time of the Battle of Passchendaele, and the draft riots in Oklahoma, and the mining strikes throughout the West, the boys pay their first visit together to the house on Sands Street. The kitchen is the waiting room. Six men sit around the table, and along the wall, reading newspapers, like men at a barbershop. The boys grab newspapers, take seats near the stove. They blow on their hands. The night is cold.

Willie watches the other men closely. Each time one is summoned it's the same routine. The man tromps upstairs. Minutes later, through the ceiling, heavy footsteps. Then a female voice. Then muffled laughter. Then bedsprings squeaking. Then a loud grunt, a high trill, a few moments of exhausted silence. Finally a slammed door, footsteps descending, and the man passes through the kitchen, cheeks blazing, a flower in his button-hole. The flower is complimentary.

When it's their turn Willie feels panic verging on apoplexy. At the upstairs landing he hesitates. Maybe another time, Happy, I don't feel so good. My stomach.

Tell her where it hurts, Willie, she'll kiss it and make it better.

Happy pushes Willie toward a pale blue door at the far end of the hall. Willie knocks lightly.

Come.

He pushes the door in slowly.

Shut the door, honey—there's a draft in that hall.

He does as he's told. The room is dim, lit only by a candle lamp. On the edge of a frilly bed sits a girl in a baby pink negligee. Smooth skin, long full hair. Pretty eyes with dark lashes. But she's missing her right arm.

Lost it when I was six, she says when Willie asks. Fell under a streetcar. That's how come they call me Wingy.

It must also be the reason she's on Sands Street. Not many other ways for a one-armed girl in Brooklyn to get by.

Willie puts a fifty-cent piece on the dresser. Wingy rises, drops the baby pink negligee. Smiling, she comes to Willie, helps him undress. She knows it's his first time. How do you know, Wingy? I just do, darlin. Willie calculates—it must be her hundred and first time. This month. As he stands with his pants bunched around his feet, she kisses his chin, his lips, his big nose. He begins to shake, as if cold, though the room is stifling. The windows are shut tight, fogging. Wingy leads him to the bed. She lies on top of him. She kisses him harder, parts his lips with hers.

He draws back. Half her bottom teeth are missing.

Merchant marine knocked them out, she says. Now no more questions, sugar lump, just you lie back and let Wingy do what Wingy does.

What does Wingy do?

I said no more questions.

Her touch is surprisingly gentle, and skillful, and Willie is quickly aroused. She drags her rich chestnut hair up his chest, across his face, like a fan of feathers. He likes the way it feels, and smells. Her hair soap, Castile maybe, masks the room's other baked-in scents. Male sweat, old spunk—and Fels?

It struck him when he first walked in, but it didn't register. Now it registers. Whoever launders Wingy's bedclothes uses the same detergent as Mother. It's a common detergent, he shouldn't be surprised, but it confuses and troubles Willie at a climactic moment of his maturation.

More confusions. Willie thought Eddie could cuss, but Wingy makes Eddie seem a rank amateur. Why is she cussing? Is Willie doing it wrong? How can he be, when he's not doing anything? He's pinned on his back, helpless. If anyone should be cussing, it's him. Wingy's abundant pubic hair is coarse, nearly metallic, and it chafes and scrapes the tender skin of Willie's brand-new penis. In and out, up and down, Wingy does her best to pleasure Willie, and Willie appreciates her diligence, but he can't stop dwelling on the gap between reality and his expectations. This is what makes the world go round? This is what everyone's so excited about—*this*? If there's any pleasure at all in the experience, it's the relief he feels when it's over.

Wingy curls against him, commending his stamina. He thanks her, for everything, then gathers his clothes and gives her a ten-cent tip. He doesn't stick around for the complimentary flower.

Photographer turns down Sands Street. The road is being repaired. He weaves slowly among orange cones, sawhorses. Anywhere along here, Sutton says.

Photographer pulls over, slips the car into park. Ninth floor, he says in an adenoidal voice—ladies' handbags, men's socks.

What happened on this corner, Mr. Sutton?

This is where Willie lost his innocence. A house of ill fame. That's what we called whorehouses back then.

Was she pretty? Photographer asks.

Yeah. She was. Though she had only one arm. They called her Wingy.

Which arm?

Her left.

Why didn't they call her Lefty?

That would've been cruel.

Reporter and Photographer look at each other, look away.

Do you want to step out, Mr. Sutton?

Nah.

Willie, Photographer says—why exactly are we here?

I wanted to visit Wingy.

Visit?

I can feel her, right now, smiling at us. At your questions. She didn't like questions.

The ghost of a one-armed prostitute. Great. That should make a nice photo.

Okay, boys, next stop. We've seen where Willie lost his innocence. Let's go to Red Hook and see where Willie lost his heart.

With the Armistice—November 1918—all of New York City becomes Coney Island. People fill the streets, dance on cars, kiss strangers. Offices close, saloons stay open around the clock. Willie and Eddie and Happy join the crowds, but with mixed emotions. The war was the best thing that ever happened to them. Peace means no more need for machine guns. No more need for them.

Laid off again, the boys scramble. They comb the wants, fill out applications, canvass. But the city is crowded with soldiers also hunting for work. Newspapers forecast another Depression. The third of Willie's life, this one looks to be the most severe. Things get so bleak, so quick, people wonder aloud if capitalism has run its course.

The boys sit on the rocky waterfront at Red Hook, fishing, while Eddie reads aloud from a newspaper he pulled from the trash. Strikes, riots, unrest—and every other page carries a grim profile of another boy not coming home.

One of every forty who went overseas, Eddie reads, won't be back.

Christ, Happy says.

At least they did something with their lives, Willie says.

Eddie stands, paces. He pitches rocks at the water. Nothin's *blunth* changed. We're *blunth* right back *blunth* where we started.

He stops, lets the rock in his hand fall to the ground. He stands still as a statue and stares into the distance. Willie and Happy turn, follow his gaze. Now they too stand slowly and stare.

Happy sprints toward her, removes his tweed cap, bows. She jumps back, but it's an act. She's not startled. A coiled cobra wouldn't startle this girl, you can tell. Besides, it's Happy. She was hurrying somewhere, walking purposefully, but now, coming upon a specimen like Happy, she's got all the time in the world.

You gotta hand it to that Happy, Eddie says. He sits, adjusts his hat, checks the poles. Willie nods, sits beside him. Every few minutes they turn and shoot a wistful look at their friend.

Happy brings her over. Okay, you bums, look alive, on your feet. Bess, this here's the Beard Street Fishing Club. Of which these are the presidents, Mr. Edward Wilson and Mr. William Sutton. Fellas, say hello to Bess Endner.

She's an ash blonde, that's how police reports will later describe her, but in the light of late autumn her hair contains every kind of yellow. Butter, honey, lemon, amber, gold—she even has golden flecks in her bright blue eyes, as if whoever painted her had some yellow left over and didn't know what to do with it. She's petite, five foot four, but with the graceful strides of a taller girl. Fifteen years old, Willie guesses. Sixteen maybe.

She's carrying a wooden basket. She shifts it, shakes hands with Eddie, then Willie.

What's in the basket? Happy says.

I'm bringing lunch to my father. That's his shipyard right over there.

Some big shipyard, Happy says.

Biggest in Brooklyn. Founded by my grandpa. He came to this country in the hold of a ship, and now he builds them.

Willie stares. He's never seen such confidence. The next time he does, it will be in men with guns. Eddie stares too. It doesn't seem to make her uncomfortable. She probably can't remember a time when people didn't stare.

She points to their poles. Fish biting?

Nah, Eddie says.

What are you using for bait?

Bottle caps, Willie says. Nail heads. Chewing tobacco.

Water's kind of icky, isn't it?

We give the fish a hot shower and a shave before we cook them, Willie says.

She laughs. Sounds delish. On the subject of food, I better run. Daddy gets cranky when he's hungry.

She wiggles her fingers goodbye. Is it Willie's imagination or does she hold his gaze for half a second?

The boys stand shoulder to shoulder, watching her walk down Beard Street. They don't speak until she passes into her father's shipyard. Then they still don't speak. They lie back on the rocks and hold their faces to the sun. Willie, eyes closed, watches the golden sun spots float under his eyelids. They remind him of the flecks in Bess Endner's blue eyes. He'd have a better chance of kissing the sun.

A cat or rat scurries in front of the car. Photographer swerves. What the—? A block later, another cat or rat. So this is Red Hook, Photographer says—people live here?

And die here, Sutton says. In the old days you'd hear two guys at a lunch counter. One would whisper to the other, I dropped that package in Red Hook. Package meant corpse.

Reporter points to a pothole that looks like a lunar crater. Look out.

Photographer drives straight through it. The Polara begins to rattle like an old trolley.

You cracked the axle, Sutton says.

Brooklyn is full of potholes, Photographer says.

Brooklyn is a pothole, Sutton says. Always was.

Reporter points at a street sign. There it is—Beard Street.

Photographer turns on Beard, slides the Polara along the curb, scrapes the hubcap. Sutton steps out, limps across the cobblestones to a raised, railed sidewalk along the water. He steps up, grabs the railing, stands like a dictator about to address a crowd-filled plaza. Now he turns back to Reporter and Photographer, who are staying by the car. He calls to them: What are there, three billion people in the world? Four? You know the odds of finding the one who's meant for you? Well—I found her. Right here. On this spot.

Reporter and Photographer cross the street, one jotting notes, the other shooting.

Boys, you're only really alive, in the fullest sense of the word, when you're in love. That's why almost everyone you meet seems like they're dead.

What was her name, Mr. Sutton?

Bess.

SEVEN

OUT OF WORK, NEARLY OUT OF CASH, THE BOYS STILL SPEND nights at Coney Island, but they skip the hot dogs, the rides. They merely pace up and down the Boardwalk, looking at the Christmas lights. And the girls. Happy has an old ukulele. Whenever a beautiful girl passes by on the arm of a soldier, he purposely hits an out-of-tune chord.

Then, a miracle. The most beautiful girl in the crowd isn't with a soldier. She's with two girlfriends. And she recognizes Happy. And Eddie. Then Willie. If it isn't the Beard Street Fishermen, she cries.

She runs over, dragging her two girlfriends. She introduces them. The first has red hair, pale green eyes, slightly recessed, and thick eyebrows. Double thick. Get a load of this bird, Eddie whispers. When they was handin out eyebrows, she must've got in line twice.

But First Girlfriend and Eddie discover that they have several friends in common, so they pair off.

Second Girlfriend, with long brown hair and a snub nose, doesn't speak, doesn't make eye contact, doesn't seem to want to be here. Or anywhere. Her aloofness sparks Happy. He takes her by the elbow, turns to wink at Willie. Meaning, Bess is yours.

She wears an aqua blue hat, the brim pulled low, concealing her eyes. When Willie compliments the hat, and her matching blue dress, she slowly raises her face to him. Now he sees the golden flecks. They capture him, paralyze him. He tries to look away, but he can't. He can't.

She makes a favorable remark about Willie's attire. Thank God he didn't pawn his Title Guaranty suits. Thank God he wore one, the black one, tonight.

They follow their friends up the Boardwalk. Willie asks Bess where she lives. Near Prospect Park, she says. Me too, he says. President Street, she says. Oh, he says, well, you live on the nice side. Biggest house on the block, she says, you can't miss it. Biggest house, Willie says, biggest shipyard. Means nothing to me, she says, it's not *my* shipyard, and it's not *my* house.

They talk about the war. Bess reads everything. She sits with her father every night, scouring the *Times*, and she never misses an issue of *Leslie's Illustrated*. She says it's criminal that bankers are balking at President Wilson's plan to grant Germany a merciful peace. Criminal.

You certainly do have strong opinions, Willie says.

Don't you think it a shame I can't express them at the ballot box?

Oh, well, women will have the vote soon enough.

Tomorrow would not be soon enough, Mr. Sutton.

Of course. My mistake.

He tries to steer the conversation away from politics. He mentions the balmy weather. Unseasonably warm winter, isn't it?

I should say so.

He asks if Bess is her proper name.

I was born Sarah Elizabeth Endner, but my friends call me all sorts of things. Betsy, Bessie, Bizzy, Binnie. I prefer Bess.

Bess it is.

They fall silent. The sound of their shoes clicking along the Boardwalk seems inordinately loud. Willie thinks about the impossibility of knowing anyone, of getting to know anyone, ever.

Say, uh, Bess. Did you know Coney Island was named by an Irishman?

Oh?

Coney is Irish for rabbit. I guess there were a lot of wild rabbits around here once.

She looks around, as if trying to spot one.

Big ones, Willie says.

She smiles weakly.

Wild, he says.

She makes no reply.

Willie racks his brain, trying to remember what he and Wingy talk about. He tries to remember what the hero says to the heroine in every Alger novel. He can't think straight. He calls to Eddie and Happy. Hey fellas—what should we do next?

How about the Whip? Eddie says.

The girls think that's a grand idea. They all hurry down to Luna Park. Luckily the line is short. The boys pool their money and buy six tickets.

The Whip is twelve little sidecars around an oval track. Cables move the sidecars slow, *slow*, then whip them around narrow turns. Each sidecar holds two people. Eddie and First Girlfriend take one, Happy and Second Girlfriend another, which leaves Willie and Bess. Climbing into the sidecar, Willie feels Bess's upper arm brush his. One brief touch—he's shocked by what it does to him.

Will it go fast? she asks.

It might. It's their best ride. Are you afraid?

Oh no. I love going fast.

The ride starts, the sidecar lurches forward. Willie and Bess press together as it slowly gains speed. The whole thrill of the ride is how slowly it starts, Bess says. They hold tight to the sides, laughing, giggling. She screams as they whip through the first turn. Willie screams too. Eddie and First Girlfriend, one car ahead, look back, frantic, as if Willie and Bess are giving chase. Eddie points a finger and shoots. Willie and Bess shoot back. Eddie is hit. He dies, because it gives him an excuse to collapse his body across First Girlfriend.

Suddenly the sidecar bucks, crawls, comes to a stop. Bess groans. Let's go again, she says.

Willie and the boys don't have money for another turn. Luckily, Willie notices that a line has formed. Look, he says.

Oh drat, she says.

The three couples again stroll the Boardwalk.

Darkness is falling. The lights of Coney Island flutter on. Willie tells Bess that there are a quarter million bulbs in all. No wonder Coney Island is the first thing seen by ships at sea. Imagine—this right here is the first glimpse the immigrants have of America.

It's also the last thing you see when you sail away, Bess says.

How do you know that?

I've seen it. Several times.

Oh.

She points at the moon. Look. Isn't the moon lovely tonight?

Like part of the park, Willie says. *Lunar* Park.

Bess speaks in the stagy voice of an actress. Why, Mr. Sutton—handsome *and* clever?

He plays along. I say, Miss Endner, would you mind repeating that?

Can you not hear me, Mr. Sutton?

On the contrary, Miss Endner, I cannot believe my good fortune at being paid a compliment by so fine a young woman, therefore I was hoping I might memorize it.

She stops. She looks up at Willie with a smile that says, Maybe there's more here than first met the eye. After a slow start he's turning her. Like the Whip.

The three couples gather at the rail and listen to the pounding waves, a sound like the echo of the war drifting across the sea. The wind picks up. It billows the girls' long dresses, causes the boys' neckties to snap like flags. Bess keeps one hand on her hat. Happy gives his hat to Eddie and plucks his ukulele.

> *I don't wanna play in your yard*
> *I don't like you anymore*
> *You'll be sorry when you see me*
> *Sliding down our cellar door*

They all know the words. Bess has a fine voice, but it's quavering, because she's cold. Willie takes off his coat and wraps it around her shoulders.

> *You can't holler down our rainbarrel*
> *You can't climb our apple tree*

People drift toward them, adding their voices. No one can resist this song.

> *I don't wanna play in your yard*
> *If you won't be good to me*

With the final notes Happy makes his battered ukulele sound like a ukulele orchestra. Everyone claps and Bess squeezes Willie's bicep. He flexes it bigger. She squeezes it harder.

Heavens, First Girlfriend says, looking at her bracelet watch, it's late.

Bess protests. First Girlfriend and Second Girlfriend overrule her. The three couples follow the crowd toward the trolleys and subways. Willie and Bess begin to say their goodbyes. Then find themselves alone. Willie looks around. In the shadows of a bathhouse Eddie and First Girlfriend are entwined. Behind a fortuneteller's booth Happy is stealing kisses from Second Girlfriend. Willie looks at Bess. Her eyes—pools of blue and gold. He feels the earth tip toward the moon. He leans, touches his lips softly to hers. His skin tingles, his blood catches fire. In this instant, he knows, in this unforeseen gift of a moment, his future is being reshaped. This wasn't supposed to happen. But it is happening. It *is*.

At last, on the street, the girls stand facing the boys. Thank you for a lovely evening. Nice meeting you. And you as well. Merry Christmas. Good night. Ta ta. Happy New Year.

And yet Bess will be seeing Willie in just a few days. They have a date. The girls walk off, First Girlfriend and Second Girlfriend on either side of Bess. Willie watches them melt into the crowd. At the last second Bess turns.

You can't holler down my rainbarrel, she calls.

You can't climb my apple tree, Willie calls back.

She sings: I don't wanna play in your yaaard.

He thinks: If you won't be good to me.

Sutton looks at his reflection in the water. He realizes it's not his reflection, but a cloud. Did you know Socrates said we love whatever we lack? Or think we lack?

Socrates?

If you feel stupid, you'll fall for someone brainy. If you feel ugly, you'll flip your lid for someone who's easy on the eyes.

You've read Socrates?

I've read everything kid. I couldn't have survived the joint without reading. When the FBI was looking for me, they had agents staking out bookstores. Somewhere in your files it must say that.

But—Socrates? Really?

He was a right guy. And boy did he hate cops.

Cops. In ancient Greece.

You tell me. He offed himself rather than confess, right?

They meet a few nights later for ice cream. A drugstore near the park. Bess wears a green dress with a kind of hobble skirt, a tall hat with one long white feather. Willie wears his other suit from Title Guaranty. The gray one.

He's relieved to find her chatty, since he's incapable of forming words. He couldn't be more nervous if he were on a date with Theda Bara. Also, he wants to know her. Desperately.

She tells him all about her family. I must've been left on their doorstep, she says, because I'm not like any of them. Daddy's a tyrant. And a bore. Mummy's a fussy old hen. And my older sister's a simp.

Willie almost says he knows about not getting along with older siblings, but he doesn't want to think of his brothers. Not tonight. He eats his hot fudge sundae in careful, measured spoonfuls, prods Bess with questions.

What's your favorite food?

Oh that's easy. Ice cream.

Me too. What's your favorite book?

That's easier. *Wuthering Heights*. I agree with Mr. Emerson—all humankind roots for a pair of lovers. Nothing quickens our attention and excites our sympathy like a Cathy and a Heathcliff.

Right. *Wuthering Heights*. That's my favorite too.

You're lying.

Yeah.

I'll loan you my copy.

Do you have any pets?

A terrier named Tennyson. That's my favorite poet.

What's your favorite place in the world?

Three-way tie. Paris. Rome. Hamburg. What's yours?

I don't have one.

Well what's your least favorite place in the world?

Home.

Oh dear.

What's your finest quality?

My memory. I can read a poem once and have it by heart. Do you have a good memory?

I'll never forget this day, he thinks. I'm bad with names, he says.

Most aren't worth remembering.

What's your greatest fault?

I can't sit still. You?

I'm from Irish Town.

He tells her about Father's failing business, Mother's endless grief, his own inability to find work. He surprises her, and himself, revealing so much in such a plainsong voice. In this lifetime it's the closest he'll ever come to a full confession.

He walks her home through the park. In a dark, secluded spot she leans against a tree and grabs his necktie, pulls him to her. He puts one hand against the tree, the other against her cheek. The scratchy roughness of the bark, the creamy smoothness of her skin—this too he'll never forget. They kiss.

She tells him that she hasn't lost her innocence yet, in case he was wondering.

I'd never wonder about a thing like that, he whispers.

Gosh, you didn't even wonder? I must not be as attractive as people tell me.

She pokes him in the ribs, to let him know she's kidding. But she's not kidding.

On their second date, at the same secluded spot, she takes Willie's hand, puts it inside her dress. She guides the hand over her breast, under. He can feel her young heart, ticking like a new watch. It will run forever.

He removes his hand, restrains himself, and her. No, Bess. No.

Why?

Isn't right.

Who decides what's right?

He has no answer for that. But still he holds firm.

All their dates arrive at this same stalemate, until their courtship becomes a kind of burlesque. After an hour or two at Coney Island, or the drugstore, they walk and walk and soon find themselves in some hidden enclave within the park. Bess undoes a button, or two, and guides Willie's hand, or else drops her hand, touches between his legs. Willie stops her, saying it wouldn't be right. She acts flustered, but Willie believes she secretly admires his restraint. Then they say good night, each of them flushed, confused, longing.

Eddie and Happy are appalled. Eddie thinks Willie has lost his mind, or his manhood. Happy calls him an ingrate. Happy gave Bess to Willie—that's the myth they share. Happy kids Willie that, if Bess is going to waste, he might just take her back.

But if anyone gave Bess to him, Willie thinks, it was God. Through divine grace—he can think of no other explanation—Bess Endner is his sweetheart, and he doesn't want God to think him ungrateful. So he behaves the way God would want. The way a hero in an Alger novel would behave.

Though it goes against his grain, though it stuns his best friends, his strategy of unwavering chivalry pays off. After weeks of courtship Bess stops Willie at their favorite tree and puts her face on his chest. Well I hope you're happy, Willie Sutton. I've fallen in love with you.

You have?

Oh yes.

Truly?

Truly, madly. You're my heart's darling.

Why, Bess?

Willie—what a question.

No. Really. I mean, I'm tough, but I'm no Eddie. I'm not bad looking, but I'm no Happy. Why me?

All right, she says. I'll tell you, Willie. I love you because you look at me the way every girl *thinks* she wants to be looked at, though I suspect very few girls could really bear such intensity. Such scrutiny. You look at me as if you want to devour me, as if you want to carry me off, keep me prisoner on a desert island, carve statues of me.

Willie laughs guiltily.

You look at me as if you want to make me happy, as if you can't possibly be happy unless I am. It's thrilling. It's frightening. It's what I want for the rest of my life. The only thing I want.

That's it?

Life is complicated, Willie, love isn't. My girlfriends do cartwheels for boys who dress nice or dance well or come from good families. They'll find out. There's only one thing that counts. How does a boy look at you? Can you see in his eyes that he'll *always* be there? That's how you looked at me on the Whip. You had *always* in your eyes. That's how you're looking at me now. I hear my mother and sister talk—they only dream about what I've got right here under this tree. Oh Willie. I just love you, that's all. Oh.

All Bess's avowals, all her sweet nothings, begin and end with this word. It's the prelude and conclusion to every endearment. Oh—she says it before kissing him. Oh—she says it after. Oh—she says it as she turns her back to him, as if the sight of Willie is just too marvelous to bear.

Oh Willie. Oh.

Sutton lets go of the railing. Okay, boys, let's go. Next stop.

You looked like you were a million miles away, Mr. Sutton.

Two hundred fifty thousand at least.

What were you thinking about?

I was thinking I could use a drink. Willie needs a Jameson.

Oh Mr. Sutton. That does not sound like a good idea.

Kid haven't you figured out by now? None of this is a good idea.

EIGHT

WILLIE HAS SEEN THE ENDNER HOUSE MANY TIMES FROM the outside— stained-glass windows, fancy balustrades, an iron gate with spikes along the top—and he's always cowered before it. At the start of 1919, wearing his black Title Guaranty suit, he steps inside for the first time.

A butler takes his coat. Willie blinks, trying to adjust his vision. If Coney Island is the brightest place on earth, Chateau Endner is the darkest.

We keep the house dim for Mummy, Bess whispers. She suffers migraines.

Bess leads Willie by the hand down a long hall and into a library, the walls of which are lined with enormous glass-doored bookcases. Willie glances at the titles: mostly rare Bibles, assorted religious texts. The floor is covered by a massive wool rug. It came from China, Bess whispers.

Mr. and Mrs. Endner stand at the far end of the rug, warming themselves before a fireplace big enough to roast a deer. The crack and pop of wood are the only sounds in the room, the flames the only light.

Mummy, Daddy, this is Willie.

Willie goes forth. Crossing the rug takes longer than swimming the East River. He shakes their hands. Nothing is said for several moments. A maid appears at Willie's side, offers him a glass of sherry. Thank you, he says, his voice cracking like the firewood.

A second maid announces that dinner is served.

Willie and Bess follow Mr. and Mrs. Endner down another long hall into a high-ceilinged dining room. The darkest room yet—only two candelabra. Willie surveys the table. It would take up half his house. Mr. Endner sits at the head, Mrs. Endner at the far end. Willie and Bess sit in the middle, on opposite sides. A third maid sets before Willie a plate of grilled lamb chops with mint jelly, scalloped potatoes.

Mrs. Endner says grace. Amen, Willie says, a little too loudly.

Mr. Endner doesn't touch his food. Instead he makes a meal of his mustaches while watching Willie. Bess warned Willie, her father plays with his mustaches when upset.

Where do you work, Willie?

Well sir. I'm looking for work right now. I was recently laid off from a munitions factory. Before that I worked for Title Guaranty.

And what became of that position?

I was laid off also.

Mr. Endner gives his left mustache a hard tug.

What faith do you practice, son?

I was raised Catholic sir.

Mr. Endner pushes the right mustache up into his nostril. The Endners are Baptist, he says. In fact Mr. John D. Rockefeller Sr. is a close friend—he's eaten at this table. His son is talking about building a new Baptist church. It's going to be glorious. Grander than anything they have in Europe.

The last thing Willie heard about old man Rockefeller: Eddie said his father bilked sick people down south, sold them snake oil. Which is ironic, Eddie said, since Rockefeller started Standard Oil. Willie fills his mouth with food, nods. Yes sir, I believe I read something about that.

Mrs. Endner looks at Willie, then Bess. William, she says— where do your people come from?

Brooklyn mam.

Yes. We know. But your ancestors.

Willie chews his lamb slowly, stalling, which heightens the suspense now gripping the table. Ireland mam.

Willie can hear nothing but the pounding of his own heart and the compounding of interest in the Endner bank accounts. Everyone around the table, even the servants off in the shadows, seems to be envisioning the same selective montage of Irish history. Druids performing human sacrifices on oaken altars. Celtic warriors running naked toward Caesar's legions. Toothless hags hurling bombs from behind the golden throne of the Pope.

The Endners hail from Germany, Mrs. Endner says, looking as though a once-in-a-lifetime migraine is coming on. Hamburg, she adds.

Willie is taken aback at her prideful tone. Even being a Hun is better than being a Mick. He stares at the potatoes on his plate, wondering if he should push them aside, defy at least one cultural stereotype. Only Bess's steady reassuring gaze keeps him from fleeing the room, the house, Brooklyn.

The next night Willie meets Bess at a soda fountain in Coney Island. Her face is pale. He's never seen her without high color in her cheeks. He knows what's coming, but it's still a shock to hear the words.

Willie Boy, my father has forbidden me from seeing you ever again.

She looks down at her dish of ice cream. Willie does the same. His senses are strangely heightened. He can feel the ice cream melt. He knows what Bess wants him to say, what he must say. And do. When he looks up, she's waiting.

Okay, Bess. I'll go talk to him.

They pile back in the Polara. Events were set in motion, Sutton whispers.

What, Mr. Sutton?

Bess and I had a talk. January 1919. Everything flowed from that talk, that moment. Everything. Look back on your life and see if you can pinpoint the moment when everything changed. If you can't? That means you haven't had your moment yet, and you better hold on to your ass, it's coming.

Where did this talk take place?

Coney Island. Mermaid Avenue. I was going to put it on the map. I don't know why I didn't. Maybe I couldn't face it. Is there anything more painful than remembering? And it's a self-inflicted pain, we do it to ourselves. Ah Christ, maybe you can say that about all pain.

But you said we should remember. That remembering is our way of saying fuck you to time.

Did I?

Willie, wearing his gray Title Guaranty suit, knocks at the door on President Street. A maid shows him into an office off the vestibule. As planned, Bess is out with her girlfriends.

The office floor is covered with a full bearskin, its mouth about to devour the floorboards, its round snout shiny and black as an eight ball. Above a brick fireplace hangs a gray wolf's head, fangs bared.

Willie stands before a mahogany desk covered with neatly stacked account books, model ships, letter openers that could slice open a man. He holds his hat by the brim, takes a step back, almost trips over the bear's paw. He wonders if he should sit. He wishes he could smoke. From a door on the far side of the office Mr. Endner enters. Willie, he says.

Mr. Endner sir. Thank you for seeing me.

Mr. Endner seats himself behind the desk. He's wearing a blue serge suit with a gray bow tie and his eyes are dull, as if he's just wakened from a nap. He gestures to a straight-backed chair across from him. Willie sits. They eye each other like boxers at the opening bell.

The floor is yours, Willie.

Well sir. I came to ask you to please reconsider your decision. I think if you'd give me half a chance, you'd see that I'm a good and decent person, that I care for your daughter very much. And I think she cares for me.

Mr. Endner spins a fountain pen on the desk blotter. He moves a few envelopes, sets a letter opener atop them, picks up a silver dollar and raps it on the mahogany desktop. What's the most valuable thing you own, Willie?

Willie thinks. This must be a trap, since every answer that comes to mind sounds wrong. He looks at the silver dollar. Sir, I don't own anything valuable.

Mr. Endner rocks in the desk chair, causing it to squeak. Well that's part of the problem right there isn't it? But let's say you did. Let's say you owned a diamond as big as this silver dollar.

Yes sir.

What would you do with it?

Do sir?

How would you treat it? Would you swap it for a root beer?

No sir.

A ten-cent cone?

No sir.

Of course you wouldn't. Would you give it away for nothing?

No sir.

Well then you understand my position. God Himself placed Bess in our hands and she's worth more than any diamond. It's our job to take the utmost care in choosing who gets her. No easy task. It keeps Mrs. Endner and me awake nights. And Bess, much as we love her, doesn't make it easier. She's a willful little girl, with a fondness for trouble. As you well know. That's why she's fond of you, I suppose.

She says she loves me sir.

I would take that *cum grano salis*, son.

But sir.

Look, I have nothing against you per se, Willie, but let's be frank. You can't possibly think in your heart of hearts that you're a suitable match for Bess.

Willie suddenly finds it difficult to breathe. He tugs at his collar.

Mr. Endner, sir, I've had a few tough breaks, it's true. Losing two jobs. I've stumbled out of the starting gate in life, I guess. But still. My luck's bound to change.

How do you know, son? How can you be sure? None of us knows what bad luck is. Or where it comes from. Maybe it's temporary, like an illness. Or permanent, like a birthmark. Maybe it's wild and random like the wind. Maybe it's a sign of God's displeasure. Either way. Let's say through sheer bad luck you're out of work, on your uppers—is that supposed to ease my mind? This is a country for lucky people. Do I want my little girl to be with someone prone to bad luck?

To address your earlier point sir. I know Bess is a diamond sir. No one needs to tell me. But it seems like you're saying she should be with a fella who can afford diamonds, and wouldn't a fella like that be liable to take a diamond for granted? Wouldn't a fella who's never so much as seen a diamond until a few months ago be more liable to cherish one? And sir I wish I'd thought to say this when you first asked, but I'm very nervous, and it hits me just now that if I had a diamond I wouldn't have any trouble figuring what to do with it. I'd give it straightaway to Bess.

Okay, Willie, I see how it is.

Thank you sir.

What's it going to take?

Sir?

To make you disappear?

I don't. What?

I'll have my attorney draw up a paper this afternoon. Legally binding. Sign it, agree to stay away from my daughter, and I'll write you a check with more zeros than the scoreboard when Walter Johnson pitches. You'll be able to live quite well until you secure another position. You'll be able to live well if you don't find work for years.

Willie stands, turns his hat in his hands, one full circle.

Mr. Endner, sir, I don't want your money. You can draw up a paper saying I can't ever have one red cent of it. That paper I'll sign.

So you're ethical then?

Yes sir.

You have *character*.

I do sir. If you'd just get to know me—

Then surely you wouldn't do anything to damage the relationship of a young girl and her parents. Surely your ethics, your *character*, will prevent you from interfering in a private family matter.

Willie blinks.

I've forbidden Bess to see you, Willie. Whether or not you agree with my decision, should you violate my wishes, should you transgress the rules of this household, you'll confirm my darkest fears about you. You want to show me who you really are? Stay away.

Willie can hear the wolf and the bear snickering.

Goodbye, Willie. And good luck.

Sutton: Did you boys know that when the astronauts got back, and they were under quarantine, someone broke into the building where they were housed and stole the safe full of their moon rocks?

Reporter: I did see that in the paper, yes.

Sutton: Stealing the moon. That's what I call a heist.

Reporter: Did anything particular bring that to mind, Mr. Sutton?

Sutton: No.

Reporter: Mr. Sutton, your handwriting is just, wow. This map. Um. As best I can tell, our next stop is the middle of—Meadowlark's Ass?

Sutton: Meadowport Arch.

Reporter: Oh. Yes. That would make more sense.

Bess tells her parents that she's going to meet her girlfriends and instead she meets Willie at Meadowport Arch. Set at the edge of Long Meadow, the arch leads to a hundred-foot-long tunnel with a vaulted ceiling and walls made of pungent cedar. Our tunnel of love, Willie calls it. Our moors, Bess says. They spend hours and hours there, holding hands on a bench, making plans, listening to their plans reverberate.

If another couple, or raccoon, is already under the arch, they retreat to a different arch, the one in Grand Army Plaza. They huddle among the statues of Ulysses Grant, Abraham Lincoln—and Alexander Skene?

Who in the world? Bess says.

Willie reads the inscription. Says here, Alexander Skene was a renowned—gynecologist?

How that makes them laugh.

They talk obsessively about what life would be like if they had complete privacy, if they could be alone whenever and wherever they wanted.

I'd let you put it in me, Bess says.

Bess.

I would, Willie. If we could be alone, I'd let you do whatever you want.

Whatever you want. The phrase runs through Willie's mind night and day.

If it's raining or snowing they meet Eddie and Happy at Finn McCool's, a bucket of blood with a picture of Ben Bulben over the bar. The barkeep knows they're underage and doesn't care. He's an old cuss in a gray felt hat and canary yellow suspenders who believes that if you can pay, you can drink. He also believes that opening an umbrella indoors causes years of bad luck. Every time a customer opens an umbrella the barkeep turns three times in a circle, then spits on the ground, to head off the jinx. Bess opens her umbrella several times a night just to see him do it. It makes Eddie and Happy howl. One hundred years from now, Willie thinks, we'll all be able to recall the sight of Bess at the bar, twirling her umbrella, taunting the barkeep. And fate.

At the end of January 1919, Eddie and Happy sit at the bar while Willie and Bess stand before them, lamenting their situation. Happy smirks. The Romeo and Juliet of Brooklyn, he says.

We're not Romeo and Juliet, Bess says. Willie's family isn't against me.

They're just against *him*, Happy says.

Knock off the Romeo-Juliet talk, Willie says. They die at the end.

At least their families build statues to them, Bess says. Like Alexander Skene.

She laughs. Willie doesn't.

Eddie insists there are solutions. You two kids should just *elope*, he says.

Bess gasps. She looks at Willie, joyful, expectant. He sees twice the number of golden flecks in her blue eyes. He shakes his head. Bess, honey, where would we go? How would we live?

She has no answer. Sullen, she lets the subject drop.

But she brings it up again the next night at Meadowport. She has an idea, she says. Her father's shipyard. They can break open the safe. Then they can run off, anywhere they want, and they'll have enough to live on for years.

Willie wonders if she's testing him. Maybe at her father's suggestion. *See how he reacts. See if the boy has a pure heart—or an Irish heart.* Willie tells Bess he's not about to commit grand larceny. She says it's not larceny. That money is her dowry.

He waves her off. Out of the question, he says.

Bess raises the idea the next night, and the next. She says they have no choice. Her father suspects that they're still seeing each other—he's threatening to send her to Germany to live with his family until their romance dies. The thought horrifies Willie, but he still can't agree to commit such a bold crime.

But why not, she says.

No. I just couldn't. No.

Finally, February 1, 1919. Bess loses all patience. Well! she says. If I don't mean enough for you to stand up to my father—

You don't want me to stand up to your father. You want me to *rob* him.

She blanches. He pulls away. Then quickly apologizes. She leans against the wall of Meadowport. Look what this is doing to us, she says. Oh Willie.

He takes her in his arms. Ah Bess. She puts her hand on his cheek, his lips. Willie, I don't know what I'll do if he sends me away. Please don't let him send me away from you.

Later that night Willie calls a summit. In a booth at McCool's he puts the case before Eddie and Happy.

Looks plain and simple to me, Happy says.

Me too, Eddie says. Either you clean out the safe or you lose her, boy.

You ready to lose her? Happy says.

I'll die, Happy. I swear I'll die.

The old man has brought this on himself, Eddie says. He could've welcomed you into the family. He could've given you a job. What can you expect from a friend of Rockefeller? Fuck him, I say.

Will you help me, fellas? I can't do it alone. I'll cut you in, make it worth your while. You'll only be out of town a few days. A week tops.

Eddie would love to help but he's landed a part-time job. As a driller, alongside his old man. Twenty a week—he can't walk away from that kind of dough. Willie understands. He turns to Happy, who takes a long drink of beer and snaps a salute: You can count on me, Willie.

We have to move fast, Willie says.

How fast?

Tomorrow. It's the day before payroll. Bess says the safe will be stuffed with cash.

Sutton steps into Meadowport, followed by Reporter and Photographer. The cedar walls are covered with graffiti. Photographer lights a Zippo, holds it aloft.

Sutton reads. Fuck the Pigs. Nixon Equals Stalin.

Power to the people, Photographer whispers.

Reporter reads. Sergio Sucks Balls. Spicks Must Die.

So much anger in the world, Sutton says.

Righteous anger, Photographer says. The anger of the oppressed.

Reporter reads. Aryell plus Jose.

Sutton smiles. They sound like a nice couple—you think they made it?

February 4, 1919. Midnight. Bess sneaks out of her house and meets Willie and Happy at Meadowport. Willie carries a plaid grip with bolt cutters from his father's shop. Happy carries a jimmy. They hail a horse cab, tell the driver not to spare the whip.

At the shipyard Willie clips the padlock on the fence. Happy jimmies the door to Mr. Endner's office. The safe is made of wood. The three of them stand before it, looking at it, then at each other, for one long moment.

The safe splinters with two chops from a fire ax. As the door swings out Happy whistles. Would you look at this, Willie. It's like the vault at Title Guaranty.

Sixteen rolls of cash. Each wrapped in brown paper. Each labeled $1,000. Four times more than Bess told them it would be. They shovel it into the plaid grip, run up Beard, hail another horse cab.

Once upon a time, Sutton says, Happy and I met Bess here. Then we went down to her old man's shipyard and cleaned out his safe.
  How much did you take?
  Sixteen large. That's a nice sum today, but back then the average Joe made fifteen bucks a week. So. You know. We were rich.
  Then what did you do?
  Went hell for leather to Grand Central.
  And then?
  Poughkeepsie. My first trip outside the city.
  Why Poughkeepsie?
  That's where the next train was headed.

The train pulls in at dawn. They ask a cabdriver to take them to the best hotel in town. He takes them to the Nelson House, a redbrick fortress.

Willie, trying to steady his hand as he holds the hotel's heavy black fountain pen, scratches the register: Mr. and Mrs. Joseph Lamb. Happy signs as Mr. Leo Holland. The name of his neighbor back in Irish Town. The prosecution will call this hotel register Exhibit A.

Since Willie and Bess plan to marry in the morning, Bess says there's no longer any sense in waiting. She closes the door of their suite, undoes the top two buttons of her dress. Then the bottom two. Willie glimpses her corset. It looks harder to open than her father's safe. She begins the process, untying one silk ribbon after another.

He lies back. He can't resist her anymore. He reminds himself, reassures himself, that he doesn't need to. She slips into the bathroom. He counts backwards, trying to calm himself.

Ready or not, she calls.

Not, he thinks.

She walks out naked, palms on her thighs, pantomiming shyness, though there's no shyness in Bess. She's got power, the vast power of beauty and youth, and she wants to use it. It's like money burning a hole in her pocket. Willie stares at her angles and curves, her pinks and ivories, the flush of rose along her collarbone. He stares at the points of her nipples, the creamy roundness of her hips, the smooth plane of her stomach. Loving Bess has already caused him agonies of pain and anxiety, but now he sees that what comes next will be a far greater test. Bess, her power, is a giant wave. Willie's boat is small.

You're staring, Willie Boy.

I am?

They're not much, I know.

What?

My breasts. I'm flat as a pancake.

No. You're perfect.

She walks to the bed, puts one knee on the mattress. She pretends to hesitate. He undoes his belt, she slides off his pants.

Are you going to have me, Willie?

If you'll let me.

I don't want to let you. I want you to take me.

Okay. I'll take you.

Is it going to hurt?

It might, Bess.

I hope it hurts.

No.

They say the hurt is how you know you're a woman.

Then I'll hurt you.

In the years ahead, in cells, in lonely rooms, whenever Willie replays this night, he'll struggle to remember his thoughts. He'll have to remind himself that there were no thoughts, only impulses and flashing images and tidal surges in his heart. That may be why it all passes so fast. Time is an invention of the mind, and with Bess his mind is off. Which is part of the joy. And the danger.

In one motion they finish and tumble into sleep as if falling down a well. He wakes three hours later to find Bess stroking his hair. I thought it was all a dream, he says. She smiles. He wakes two hours later to find Bess sliding her head onto his chest. He sighs. She kisses his fingers. He wakes an hour later to find Happy sitting on the edge of the bed. Happy—what time is it?

Happy smiles at the bloodstained sheets. Time to skedaddle.

Bess looks at the sheets, puts a hand over her mouth. We can't leave these. They'll think there's been a murder.

They strip the bed, stuff the sheets into the plaid grip. Blood money, Happy jokes.

Over breakfast in the hotel dining room they take stock. Surely the safe has been discovered by now. Surely Bess's father has called the police. So the chase is on. They'll need to stay off the trains, and that means buying a motorcar.

Can we afford a motorcar? Bess asks.

Willie and Happy laugh. We can afford eight, Happy says.

They find a dealership at the edge of town. Francis Motors. They pick out a brand-new Nash, open-topped, pine green, with shining nickel headlamps and a spare tire covered in white leather. The salesman chortles when Willie says he'll take it. The salesman stops chortling when Willie counts out two thousand on the hood.

Son, I don't know—and I don't *want to* know.

They drive to the next town, shop for clothes. Four new suits for Willie and Happy, eight new dresses for Bess. They pass a store with a three-quarter-length squirrel coat in the window. Bess presses her face to the glass. Nine hundred, she says, marked down from fifteen hundred—that's a *steal*.

It's a steal all right, Willie says.

The coat is a drab gray, the color of rain clouds, of dishwater—of Mr. Endner's mustaches. But Bess is already inside the store, burying her face in the fluffy collar.

Standing before the astonished salesman Willie counts nine hundred on the counter. Don't bother wrapping it, Willie says, taking the receipt, which the prosecution will call Exhibit B, she'll wear it out.

They head northeast, to Massachusetts, where the age of consent is younger. So they've heard. The motor-roads are bad. They're not motor-roads, but Indian trails. The Nash gets a flat. Happy wrestles with the jack and the spare. Bess wrestles with Willie. He catches her hands, tells her to be good. My being-good days are over, she says.

At dusk they stop at a four-room inn. There's still an hour of daylight. Bess wants to go right away to the nearest justice. Happy says he's worn out from changing the flat.

We'll go without you, Bess says.

Happy's offended. How you going to get married without the best man?

Willie hugs her. First thing in the morning, Bess. That way we'll be able to buy you a proper wedding dress.

Oh Willie. Yes.

Then, he thinks, Niagara Falls, and on to Canada, far beyond her father's reach. Willie's not sure what they'll do with Happy at that point.

They all turn in early. Big day tomorrow, they say at the top of the stairs. Willie falls asleep instantly. Hours later he wakes, Bess nudging him. Willie Boy, I can't sleep.

Yeah. Me either.

She laughs. He gropes for his suit on the floor, finds his cigarettes. Lights one, lies on his back, takes a long drag. Bess confiscates the cigarette, puffs it, hands it back. The room is ice cold.

She spreads the squirrel coat across them as an extra blanket, lies on her side facing him. We're outlaws, she says.

I guess so.

Never thought I'd be an outlaw.

It wasn't in my plans either.

She jabs a finger into Willie's ribs. Stick em up.

Bess.

You heard me.

He puts the cigarette in his mouth, raises his hands.

Put the money in the bag, she says.

Say, you've got the act down pretty good.

Your money or your life?

Those are my options?

Yup.

My life.

She props herself on one elbow. Have you ever committed a crime, Willie?

He sighs. Not for a while.

What'd you do?

Eddie used to shoplift, break into stores. Happy and I would stand lookout sometimes.

She twirls his chest hair. Have you ever been with anyone else, Willie Boy?

He blows a smoke ring. It encircles her face like a cameo. I don't know.

Who? Who was she, Willie?

Ah, no one, Bess. She was just—no one.

Who, Willie?

If you must know. A whore lady. On Sands Street.

Sands Street?

Happy. He took me and Eddie.

Figures.

It wasn't anything.

What was she like?

Skip it.

Tell me.

She was nothing like you.

How did she do it?

Ah come on.

Tell me.

What's it matter?

How?

Bess.

Willie.

God you're stubborn. Your old man said you were willful.

You don't know the half. How?

On top mostly. There. You satisfied?

Bess takes the cigarette from his hand, puts it in the ashtray on the nightstand. She climbs on top, the squirrel coat around her shoulders. She takes him, guides him. He doesn't last. She falls on top of him, buries her face in his neck. He holds her tight. She's trembling, her hair is damp with sweat. This is what the whole world is after, he says, breathless. Yes, she says. This is why everyone's trying to beat everyone else, Bess, this is why people are ready to lie, cheat, kill. For this, Bess. This is what makes the world go round. This, Bess. This.

Sutton adjusts his glasses, brushes away the dirt on the cedar wall. Ah—I knew it'd still be here.

Reporter moves closer. What?

Bess's initials. I carved them. There.

Photographer moves closer. I don't see anything, brother.

Right there. S-E-E. Sarah Elizabeth Endner.

Photographer hands his Zippo to Reporter, takes a folding knife from his back pocket. He scrapes at some dirt on the wall. There's nothing there, he says.

You're blind, Sutton says.

Photographer closes his knife. He fires the flash on his camera, illuminating the wall. Nothing, he says.

Get your eyes checked kid.

In the morning they go for a walk around town, wearing some of their new clothes. Bess has never looked more dazzling—black cloche hat, black silk skirt, white blouse with a chou of chiffon. She wears the squirrel coat like a tunic. They buy the papers, read them on a bench in the square. The headlines are grim. Half the country looking for work, the other half striking. Nearby, Boston cops are incensed about their wages. They're threatening a walkout.

Willie folds back the newspaper, smoothes the page. Says here the average cop earns a thousand bucks a year.

Happy pats the plaid grip. We could buy ourselves thirteen cops.

Bess points at a photo of Calvin Coolidge, the governor of Massachusetts. What a sourpuss, she says.

Willie can't find one line in any of the papers about a robbery in Brooklyn. Which seems ominous. How could it not be in the papers?

I have no doubt, Bess says, that my father is doing all he can to keep it quiet.

He has that kind of influence?

She frowns. They look around the square, as if Bess's father might jump out from behind a tree or the Civil War cannon.

They spend the rest of the morning shopping for a wedding dress. Bess doesn't see anything she likes. She stomps her foot. The stores were so much better back in Poughkeepsie, she says.

Then we'll go back, Willie says. Whatever my Bess wants.

Willie drives. Bess sits in the passenger seat, Happy in the rumble. They pass through virgin forest filled with overnight snow. The ancient trees look as if they've been splashed with white paint. And yet the air is warm. February thaw, says the young attendant at the Esso station when they stop for gasoline.

Bess lights one of Willie's cigarettes. The attendant stares as if she's removed her blouse. Women don't smoke in public in 1919. Especially not in backwoods Massachusetts. As they chug away from the Esso station, Bess gives the attendant something else to remember. She stands and arches her back and whips her hair in a circle. She looks like the hood ornament, Happy says.

That wind in my hair is *heav*-en, she shouts.

Willie yells over the engine: Your hair in that wind is heaven.

She leans over, kisses Willie. You two are making me sick, Happy says. She leans into the backseat, kisses Happy.

Bess, Willie says, why don't you take a turn.

Finally, she says.

They pull onto the shoulder and she and Willie trade places. He tries to explain the clutch but she says she's got it, she's got it. In no time she's smoothly shifting gears, though she's still gripping the wheel too tight. Relax, Happy says, relax. As she does, as she gains confidence, she goes faster and faster. Then nearly drives them into an oncoming logging truck.

They stop for lunch at a roadside diner. Deviled eggs, tomato soup, grilled cheese sandwiches. Pecan pie for dessert. The bill is three dollars. Willie leaves a five-dollar tip. The prosecution will call this Exhibit C.

In Poughkeepsie they buy Bess's wedding dress. Lace-embroidered, a bodice of silk and taffeta. Then they drop into the courthouse, inquire about the local marriage laws. The clerk says the age of consent in New York is the same as in Massachusetts, fourteen for males, twelve for females. So there's no need to drive back to Massachusetts. Except that Justice Symonds has left for the day. Family illness. He'll return in the morning. They check back in to the Nelson House, eat dinner in the formal dining room. Over two bottles of red wine they talk about Prohibition. By this time next year alcohol will be against the law. What a gyp, Bess says, just when I was developing a taste for it. Don't worry, Willie says, we'll be in Canada by then, you can get good and stiff every night.

They take their coffee into the hotel parlor. Happy wants to plink at his ukulele, but there are older people sitting around the fire, reading, playing checkers. He entertains Willie and Bess with jokes, stories, which make them laugh so hard that Bess gets the hiccups. When the old people leave at last, Happy tunes his ukulele. My dog has fleas, my dog has fleas. Bess asks him to play her favorite. She stands with her back to the fire and while Happy plays she serenades Willie.

> *You can't holler down our rainbarrel*
> *You can't climb our apple tree*
> *I don't wanna play in your yard*
> *If you won't be good to me*

She's wearing another of her new dresses, a gray-green tweed, and the long skirt swishes as she sways to the music. Willie wants to watch her, listen to her, forever, but she makes him get up, dance. Happy plays fast numbers and she teaches Willie the latest steps, including something called the Bunny Hug, a kind of tango that started in Paris. Willie twirls her around the parlor, his head whirling, Happy strumming, the bellman laughing. They ask the bellman to throw more logs on the fire. They order hot toddies. Then more hot toddies. Bess can't dance anymore. She can't stand. Uh-oh, she says—someone had too many *tooodies*. Happy stops playing. He helps Willie carry Bess up the carpeted stairs to the suite. She smells of buttered rum and tweed and youth. Happy and Willie drop her on the bed. Happy laughs. Willie puts a finger to his lips, steers him into the hall.

Happy, leaning against the doorframe. So how's about letting me have a turn?

Willie stares. What?

You know. Let old Happy have some fun.

Happy, what the?

She won't even know the difference.

I'm getting married to her in the morning.

That's tomorrow. This is today.

No, Happy. This isn't just some— I love her.

Of course you love her. Everybody loves her. The bellman loves her. Christ, look at her.

Happy—

I gave her to you, Willie, didn't I?

Yeah. Sure. But.

Happy sends Willie a hard look, something between a snarl and a sneer. It's a look Willie has never seen on Happy. Who are you? Willie whispers.

I'm the guy who helped you pull off this whole caper, that's who I am.

Yeah. But.

We're like brothers aren't we?

Yeah. Sure.

We share everything don't we? The girls on Sands Street?

This is different.

Happy moves forward. Willie blocks the door, braces himself. Happy puts a hand on Willie's chest, pushes him into the door, hard, then staggers away down the hall to his room.

Lying in bed beside a sleeping Bess, Willie strokes her hair and goes over and over the scene with Happy. At first light there's a knock. It's Happy, ready to apologize. Then Willie remembers. Happy doesn't knock. It's the sheriff. With two private detectives from Brooklyn who drove all night. They put Willie in handcuffs. They put Bess in handcuffs. They drive them in separate cars to the same courthouse where they inquired about getting married.

Handcuffed, standing before the judge, Willie hears a side door bang open. Two cops drag in Happy, who doesn't look frightened, doesn't look worried. They stand him next to Willie.

Young man, the judge tells Happy, do yourself a favor. Wipe that goddamn smirk off your face.

We were caught within a week, Sutton says.

How?

We left quite a trail of bread crumbs.

What did they do to you?

Dragged our asses back to Brooklyn, threw us into Raymond Street Jail. The Brooklyn Bastille they called it back then.

They tore it down. Not long ago.

Good. But we'll still go have a look.

Photographer groans. Willie—why? If it's not there, what's the point?

Sutton rises to his full five foot nine, peers at Photographer. You know kid, a couple years ago, I got to know an old Indian. He was doing a twenty-year bit for setting off bombs to protest the war. He told me that whenever an Indian is lost, or sad, or near death, he goes and finds the place of his birth and lies down on top of it. Indians think that gives a man some kind of healing. Closes some kind of loop.

We've already been to the place you were born.

Each of us is born many places.

Did the old Indian say that?

Sutton stares at Photographer. It just hit me kid. You remind me a little of Happy.

NINE

BESS IS KISSING WILLIE. HE FEELS HER EYELASH FLUTTERING against his eyelid. He smiles. Stop, Bess, I'm sleeping. He opens his eye. A cockroach is crawling across his face. He swats it away, sits up. He's on the floor of a small cell. The only light comes through a Judas hole, but it's enough to see that the floor is alive with cockroaches.

A cup of water sits next to the door. He crawls to it. His throat is raw, scorched, and yet he can't drink the water. It smells like piss. The cops tell him later: they pissed in it.

The cops appear at the Judas hole once an hour and torment him. They ask about his whore. They tell him what they'd like to do to his whore. She's in a cell down the hall, his whore. Any message for his whore?

Mr. Endner bails out Bess right away. Willie's family can't afford bail, nor can Happy's. After several days the cops bring Willie to a visiting room. Mother sits at a scarred wood table wearing her mass dress. She hasn't slept in years. She's lost another child. First Agnes, now Willie. She asks Willie what he has to say for himself.

Nothing, he says. Not a thing.

It's not just *your* name in the newspaper. It's ours too. They printed our *address*. The neighbors, the priest, the butcher, they all look at us different.

Willie lowers his gaze. He apologizes tearfully. But he also asks for her help. He needs a newspaper, a magazine, a book, a pad and pencil—something. He's going crazy in here with nothing to do but swat cockroaches and listen to cops say horrible things about Bess.

You want something to do? Mother says.

Yes.

Pray.

She stands, walks out.

Willie, Happy and Bess are charged with burglary and larceny. Willie and Happy are also charged with kidnapping. They're assigned a public defender, who smells of castor oil and liver pills. Stiff white hairs poke from the tip of his pink nose. Willie doesn't catch his name. He's too eager to know if the man has spoken to Bess.

No, Lawyer says. But I've spoken to her family's attorney, who says Mr. Endner is keeping the young lady under lock and key.

Lawyer hands Willie a stack of newspapers. The story is on every front page, though each paper slants it differently. One turns it into a tale of two Irish Town thugs and their gorgeous accomplice. Another makes it a tale of two Irish Town thugs who kidnap an heiress. The one constant in every telling is that Willie and Happy are Irish Town thugs.

The story also makes the papers in St. Louis, Chicago, San Francisco. Even Europe, via the telegraph. Everyone, everywhere, can find something of interest in this yarn. Crime, class, money, sex. So the trial, months later, is a sensation. As Willie and Happy walk into the courtroom they find hundreds of spectators, roistering, laughing, eating. It's like a damn Giants game, Happy says.

Willie and Happy, wearing suits bought with the stolen money, sit on either side of Lawyer. Willie turns, scans the faces in the gallery. Mother and Father, Happy's family, all sit in the front row, frowning. Two rows back, his eyebrows a deep V above the stormy royal blue eyes, is Eddie. He's about to give someone, everyone, an Irish haircut.

A hush falls as Mr. Endner enters. Guided by a nurse, he

moves slowly down the aisle. Lawyer leans over to Willie: The man's not well, I hear.

He's well enough to glare. Willie tries to look contrite. It has no effect. Mr. Endner continues to glare. Willie sighs, faces front, counts the stars on the American flag. He senses a commotion behind him. He turns in time to see a blur. Two of the cops who called Bess a whore grab Mr. Endner just before he wraps his hands around Willie's throat.

Willie and Happy will not take the stand. Their codefendant, however, will. Her lawyers have struck some sort of deal for her cooperation. She enters the hushed courtroom, makes her way to the stand. She wears a gray dress with a blue collar and blue cuffs, black patent leather shoes with white tops, and she holds a blue clutch purse with both hands, tight, as she held the steering wheel of the Nash. Her hair is curled in ringlets that brush her shoulders as she leans forward to put a kid-gloved hand on the Bible.

Willie hasn't seen her since the morning they were arrested. Yes sir—those were the last words he heard her speak, when the sheriff of Poughkeepsie said, Put some clothes on, young lady. Not one visit, not one letter or card. Willie wants to leap across the table, run to her, scold her. He wants to caress her, kiss her. He wants to shout, You ruined my life! He wants to whisper, You are my life. He blames her for leading him into this mess. He rues not marrying her when he had the chance.

Do you swear to tell the whole truth and nothing but so help you God?

I do.

Willie imagines her saying *I do* in a different courthouse, on a different occasion. If only. He bows his head.

In a halting voice, guided gently but firmly by the district attorney, Bess tells her story. The courtroom is rapt, even though this isn't the story they came for. It's not a salacious story, as Bess tells it, but a chaste story of first love. It's the original human story, the only story. With a capitalist twist. Rich girl, poor boy. They want to get married but her father stands in the way. So they risk everything to be together. And yet they do nothing improper, Your Honor. The boy is a perfect gentleman. Also, it's all the girl's idea. *She* breaks the safe. *She* keeps the stolen money on her person at all times. The boy does nothing more than drive.

And this boy's friend, says the district attorney—why bring him along?

We thought we needed a witness, Your Honor. We thought the law required it.

She swears that if she could go back and undo it all, she would. Love clouded her mind. Love made her unwell. Love made her do what she didn't know she was capable of doing.

She pauses, asks for a glass of water. Willie knows she's not really thirsty. He knows this is purely for effect, for sympathy. But anyone who didn't know Bess would think she was dying from dehydration. It makes Willie wonder if any of this, of her, is real. It makes him think that maybe Bess is a true criminal, that maybe love is a crime. Maybe when lovers say, You stole my heart, it's not just pretty words. As surely as they stole her father's cash, Bess stole Willie's heart. And now she shows no remorse. Not the kind Willie wants to see.

The judge peers over his spectacles at the defense table. Lawyer touches the white hairs on his nose, puts a liver pill on his tongue. No questions, Your Honor.

You may step down, young lady.

Bess stands. She looks at her father. Then Willie. The first time she's looked in his direction all morning, the first time their eyes have met in months. He tries to read her face. He can't. She then floats up the aisle, out of the courtroom, onto the front pages. In Brooklyn, in San Francisco, in London, people will soon read about the little flapper's charmingly innocent tale of first love and heedless crime. She'll share the front pages with the bankers and their proxies haggling over the spoils of war. Because of her stirring testimony, however, there will be little mention of Willie and Happy in the newspapers. Reporters will turn Bess's story of star-crossed lovers into the debut of one beautiful star.

It doesn't matter if the judge believes Bess or not. The judge himself doesn't matter. Mr. Endner and his cronies have already told the judge, over ten-dollar cigars in his chambers, what to do. After some pointless testimony from the sheriff of Poughkeepsie, some dithering about the evidence, the squirrel coat, the receipts, the judge finds the boys guilty and sentences them to three years probation. He further orders Willie and Happy to stay away from Bess.

William F. Sutton is released from Raymond Street Jail a few days before Christmas, 1919. He stands on the top step of the jailhouse, looking at the city. Free at last—so what? The Depression awaits him. It's the only thing that awaits him. Under the best of circumstances he wouldn't be able to find work. With a criminal record, forget it. Besides which, he's lost Bess. He might as well turn around and ask to stay at Raymond Street.

The reality is a little worse than he imagined. He misses Bess so much that he can barely function. He wants to die. He plans his death. He writes goodbye letters to his family, to her. At the last minute, walking to the river, he tells himself: If only I could speak to her, for even one minute. He goes to the house on President Street. To hell with his probation. He stands on the sidewalk. The stained glass, the fancy balustrades, the iron fence. He prays for her to pass by a window.

They're all dark.

Mr. Sutton? Are you crying?
    No.
    The Polara is parked outside Kings County Criminal Justice Center. Formerly Raymond Street Jail.

Reporter turns. Mr. Sutton, you're crying.

Sutton puts his hand to his cheek. I didn't know I was crying sir.

Sir?

Kid.

Sutton looks for a Kleenex. He opens the camera bag. Expensive lenses. He opens the cloth purse. Billfold. Baggie full of joints. Armies of the Night. Malcolm X. *Photographer has dog-eared page 155. And underlined a passage.* Any person who claims to have deep feeling for other human beings should think a long, long time before voting to have other men kept behind bars—caged.

He stakes out Coney Island, finds Bess's girlfriends. They tell him that Mr. Endner has taken Bess out of the country until the scandal subsides.

She sailed for Hamburg last week, First Girlfriend says.

She's going to live with Mr. Endner's family, Second Girlfriend adds. Say—how's Happy?

Willie's parents offer no comfort, no quarter, no mercy. When they speak at all in his presence, it's not to him, but about him. They say he's disgraced them, betrayed them. They won't throw him out, but they want no part of him.

Daddo would understand, but Daddo is failing. Half the time he thinks he's back in Ireland with the witches and the mermaids. The little men—they've stolen Daddo's mind.

Thank God for Eddie. He's still working at the shipyard, and he's held in such high regard that he's able to get jobs for Willie and Happy. A nice piece of luck, but also strange. Being in a shipyard reminds Willie of Endner and Sons, which reminds him of Bess, which makes him want to cry. Still, he's working. He tells himself that this, *this* is all he needs. This is all he ever really wanted.

As the new decade begins he's standing on a hooded platform, dangling from the side of a freighter, wielding a purple flame of five thousand degrees. He's cutting the freighter into pieces, cutting the pieces into littler pieces. The job is dangerous, grueling, exhausting, and thus a blessing. At the end of each day he has no choice but to sleep. Also, in his current frame of mind, he finds it therapeutic to destroy, to burn and break stuff apart.

Most mornings, before work, he meets Eddie and Happy at a diner near the shipyard. They clap him on the back, tell him he's good as new. He knows better. He knows that something inside him is broken, something more than his heart, and it's like a scrapped freighter, there's no putting it back together.

He earns enough for a furnished room. His parents don't bother to pretend they're sorry to see him go. Mother says good luck, her tone is good riddance. Father stares, eyes filled with disappointment. On his day off Willie goes for walks along the river. He saves his pennies for a ball game now and then with Eddie and Happy. It's not much, but it's enough. No one will ever hear him complain.

Then he gets laid off. Eddie and Happy too.

With nowhere else to go, the boys meet at the diner every morning. They talk about the Depression as if it were a punk they'd like to rough up. Eddie, on his soapbox: Crops failin, prices fallin, and banks, when they're not goin under, foreclosin on everythin in sight. Banks, he tells everyone along the counter. Fuckin banks.

Willie rations his savings. He has enough for three months, he figures, if he eats once a day, sticks to sardines and crackers. It's some consolation that his pals are in the same fix, until they're not. Eddie and Happy catch on with some high-flying bootleggers, driving beer trucks. Prohibition is now in full force, and though thousands of barkeeps and brewers are thrown out of work, all kinds of new jobs are created, for those not squeamish about the law.

Eddie and Happy are transformed. They have suites at the St. George, bankrolls as big as ham sandwiches. They urge Willie to join them, but no. The newspapers are filled with stories about bad hooch. It's made with rat poison, embalming fluid, gasoline. Fourteen people just died from a batch last month. They were lucky. Others wake up blind. After a night on the town, young men and women grope for the lamp on the nightstand, turn it on—and the room is still dark. I think about my Daddo, Willie tells Eddie and Happy. I don't want to be the cause of someone spending his days in darkness.

Eddie and Happy harass him, berate him—but they also understand. They float him loans, stand him meals. When the three get together at a chop suey joint, or a steak house near the bridge, they don't even let Willie see the check.

Thanks fellas, Willie says, glum. I owe you.

At every meal Eddie and Happy wear brightly colored ties, fancy hats, pointy shoes. Willie wears pants that need mending in the seat. He pawned the suits he bought with Bess.

Sutton sits on the curb across the street from the justice center, between Reporter and Photographer. When I got out of this joint, he says, I just about starved. There were no jobs, boys. None. Except running beer.

Prohibition, Photographer says, rocking back and forth angrily. Big Brother butting into people's personal lives. Back then it was booze, today it's drugs—it's all the same fascist ideology.

Sutton grins. You've got strong opinions kid.

And you know the worst thing about Prohibition, Willie?

Sutton stubs out his Chesterfield. What's that kid?

Banks. Who do you think was laundering all the bootleggers' cash? Banks were always bad, but during Prohibition they went hog wild. The fat cats got fatter. Am I right, Willie?

Sutton shrugs. One thing is for sure, kid, nothing happened quite the way it was supposed to back then. The government banned drinking, but people drank more than ever. Women got the right to vote, but they didn't really use it. The radio was invented—suddenly you could listen to Dempsey wallop a guy two thousand miles away—and they promised it was the end of loneliness. Hell it only made people lonelier. People sat in their rooms, listening to dance music, and theater plays, and laughter, and they felt more alone than ever. Nothing went according to Hoyle, nothing turned out as advertised. That's when people started to get cynical.

Reporter stands, checks his watch, checks the map. Our next stop is Manhattan, Mr. Sutton?

Sutton nods. Yeah. We're done with Brooklyn.

Until the Schuster thing.

Mm hm.

Mr. Sutton. We made a deal.

Deal. Yeah.

Readers want to know what you have to say about Schuster.

He was a nice kid who happened to be in the wrong place at the wrong time. Which can also be said of the rest of us. What else is there to say?

Any idea who might have killed him?

Sutton stands, glowers at Reporter. Chronological order kid.

But Mr. Sutton—

Did you ever notice, kid, that the words obit *and* orbit *are separated by one little letter?*

Down to his last two dollars, Willie walks into the recruiting center in Times Square. A burly sergeant tells him to have a seat, hands him some forms, asks how many chin-ups he can do.

Plenty, Willie says.

Push-ups?

Stand back, Willie says, spitting on his palms, falling to his knees.

The sergeant asks casually if Willie has a criminal record.

Willie, still on his knees, looks off through the glass door at all the people bustling back and forth through Times Square.

Sorry, the sergeant says, taking back the forms. Uncle Sam likes em squeaky clean.

Eddie and Happy tell him to wise up. He can have pockets full of jack by this time tomorrow.

Quit bein such a goddamn Boy Scout, Eddie says.

Do you have any idea how much we're making? Happy says.

Before I peddle poison, Willie says, I'll starve.

From the looks of you, Happy says, that should be about two days.

Then, May 1921. An uncomfortably warm day. Willie is in his room, lying on his bed, reading the sports pages. He's two months behind on the rent. The door bursts open and he reaches for a bat to fend off the landlord, who's barged in before. But it's Eddie, out of breath. Sutty, grab your hat—Happy just got pinched.

Shit. The beer truck?

The truck, yeah. And assault.

Who'd he assault?

Nobody. The cops say he mugged some guy in an alley, hit him over the head and took his billfold, but it's a dirty lie.

In the cab to the station house, Eddie explains. The cops saw an opportunity. They figured they could use Happy to clear an old case off the books, and they knew he was good for some headlines, because of the Endner case.

So what can we do, Willie says.

Sometimes, Eddie says, if you just show up at the cop house, the cops know the prisoner has friends. He's not a nobody. It keeps them from beating him too bad.

Not this time. The cops nearly beat Happy to death. They keep beating him until he confesses to the assault, and another one to boot. Weeks later, in the same courthouse where Willie and

Happy were tried for kidnapping Bess, a judge sends Happy to prison for five years. Willie and Eddie are in the front row. Happy gives them half a wave as he's led from the courtroom in chains.

Eddie taps Willie on the shoulder. Let's go, Sutty.

Yeah, Willie says, but he doesn't move. He stares at the witness chair. He feels terrible for Happy, and partly responsible, but mainly he can't stop thinking of the gray dress with the blue collar and blue cuffs. And the matching blue purse. She held it like a steering wheel.

They drive half a mile, turn onto the Brooklyn Bridge. Sutton still doesn't like the view from this bridge. He sits in the exact middle of the seat, where he can't see the river below, and where much of the skyline is obscured by the heads of Reporter and Photographer. He does what he often does when he's somewhere he doesn't want to be. He recites a poem.

He lunged up Bowery way while the dawn was putting the Statue of Liberty out—that torch of hers you know.

What's that, Mr. Sutton?

Hart Crane. The Bridge.

What's it mean?

Search me.

Photographer aligns Willie in the rearview. You know any Beats?

What am I, a jukebox?

The Beats are where it's at, brother. I shot Ginsberg once. Meditating.

Prison is where you promise yourself the right to live. That's Kerouac—he Beat enough for you?

Photographer nods. Kerouac is cool, he says.

Sutton leans sideways, sneaks a quick look at the city, leans back. Grunts. New York, he says. No matter how many times you see it, you never quite get over how much it doesn't fuckin need you. Doesn't care if you live or die, stay or go. But that—that indifference, *I guess you'd call it—that's half of what makes the town so goddamn beautiful.*

Reporter turns to look back at Sutton. He opens his mouth, closes it.

Sutton chuckles. You got something on your mind kid? Out with it.

I just have to say, Mr. Sutton, you are nothing *like what I expected.*

Photographer snorts. Amen to that, brother.

What did you expect?

You just don't seem—like a bank robber. No offense.

None taken, Sutton says.

I didn't expect you to be quite so—romantic, Mr. Sutton. I mean, poetry? Socrates? And so nostalgic—the tears? Honestly, it's just hard to imagine you with a gun, robbing banks, terrorizing an entire city.

At the center of the bridge they hit a wall of traffic. Photographer turns to Reporter: Maybe you picked up the wrong guy in Buffalo last night. Did you ask this joker in the backseat for his ID?

They both laugh.

Sutton watches a cloud sail across the bridge. He puts on his glasses, takes them off, plays with the Scotch tape that holds them together. He looks down. He opens Photographer's cloth purse. Malcolm X, Armies, baggie, billfold. He opens the camera bag. He takes out two telephoto lenses. Long sleek black metal—he holds one in each hand, tests their weight, then presses one to the back of Reporter's skull, the other to Photographer's.

OKAY, YOU MOTHERFUCKERS, DO WHAT I SAY AND NO ONE GETS HURT. PUT YOUR HANDS IN THE MOTHERFUCKIN AIR!

Reporter raises his hands. Photographer lets go of the wheel as if it's scalding. The Polara swerves. Car horns blare from the next lane.

Holy shit, Reporter says.

Put the MONEY in the FUCKIN bag!

WHAT money? Photographer says. WHAT bag?

Holy shit, Reporter says again.

Sutton laughs. Reporter and Photographer turn and see the lenses. Reporter puts a hand over his mouth. Photographer grabs the wheel.

Funny, Photographer says. Hilarious.

Mr. Sutton, was that really necessary?

You said you couldn't imagine, Sutton says, dropping the lenses. Now you can imagine.

Hours after Happy's trial, Willie tells Eddie he needs to be alone. He walks the length of Brooklyn, walks through Prospect Park, walks all night until he can't walk another step, then walks some more. As the sun oozes above the river he finds himself walking down Sands Street. Jeepers, Wingy says, opening her bedroom door. Last I heard, you were a wanted man.

You heard wrong. No one wants Willie.

I'll show you want. Buy an hour?

I'll pay for the whole morning.

Big shot.

Och, it's Eddie's money.

All the same, I don't think I can go all morning, sugar lump.

Nah, nothing like that. I just need someone to talk to. I need a friend, Wingy.

She puts her one hand on her hip, gives her head a sympathetic tilt. Come on in, Willie.

They lie on her bed, Wingy propped against the headboard, Willie against the footboard.

Wingy, did you ever wish you could just start your life over?

You and your questions. Let's see. About thirty times a day.

That's my dream.

That's everybody's dream, Willie.

How do you know?

People tell me their dreams.

How come no one ever does it?

It's quite a trick. You figure out how to manage it, you let me know.

Eddie says the whole thing's rigged.

Eddie's a wise man.

I should've listened.

To who.

To him. To anybody. Except myself.

You've always been cockeyed.

I have?

Sure. Remember when you worked at the bank? You used to tell me how wonderful it all was, how you were going to be the bank president one day. The *president* for Pete's sake. You were a dreamer, Willie. You were like some potato-eater fresh off the boat.

She stands, wraps herself in a sheet, holds forth her arm. The laaand of *lib-er-tee*, she says in an operatic voice. Send me your huddled messes and misses and asses.

Willie laughs, rolls onto his side. I always wanted to go up inside her, he says.

Wingy laughs, lies down beside him. The Fels smell—still. He takes her arm, wraps it around himself. They both fall asleep laughing.

In the morning he rides the trolley to Thirteenth Street. It's just his parents now. His brothers have left the city, gone out west. Older Sister is married, Daddo has passed. Willie sees the cane in the corner, gives the empty rocking chair a push. House feels strange without the old chatterbox, he says. Mother doesn't answer. She sits at the kitchen table with a cup of tea, refusing to make eye contact. Father stands behind her, saying nothing loudly. They've both read about Happy in the papers. They assume Willie is mixed up in it somehow.

That Happy business had nothing to do with me, Willie says.

They don't answer.

You know me, Willie says. You know I'd never hit a guy on the head and take his billfold.

Know you, Mother says. *Know* you? We don't have the slightest idea who you are.

Father nods, grinds his jaw.

How many times can I apologize for the Endner thing, Willie says.

Not enough, Mother says. And isn't that the problem.

Please, Father says, if you care about us at all, Willie Boy, you'll leave us alone.

He walks to Meadowport, sits deep inside the tunnel, replaying the last three years. At dusk he walks out, through the meadow, through the park, and soon finds himself on Eddie's doorstep at the St. George. Eddie throws open the door. Pleated slacks, a sleeveless white undershirt, white suspenders hanging down. He's been doing push-ups. His arms are the size of Willie's legs. Where you been, Sutty?

Everywhere. Nowhere. Wingy says hi.

They go up to the roof. Eddie has a pint of bootleg in his back pocket. He takes a swig, offers it to Willie. Willie shakes his head. But he smokes Eddie's cigarettes greedily. He's been denying himself tobacco, trying to economize.

The sun is nearly set. They watch the lights come on in Manhattan, cars going back and forth across the bridge. An ocean liner, lit up like a miniature Manhattan, heads off to sea. Willie imagines the passengers: gentlemen standing along the upper decks, taking the air, ladies below sipping illegal cordials. On the Brooklyn side of the bridge steam bubbles from the Squibb factory, where they make stuff for bad stomachs. The air is heavy with milk of magnesia.

Willie looks at Eddie: I can't stop remembering Happy's face when they dragged him off in bracelets.

Yeah. Me either.

Sing Sing. Christ.

It's a war, Sutty. Us, them. How many times do I have to tell you.

They watch the bloodred sun slide into the river. Every day, Eddie says, that fuckin sun goes out the same way. A blaze of glory.

Mm.

Hey, Sutty.

Yeah.

Look at me.

Huh.

I got somethin I need to tell you.

Shoot.

You're a fuckin skeleton.

Willie laughs. I am kind of hungry.

I think if you ate a grape you'd have a paunch. We need to get some groceries in you, boy. Fast.

No can do. I'm broker than broke.

My treat.

At the speak on the corner Eddie orders for Willie. Meat loaf, oysters, creamed potatoes, garden salad, a wedge of apple pie à la mode. Eddie was right, the food helps. Willie feels alive. Then comes the check. Dead again. He's twenty years old, no job, no hope of a job, sponging off his friend.

He stabs the pie. Ed, what am I going to do?

Move in with me. Stay as long as you want. You know you're like a brother.

Thanks, Ed. But long-term. What's any of us going to do?

Eddie leans back. I might have a solution. For both of us.

Eddie tells Willie that he's leaving the bootleggers. Happy's arrest has given him pause. Prohibition is no joke, the government isn't playing. If you're going to take the risk, you better make sure the reward is worth it.

Meaning?

One of the other drivers introduced me to a guy. Horace Steadley. Goes by Doc. A box man out of Chicago, and a great one at that—a true genius. Though he made his bones running the glim-drop back in Pittsburgh.

The what?

The glim. A nifty little two-man con. First man goes into a department store, dressed real sharp, wearin an eye patch, says he lost his glim—his glass eyeball. Tells the clerk he'll pay a thousand bucks if anyone turns the eyeball in to Lost and Found. Leaves his callin card, fancy, gold-embossed with his phone number. Next day, the second man goes up to the clerk carryin a glass eyeball. Anyone lookin for this? He gets the clerk to give him three hundred. Why not? The clerk knows the glim's worth three times that much. But when the clerk dials the number on the first man's callin card, disconnected. Doc had it down to a science. But then he started crackin safes, takin down jewelry stores, and he liked that a whole lot better. Now he runs a topflight box crew and he needs a couple more men. He's a right guy, Sutty. A real right guy. And he knows his potatoes, so he can *teach* us. Then we can start our own crew. Move up to the bigs.

Bigs?

Banks, Sutty. Banks.

Oh Ed. I don't know.

The waiter comes, clears the table. Eddie orders two coffees. When the waiter goes away he hisses: What don't you know?

Isn't it—*wrong*, Ed? I mean, hell. What about right and wrong?

The world is wrong, Sutty. I don't know why, I don't know when it went wrong, or if it's always been, but I know it's wrong, sure as I know you're you and I'm me. Maybe two wrongs don't make a right. But answerin a wrong with a right? That just makes you poor and hungry. And nothin is as wrong as that.

Neither says anything for several minutes. Eddie lights a cigarette, puts on his hat. Just come meet him, he says.

Minutes later Willie is letting Eddie push him into a cab.

Doc's apartment is all the way over in Manhattan, near the theater district. As they approach Times Square, Willie looks out the window. Men in tuxes, women in evening gowns, hurrying from luminous motorcars into cafés, clubs, theaters. The looks on their faces say: Depression? What Depression? Willie wishes he were going to see a show. He's never seen a show. One of the million things he's never done. He should level with Eddie, tell him this is a waste of time. Heisting jewels isn't his line. He doesn't know what his line is, but it isn't this.

Too late. They're outside Doc's building, under the awning. The doorman is buzzing upstairs to announce them.

Sutton peers at the tops of the new skyscrapers in midtown. OK, boys, pop quiz: What drove Jack Dillinger to rob his first bank?

No clue.

A girl broke up with him.

Left at the next light, Reporter says to Photographer. Then straight until Fifty-Third.

It's on the corner, Sutton says.

What's the significance of this next stop? Photographer asks.

It's where Doc lived, Sutton says.

Doc?

My first teacher.

Happy, Doc—when do we get to hear about Sneezy and Dopey?

You two are Sneezy and Dopey.

Har har.

Willie and Eddie stand at attention, Willie straightening his tie, Eddie brushing dandruff off his shoulders. The door opens. A liveried butler takes Eddie's topcoat and fedora. Willie says he'll keep his. They follow the butler down a long hall into a sunken living room. Willie does a triple take at the furniture. End tables, side tables, coffee tables—it's all safes. Big, little, metal, wood—safes.

A man enters from a hall on the other side of the living room. He has an oversize head covered with thick marshmallow hair, and a mouth full of crooked teeth, which he tries to conceal with an equally thick white mustache. Come in, he says in a booming voice, come in, boys.

Doc, Eddie whispers to Willie.

Doc waves a crystal rocks glass full of whiskey. What'll you have?

Nothing, Willie says.

A double of whatever you're havin, Eddie says.

Doc pours Eddie's drink at a bar underneath oil paintings of black-hatted horsemen chasing lithe foxes. He motions for Willie and Eddie to join him in the center of the living room. The windows look onto the theaters. Fluttering marquees make the room brighter, darker, brighter, darker. Willie sits in a chair with curved legs and a silk seat cushion. It feels like sitting on a beautiful woman's lap. Doc and Eddie take the sofa. Bending at the waist and lowering himself, Doc grunts and groans as if sliding into a warm bath.

Pleasure to finally meet you, he says to Willie. Eddie here tells me you're the brightest lad to come out of Irish Town.

Eddie tells me you're the best thief to come out of Chicago.

Silence.

That's a dirty lie, Doc says. I'm the best anywhere.

Eddie smiles. Doc smiles. Crooked smile to go with the crooked teeth. Willie lights a Chesterfield, looks for an ashtray. There's one on the safe at his elbow. Nice place you got here. Who's your decorator, Wells Fargo?

They're all functional too, Doc says. I practice on them, take them apart, put them together, time myself. I'm like a boxer who lives in his gym. The best ones do, by the way.

What's with all the paintings?

Ah. They're from my first boost ever. An estate in Oak Park. They lend a touch of class, I think. They give me hours of pleasure. Sometimes I sit here all night, having a libation, rooting for that fox.

Willie gives Doc a fast once-over. He does seem like a right enough guy. But what's with that getup? He's dressed like a manager at Title Guaranty. Cutaway coat, gold watch chain, plaid bow tie. Plus—white opera gloves? Willie cocks an eyebrow, asks about the gloves. Doc holds out his hands and spreads his fingers, as if Willie has asked a question to which the answer is an emphatic *Ten*.

Willie, he says, my fingers are my life. I'm a box man, I make no pretense of being anything else. On the contrary I'm proud of my art, which goes all the way back to the ancient Egyptians. Did you know the pharaohs were the first to use a lock with pins? I guess they were the first people with valuables. Ach, kids today don't care about the history. They just want to peel a box, shoot a box—put some nitro in the cracks and boom. It's loud, it's vulgar, and frankly you're more likely to get caught. I still think the old ways are best. Stethoscope, fingers, let the tumblers talk. A safe is like a woman. She'll tell you how to open her, provided you know how to listen. So if anything happens to these fingers, well, I'm sleeping under bridges. Naturally I take care of them. Polish the nails. Sandpaper the tips. Keep them warm and well-wrapped. Hence—opera gloves. They're from D'Andrea Brothers, by the by. Do you know their stuff? I think they're the tops.

Willie has never heard anybody talk like Doc. He's either a genius, as Eddie said, or else just full of hot air. Willie fears it's the latter. He wants to stand, tell Doc thanks but no thanks, and he's on the verge of doing just that when Doc says:

Eddie tells me you're mooning over some bird.

Willie frowns at Eddie. Eddie shrugs.

It's been a tough couple of years, Willie says. Let's leave it at that.

Eddie says it's a lost cause. The bird's some rich man's daughter. Please don't call her a bird.

Eddie says she's out of the country, no hope of finding her.

Willie remembers a line from his Latin class at St. Ann's. Where there's life, he says, there's hope.

Uh-huh.

Doc stares at one of his safes, deep in thought. He looks as though he's placed his mind inside the safe and locked the door. His eyes turn glassy, his bottom lip goes slack. Thirty seconds. Forty.

And now he's back. Here's the thing, Willie. I need men on my crew who think straight.

Willie rises out of his chair, points a finger at Doc's chest. When I'm on someone else's time I think plenty straight. When I'm on my own time what I think about is *my own* business.

The idea of being rejected again, for yet another job, has triggered a deep reflex. The thought of adding this popinjay safecracker to the growing list of people who don't want him, who have no use for him, is more than he can take.

Eddie glares at Willie. Easy, boy.

But Doc isn't a bit ruffled. Willie, he says calmly, sit. I didn't mean to offend.

Willie lowers himself back onto his chair. Doc takes a slug of whiskey, looks at the fluttering marquees outside the window. Light, dark, light, dark. Then:

What's your angle kid?

Angle?

Why do you want to work for me? Are you like Eddie, looking to learn? Are you looking for thrills? Or—do you just want money?

Doesn't everybody want money? Sure, I'd like to eat three squares a day. Have my own place, one that's bigger than a washtub. Not have to hide from my landlord. Not wear these stinking clothes. I'd like to salt away enough to maybe see something of this world.

Eddie leans forward. News to him. A trip?

Where to? Doc says.

I'd like to go down to the harbor one day and get on one of those great big liners. Just—sail away.

Who wouldn't, Doc says.

I always see the ads in the papers, Willie says. *The Aquitania sails every second Wednesday at midnight.* That always gives me a tingle. Whenever the second Wednesday rolls around, I find myself looking at a clock.

Anyplace special?

Europe, maybe. Ireland. I don't know.

Eddie smirks. Hamburg, he mutters.

Doc sets his drink on a safe, tugs at his white gloves. He waggles his fingers, cracks his knuckles. Okay, he says. I get the picture. I can see who you are, Willie, I can see you're a right guy. I could see it when you came through the door. I was just testing your motor. Runs plenty hot. That's usually a good thing. Welcome aboard.

You mean—I'm in?

You're in. Both you and Eddie. We pull strictly out-of-town jobs. Boston, Philly, Washington. Sometimes upstate. Staying out of town keeps the bluecoats off balance. A bluecoat is a poor tourist. We use the same routine every time. Break into a jewel store in the wee hours, crack the safe, sweep out the good stuff, make for the train. We're home in bed before the first salesman shows up to fill the showcase in the morning. Our next job's in Philly. A store I've been casing for months. Ever been to Philly?

I've never been anywhere. Except Poughkeepsie.

After this job you still won't feel as if you've been to Philly. In and out. Two hours. Tops.

And so it begins.

PART TWO

The saddest thing about love, Joe, is that not only the love cannot last forever, but even the heartbreak is soon forgotten.

WILLIAM FAULKNER, *SOLDIERS' PAY*

TEN

HE LIKES EVERYTHING ABOUT IT. HE TELLS HIMSELF HE shouldn't. But he does.

He likes checking in to a fancy hotel, requesting one of their best suites, lying on the bedspread with a newspaper and getting his rest like a prizefighter before a fight. He likes keeping one eye on the clock, then coolly putting on his topcoat and walking out at two in the morning, reconnoitering with Doc and the crew at the back door of the jewelry shop. After Eddie jimmies the door, he likes watching Doc carefully remove his opera gloves and flutter his fingers around the dial of the safe. He likes that first sight of those jewels. People are already mad for diamonds, but people don't know the half. The haunting beauty of stolen diamonds in a black silk purse at two in the morning—it's like being the first person ever to see the stars.

He even likes the planning and studying that go into a job. The safe, as an intellectual subject, as an abstract concept, fascinates Willie. Everything in life is a safe, he thinks. His parents, his brothers, Mr. Endner—if only he'd known the combination.

Above all he likes having a job. Though most times it doesn't feel like a job. Doc was right. It's an art.

Within weeks Willie is an indispensable member of Doc's crew. He's the first to show for the weekly planning sessions, the last to leave. He asks smart questions, gets the answers right away, and sometimes thinks of things that Doc missed. Eddie and the other two men on the crew tend to get bored. Not Willie. He can sit in a coffee shop all night, poring over maps, blueprints, brochures from safe manufacturers. Let's go over it one more time, Doc always says, and Willie is the only one who doesn't kick.

Sutton: *It looks exactly as it did when Doc lived there.*
Reporter: *Which one is it?*
Sutton: *That one, with the white awning and the skinny doorman. Doc always gave a big Christmas tip to the doorman, to make sure the kid would buzz up and warn Doc if the cops were ever on their way. Wait here.*
Reporter: *Wait? Mr. Sutton, where are you—? And there he goes.*

Willie buys a shiny new Ford, black with burgundy seats, and a gold wristwatch, and ten pairs of handmade shoes, and a dozen custom-made business suits, all midnight blue and gray flannel. He buys a tuxedo and attends a new Broadway show every other night. He rents a six-room apartment on Park Avenue for three thousand dollars a month and fills one of the walk-in closets with silk-lined topcoats and hand-painted ties, pastel shirts, cashmere scarves. And two of every kind of hat. Boaters, fedoras, panamas, leghorns. He's never owned more clothes than would fit in one grip. Now his closet looks like Gimbels.

Mornings, he likes to sit in his new leather chair by his new living room window, looking out across the rooftops and chimney pots, the clotheslines and telegraph lines and office towers. It's the first time Manhattan, from high above, hasn't crushed him with desire. On the contrary the view makes him feel smug. All those people down there, striving, hustling, pushing, shoving, busting their asses to get what Willie's already got. In spades. He lights a cigarette, blows a jet of smoke against the window. Suckers.

For several months he's happy, or as close to happy as he

thinks himself capable of being without Bess. He takes none of it for granted, the pleasures of dressing well, eating well, sleeping on silk sheets that cost more than most people pay in rent. He's never felt stronger, more alive, and he covets the effect it has on other people—the looks he gets on the street, women sending him engraved invitations in the form of over-the-shoulder smiles, men openly gawking with fear and envy. Waiters come to attention, doormen bow deeply, cigarette girls bend over and give him peeks at their cleavage as though it were his birthright. And yet, and yet. One morning his aerial survey of Manhattan doesn't afford the same jolt. His mind is restless, his heart troubled. King of all he surveys? What of it? He thinks of the old neighborhood. Suddenly he's up, out of the chair, ringing the doorman to bring his car around. An hour later Wingy is gawking, barking with laughter. Don't you look like Sunday, she says.

Hiya kid.

Some getup. Your ship come in?

Rich uncle died.

You don't say. And you want to spend some of your inheritance on a little Wingy love?

Nah. Just came by to say hello. I had a hunch you might like a visit.

He drops his new hat on the bed.

I was just going to have breakfast, she says.

I'd love some.

She pulls a bottle of bootleg from under her mattress, pours two glasses, hands one to Willie. She tells him that his hunch was spot-on, she's feeling blue this morning. The quality of her clientele is in steep decline. The Depression is ending, the markets are roaring, and suddenly the men who visit her are very different.

Different how?

Wall Street, Willie. They're a bad bunch.

I'm surprised they venture across the bridge.

They come to Brooklyn for—something different. On this side of the river, the plainer the girl, the better the business. They feel they can make bold with us plain ones. Be more themselves, I guess.

Don't lump yourself in that group. Nothing plain about you, Wingy.

You're sweet, Willie. But I know who I am. What I am. And as such, I'll take a sailor over an investment banker any day.

Why's that?

Bankers don't *ask*, Willie. They take.

I'm sorry you're having to deal with such fellas.

Don't be. It makes me feel less guilty when I rob em.

Willie laughs.

Wingy asks if he's got any smokes. He takes out a pack, lights one for her, leaves the pack on the bed.

I wish they could all be sweet as you, she says. That first time? I still remember you walking through that door, polite, shaking—grateful. Yes mam, no mam. Like it was the first day of school. Like I was your teacher.

It was. You were.

Willie sits in a chair, Wingy sits on the edge of the bed. She runs her one hand through her hair. I miss that Willie Boy, she says. The only weird thing he ever wanted to do was call me Bess.

Willie looks off. That Willie Boy is dead, he says.

Along with your rich uncle.

Sure, he says. Right.

Was there a funeral?

Yeah. No one showed.

She moves over to her makeup table. Watching her cross the room Willie thinks she looks much older than her years, though he has no idea how old she is. She sits, powders her nose, asks his reflection about Happy. Willie frowns. She asks about Bess. His frown deepens.

I wrote her a letter. But I had nowhere to send it.

You'll hear from her, Wingy says. If she's as smart as you always said, she'll get in touch.

He taps his new gold watch. I better be going.

Short visit.

I've got a meeting.

He stands, straightens his tie, reaches into his breast pocket. He comes out with a neat stack of new bills, holds it forth with two hands. Wingy turns on her stool. She doesn't stand, doesn't take it.

The hell is that, Willie?

Christmas gift. Belated.

What's the punch line?

I thought you might like to go somewhere. Like we talked about. Start over.

He steps forward, places the money on Wingy's lap. She touches it, flips the bills like pages of a book. She looks up. I don't want your pity, Willie.

It's not my pity. It's my money. Hell it aint even my money.

She stands, lets the money fall. She covers the ground between them in one step, wraps her arm around Willie. Surprised, Willie stiffens. Then lets his body go slack. Gives her a brotherly hug.

He's not dead, she says.

Who?

Willie Boy.

Doorman: Merry Christmas sir.

Sutton: Merry Christmas to you kid. Say, is there any chance 8C is vacant? A friend of mine used to live up there and I was hoping to take a quick look around. For old times' sake.

Doorman: Wait a second. Hold the phone. Aren't you Willie the Actor?

Sutton: Yeah.

Doorman: Willie the Freakin Actor?

Sutton: Some people call me that.

Doorman: Willie the Actor at my freakin door? Okay, this right now is blowing my mind. My old man is not going to freakin believe this. He's your biggest fan, Mr. Sutton. Run, Willie, run, that's what my old man says whenever you're in the papers. Three greatest Willies in New York, my old man says—Willie Mays, Joe Willie Namath, and Willie the Actor.

Sutton: You're very kind.

Doorman: Hey—wow. I mean—wow. Could you sign my newspaper?

Sutton: Sure thing.

Doorman: Here. Sign it right here. Under your picture. There you go. Put—To Michael Flynn, That's where the money was. Michael Flynn, that's my old man. I'm Tim Flynn. What the heck are you doing here, Mr. Sutton?

Sutton: I got out yesterday.

Doorman: Who doesn't know that? But here?

Sutton: I'm reminiscing. Visiting old haunts. I used to know a guy in this building, and I was just hoping to see his place.

Doorman: Eight C? Okay, that's the Monroe place. Between you and me the Monroes are some Grade A world-class WASP prick motherfucks.

Sutton: Is that a fact.

Doorman: If they weren't home I'd be happy to show you around. On the q.t. Hell, I'd let you use their toilet. But they're definitely home. Guests have been going up all morning.

Sutton: Maybe there's another way? That's a handsome uniform you're wearing. What size are you kid?

Doorman: Thirty-eight.

Sutton: What say we trade outfits? This suit is brand-new.

Doorman: You serious?

Sutton: Dead serious. I'll go up as the new doorman, invent

some reason for knocking on their door, and be out before they know what's what.

Doorman: Gee, I don't know, Mr. S. I could lose my job. And who are you?

Reporter: I'm writing an article about Mr. Sutton.

Photographer: And I'm taking his picture.

Sutton: Oh. I didn't know you boys were behind me. Kid, meet Commanders Armstrong and Aldrin.

Doorman: Merry Christmas.

Photographer: Same to you.

Sutton: Well, okay kid. I understand. I'd love to give you a tip, but all I've got is a couple of checks from Governor Rockefeller.

Doorman: Please, Mr. Sutton. I wouldn't take your money.

Sutton: Don't say that kid. Don't ever say that. Never turn down money.

Eddie was right, Doc does know his potatoes. He can talk all night about safes. And Willie can listen all night. After their regular planning session at the coffee shop on the corner, Willie often follows Doc back to his apartment for private tutorials.

In addition to safes, Doc is a collector of quotations. He has one to illustrate every teaching point. He's fond of Gibran. *Work is love made visible.* And Novalis. *We are near waking when we dream we are dreaming.* He knows pages and pages of Plutarch, Epictetus, Emerson. When he's had too much to drink he'll say this over and over: *Commit a crime, and it seems as if a coat of snow fell on the ground, such as reveals in the woods the track of every partridge and fox and squirrel and mole.*

One night Doc pours himself a whiskey, lights a thin cigarillo, eases back on his sofa. It's all a kind of sad joke, Willie Boy. Americans are a trusting people, so your average safe is an impediment at best. It's not meant to stop you, just slow you down. If you know boxes, really know them, this whole game is child's play. Every box is flawed *by design*. Even if you can't crack it, there's always at least one way around the lock, a back door installed at the factory, in case the owner croaks, the tumblers quit working. Or else the combination is obvious, the owner's birthday, say. Or else it's writ down someplace obvious. You'd be flabbergasted how many times it's right there on the wall above the safe. The rule with safes is a rule you can apply to everything, Willie. There's always a way in.

Along with all that's worth knowing about safes, Doc teaches Willie about alarm systems, door locks, padlocks, cops. He teaches Willie which lawyers are best for which charges, and which ones to avoid. He leads him around town, introduces him to the fraternity. Hard-eyed killers, flashy bootleggers, wizened yeggs. Cracksmen, petermen, heistmen, bookies, flickers, conners, buzzers, overlords. He presents Willie, like a minister without portfolio, to the bosses. Legs Diamond. Owney Madden. Dutch Schultz.

Lastly Doc carefully and patiently educates Willie about the logistics of offloading stolen goods.

Your most important tool, Doc says, isn't your tension wrench, your stethoscope, your jimmy. It's your off man. Whosoever converts your boost to cash knows as much about you as anyone in the world, including your mother, so choose that person as you choose your partners. With double care.

Doc's off man is a woman. A well-known socialite, she's in the society columns every week for giving truckloads of money to the church, the ballet, the library. Newspapers call her a doyenne, a dowager, a pillar of the community. Doc says she's also a sicko. She gets a thrill from diamonds with a sordid provenance. She has a particular fetish for other women's heirlooms.

Willie goes with Doc one day to meet Socialite at her home, a gorgeous town house in the East Sixties. For the better part of an hour they sit in her Art Deco living room, on white leather

Barcelona chairs, drinking tea, eating lemon cookies. Half the walls are paneled with mirrors, so Willie finds fifty Willies eyeing him from all directions. He feels outnumbered. Outmanned.

He sees a book lying facedown on the coffee table. He picks it up. Socialite says it's a collection of stories and poems you can only find in Paris. The young writer's name is Heming-something. Willie studies the author photo, sets the book down. Looks like a tough mug, he says.

Ravishing, Socialite says. Every sentence is *ravishing*.

Willie isn't entirely sure what this word means, but Socialite uses it a lot. Paris is ravishing this time of year. Clara Bow is ravishing on the silver screen. These new puzzles everyone is doing, crossword puzzles, are a simply *ravishing* way to pass the time.

A puzzle book is lying facedown near the short stories. She picks it up. Do either of you know a four-letter word for *Europe river*, starting with *a*?

Arno, Doc says.

Socialite's eyes grow large. While she fills in the word, Doc shoots Willie a look. Willie removes a silk purse from his breast pocket and puts it on the coffee table. Socialite drops the puzzle book, scoops the bag. She carries it across the room and empties it onto a writing table that looks as if it was boosted from Versailles. Diamonds, sapphires, emeralds go skittering across the table's wood surface. She sorts them, examines each one through a lorgnette. Then she and Doc haggle.

I can't do it, Doc says. I'd be in the poorhouse if I settled for that price.

You're robbing me blind, Doc.

It's the best I can do, I'm afraid.

All right, all right.

She opens a safe behind one of the mirrored panels. She removes a brick of cash, wraps the brick in butcher paper. Willie takes one last look at the jewels on the table. An impulse overcomes him. He shoots out his hand, seizes a three-carat Old European-cut diamond ring.

Please mam. Not this one.

Doc wheels. His eyes dart from Willie to the ring and back to Willie. They both turn and look at Socialite. Doc gives a pained smile. Well now. Uh. Apparently my associate has grown—attached—to that item.

Socialite purses her lips. She doesn't like to lose out on even one piece of ice. She glares at Doc. Then Willie. Willie fears he's queered the deal. He's kiboshed Doc's vital relationship with his off man.

Socialite sits at the writing table. A girl? she says.

Yes mam. She's ravishing.

Sutton walks to the corner. There used to be an out-of-town news-stand right here, he says. We'd step off the overnight train, wearing our long topcoats, snap-brims wide as sombreros, and walk straight to this newsstand.

Who?

Doc's crew.

Why?

We wanted to read our reviews. We liked being famous. Most people suffer from a fear that they're not really here, that they're invisible. Being famous solves that. You must be here, it says so in the newspaper.

Sutton looks once more at the spot where the newsstand used to be, as if it might materialize. Shit, he says, people dove out of our way as we came up this sidewalk.

Why?

We looked bad. And we knew we looked bad. We were trying to look bad. Every criminal is playing some criminal he saw in a movie. I can't tell you how many guys I met in the joint who saw

Bogart or Cagney at an impressionable age. No one loves Bogart more than me, but the man's caused more bloodshed than Mussolini.

I'm confused, Photographer says. What reviews?

We'd buy the papers from whichever city we'd just hit and read the stories about our heist. Police say they have no leads—we always busted a gut about that one. Police say it looks like an inside job— we'd smack our knees over that one. But the bad reviews, we took those hard. If the cops said the robbery looked like the work of amateurs, we'd go into a funk for a week. Everyone's a fuckin critic.

Reporter checks Sutton's map. Mr. Sutton, speaking of newspapers, it looks like our next stop is Times Square? Now that's the home of The New York Times. *That's the belly of the beast. Times Square is to reporters what a statue is to pigeons, so please, Mr. Sutton, I beg you—not Times Square.*

Sorry kid. Willie has to see Times Square. Willie isn't even officially out of prison until he hits Times Square.

Doc waits until they're out on the street and almost to Times Square before he explodes. For the love of God, Willie Boy, what in blazes were you thinking?

I'm sorry, Doc—the ring just spoke to me.

Willie pulls the ring from his breast pocket and holds it to the spring sun.

Stow that thing, Doc hisses. Damn it, I thought your bird was out of the country.

Please don't call her a bird. Yes, she's out of the country. But I mean to find her. And when I do, I mean to be ready. To have a ring on me.

Doc squares his shoulders, pushes back his hat, looks as if he wants to hammer some sense into Willie. But then he sighs, rakes his fingers through his marshmallow hair. Okay, okay. I'll deduct the ring from your next nick.

He shadow punches Willie a right to the jaw.

But in the future, he adds, if a piece of ice should *speak* to you, don't answer, Willie Boy. Get me? Come on, let's hit the Silver Slipper. You need to buy me a fuckin drink.

I should have never left Doc, Sutton says. I owed him. I was never good at anything until I met him. A man has to feel good at something or he's not a man, and with Doc I discovered that I was good at stealing diamonds. Nah—I wasn't good at it. I was great.

So why did you leave?

We were making nice jack, but I needed a big score. A bunch of big scores, actually, if I was going to find Bess and show her that I could take care of her. That was always in the back of my mind. That was my dream. Also, if I'm being honest, Doc was slipping.

It happens in Boston. The safe is a battered old Mosler, child's play, but Doc just can't find the numbers. He rolls the wheel, back and forth, nothing doing. Don't know what's wrong with me tonight, he says. His voice is different.

They bring out the drill. Eddie starts, puts three quick holes in the plate, but Willie is pointing to his gold watch. Time. They leave everything, walk out.

On the overnight train back to New York they sit together, saying nothing. Willie watches a Model A in the distance, trundling along a dark country road, one headlamp out. He turns and watches Doc, removing his white gloves, taking several pulls from a silver flask. The flask is shaking.

Willie gives himself a week off. He sits in his leather chair, looking out at the city, thinking. At last he puts on his best suit and walks down to Doc's. They sit among the safes, drinking coffee, talking shop. Doc mentions the next job. Willie shakes his head.

Won't be a next job for me, Doc. I'm out.

Ah Willie, no.

Doc. You knew I wanted to go out on my own eventually.

But why now? Why on earth now? We've got a bang-up thing going here.

Do me a favor, Doc. Hold out your hands.

Willie.

Do it, Doc.

Doc extends his arms, spreads his white-gloved fingers.

Look, Willie says. You're playing ragtime.

Fuck kid—age. Happens to the best of us.

You blew that score the other night.

First time.

All the more reason.

Doc stands, walks to the bar. He throws down a whiskey, stares up at the hunters, the fox leaping a hedgerow. You may be right, Willie. Probably are right. But I can't quit. I love it too much.

Willie nods.

Godspeed, Willie. I'll watch the papers for your reviews.

Days later Willie meets Eddie for lunch at a chophouse in Times Square. Over porterhouses smothered in onions Willie tells Eddie it's time. Time to start their own crew.

Eddie nods.

What gives, Ed? I expected a little more vim. This is it, what you've always wanted, the real raw-jaw stuff. Banks.

Eddie shakes a Chesterfield out of Willie's pack, lights it, takes a hard drag. I got some bad news, Sutty.

Shoot.

Old friend of yours is back in town.

Oh.

She's gettin married.

Willie pushes away his steak. He looks at his hands. Ragtime.

Where?

Baptist church.

When?

Today kid. What I'm hearin, it's an arranged thing. The groom comes from money. His family owns warehouses all along the waterfront.

Willie stands, staggers out of the chophouse. A produce truck comes barreling down the street, smashing through puddles. Willie and Eddie will always disagree about whether Willie changed his mind at the last second or Eddie ran out of the chophouse just in time.

They walk around Times Square, Eddie urging Willie not to crash the wedding.

Never mind that seein it will kill you, Sutty. Her old man could have you pinched.

For what? I'm not on probation anymore.

He owns Brooklyn. He don't need a reason.

Eddie makes a good point. Willie considers wearing a disguise. He even steps into a theatrical shop, tries on a homburg and fake beard. But then he decides that he wants Old Man Endner to see him. He wants Bess to see him—at his best. He splurges on a scalp massage, a barber shave, a haircut. He puts on his newest suit, chalk-striped, with wide, dramatic lapels. At four o'clock, as the little old lady in the flowered hat presses down on the organ keys, Willie is five rows from the altar, two rows from the Rockefellers, the Old European–cut diamond ring in his breast pocket. Just in case.

Mr. Endner, escorting Bess down the aisle, sees Willie first. He tugs on his mustaches. He's going to halt the ceremony, call the cops. No—his eyes narrow to watery slits, his mustaches fan out across a yellow grin. Because Willie is too late.

Now Bess sees Willie. She stops, lowers her bouquet. Golden flowers to match her golden-flecked eyes, which quickly fill with tears. She mouths something at Willie, he can't be sure what.

No Willie no.

Oh Willie oh.

Go Willie. Go.

Then she presses on. She keeps walking, past Willie, past the Rockefellers, and with each step Willie feels another year clipped off his life. At the altar she turns, faces her groom. Willie bolts from the pew, up the aisle, out of the church. He doesn't stop running until he comes to Meadowport. He sits for hours staring at the ring. He sets it on the ground, walks out.

Then he turns around, retrieves it. He slips it into his breast pocket, decides to keep it. Just in case.

Photographer: He's asleep.

Reporter: You're joking.

Photographer: Snoring too.

Reporter: Unbelievable.

Photographer: Willie the Actor.

Reporter: Can we please turn down this radio? I've got a splitting headache.

Photographer: That's the Rolling Stones, brother.

Mick Jagger: Oh! Yeah!

Reporter: What does this song mean anyway? Why are rape and murder just a shot away?

Photographer: See there's your problem—everything has to mean something. Where are we going again?

Reporter: Times Square. Against our will.

Photographer: Maybe we've been kidnapped and we just don't know it.

Reporter: It's entirely possible.

Photographer: Hey, did you get a load of Laura in that purple skirt the other day?

Reporter: Make your next right.

Photographer: She's the best-looking chick at the paper, if you ask me.

Reporter: I didn't.

Photographer: Didn't what?

Reporter: Ask you. Turn right I said. Great. You missed the turn.

Photographer: Speaking of chicks, how's yours?

Mick Jagger: Oh!

Reporter: I have got to turn down this music. Where's the loudness knob?

Photographer: Fell off.

Reporter: This Polara is messed up.

Photographer: This assignment is messed up.

Reporter: May I remind you that you asked for this assignment.

Photographer: I asked for Al Capone. Not Vic Damone.

Reporter: Nice.

Photographer: Empty tunnels, murdered sheep, stories about some jive chick from the horse-and-buggy days.

Reporter: He loved her.

Photographer: Yeah.

Reporter: He's not making my life easy, you know. It's noon and he's hardly said anything I can use. Chronological order kid. At least you've gotten some good shots. I've got nothing.

Photographer: All my editor really wants is Sleeping Beauty standing at the scene of the Schuster murder. Schuster, Schuster, Schuster—that's what my editor said as I walked out the door.

Reporter: Mine too.

Photographer: You think Willie killed Arnold Schuster?

Reporter: He doesn't seem like a killer.

Photographer: He doesn't seem like a bank robber either—you said so yourself.

Reporter: Point taken.

Photographer: Can I turn here to get to Times Square?

Reporter: No. It's one-way.

Photographer: Do me a favor. Get my billfold out of my bag.

Reporter: Why?

Photographer: I want to buy something in Times Square.

Reporter: What?

Photographer: Something for the lotus-eater back there.

Reporter: I can't get your bag. He's using it as a pillow.

Photographer: Rip Van Willie.

Reporter: He looks so peaceful.

Photographer: He's probably dreaming about—what was her name?

Reporter: Bess.

Photographer: I thought it was Wingy.

Reporter: That was the prostitute. Must you get stoned every time we do a story together?

Photographer: I've got it. Why don't we wake up Willie the Napper and tell him we've already been to Times Square. Tell him we've been to all the places on his map and now it's time to do Schuster. He won't even know.

Sutton: I can hear you.

ELEVEN

WILLIE IN A SUIT AND TIE, CARRYING A BRIEFCASE ONTO
the Long Island Rail Road. With all the other commuters. Except
the other commuters are going to jobs, and Willie is going to
case a job. February 1923.

He learned from Doc the importance of scouting targets carefully. Also, the benefits of working out of town. Unlike Doc,
however, he wants to avoid large cities. In the sticks, Willie
reasons, cops will be slower.

He goes on walkabouts, carrying a map, a notebook, searching
for the ideal backwater. He soon stumbles on Ozone Park. The
town founders hoped the name would attract city folk in search
of clean air, greenswards. It also attracts Willie Sutton, because
it sounds like a place founded by simpletons.

He strolls Main Street. Soda fountain, cigar store, coffee stand.
He buys a cup of coffee and sits on a bench, admiring the old
enamel factory with the brick clock tower. It bongs every half
hour. Residents don't seem to hear. They seem out of it, their
heads in the clouds. In the ozone.

He finds his way to First National Bank of Ozone Park, stands
in line. When he gets to the teller's cage he slides a dollar under
the bars, asks for change. The teller has buckteeth, a cowlick, a
necktie covered with Old Glories. A brass nameplate on his shirt:
GUS. While Teller roots in his drawer, Willie pockets the bank's
fountain pen, looks around. He peers at the safe behind Teller.
A music box would be harder to open.

Best of all, First National is next door to a dilapidated movie theater. Willie buys a ticket for the matinee. During the car chase he slips down the back stairs. Just as he hoped, the bank and theater share a basement.

Later that day he and Eddie journey into the wilds of New Jersey. They buy a powerful torch, extra-large oxygen tanks, helmets.

While doing all this legwork and procurement, Eddie says they need a quick score. To keep the cash rolling in. To stay sharp. He suggests a jewelry shop in Times Square, next door to the Astor Hotel.

Sutton stands on a pedestrian island, looking up. This is Times Square? Where are all the fuckin signs? Where are the lights?

They took a lot of them down, Reporter says. The economy.

What a damn shame, Sutton says. This used to be one of the most magical places on earth. Right there was the BOND Clothing sign. All over the world people knew that sign. BOND—in big red letters. When you came to Times Square from another borough, or from Timbuktu, you could count on the trolley cars looking like great big loaves of bread, and the BOND sign being—right—there. And above it were two giant statues. Five stories tall. Like two Statues of Liberty. Nude Man, Nude Woman. The prudes got all lathered up about those statues. And between them was a huge waterfall, modeled on Niagara Falls. And right over there was the Wrigley sign. All different colored fish—green, blue, pink—and above them was a beautiful mermaid. She looked like Bess. A neon Bess. Imagine kid? And right there was the Camel sign. Blowing smoke rings. When there was no wind, the ring would keep its O shape all the way across Broadway. Christ almighty, Times Square was my everything. I came here to think, to meditate, to get my bearings. When I was young I'd come here and look at the lights and say to myself: I've got to be a part of this. If I don't find some way to become a part of this, my life will mean nothing. When I was older, and lonelier, I'd come here to dance.

Dance?

Sutton rises on his toes, slides his hips. I was quite a hoofer. Back when I had two good stems. And there were a hundred places within a few blocks of here where you could give a girl a nickel and twirl her across the floor. Ten cents, you could feel her up. A dollar—well. You know. They called them taxi girls, because you rented them.

He turns in a circle, sees a marquee that reads: SEX. *A woman totters past it. She wears red plastic pants, chunky platform heels, a purple wig. Ah, he says, some things haven't changed.*

He walks toward her.

Hey, Mr. Sutton, we really shouldn't—oh boy.

Hello, the woman says to Sutton.

Hello.

You looking for a date?

You're working on Christmas?

Is it Christmas?

That's what all the papers say.

Well. What of it. People get horny on Christmas. Fact, Christmas is the horniest holiday.

Is that so? I would have thought July Fourth.

Hubby tells wifey he's running out for eggnog. I'm eggnog.

I'm Willie.

He reaches out his hand. She stares at it.

What's the going rate, Eggnog?

Eggnog steps back so abruptly on her heels that she almost tips over. Hold up, she says. Hold up, hold up—you Willie Sutton!

That's right.

Willie the Actor!

Yes mam.

I just read about you. You got out yesterday. Now what? You want a little Eggnog?

No, thank you, sweetheart, I was just curious. I had a friend once in your profession. And I used to spend a lot of time with a few—girls—here in Times Square.

Damn. Willie Sutton. You was one badass.

Still am.

What you doing in Times Square?

Reporter steps forward, clears his throat. Sutton wheels, grins. Actually, he says, I'm giving this boy a tour of my life. The scenes of my highs and lows, my heists.

I'm working the same street Willie the Actor worked? Aint that something?

Sutton points. I actually pulled a job on that corner over there, he says.

Eggnog and Reporter look.

Stride Rite Shoes? Eggnog says.

Nah. The Astor Hotel used to be there. Next door was a jewelry store. They kept the good stuff in the front window.

So do I, Eggnog says.

They were just asking for it.

So am I, she says.

We smashed the window. Tire irons. Made off with a sack of diamond watches. Easy score.

You fence it? Eggnog asks.

Sutton nods.

How much?

Ten grand. Give or take.

You know how many Shriners I got to make happy for ten grand?

I shudder to think.

Who was your off?

Dutch Schultz.

Reporter coughs. The—Dutch Schultz?

Dutch owned a speak not far from here, Sutton says. They all talk about how ugly Dutch was, but he was no Monk Eastman.

To me he looked sort of dapper. Like a British lord. Of course, he had the most horrible little claw hands. And an ugly heart. Dutch invented the gonorrhea rubout.

Eggnog's eyes grow wide. The what?

Dutch would get a bandage infected with gonorrhea and tape it over a guy's eyes. Make him blind. He was one mean SOB, but for some reason he liked me.

Eggnog points. Who this?

Photographer, carrying a brown bag, is running toward them from Forty-Third Street. He reaches them out of breath, hands the bag to Sutton. Little gift for you, Willie. Merry Christmas.

Sutton opens the bag, pulls out a pair of fur-lined handcuffs. Bracelets, he says, laughing.

So you won't feel so quote unquote naked, Photographer says. Try them on.

I'll wait till we get in the car.

So long as I get a shot of you wearing them.

Okay, Sutton says. Sure thing.

Eggnog looks at Photographer. She looks at Reporter, Sutton, the handcuffs. She holds up one finger. Hn, hn, hn, she says, walking away slowly. Willie Sutton into some kinky shit.

Willie and Eddie stand outside a back door of the Loews theater in Ozone Park, a cold rainy night. Late.

You ready? Willie says.

Eddie nods.

Willie slides the tension wrench in the keyway, then the hook pick. Just the way Doc taught him. The lock pops. Eddie lugs the torch down the stairs, into the theater basement, along with the hoods and tanks, while Willie grabs the sawhorses.

Beneath the bank lobby they slap together a crude platform. Willie, hooded, climbs on, fires the torch. He trains the violet flame on the ceiling. Right away he knows he's miscalculated.

An article in *Popular Mechanics* said concrete melts like butter under the newest acetylenes, but not this concrete. After two hours he's not halfway through and his arms are killing him. Eddie takes a turn. They trade, back and forth, until finally they've cut a hole big enough for them to wriggle through.

Standing inside the bank at last, they hear the clock tower on top of the enamel factory bonging seven times. The guard will be here in half an hour. There isn't enough time to tackle the safe. Willie presses his palms against the safe door. They've come so far. They're so damn close. On the other side of this door lies fifty thousand, maybe seventy-five.

They put on their topcoats and fedoras, walk out into the pouring rain. They leave everything—torch, platform, oxygen tanks. They can't carry all that gear through the streets in the daylight. But it's not a problem. They used gloves. No fingerprints.

For weeks they lie low, reading every word of the newspapers. They can find no mention of a break-in at First National in Ozone Park. Maybe the bank is keeping the story under wraps, Eddie says. Maybe they don't want to scare off customers. Maybe, Willie says, maybe.

Eddie suggests they go out, blow off steam. We need a break, he says.

A ball game, Willie says.

A beautiful new ballpark has just opened in the Bronx. The whole city is talking about it.

Swell idea, Eddie says. You're always thinkin, Sutty.

It's April 24, 1923.

Sutton looks up at the CANADIAN CLUB *sign, above the fluttering* COCA-COLA *sign. He looks at the theater where he used to see silent films. It's now showing a twin bill:* Daniel Bone *and* Davy Cock It.

He looks at the headlines scrolling around the building to his

right. He reads them aloud. POPE CALLS FOR WORLD PEACE IN XMAS
MASS . . . *Good luck with that* . . . NIXON TO CUT FUNDING FOR
NASA . . . *Sure, that figures, what's NASA ever done for us?* . . . TRIAL
OF CHICAGO SEVEN RIOTERS WHO DISRUPTED DEMO CONVENTION
RECESSES UNTIL MONDAY . . . *Just delaying the inevitable.*

*Mr. Sutton, at the risk of being redundant, can we please move
on to our next stop? The New York Times is right over there. It's
a miracle we haven't been spotted yet.*

BANK ROBBER WILLIE THE ACTOR SUTTON FREE AFTER 17
YEARS . . . *Hey! HEY! That's me! Can you beat that? I'm famous.*

You've been famous all your life, Mr. Sutton.

Touché kid.

*A Chesterfield dangling from the corner of his mouth, the bag
of handcuffs tucked under his arm, Sutton flips up the fur collar
of Reporter's trench coat and walks off, a new bounce in his hobbled
step.*

Where to? Photographer calls after him.

The Bronx, Sutton says.

*Oh good, Reporter says. I can just see tomorrow's zipper head-
line.* JOURNALISTS SLAIN IN XMAS MUGGING.

Yankee Stadium is packed. It's a special occasion and every man
dresses accordingly—finest suit, sharpest necktie, best boater.
Willie has chosen a yellow linen three-piece with a lavender
four-in-hand, Eddie a gray tweed with a lime-green tie. Each of
them wears a white hat with a wide black band. Eddie's cost four
hundred dollars.

They splurge on premium seats, third base side. The guy in
the parking lot wants two hundred bucks. Pricey, but what choice
do we have, Eddie says. We can't sit with the bleacher bugs.

The seats are three rows from President Warren G. Harding,
whose box is draped with red, white and blue. Eddie cranes his
neck. He doesn't like Harding, a hypocrite, a connoisseur of

women and whiskey despite his wife and Prohibition. He doesn't like that Harding is tight with Rockefeller. Nor does Willie. Before the first pitch Harding tries to shake hands with New York's young star, Babe Ruth. Eddie howls as Harding mugs for the cameras and Ruth pointedly doesn't.

Would you get a load of that, Sutty. Rich as Croesus and Ruth's still a Democrat. Mark me down for a Ruth fan.

A boy in a white paper hat comes down the aisle selling Cracker Jacks. Eddie hails him, buys two boxes, hands one to Willie. Aint this the life, Sutty? Only thing that could make it better—a couple of ice-cold beers. Goddamn Prohibition. I think I hate the Drys worse than the Dagos.

In the bottom of the fifth Ruth whipsaws a speedball high into the spring sky. For a moment it hovers like a second moon. Then it descends swiftly and lands with a plonk against a right-field seat, near the Edison Cement Sign.

That swing! Eddie says. Mother of God, Sutty, the *violence* in that swing.

Willie and Eddie are lifelong fans of the Brooklyn Robins, but they can't deny that this Ruth fella is the genuine article. As Ruth saunters around third base, Willie and Eddie stand and respect-fully applaud. They're close enough to see the seams in Ruth's socks, the stains in his flannel jersey, the pores in his nose. Willie can't take his eyes off that nose. It's wider than Willie's, double wide, which makes Willie double fond of Ruth.

The crowd is quieting down, settling back into their seats. Wally Pipp is striding to the plate. Willie feels a hard tap on his shoulder. Leaning over him are two Ruth-size men.

You Sutton?

Sutton who?

This Wilson?

And who might you be?

Come with us.

Where to?

We'll ask the questions, Skeezix.

Look, mister, we paid good money for these seats.

You wouldn't know good money if it bit you on the ass.

Who are you to be saying—?

The men grab Willie by the lapels and lift him out of his seat. They do the same with Eddie. Fans gawk. Photographers kneeling around home plate turn and look to see what the commotion is about. Pipp calls time, watches as the men push Willie and Eddie up the ramp. Holding on to his box of Cracker Jacks, Willie reaches into his pocket, palms Bess's diamond ring, then digs into the Cracker Jacks as if for one more handful—and stuffs the ring deep down in the box.

Just outside Gate 4, before the men throw him into the backseat of their car, Willie tosses the box in the trash.

Sutton stands before Gate 4. They ruined it, he says.

I was going to mention, Reporter says. While you were away, they remodeled.

You say remodeled, I say ruined.

It was old.

It was younger than me.

Photographer shoots the façade, the flags along the upper deck. You know the Yankees aren't playing today, right, Willie?

Sutton gives him a cool stare.

Just checking, Photographer says under his breath. But since every place we visit is totally changed, and since all of New York is totally and completely different on a subatomic level, what's the point of all this driving around?

I'm totally changed too, Sutton says. On a subatomic level. But I'm still me.

Photographer and Sutton look at each other, like strangers on a subway, then look at Reporter.

Every generation, Reporter says, thinks the world used to be a better place.

Every generation is right, Sutton says.

Reporter flips his notebook to a clean page. So, Mr. Sutton, what happened here at the stadium?

This is where Eddie and I got pinched after our first bank robbery. Life was about to change—to end, really. But when the Pinkertons grabbed us here, and drove us downtown, you know what was on Eddie's mind? Ruth. He kept talking about what Ruth would do his next time at bat. The jig was up and Eddie was still thinking about a baseball game.

Didn't cops call you the Babe Ruth of Bank Robbers?

That was later. Jesus was Eddie sore about missing the rest of that game. He kept talking about how much we paid for those seats. The cops at the jailhouse had the game on the radio, and every time the crowd cheered, Eddie would moan. He didn't get it. I guess I didn't either. I was thinking about that ring.

What ring?

I chucked it in the trash right there. It was a miracle those Pinkertons didn't see me do it.

Mr. Sutton—what ring?

A diamond ring. I was going to give it to Bess. If I ever got the chance.

Were you still in touch with her?

Nah, she was married by then.

To whom?

Some rich guy. In case she was ever unmarried again, I wanted to be ready. With a nice big diamond ring. But the ring was from a job I'd pulled with Doc, meaning it was evidence, so I had to ditch it.

Photographer points to the overflowing trash cans. So many garbage strikes since then, he says, maybe it's still here.

Sutton turns his back to Reporter and Photographer, looks into the breast pocket of his suit. The white envelope. He closes his eyes. Over his shoulder he says:

Bottom line, I shouldn't have been thinking about rings, or Bess, or anything but my legal situation. Clearly my head was up my ass. I was too cocky.

He turns again, faces Reporter. You have a girl?

Yes.

You love her?

Well—

That's a no.

Wait—

Too late. I'm marking you down for no.

It's not that simple, Mr. Sutton.

It is kid. Life's complicated, love isn't. If you need to think about it for one half second, you're not in love.

She treats him like shit, Photographer says. I've been telling him he needs to break it off. He thinks he can't do any better. He has no confidence.

Oh kid, it's all about confidence. That's the whole shebang right there. Whatever you do, do it with your nuts. That's how Ruth swung a bat—with his nuts. Court a girl, rob a bank, brush your teeth, do it with and from your God-given nuts, or don't do it at all.

Photographer puts his camera inches from Sutton's face, shoots him with Gate 4 in the background. Audacity, audacity, audacity, he says.

Sutton lifts his chin. What?

Che Guevara said that.

Audacity, eh? I like it.

Reporter frowns. But, Mr. Sutton, you just said you had too much audacity here the day you were arrested. You were too cocky. Isn't that a contradiction?

Is it?

* * *

Willie and Eddie are shackled together, loaded onto a train. September 1923. Neither speaks as the train rumbles up the Hudson. Each stares out the window at the russet and gold hills, the trees wavering in the mirror of the river. The way the gold leaves sparkle in the blue water—Willie thinks of Bess. He wonders if he'll ever see her again. It doesn't look promising.

He wonders if she read about the trial. It was in all the papers, partly because he and Eddie were able to afford a top lawyer. But Clarence Darrow couldn't have gotten them off. The Pinkertons had them dead to rights. Brought in quietly by First National, the Pinks had no trouble tracing the oxygen tanks. Though Willie and Eddie used aliases when they made the purchase, the Pinks showed the salesman a book of mug shots—local boys convicted of breaking and entering. The salesman fingered Willie, the Pinks staked out Willie's apartment, tailed him to Yankee Stadium. After the arrests they searched Willie's apartment. Then Eddie's. In a wastebasket at Eddie's they found the receipt for the tanks. Open, shut.

Willie and Eddie didn't steal any money, but they broke into a bank and their intent was clear. A botched bank robbery is still a bank robbery, the judge said. Five to ten years. Sing Sing.

During the forty-mile ride Eddie stares at the river and speaks only once:

Bet they got a lot of Dagos in Sing Sing.

He and Willie had both hoped for one small silver lining. A reunion with Happy. But their lawyer checked and found that Happy was released from Sing Sing six months ago. No one's heard from him since.

A truck takes Willie and Eddie from the train station through the front gate of Sing Sing. When Willie sees those soaring walls, those black-uniformed guards holding black batons and black Thompson submachine guns, his mouth goes dry. This isn't Raymond Street. This is real live hard-ass prison. He might not be able to take it.

Just as the gate swings open, the prison begins a routine test of Big Ben, the deafening siren that sounds whenever there's an escape attempt or riot. Big Ben can be heard for miles, up and down the river, alerting people in nearby villages to stay indoors, savage convicts are on the loose. Within the prison walls it makes men clap their hands over their ears, pray for silence. As Big Ben cleaves the air, as guards strip-search Willie and Eddie, and shave their heads, and spread their ass cheeks, Willie turns. Eddie, bent over a chair, meets his gaze for one long moment—and winks.

One wink. The slow closing of one eye. Years later it will seem impossible to Willie that it could have made such a difference. But in those first days at Sing Sing, those pivotal moments when every man adjusts to his new reality or loses his mind, Willie lies in his seven-by-three cell, beside the bucket filled with disinfectant that serves as his toilet and washbasin, and listens to the thousand men above and below, cursing and crying and pleading with God, and he remembers Eddie's wink, and the quiet center of his mind holds.

After one week Willie and Eddie are brought to meet the warden, though they already know what he looks like. Warden Lawes is a celebrity, every bit as famous as Harding or Ruth. With his oddly perfect name, his raptor eyes, he's become a symbol of law and order, especially to Americans alarmed by the exploding prison population. He's written acclaimed magazine pieces and a smash bestseller about his quest to reform Sing Sing. A movie is said to be in the works.

To the outside world Lawes is a saint. Having done away with some of Sing Sing's older, harsher punishments, he's now sprucing up the library, organizing a prison baseball league. Inside, however, old-timers warn Willie and Eddie that Lawes is insane. Simply to demonstrate his manliness, his fearlessness, he lets a lifer with a straight razor shave him every morning. He's also recently declared a ban on masturbation. He thinks it leads to insanity, blindness. Prisoners caught in the act are thrown into solitary. The irony is lost on Lawes.

Standing before Lawes's desk, Willie and Eddie play stupid. They pretend to know nothing about him. They answer no sir, yes sir, and Lawes is fooled, flattered, or else just playing along. He gives them each a plum job. Eddie is assigned to the dining hall, where he'll be able to get extra chow. Willie is designated to help Charles Chapin, Sing Sing's most celebrated inmate. Chapin might be more famous than Lawes.

Not long ago Chapin was America's finest newspaperman. As editor of Pulitzer's *Evening World* he made his reputation by having no heart and few scruples. He reveled in human misery, took glee in exploiting the victims of sensational crimes and tragedies, and in crushing his competition on all the big stories of the age. He even somehow had a man onboard the *Carpathia*, which pulled survivors of the *Titanic* from the North Atlantic. While the *Carpathia* steamed back to New York, Chapin's man conducted the first-ever interviews with those survivors. And when the *Carpathia*'s tight-assed captain wouldn't let Chapin's man wire his notes to shore, Chapin rented a tug and met the *Carpathia* as it entered New York Harbor. Maneuvering the tug alongside the ship, Chapin shouted to his man to toss his notes overboard, then caught them just before they hit the water. Chapin got an extra on the streets before the survivors were disembarked and fully dried off.

Chapin had the brains, the nerve, the drive to become another Mencken. His brilliant career, however, came to an abrupt end in 1918. About the time Willie was courting Bess, Chapin was killing his wife. One shot to the head while she slept. Chapin told cops that he was secretly bankrupt and didn't want his wife to suffer the scandal and indignity of poverty. He considered the murder an act of mercy. The judge did not. He gave Chapin life.

Lawes, however, makes life soft for Chapin. He gives the old newsman free run of the prison, lets him do what he pleases, go where he likes, so long as Chapin ghosts Lawes's magazine pieces and memoirs. Recently Lawes even granted Chapin permission to turn Sing Sing's south yard into an English rose garden. Now he's making Willie the assistant gardener.

The first time Willie visits Chapin's cell, in the old death house, he sees that it's not one cell but two, the wall between them knocked out. It's also lavishly appointed—bookshelves, leather chairs, a rolltop desk. Suites at the Waldorf aren't half so nice. Willie raps lightly on the barred door, which stands open. Chapin, an elegant, bespectacled man in his mid-sixties, wearing gray flannel slacks and a tan cardigan, is entertaining visitors. They're all actors, including one in a natty Panama coat who played in a film Willie quite disliked. *Danny Donovan, the Gentleman Cracksman*—it was the story of a safecracker with style. The details, the nitty-gritty were all wrong. Willie is about to introduce himself, set the actor straight, when Chapin cuts him short.

You're Sutton.

Yes sir.

I'm frightfully busy at the moment. Come back at four.

As if Willie is dropping by Chapin's stateroom. To see about a game of shuffleboard. Willie wants to tell Chapin to kiss his Irish ass, but he holds his tongue. Chapin is the warden's pet, it won't do to cross him.

In the weeks that follow, Chapin high-hats Willie time and again, and Willie merely smiles, takes it. A small price to pay, he thinks, for peace with Lawes, and the privilege of working outdoors.

Then, gradually, Willie finds his dislike of Chapin ripening into a perverse fascination. Kneeling beside Chapin, planting tumbleweeds that Chapin claims are rosebushes, Willie steals frequent sidelong looks at that famous face. He studies Chapin's wide brow and alert gray eyes, marvels at Chapin's immaculate grooming. Most prisoners don't bother combing their hair, but Chapin never leaves his cell without his gray locks sliced precisely down the middle and wetted with fragrant oil. Just as he refuses to look the part of a prisoner, Chapin also never speaks like one. His voice is commanding, musical, a deep basso. It puts Willie in mind of this new invention everyone's so excited about—the radio. Except that Chapin is better than the radio, because he's less staticky. Sometimes Willie asks Chapin a mundane question to which he already knows the answer, just to hear him vocalize. He especially enjoys the way Chapin intones the names of different roses.

What did you say these bushes are going to be sir?

Those, Chapin says, will be General Jacqueminots.

Is that so sir? And these?

Lovely Frau Karl Druschkis. Some Madame Butterfly as well.

And here sir?

Ah. Yes. Dorothy Perkins.

You have a very fine voice, Mr. Chapin.

Thank you, Sutton. Before becoming a journalist I was an actor. Pretty fair one too. I played Romeo. I played Lear. That's why Warden Lawes permits us to stage a few plays each year.

Oh?

If you're interested, we need a new Regan. The governor pardoned our last one.

Uh-huh.

Willie spreads a bag of bonemeal, embarrassed. Chapin, catching the silence, frowns. I have a copy of the play in my cell, Sutton, you're welcome to it.

Thank you sir.

How far did you get in school, Sutton?

Eighth grade sir.

Chapin sighs. Every man in here tells the same tale—little or no schooling. The surest first step on the road to crime.

What's your excuse? Willie wants to ask.

You must use this time to read, Chapin says. Educate yourself. Ignorance landed you here. Ignorance will keep you here. Ignorance will bring you back.

I love to read sir. I always have. But when I walk into a library or bookshop, I get overwhelmed. I don't know where to start.

Start anywhere.

How do I know what's worth my time and what's a waste?

None of it is a waste. Any book is better than no book. Slowly, surely, one will lead you to another, which will lead you to the best. Do you want to spend your life planting roses with me?

No sir.

Then—books. It's that simple. A book is the only real escape from this fallen world. Aside from death.

Working together under the hot sun, both of them dizzy from the fumes of manure, Chapin entertains Willie with the raciest plots from Shakespeare, Ibsen, Chaucer. He unfolds the plots like lurid newspaper stories, and when he comes to the climax, when Willie is salivating to know what happens next—Chapin stops, tells Willie to read the book. Willie gets the feeling that Chapin is trying to fertilize his mind.

It's a shame Chapin can't fertilize anything else. Clearly the old newsman has a black thumb, black as the plague. Willie and Chapin have been hard at work for weeks and all they have to show for it is row after row of purported rosebushes, each of which looks irredeemably dead.

At the start of summer Willie is stricken with the flu. For ten days he's unable to work in the garden, too weak to get off his cot. He loses eight pounds and vomits so often that he hears the guards talk about transferring him to a hospital. Or morgue.

When his fever finally breaks it's a bright windy morning.

June 1924. Walking slowly to the death house just after breakfast, he stops in his tracks. Before him rolls a sea of scarlets and creams, pinks and umbers, deep purples and delicate corals. A breeze wafts over the new roses and carries to Willie a soft sugary scent.

Willie now sees Chapin sauntering toward him from the death house. Ah! Sutton. Good to see you back among the living.

Thank you sir. But the gardens sir—how? In just the short time I was away.

Such is the nature of roses, Sutton. You're surprised?

I am sir. Not that I doubted you. They're just so—beautiful. It's been a while since I've seen anything I could call *beautiful*.

Chapin adjusts his spectacles. Yes, he says. True. That's why I told, er, asked Warden Lawes for this garden. A man requires *some* beauty to survive.

What a shame though sir. That something so beautiful is surrounded by these ugly walls.

Every garden is surrounded by walls, Sutton. Read your Bible. Read your classics. If not for walls there would be no gardens. If not for gardens there would be no walls. The first garden ever was engirded by a wall.

Days later, as the blooms round to the size of baseballs, Willie mentions to Chapin that his favorite is the Dorothy Perkins. It's a shade of vibrant pink he's seen only once before. A ribbon Bess wore in her hair at Meadowport.

Chapin grimaces. The Dorothy Perkins, he says, is a tramp. A rambler. Wild, untamed, it wanders up walls, down trellises. But—it expends all its energy rambling. That's why it has energy to bloom just once. I hope you're not a Dorothy Perkins, Sutton. I hope you have a second bloom in you.

Yes sir. Me too sir.

Weeks later, while planting coneflowers and salvia around a meditation bench, Willie watches Chapin clip a new Dorothy

Perkins to bring back to his cell. Willie does the same. Then, on an impulse, which surprises even himself, Willie asks about Chapin's crime. Chapin blinks hard, waits a long time before answering. He waits so long that Willie fears he's overstepped. Money, Chapin says at last.

Sir?

What a world it would be without money, Sutton. After I lost all of mine—bad investments, risky ventures, nefarious advisers—I lost my mind. That's the long and short of it. I didn't know how I'd live. I didn't know how my wife would live. She was accustomed to fine things. We both were. The love of *things*—I daresay that's claimed as many victims as the love of drink. I intended to kill myself—after. That was my plan. Nellie and I were to be reunited on the other side. Did I tell you that she once played Juliet to my Romeo on the stage? That's how we met, in fact. But I lost my nerve. It's easy to romanticize the other side. Until you're on the threshold.

Willie makes no reply. He senses Chapin has more to say. He waits, expectant, as if Chapin is about to unfold one of his Shakespeare plots. But then over Chapin's shoulder he sees Eddie.

Mr. Chapin, Eddie says—may I have a word with Willie?

Chapin looks at Willie, then Eddie. He nods.

Willie and Eddie walk off to a corner of the yard, Willie carrying his snipped rose.

Did you see the new Dorothy Perkins, Ed?

The what?

Nothing.

I got news, Sutty. A couple of guys on my tier have found a way out.

You don't say.

Food trucks. They come and go every day and there's a way we can stow inside em. It's legit, I checked, and I told these fellas we're ready anytime.

Not me, Ed.

Eddie rocks back on his heels. What? Is this a kid?

No.

Don't tell me you want to keep on plantin petunias.

Beats pushing up daisies.

Sutty.

Ed. With good behavior, and a little help from Lawes, we can be out of here in four years. We'll be young yet. We'll have lives.

Eddie starts to argue but Willie hands him the Dorothy Perkins and strolls back to Chapin.

The next morning Willie and Eddie are called to Lawes's office. A vase on the desk is filled with new Madame Butterfly. The window over the desk looks down on Chapin's gardens. Lawes stands at the window, his back to Willie and Eddie.

Someone overheard you two clowns yesterday. In the gardens no less—there's gratitude for you. Well, I'm not going to have some mutts from Irish Town sully my reputation with a crash-out. You're both gone. Today. I'm shipping you north to Dannemora. Hard by the Canadian border. You don't like Sing Sing, eh? Trust me, this place will soon seem like Shangri-la.

A guard gives Willie five minutes to pack his things into a paper bag. Then he and Eddie are loaded aboard a bus. Hours later Willie finds himself on the floor of a stone cell, being spit on by two French-speaking guards who stink of cheap wine. The cell is smaller, colder, nastier by far than Willie's cell at Sing Sing. And there isn't a rose within two hundred miles.

Sutton watches a car cruise up to Yankee Stadium. The window rolls down. Two men appear from nowhere, pass a brown paper bag into the car. Money comes out. The car speeds away.

Sutton shakes his head. Say—what's a beer cost these days at Yankee Stadium?

Fifty cents, Photographer says.

And they put me in jail for robbery.

Photographer fumbles in his camera bag for a new lens. What was Sing Sing like, Willie?

If you wanted to learn how to be a criminal, there was no better place. It was the Princeton of bank robbery. There were bank robbers who'd been there so long, they were called bank bursters. That was the old-time term, back in the last century.

How long were you there?

That first time? Less than a year. It went by fast. I became friends with an old newsman, Charlie Chapin, and I was learning a lot from him. But then Eddie and I were overheard talking about escaping. Well, Eddie was talking, I was listening. I always worried it was Chapin who ratted us. I hope not. Anyway, the warden shipped us to Dannemora, a dungeon up north. That's when things got rough. Stone cells, no heat. They beat us with metal sticks, fed us undercooked mountain goat. Judas goat.

Sutton smacks his lips, as if tasting the goat, sets off for the Polara.

Photographer runs ahead, walks backwards, shoots Sutton in stride. Yeah, he says. That light bouncing off the stadium is cool, Willie. Kind of spooky.

Reporter walks just behind Sutton, holding open a file. Mr. Sutton, this file says that while at Dannemora you met a future accomplice? Marcus Bassett?

Sutton grunts.

What was he like?

Typical yegg.

A what?

Stickup man.

He sounds, from these clips, like a character.

His head was shaped like a triangle, Sutton says. A perfect triangle. Imagine? And his eyes looked like waterbugs. And they never stopped moving. You meet someone whose eyes are like waterbugs, walk the other direction. But somehow I thought Marcus was a right guy. I was fooled, I think, because he was a writer. I had respect for writers back then. I should have wised up when he showed me some of his stories.

No good?

The literary equivalent of undercooked mountain goat. He became a stickup man because he couldn't sell anything.

Sutton stops, takes one last look at the stadium façade. Walled garden, he says. I think it was at Dannemora that I first became angry. A cell is a bad place to be angry. When a man's angry, he needs to move around, burn it off. Lock an angry man in a cell, it's like locking a stick of lighted dynamite in a safe.

Who were you angry at?

Everyone. But mostly myself. I hated myself. The unhealthiest kind of hate.

Were you angry with Eddie? For messing up the good thing you had going with Chapin?

Nah. I could never be angry with Eddie. Not after that wink.

What wink?

TWELVE

WILLIE SITS BEFORE THE PAROLE BOARD, FIFTEEN POUNDS underweight, shivering. He's been shivering for three years. He tells the board that he wants to go straight. He tells them that he wants to get married, get a job, become a contributing member of society. He tells them that the last four years in Sing Sing and Dannemora have been a torment, but also a godsend, for which he thanks them. He didn't know himself four years ago, but he does now. He knows who Willie Sutton is, and who he isn't. It's June 1927, he'll soon turn twenty-six, and he's sick about how much of his twenty-six years he's wasted. Fighting to keep his voice steady, he tells the board that he's determined not to waste one minute more.

He sees the effect of his performance. He sees the members of the parole board lean forward, soak up his words, conclude that Sutton, William F., no longer poses a threat to society, that he should be released at once.

Days later it is so ordered.

As to the matter of Sutton's accomplice, Edward Buster Wilson. Parole denied.

Willie packs his books into a paper bag. First the Tennyson. He's memorized the ballad Tennyson wrote about the great love of his youth. *Come into the garden, Maud, I am here at the gate alone.* Next his heavily underlined copies of Franklin, Cicero, Plato—all recommended by Chapin.

A keeper walks Willie over to the prison's parole agent, who hands him a ten-dollar bill wrapped around a train ticket. The keeper then walks Willie to the prison tailor, where he's given a release suit. Gray, with a brown tie. At the front gate Willie stops, asks the keeper: Would you please tell Eddie Wilson goodbye for me?

Hit the grit, asshole.

Willie walks to the station, boards the local, arrives in Grand Central at dusk. He walks to Times Square, marvels at the new signs, the dozens of new marquees. And the *lights*. Someone apparently decided while he was gone that Times Square should outshine Coney Island. He sees a towering sign: WELCOME TO NEW YORK, GREATEST CITY IN THE WORLD. He stops at a newsstand, buys the papers and two packs of Chesterfields. Settles into a coffee shop. At a corner booth, not touching a plate of pastries and a cup of coffee, he stares out the window at the men and women passing by. The population of New York City must have doubled since he left. The sidewalks seem twice as crowded. And everyone looks different. They're all wearing new clothes, using new words, laughing at new jokes. He wants to ask each of them, What's so funny? What'd I miss?

He wolfs a cruller, opens the *Times*. He reads the sports page. Gehrig homered, Ruth doubled, the Yanks clobbered the Sox. He reads about Lindbergh's triumphant return to the U.S. The aviator was just in New York City days ago, the papers say, and Mayor Walker and the whole city turned out to shower him with adulation and ticker tape.

Willie turns the page. Ads for vacation packages. A berth on a train to Yosemite costs $108.82. On a train to Los Angeles— $138.44. He thinks of the crumpled dollars in his pocket. He flips to the wants, runs his finger up one column, down another. Griddle man—experience required. Bookkeeper—experience a must. Driller—references only. Store detective—experience, references, background check.

He looks around the coffee shop. People are staring. He didn't realize he was cursing aloud.

He walks around the theater district, reading every marquee, every lobby card, listening to the new jazz spilling out of the clubs. He watches gentlemen and ladies skipping across the street, dancing in and out of new theaters, laughing. They walk past him, through him. When he got out of Raymond Street Jail seven years ago he felt bleak. Now he feels invisible.

Bleak was better.

He stands outside the Republic Theater on West Forty-Second Street. The show is *Abie's Irish Rose*. He can hear the overture. He pictures the dancers and actors warming up, the audience nestling into their seats for an hour and a half of fun. He stuffs his hands in his pockets, shuffles along. He comes to the Capitol Theater. NOW PLAYING: LON CHANEY AS A FUGITIVE IN *THE UNKNOWN*. Also, as an added bonus, newsreels of Colonel Lindbergh.

Willie feels as if the world is a novel he set down years ago. Picking it up again, he can't recall the plot, the characters. Or why he cared. He tells himself that he'll remember, he'll feel like part of the world once more if he can just find work. A job, that's the answer, it always was. He has no experience, no education, and no one will hire a guy coming off a four-year bit. But maybe he can find something legit through his criminal associates. Maybe in another city.

He snaps his fingers. Philadelphia. He went there often with Doc, and though he only had glimpses late at night from the windows of moving trains, he liked the town. Brotherly Love. The Liberty Bell. Ben Fuckin Franklin. He walks to Penn Station, boards the Broadway Limited. He slips into the barber car, pays a dollar for a haircut and face massage, then finds a seat in the parlor car, by a window. He pulls Franklin's autobiography from his paper bag. Chapin told Willie that Franklin built his life around one simple idea—happiness. Before doing anything Ben asked himself, Will this make me happy? Now, reading about

Young Ben running off to Philadelphia, Willie grins. He guesses there are worse footsteps to follow in.

Outside the train station in North Philadelphia he asks people how he can find Boo Boo Hoff, the erratic mobster who runs this town. Boo Boo's headquarters, people say, is a gym. He surrounds himself with fighters as a king surrounds himself with knights. Willie walks into town, finds the gym, finds Boo Boo in a humid corner working out a densely muscled featherweight.

Approaching with caution, Willie introduces himself, explains that he's out of work.

Boo Boo grins. He has one of those grins that descend from left to right at a ninety-degree angle, like a knife slash. Yeah, he says with a kind of affected impatience, yeah, yeah, Willie Sutton, Doc mentioned you. Said you was smart. Said you was a right guy.

Yes sir, Mr. Hoff. How is old Doc? Is he well?

He's getting three squares and plenty of rest if you call that well. He was pinched a couple years ago. The judge gave him a long bit. Doc being a repeat offender.

Boo Boo turns back to the featherweight, whose body has less fat than a leather belt. The featherweight stands before a speed bag, thrums it with his fists, makes it purr. He looks well-tuned to Willie, ready to step in the ring right now, but Boo Boo chides him.

Don't make love to the fuckin bag kid. What are you gun to do next, kiss it?

No, Boo Boo, the featherweight says, smiling, exposing his mouthpiece, which glistens with saliva and blood.

Why don't you kiss it kid? You seem to be kind of sweet on that bag, so gwan, kiss it.

Gee, Boo Boo. I'm doin my best.

Your best? I'm not paying you to do your best, you bum. I'm paying you to hate that bag. Why will you not hate that bag?

Why will you not hate and maim and kill that bag like I fuckin told you?

Okay, Boo Boo, okay. I'll hate da bag.

Boo Boo turns from the featherweight. I might have something for you, he says to Willie.

Really? Say, that's great, Mr. Hoff.

Willie hopes it's something in the fight game. Maybe he can manage some ham-and-egger. Boo Boo is one of the best fight promoters in the country. *Impresario*, that's what newspapers always call him, though it seems to Willie like an awfully fancy word for a man whose face looks like an ass. Fat, pale, globular, the only thing missing is a line down the center. Boo Boo must know he has an ass face too, which is why he wears that extra-large boater and that bow tie the size of a box kite. He's trying to distract from the obvious, even though it's futile. His face looks like someone took a great big heinie and put a boater and bow tie on it. Talking to Boo Boo, Willie thinks, is like being mooned.

It's a little job, Boo Boo is saying.

No job too small sir.

Real little.

Well. Like I said.

I need for you to bump someone off.

Uh.

A real little—*pest*.

Well.

A fuckin pisher.

Er. Gee.

What. You just said.

I know. But I don't think. Kill a guy? Holy.

Relax. It's not what you think.

Okay. Phew. For a second there.

It's only half a guy.

I'm lost again.

Half man. Full pay.

I don't think. See, I'm not.

A dwarf. A little hunchback dwarf traitor cocksucker who works for me but also for the cops, which therein lies the problem. Ooo what a mouth on this little pest. He tells cops whatever they want to know about my operations, they don't even have to slap him, they just pinch his little cheek and he sings like Jolson. Plus I think he's skimming. He needs offing in the worse way. Look. Here's his name. I'm writing it down for you on this piece of paper. I'm also writing down the name of the gin mill he owns. Go say hello, look him over. But do not let on that I'm wise. Let me know if you're interested.

Willie walks around Philadelphia, staring at the piece of paper, the name scratched in Boo Boo's globular handwriting: Hughie McLoon. Willie tries to picture McLoon, but he can only think of Daddo's stories about the little men back in Ireland. Willie's been afraid of little men ever since. Still, he needs a job. What would Ben Franklin do if offing a dwarf were the only way to be happy?

By nightfall Willie finds himself at Tenth and Cuthbert, standing outside Hughie McLoon's Dry Saloon. He forces himself to walk in, take a seat. He orders a whiskey, asks for Hughie. Who wants to see him? Friend of a friend. He'll be along. Willie orders another whiskey. He orders a bowl of turtle soup. Around eleven he sees a hat floating toward him along the bar, like the dorsal fin of some languorous tropical fish. You lookin for me? the fish asks.

Willie hops off his stool. Mr. McLoon? Hello, my name's Sutton. Willie Sutton. Boo Boo Hoff sent me. Said you might have a job for me.

Hughie gives Willie the head-to-toe. More like the hip-to-toe. Oh yeah? Hnh. Fine, fine, welcome to the Dry Saloon kid. Let me buy you a drink.

Roughly Willie's age, Hughie is two-thirds as tall. He can't be four feet. More than merely short, he's all out of proportion. His brow is too big for his face, his hat is too big for his head—his voice is too high for his mouth. He sounds like a Josephine Baker record played too fast.

He tries to hop on the barstool next to Willie. He can't. He needs help, and he's not shy about asking. He places his palm on Willie's, like a deb stepping into her cotillion.

Despite Willie's nerves, despite Hughie's distracting appearance, they get on well. Hughie, it turns out, is a fine conversationalist. He reads the papers, thinks deeply about current events, politics. He's rooting for Al Smith, of course, the first Irish Catholic to be a serious candidate for president. But he also likes Coolidge, thinks Coolidge will go down as one of the best presidents in history.

Kind of a sourpuss, Willie says.

Nah, Hughie says with a wave of his hand, Silent Cal's just serious izzall. I like that. Life's serious. Cal wants what he wants, and anyone duzzen like it can jump straight up his Vermont fuggin ass. And Cal wants you to get rich.

Me?

You, me, everybody. Cal takes the handcuffs off businessmen, so we can do what we gotta do. I marked him down as my kind of fella back in '19. When he stood up to them Boston cops. Any man who stands up to cops is all right by me. You wimmee?

Hughie lets out a laugh. A disturbing sound—like a Thompson machine gun. A few staccato bursts, then an ominous smoky silence. Willie makes a point to avoid saying anything funny.

The talk swings around to baseball. Like Willie, Hughie is a fan. He stabs a thumb the size of a baby carrot into his chest.

I used to be in the game, he says.

That so?

I was batboy for the A's. I was fourteen. Skinny as a bat back then too. Which made my hump look bigger. One day we're playin Detroit, see? And here comes Ty Cobb walkin up to the plate. All of a sudden he stops, gives me the stink eye. Before I know what's what, he's rubbin my hump for luck. The fans is laughin, all the other Tigers is laughin. Even my own team is laughin. Then, wouldn't you know, Cobb laces a triple up the gap. Goes on to get four hits that day. Well you know how superstitious ballplayers can be. From then on, every player has to rub my back. For luck. They practically rubbed the skin off.

Willie takes a long look at Hughie. Poor little fella, Willie thinks. He should rub his own back, because his luck's about run out.

Hughie's favorite topic is women. He's girl crazy, he admits, and girls are twice as crazy for him. They like to pick him up, cradle him, cootch him under the chin. He's a half-pint Valentino, he claims, but he can't enjoy it, because his heart belongs to one heartless bitch.

She comes in here once a week, Hughie says morosely. With her husband. She's got long red hair, stands about five nine in her silk stockings. She's my Everest. I don't want to go on livin if I can't never make it to the top.

Plant your flag.

Zactly.

Have you told her how you feel?

Teller all the time. Teller I'd be the happiest man inna world if only she'd lummy. She don't lummy. Says I'm *cute*. Says she'd like to put me on a charm bracelet. Aint that a low blow?

Hughie is drunk. Willie too. At last call they stagger out, arm in arm, and say a fond good night on the sidewalk. Before waddling away Hughie tells Willie to come by in the morning about that job. Willie watches the hump fade slowly into the darkness, then staggers in the opposite direction. He keeps staggering until he finds a two-dollar flop. He falls onto the filthy bed, his clothes still on, and before passing out he realizes he can't kill Hughie. He's ashamed to admit it, but he can't kill anyone, especially not Hughie.

On the other hand he also can't warn Hughie. As he told the parole board, he knows who Willie Sutton is, and who he isn't. He thought briefly that he might be a killer, but he knows he's no rat.

A few light snowflakes fall as the Polara pulls away from Yankee Stadium. Photographer turns on the wipers. Reporter turns on the AM radio. News. The announcer sounds as if he's had too much coffee. And a line of cocaine. His jangled nerves can't be helped by that Teletype machine clacking in the background.

Our top stories this hour. Willie the Actor Sutton is a free man today. Governor Rockefeller pardoned the sixty-eight-year-old archcriminal late last night. No word where the most prolific bank robber in U.S. history is spending Christmas. Checking holiday traffic . . .

Reporter and Photographer look at each other, look in the backseat. Sutton smiles sheepishly. Archcriminal, he says. He looks out the window—the Bronx. In the distance he sees a building on fire. Flames pour from the top floor. Where are the firefighters? In a vacant lot along the highway he sees a dozen boys tossing a football. Collarless shirts, ragged shoes. Not sneakers, not cleats—but old dress shoes? A bum lies sleeping in the end zone.

Dark clouds move in from the north.

When I got out of Dannemora, Sutton says, almost to himself, that summer of '27, I couldn't find a job.

Even in the roaring twenties?

Everybody thinks the twenties were roaring. People getting rich overnight, all that F. Scott Fitzgerald bunk, but you boys listen to Willie, the decade started with a Depression and it ended with a Depression and there were plenty of white-knuckle days in between.

A few people were living high, but everyone else was circling the drain. Times were hard, and you could see worse times dead ahead. A crash was coming, you could feel it. Of course, that's always true. You want to be a prophet? You want to be fuckin Nostradamus? Predict a crash. You'll never be wrong.

Reporter spreads the map. Our next stop is Madison and Eighty-Sixth. What happened there, Mr. Sutton?

That's where Willie finally found one of the two sweetest things a man can hope to find.

In a phone booth at Penn Station, Willie calls Boo Boo. Collect. He says he won't be able take that job they discussed. Suit yourself, Boo Boo says. Godspeed.

Click.

Willie hits a newsstand, buys all the papers, folds them into a thick wad under his arm, walks to Times Square. He gets a room in a flop, spends two days combing the wants. Bus driver—experience. Griddle man—experience. Child caretaker—experience, references, background check.

In the margins of one classified section he drafts a letter to Bess. He runs out of room, out of words. He tosses the newspaper aside.

On the third day, when he goes out for food and the evening papers, he steps into a speak. Orders a beer, opens the paper. GANGLAND SHOOTING IN PHILADELPHIA. Police say Hughie McLoon, local saloonkeeper, was gunned down outside et cetera. Willie shudders. He imagines Hughie's machine-gun laugh being cut short by the real McCoy. He feels a moment's pang of conscience, but he reminds himself: nothing he could do.

He flips to the wants. Dishwasher—experience required. Fry cook—references. Landscape gardener—hmm. *Small Upper East Side firm seeks man. Must be knowledgeable about shrubs, flowers. Funck and Sons. Ask for Mr. Pieter Funck.*

Willie goes to the drugstore on the corner, buys a tin of shoe polish. He shines his one pair of shoes to a high gloss, hangs his release suit neatly over the chair, hits the sack.

At first light he rises, breakfasts on water from the tap, walks uptown, forty blocks. The address is 42 East Eighty-Sixth. An old redbrick building. On the third floor he finds a frosted door stenciled with the name FUNCK. He discovers the apparent proprietor behind an industrial desk that holds an adding machine, an ashtray, several skin magazines. Examining one magazine through a magnifying glass.

Pieter Funck?

What do you want?

I'm here about the job?

Sit.

Funck stows the magazine. Willie takes a wooden chair. The office smells pleasantly of potting soil and hay. I'll tell you straight, Funck says—no sons.

Excuse me?

Funck and Sons, I got no sons. I thought *and Sons* gave the business class, but Mrs. Funck is not fertile and so now you're knowing and I don't want you later asking me where are the sons and calling me liar. I can grow anything, anywhere, except a baby inside Mrs. Funck.

Forty, gone to fat, the shape and color and texture of a mushroom, Funck rambles on and on in something like English. He says he came to America eight years ago from Amsterdam, and he's still not fluent. No fooling, Willie wants to say. When he's not bunching words in strange clusters, Funck is planting them upside down in sentences, their roots showing. And yet sometimes they thrive. He says he learned *landescaping* back in Holland. He says he knows everything worth *nosing* about tulips.

Eventually the interview goes the way Willie feared. Funck

asks about Willie's recent experience. Willie takes a cleansing breath. On the level, Mr. Funck, I've spent the last four years in prison.

Hurrying to bridge the inevitable silence, Willie swears he knows *landescaping*, knows it well, learned it from a fellow inmate, Charles Chapin.

The editor? Funck says.

Willie nods.

Funck leans back in his creaky wooden desk chair. A row of cigars pokes from his shirt pocket, all different sizes, like a cigar skyline. Say now how do you like that, he says. I followed the Chapin case real close.

Well, I can tell you, he's a very interesting man. His gardens are—

I'm all the time wondering how many men dream of doing what Chapin does. It's taking real guts, no? To bump off the missus? How many thousands of husbands you think watch their wives asleeping and fantasy about putting in the brain one little bullet? And then the crabbing is stopping forever, no? *Heb ik gelijk?* How wives *crab*, am I right? All the time wanting something, but when *you* are wanting something, say a little *affectioning*, they can't be bothering? Too busy crabbing!

Willie straightens his necktie, tugs his earlobe, focuses on a spot in the wall just behind Funck's head. Mrs. Funck, he thinks, should not buy any green bananas.

Funck flips through a card file, says he's got just the thing for Willie. Samuel Untermyer, he says. Big-shot lawyer. You ever heard of his house up in Yonkers?

No sir.

Greystone it's called. This place you never seen nothing like. It's the Eden Garden. Dozens of men it's taking to keep this place shape ship, so Untermyer is using lots of firms, us including. I'm sending a crew every two days and this day I'm short. One of my mens is having a rupture. So. You take his place. Tomorrow morning, four o'clock, if you're late you're being fired.

Photographer is looking out the back window, changing lanes, trying to exit the highway. He checks the clouds. Hey, Willie? Couldn't we just swing by the scene of the Schuster murder real quick? While the light is good.
  You and your light.
  The light right now is ideal, Willie. Look. Look at that sky, brother.
  Haven't you learned anything so far from Willie? You make your own light in this fuckin world.

Willie is an hour early for his first day. He carries a kerchief, an apple he found in the trash, a dog-eared copy of Cicero. He's still wearing his release suit.

Funck smacks his palms against his cheeks. A suit? Jezus the Christ! Greystone is not formal gardens!

These are my only clothes, Willie says.

Funck loans Willie gray coveralls, gardening boots, a hat. Willie climbs into the back of Funck's truck, which seems made of cardboard and pie tins. There are four other workmen sitting along a wood bench. None says hello. An hour later, just as the sun is rising, the truck rolls through the front gate of Greystone and Willie can't help himself—he gasps. Funck lied. This isn't the Garden of Eden. This makes the Garden of Eden look like Irish Town. There are Grecian temples, Roman statues, marble rotundas, fountains of burbling silver water and brightly colored tile. There are dark green ponds dotted with lily pads and calm ponds of limpid blue. There must be one of every flower and tree in existence, and every variety of hedge and bush, trimmed and planed into all manner of sizes, shapes. And containing it all, lending it all a touch of drama, is a sheer cliff that plunges straight down to the majestic Hudson.

The foreman is a tall man with a neck goiter the size of a radish. He starts Willie mulching, raking. Willie quickly breaks a sweat. It feels good to be using muscles, breathing hard. He whistles under his breath, lost in the joy of having a real job. Until the workman on his right interrupts.

Foreman's a prick, the workman says.

Oh? Willie says.

Don't get on his bad side. He'll fire you for nothing. Less than nothing. Sick wife? Sick kid? He don't care.

Okay. Thanks for the warning, friend.

Some place, eh?

Yeah. Beautiful.

You know how many rhododendron they got in this joint?

No.

Thirty thousand. You know how many tulips?

Nope.

Fifty thousand.

That a fact?

You know how many fireplaces?

Nuh-uh.

Eleven. One's made of rubies and emeralds.

Really?

You know how come Old Man Untermyer built these gardens?

Can't say as I do.

For his old lady. He was crazy in love. But then she croaked before they was done. Old Man Untermyer lives here all by his lonesome.

Sad.

That's life.

The workman points to a winding path that leads to a gazebo at the edge of the cliff. Mr. Untermyer calls that the Temple of Love.

Now the workman on Willie's left chimes in. Don't listen to this mug, he's talkin through his hat. These gardens aint just for Mrs. Untermyer. Old Man Untermyer also wanted to one-up the Rockefellers. They live just north of here. Mr. Untermyer hates Rockefellers worse than he hates rabbits.

At noon the foreman hands out onion sandwiches, bread, a cup of thin vegetable soup. Willie takes his lunch and climbs to the Temple of Love. He sits on a green metal bench. To his left are the gardens, to his right is the river. At his feet, painted on the floor of the Temple, are pale pastel nymphs and naiads, sporting and calling to sailors. Beyond, at eye level, are the palisades of Jersey. He looks at the water, watches a yacht gliding upriver. He makes a note to send Eddie some cigarettes and magazines when he gets his first paycheck.

He lies back, opens Cicero. An essay on happiness. What is it about the great men, all they can think about is happiness? A line jumps off the page. *But no one can be happy if worried about the most important thing in one's life.* Willie mulls this line, trying to see how it applies to his experience, and suddenly a clammy feeling comes over him. He's being watched. He lowers the book, sees a second foreman thirty feet away, staring. Where the hell did that second foreman come from? He must live here on the estate. Willie sits up. He has twenty minutes remaining on his lunch break, but he wads up his bag and shuts his book and hurries back to work.

The first foreman sends him to help plant boxwoods along the front path. Before long he feels a prickling gaze on his neck. He turns. The second foreman again. He barks at Willie: Careful, those boxwoods are a century old.

Yes sir.

Gentle with that one.

Yes sir.

Cicero had boxwoods on his estate, you know.

Willie stops, peers from behind a boxwood. He sees the trace of a smile on the second foreman's face. At least Willie thinks it's a smile. Hard to know exactly what's going on behind that mustache, which is so wild and furry that it must have its own full-time gardener. Above the mustache sits a massive nose, sheer as the cliff that forms Greystone's western border.

Can I ask sir, is this by chance *your* boxwood?

My boxwood. My house.

Very pleased to meet you, Mr. Untermyer.

I must say—we haven't had many gardeners reading Cicero during their lunch breaks.

Brilliant man sir.

Indeed.

Wish I could have known him.

Why is that?

They say he was the best lawyer who ever lived.

He was.

In which case, he might have kept me from getting sent up that river down there.

Willie can't believe he said it. Something about Mr. Untermyer's gaze made him forget himself. He waits for Mr. Untermyer to flinch, maybe call over the first foreman and have Willie fired on the spot. Instead Mr. Untermyer smiles with his eyes.

If I may ask—what was your crime?

Bank robbery sir. Attempted.

Mr. Untermyer stares. When was this?

Nineteen twenty-three sir. Ozone Park.

When did you get out?

This month sir.

What's breaking into a bank compared with founding a bank?

Sir?

It's a line from a new play. Bertolt Brecht.

I haven't been to the theater in a while, Mr. Untermyer. Though

I was Regan in a production at Sing Sing. *Jesters do oft prove prophets.*

Mr. Untermyer tugs his mustache, not unlike Mr. Endner. What's your name son?

Sutton sir. William Francis Sutton Jr.

Photographer double-parks on Madison, just off Eighty-Sixth. Sutton looks out the window at the former home of Funck and Sons. I'll be damned, Sutton says. It's still there.

What is?

I got a job with a landscaping firm in that redbrick building. Forty-two years ago. The boss sent me to Greystone, a famous estate. Terrible soil. We had to dig out and blast out truckloads of rock. I don't know how much poop we had to mix into the topsoil.

Sutton opens the car door, puts one foot outside. He smiles. The place was so beautiful, I begged the boss to put me on permanent. I actually got down on my knees.

Get off your knees, Funck says. I'm not putting you on permanent.

Why not?

I don't need you there. My man with the rupture is back.

Please sir. This is the right job for me. The grounds, the air, the owner. After prison a man needs to heal—they should send prisoners straight to the hospital—and Greystone is a place where I can do just that.

Heal on your own time.

Willie doffs his cap. If that's how you feel sir.

It is.

Willie gets off his knees, walks toward the door. So long, Funck. I hope the missus doesn't make too much trouble.

So long . . . Wait. Why trouble?

When I shoot her a wire—relating our conversation about Chapin? When I tell her that her husband thinks it's a swell idea to blast a wife in her sleep?

Funck turns the color of a poinsettia. You wouldn't.

Willie leans against the door's frosted panel. Wouldn't I?

She won't believe.

Probably not. She sounds like a very sweet woman.

He's laughing, Photographer says to Reporter. He's just standing in the middle of Madison Avenue, laughing.

Mr. Sutton, why are you laughing? And would you please be careful—there are cars coming.

I was remembering how I got the boss to put me on full-time at Greystone. Ah boys, score one for Willie. Finally things were turning around for me. A job I loved. A job I was good at. Money in my pocket. I started getting in shape, putting on weight, and on my day off I'd spend hours and hours at the library. Reading. What bliss.

Reading what?

Everything.

Photographer holds the map against the wind. Oh brother, holy shit, is that why our next stop is—the library? Seriously? Willie— we're going to the library?

The first chance Willie gets, he pulls newspapers, magazines, business journals, everything he can find in the library about Mr. Untermyer. He's shocked by what he learns. Willie and Eddie thought they were pretty slick, breaking into a bank, but Mr. Untermyer *breaks up* banks. As a special prosecutor, Mr. Untermyer became the all-time bank buster, the scourge of America's most notorious robber barons. During tense hearings before the United States Congress, hearings that riveted the nation, Mr. Untermyer, a fresh orchid from Greystone in his lapel, called one banker after another to the stand and exposed them as conspirators, liars, thieves. Over a span of several years, through a secret money trust, the bankers had hijacked the financial system. They'd appointed one another to the boards of their various banks and corporations, essentially merging them all into one secret superbank. Mr. Untermyer had the audacity to expose this skulduggery, to publicly interrogate the perpetrators, who happened to be the richest men in America, among them J. P. Morgan and one of the Rockfellers. What was more audacious to Morgan than the questioning itself—Untermyer was a Jew.

The hearings didn't end in criminal charges, but they did ruin Morgan's health. Shaken, humiliated, he fled to Europe. Weeks later, in a lavish hotel suite in Rome, he breathed his last. His heirs and partners openly blamed Mr. Untermyer. While Mr. Untermyer never accepted the blame, he never denied it either.

Whenever Willie sees Mr. Untermyer on the grounds of Greystone, he tries to catch his eye. Now and then Mr. Untermyer comes over and chats. Willie can't believe a man so important, a man busy slaying Morgans and shaming Rockefellers, makes time. But Mr. Untermyer seems amused by Willie, intrigued by his stories about Irish Town, Sing Sing, Dannemora, Eddie. When Willie runs out of real stories, he makes up new ones. In the middle of just such a story, a querulous look comes over Mr. Untermyer. Willie, he says, I think you're a modern seanchaí.

Willie, kneeling in the shadow of the Temple of Love, planting delphiniums, looks up. He can see the nymphs dancing behind Mr. Untermyer. My grandfather used to talk about the seanchaí sir.

I don't doubt it. Your grandfather was from Ireland of course.

Yes sir.

The seanchaí was a holy man in Ireland. He made the long

nights shorter. And he didn't always care if his stories were true.

Is that bad?

Not necessarily. Truth has its place. In a courtroom, certainly. A boardroom. But in a story? I don't know. I think truth is in the listener. Truth is something the listener bestows on a story—or not. Though I wouldn't recommend you try that argument on a wife or girlfriend.

Willie laughs. No sir. Is it true sir that you planted these gardens for your wife?

It is. Every time they bloom, I grieve anew.

Yes sir. Sorry sir.

Mr. Untermyer clears his throat. May I ask you something, Willie?

Sure thing.

What's it like to rob a bank?

Willie starts to answer. He sees the look on Mr. Untermyer's face, stops himself. He wipes his brow, stabs his spade into the ground.

Honestly, Mr. Untermyer, it's a job. Other bank robbers in the joint, they like to say how thrilling it is to rob a bank, how nothing makes a man feel more alive. That's the bunk sir. The idea is to do it well, do it fast, get home safe.

Mr. Untermyer smoothes his mustache. I thought you might say that.

May I ask you something sir?

Of course.

What's it like to make a Rockefeller squirm?

Mr. Untermyer smiles upriver. Nothing makes a man feel more alive, he says, then walks away.

Sutton takes one last look at the former home of Funck and Sons. Okay, he says. Let's scram. Next stop: New York Public Library, Central Branch.

Photographer shakes his head. Honestly, Willie, I can't think of anything less visually compelling than the damn library.

Visually compelling.

Yeah. I'd rather shoot you talking to some more prostitute ghosts. I mean, a bank robber in front of a library? I don't see the point, brother. And my editor won't either—unless you happened to hit the library back in the twenties.

I would have, if they'd kept books locked up the way they did money.

Also, while we're at it, I've got no idea why we needed to come here.

I wanted to tell you about Mr. Untermyer, the owner of Greystone. He was an American Cicero.

You couldn't tell us about him at Yankee Stadium?

I wouldn't have remembered everything without seeing this building. I wouldn't have remembered that Mr. Untermyer killed J. P. Morgan. I think he secretly wished he'd offed Rockefeller too.

Photographer squints at Reporter. Reporter shrugs. They all get in the car.

Sutton taps Photographer. You'd have loved Mr. Untermyer kid. He really spoke your language. Boy did he hate banks. He told me once that the Founding Fathers worried more about banks than they worried about the British. They knew that banks had been causing chaos, bringing empires to their knees, for centuries, all in the name of free enterprise.

Photographer snorts. Willie, are you—a Communist?

Fuck no kid. They asked that question once of Capone and he went crazy, almost brained somebody, and I know how he felt. Commie? I don't want to give ninety percent of my nick to the government. Mark me down as a believer in small government. Mark me down as a believer in free enterprise. But when a few greedy bastards make up the rules as they go, that aint free enterprise. It's a grift.

You sound at least a little socialist.

What's your political bent kid?

I'm a revolutionary, Photographer says.

Sutton laughs. Of course you are. That's a grift too. Did you boys know that old man Morgan was obsessed with his nose? It was covered with carbuncles, pockmarks, veins—it was the bane of his existence. He couldn't stand having his picture taken. If he'd seen you coming with your camera he'd have run away like a little sissy. A camera scared Morgan more than Communism.

Photographer laughs, pulls into traffic. J.P. Morgan running away from me. Now that I'd like to see.

They begin to head downtown. Photographer lines up Sutton in the rearview:

Hey Willie—you told us Untermyer hated banks. But I haven't heard you say that you did.

Haven't you?

Sutton looks out the window at the sky. Look, he says. The moon is rising.

THIRTEEN

WILLIE IN THE READING ROOM, HIS HEAD UNDER ONE OF the brass lamps. July 1929. He scans the headlines in the *Brooklyn Daily Eagle*.

> COOLIDGE SUMS UP HIS ACHIEVEMENTS
> FORMER SLAVE DIES AT 109
> BESSIE ENDNER HAS HUSBAND ARRESTED

The light from the brass lamp grows blurry. Willie's line of vision narrows. He brings the newspaper closer to his face, reads as fast as he can, but the words don't make sense. He has to read the first paragraph four times before it sinks in.

Bessie Endner is again in trouble. She tells a judge that her husband has mistreated her, threatened her life . . .

Next comes the boilerplate reference to her criminal past. *The pretty young woman, who astounded friends and the public by running off . . .*

Then a bit of reporter snark. *She tells a judge that shortly after she married she found that life instead of roses was a mere hail of ripe chestnut burrs.*

Finally the newspaper lists her new address, where she's said to be hiding from her abusive husband—15 Scoville Walk, Coney Island.

Willie staggers home to his flop. He takes a tepid shower, the only kind possible in the communal bathroom, shaves his jaws carefully. Combs Wildroot into his hair. Splashes lavender water on his cheeks. Puts on his release suit. Lights out for the subway to Coney Island.

Stepping off the train he realizes he's a wreck. Too emotional, too keyed up to see Bess right now. In this state he'll scare her. He walks up and down the beach, taking long draughts of sea air. He stops at Luna Park, stands outside the front gate and relives that triple date of a decade ago. Eddie and Happy. First and Second Girlfriends. He lingers beneath the giant heart-shaped sign above the park entrance. THE HEART OF CONEY ISLAND. He watches the moon slowly rise out of the sea.

He walks to the brand-new Half Moon Hotel, at the far end of Coney Island, its golden dome shining in the twilight. He sits in the lobby, watching people come and go. Most seem to be honeymooners. They stroll arm in arm through the lobby, up to their rooms, out to the beach. He can't bear it. He flees the hotel, walks until he finds a dark, divey little speak. Two whiskeys, bang bang, now he's ready. He strides up Mermaid Avenue, hangs a right on Twenty-Fourth, left on Surf, turns down Scoville, comes to Number 15. A salt-stained bungalow. The wind is picking up. It blows sand into his eyes. He looks once more at the moon. At the library he read an article that said there's no wind on the moon.

He knocks on the screen door.

No answer.

He opens the screen door, knocks on the main door.

No answer.

He closes the screen door, backs away. He turns, walks slowly up Scoville. At the corner he hears his name in the wind.

Oh Willie.

He wheels. She's fifty feet away. He takes one step toward her, she takes two toward him. She's wearing a sundress, green and blue, form-fitting, like a tail fin. She looks as if she rode the moon out of the sea. They both break into a run, colliding in the middle of the street. The feel of her taut body under the thin sundress—Willie has never known such desire. He didn't know that he was prey to such desire.

He sets her on the ground, looks at her.

Ah Bess. No.

Her eye is black, her lip bloodied.

Sutton touches the base of the lion outside the New York Public Library, stares at the lion on the other side of the entrance. I can never remember which one is called Patience, which one is called Fortitude.

I didn't even know they had names, Photographer says.

You know who named them kid? Mayor LaGuardia. During the Depression. He said that's what New Yorkers would need to survive the hard times—Patience and Fortitude.

Photographer tries to shoot Sutton from the sidewalk. A line of tourists gets in the way. They're speaking what sounds like German. They notice Photographer shooting Sutton and assume Sutton must be famous, so they take out their cameras. Reporter and Photographer yell at them, shoo them away like pigeons.

No pictures! Ours! Exclusive!

Sutton watches the Germans scatter. He laughs. Now he turns to the lion. The old lion, he says. The old lion perisheth for lack of prey.

Say something, Willie?

No. Must've been the lion.

Mr. Sutton, what happened here? In what way was this a—what did you call it? Crossroads?

This is where Willie ran out of patience and fortitude.

They walk along the ocean. Bess tells Willie that Eddie was right, her father did force her into the marriage. Heavily in debt, her father faced losing his shipyard, so he found a rich family with a dissolute bachelor son.

A match made in economic heaven, Bess says. If Daddy could've married me off to old Mr. Rockefeller, he would have.

She might have said no. She nearly did. But she felt beholden to her father after the scandal with Willie and Happy, which was the start of his health problems.

She went into the marriage with no illusions. Every bride and groom are strangers, she says. But on my wedding night my husband was literally a stranger. Still. The yelling, the beatings, that I never expected.

Bess.

I thought it would stop, she says. When I got pregnant.

Pregnant?

She touches her stomach. It didn't, she says. It got worse. So I went to the police. Then came here. Coney Island was always a special place for me.

For us.

She rubs his arm. Happy memories, she says.

They sit on the sand and watch the moonlight spill like milk across the water.

How are the other two merry fishermen? she asks.

Eddie's still in Dannemora. Happy got out of Sing Sing a while ago but no one's seen him.

All my fault, she says.

Nah.

They talk until the wind turns colder, then retreat to the bungalow. Along the way Willie tells her about his time at Sing Sing, the horror of Dannemora, his job with Funck.

Bess warms a can of soup, opens a bottle of bootleg wine. Willie lights a fire using driftwood and a *Brooklyn Daily Eagle*. There's a suitcase open on the sofa and beside it a canvas bag filled with books. He looks through them. Tennyson, he says. Still?

Always, Bess says. Once I'm in love, it's forever.

He reads: *And ah for a man to arise in me, That the man I am may cease to be.* He sets down the book, picks up another. Ezra Pound?

Bess comes toward him, swirling wine in a glass. She hands the glass to Willie, closes her eyes: *You came in out of the night, And there were flowers in your hands, Now you will come out of a confusion of people, Out of a turmoil of speech about you.*

Willie stares at the book. A confusion of people, he says.

They put pillows on the floor and sit by the fire. When the embers turn to ashes, when the clock on the mantel says three, Willie has to go. He's due at Funck's in two hours. Bess walks him outside. They stand, shivering.

Run away with me, Bess.

She throws back her head. We both know that's not possible.

Why not?

No money.

There are places where that won't matter.

Places where money doesn't matter? Make me a list.

Poughkeepsie.

She gives a pained smile. My husband's family is powerful. They'll see to it that your parole is revoked. They'll have you locked up forever. I won't be the cause of that. I've done enough damage to your life.

He looks at the sky. He tries to think of something to say that will change her mind. He tries to put his feelings into words. She stops his thoughts with a touch, tracing her finger down his sideburn.

He takes a pad and pencil out of his breast pocket, writes the number of the telephone in the lobby of his flop. I'll be back tonight to check on you, he says. Until then be careful.

I'd feel a whole lot safer if the newspaper hadn't printed my address.

He nods. Damn newspapers, he says. On the other hand, if they hadn't printed your address, I never would have found you.

She kisses him on the cheek, then steps back and aims a finger gun at his chest. She smiles. Your money or your life?

My life, Bess. Always.

Her smile fades. Oh Willie.

That night, as soon as the Funck truck returns from Greystone, Willie leaps off, dashes to the subway. Still wearing his gray coveralls, he rides to Coney Island and finds the door to the bungalow flapping open. The empty wine bottle is on the floor. Bess's things, her books, are gone. He picks up the bottle, sets it on the table. He walks down to the Half Moon and watches the honeymooners come and go.

Oh no, Photographer says. Guess who's crying again.

No.

Look.

Reporter walks toward Sutton timidly. Mr. Sutton? You okay?

Sutton, leaning against the lion: Do you know the Half Moon Hotel kid? In Coney Island?

Where that mob hit happened? Back in the forties?

Yeah.

That nut job, Albert Anastasia, killed some informant?

Yeah. Abe Reles. Rat of all rats.

Anastasia tossed Reles off the hotel roof, didn't he?

Right, right. Imagine—the Half Moon used to be the place to honeymoon in New York.

Did you know Anastasia?

We had—mutual friends.

What brought the Half Moon to mind?

I was bumped off there too. In a manner of speaking.

* * *

Willie punching the time clock at Funck and Sons. February 1930. From Funck's office he hears maniacal laughter. He walks down the hall, finds the frosted door standing open, Funck sitting with his feet on his desk, cradling a bottle of something. Well well, he says to Willie, if it isn't Mr. Blackmailer! Come in, come in. Guess what, Mr. Blackmailer, you can be blackmailing me all you want, it don't matter. We're out of business. You want to call my wife? It don't matter neither. She's going to divorce me anyhows.

But why?

The market, genius. Half our clients is canceling. When bad times is coming, gardens is the first to be going. No azaleas in recessions. Fuck the daisies in Depressions. Motherfuck the peonies. Cocksuck the daffodils. Nice knowing you. Here's your last check, Mr. Blackmailer. Hope you're having a nice life. I should've stayed in Amsterdam.

Funck puts his head on the desk, starts to cry.

Willie walks straight to the library, holes up in the reading room, opens the wants. But there are no wants. Just pages and pages of people looking for work, advertising themselves, their skills. The few available jobs listed are for specialists, professionals, people with spotless pasts. Willie lights a cigarette. Banished from another garden. He wishes there had been time at least to say goodbye to Mr. Untermyer. Then he thinks—maybe there is.

The next morning he takes a bus to Yonkers. He walks from the bus stop to Greystone, asks the guard at the gate if he can see Mr. Untermyer.

And who might you be?

I'm a—friend.

Aint you one of the landscaping crew?

Yeah. But also a friend.

Fuck off.

If I could just see Mr. Untermyer for five—

Look, pal, everyone's hurtin. Everyone's workin an angle. But I'm not gonna lose *my* job pesterin Mr. UN-tuh-my-uh about some fuckin gardener. Screw.

Willie rides the bus back to Manhattan. He walks from the Port Authority to his flop. Along the way he sees a newsboy waving an extra.

HOOVER URGES CALM.

He grabs the paper from the newsboy's outstretched hand. President Hoover insists that the American economy is solid. The fundamentals are sound. Willie would like to buy the paper, but he knows it will only make him angrier. Besides, he needs to save his nickels.

In his room Willie stands at his bureau and counts his savings. He stacks the coins, puts the bills in neat piles. One hundred and twenty-six dollars. Enough for four months' rent and food. If he eats sparingly. He sits down, writes a letter to Mr. Untermyer, explaining that he tried to see him, that he'd like to continue at Greystone, even at reduced pay.

He never will get a reply.

Starting at sunrise he hits the streets. He visits landscaping firms, factories. At every gate and loading dock he finds one hundred, two hundred men already waiting. He goes to employment agencies. The buildings in which they're housed are so mobbed, so crammed full of people begging for work, he can't get inside.

Every few days he swings by the library to check the wants. Chauffeur-mechanic—must have best of references. Paint salesman—only those with first-class experience need apply. Junior bank clerk—fair wages, luncheon provided, high school degree a must.

He asks himself why he keeps checking.

One foggy morning, walking in a daze down the library's front steps, Willie trips, nearly faints. He hasn't eaten in two days. But he can't bear the thought of rummaging through a trash can—again. He sits heavily under the lion, puts his head in his hands, prays.

He hears his name.

He looks up. A familiar face floats out of the fog. A triangular face. Waterbug eyes. It's Marcus Bassett—from Dannemora. He's running up the steps with a book tucked under his arm. *Now you will come out of a confusion of people.* Willie stands, surprised how glad he is to see someone, anyone he knows.

How's tricks, Marcus?

Willie! How you doing, old pal?

Willie takes the book from under Marcus's arm. *The Decline of the West.*

It's due today, Marcus says.

Sorry, Marcus. Library just closed. You'll have to pay the fine.

That's about how my luck's running.

Same here.

Marcus invites Willie back to his place uptown. He has a pint of bathtub juniper juice he's been saving.

Another time, Willie says. I'm not feeling well.

Marcus isn't taking no for an answer. He drags Willie up Fifth Avenue.

Along the way they pass a silver-haired man in a bespoke suit selling apples. They pass a group of soot-faced kids selling pencil stubs. Penny apiece, mister? They pass a woman in a stained housecoat and bedroom slippers, talking to her slippers. They pass a conclave of men at a taxi stand, newspapers spread across the hood of a cab, deep worry lines etched in the corners of their eyes.

They come upon an ambulance parked outside a rooming house. Willie asks a roly-poly man with cauliflower ears what's going on, though he already knows. He can smell the gas.

Nother suicide, the man says. Thoid this month on this block.

They see furniture stacked on curbs, nests of toys and clothes, the belongings of families who couldn't make the rent, couldn't hang on. It looks like the detritus that washes ashore hours after a ship sinks.

I'm almost on the street myself, Marcus says. I was doing okay till a few months ago. I was a proofreader at an ad agency. My boss was a rummy, the work was dull, but I loved that job, Willie. It was decent pay, honest work, and it was the only thing standing between me and the edge.

What happened?

Business fell by forty percent. It came down to me and another guy. The other guy had never been in the joint.

When Willie sees the basement apartment where Marcus lives, at Eighty-Third and Broadway, he thinks Marcus might be better off on the street. The front walk is covered with trash, the halls smell of urine. Old urine. Marcus's one lightless room is a rabbit cage, its walls papered with newspapers. Old newspapers. Over Marcus's hot plate are headlines about President Taft.

On the other side of the wall a woman or wild animal is wailing. The walls are so thin, the wailing so loud, she sounds as if she's right there in the room with Willie and Marcus. She sounds like Big Ben.

Make yourself at home, Marcus says.

Willie looks around. Home? There's no furniture, just a couch that looks like a park bench, an unmade Murphy bed, a card table bowing under the weight of an Underwood. Scattered around the Underwood are rejection letters from all the slicks. Willie unrolls the page in the typewriter. It's covered with x'd sentences.

How's the writing coming, Marcus?

I'm working on a story about a guy with no job who lives in a rathole. I need an ending.

Willie is about to say something sympathetic when the door bangs open and in walks a shockingly plain woman. No waist, no breasts, cheeks specked with so many dark moles that she looks splashed with mud. Her hair is set in a kind of finger wave, but the fingers that did the waving must have been arthritic. Willie's heart goes out to her. She must be the wailing neighbor. Then he hears the neighbor send up a wail. Big Ben. Convicts on the loose. Confused, he watches Marcus rush to the woman's side and plant a kiss on her mole-splashed cheek.

Willie, I want you to meet my bride. Dahlia, say hello to my old pal Willie Sutton.

This is where it happened, Sutton says, stepping away from the lion, gazing up at its broad nose, which always reminded him of his own. Talk about your crossroads, boys—I bumped into Marcus on these steps, with these lions watching, in the spring of 1930. How many times I've looked back on that moment and thought, What if? What if I hadn't decided to sit in the shadow of this lion at the very same moment Marcus was returning a book? What if Marcus had decided to finish The Decline of the West? *What if I'd stopped in the library men's room, or spent a few extra minutes combing the wants, or said hello and goodbye and gave Marcus the air? The things I might have said. The things I shouldn't have said. So much would be different.*

Sutton glowers at the lion. You saw it happening, he says. Patience, or Fortitude, whatever the fuck your name is. How come you didn't warn me? One little roar?

FOURTEEN

WILLIE SITS ON THE STEPS OF THE LIBRARY, WAITING FOR it to open. In the last few months he's managed to scrounge a few temporary things in the wants. A job mopping floors in an office building—then the boss had to cut back. A job cleaning toilets at the bus station—then the regular guy returned. He's nearly out of money. He has no family, no friends, besides Marcus, who's in even worse shape than Willie. He needs to find something permanent, right now, or else.

The library unlocks its doors. Willie runs upstairs to the reading room, grabs an armful of newspapers, settles into a chair. He goes through the wants slowly, hopefully, twice. Nothing. He rubs his eyes, massages his temples.

He turns briefly to the news pages. Four million out of work. Thirteen hundred banks belly-up—this year. Next year the number is expected to be two or three times higher. He crumples the newspaper, tosses it on the floor. The librarians give him a look. He storms out.

He feels the sidewalk poking through a new hole in his shoes. Before he can think about the hole and how he's going to afford new shoes, his infected tooth starts to throb. He puts a hand to his jaw. He can bear it most days, but today it's pulsing. He walks and walks, fighting his rage, his hunger, and eventually finds himself before a bank. He gazes at the marble columns, the gold and brass eagles around the front door. He watches customers come and go. He watches the security guard lock up.

Closing time—already? How many hours have passed? He must have fallen into a stupor.

He stumbles back to his flop. He's paid up for one more week. Then what? He lies on the lumpy bed, pulls the sour-smelling coverlet to his chin. It smells of the previous occupant. And the previous, and the previous. He imagines them all lying here, worrying about the same thing. He nods off.

He wakes drenched with sweat, his neighbor banging the wall. Shaddap in there! Willie must have been screaming in his sleep again. The room is pitch dark. He doesn't know what time it is. He pawned his clock. But he can tell from the number of lights in the buildings across the street—it's late. He goes to the basin, wets his wash rag, presses it to his face and neck. He puts on his coat and hat, goes for a walk. He finds himself back at the bank. Across the street is a drugstore. Its front window casts a trapezoid of white-purple light on the sidewalk. Willie stands just outside the trapezoid. He looks at the windows of all the buildings around him. Each window is a story. Probably like his. He makes up the stories, tells them to himself, one after another, stories about people tired, sick, scared, broke. Then he looks at the bank. And looks. An hour passes. Three. The bank's security guard appears. Willie sees him unlock the door. Creeping from the shadows Willie peeks through the bank's front window, watches the security guard cut the alarms, make a pot of coffee. Willie sidles back across the street, waits for the first tellers to arrive, then the assistant manager, then the manager. Just before the bank opens for business a Western Union boy knocks. The security guard opens wide, jokes with the boy, signs for a telegram.

And then it happens. A feeling comes over Willie, something like the feeling when he first walked into the south yard of Sing Sing and saw Chapin's explosion of roses. He runs all the way to Marcus's apartment. While Dahlia sleeps Willie and Marcus sit at the card table and Willie lays it all out.

It's so simple, Marcus. I don't know why I didn't think of it before. I don't know why no one else has thought of it. We stand outside the bank, see? Early. When that security guard comes, when he cuts the alarms, the bank is defenseless. A sitting duck. All we need to do is get in. So how do we get in? We *trick* our way in. No one's ever done it that way. Dillinger, Floyd, Barrow, all those boys shoot up a bank, scare everybody out of their wits. Or else they break in, middle of the night, blow the safe—risky. A hundred things can go wrong. But it doesn't have to be that tough, Marcus. It's all so much easier.

What is?

A uniform. *Any uniform.* Western Union. Post Office. The guard will open sesame, abracadabra, because guards obey uniforms blindly, they don't check, and once that guard opens that door, it's over. *We own that fuckin bank*. I back the guard in, tie him up. Then you come in. As each employee arrives we tie *them* up. Then the manager comes. We make him open the safe. Then we tie him up and out we go. No torch, no nitro. No violence, no evidence. Clean. Cool.

Marcus strokes the sloping sides of his triangular face. His waterbug eyes are skittering. It's a thing of beauty, Willie.

Say you're in.

Oh I'm in, Willie. I'm in.

They agree, there's only one problem. Guns and uniforms aren't cheap. They'll need seed money for this new venture. Not to mention rent, food, cigarettes. Also, they could do with a dress rehearsal. Besides murder one, no crime carries a stiffer penalty in 1930 than bank robbery. The bankers and their lobbyists have seen to that. If you're going to rob a bank, you'd better be damn smooth about it.

If Eddie were here, Willie says, he'd recommend a jewelry store. I know just the one. Rosenthal and Sons. It's on one of the busiest corners in midtown.

That seems like asking for trouble, Willie.

I'll bet you a fin that busy corner makes them smug. They think they have nothing to worry about.

He's also willing to bet there are no sons.

Why do you think bumping into Marcus Bassett was so fateful, Mr. Sutton?

We were both out of work, desperate—stupid. It was the fuse meeting the match.

Did you have any qualms about going down that road again? Getting back into a life of crime?

Qualms? Yeah kid. I had qualms.

I mean, did you think about ethics? Morals? Did it occur to you that taking something which doesn't belong to you is, you know, immoral?

People took plenty from me.

I don't mean to—I'm just trying to get a sense, Mr. Sutton, of your thinking at the time. Did you ever stop and think it was wrong?

I didn't think it was wrong. I knew it was wrong. But it was also wrong that I was hungry. It was wrong that I was about to be on the street. It was wrong that half the country was in the same boat as Willie, that half the fuckin country was out of work. You know how they say character is destiny? That's the bunk. Work is destiny. A man talks about the woman he loves, he might sound excited, but get him talking about his job, then check his eyes— that's the real him. A man is his job, kid, and I had no job, so I was a bum. A loser. America's a great place to be a winner, but it's hell's basement for losers.

Three Salvation Army workers appear outside the library. They set up their kettle, begin ringing bells, shaking tambourines.

Besides, Sutton says, I had it all worked out. I wasn't going to hurt anyone. I went out of my way like no bank robber before me

*not to hurt anyone. Marcus and I robbed banks before they opened.
When that wasn't possible, we did everything we could to make
sure there was no violence.*

*Reporter opens a file. According to this one clip, Mr. Sutton,
you and Marcus had some kind of policy? If someone got sick
during one of your robberies, if an old person or a pregnant woman
got faint, if a baby was crying, you'd call off the job and walk out
of the bank.*

That's true.

It seems such a contradiction, Reporter says.

*I don't really like people, kid, but I don't want to hurt them
either. Do unto others—I believe in that shit.*

*But you were hurting people, Reporter says. You were taking
their money. And this was before people had deposit insurance.*

*Nah, Sutton says, banks back then insured themselves against
robberies.*

Photographer sighs. He doesn't get it, Willie.

And you do kid?

*Photographer turns to face Reporter: Around the time Willie
and this Marcus cat went on their rampage, the Bank of United
States collapsed. People today don't remember—the government
doesn't want us to remember. The Bank of United States just
vaporized—with $100 million of people's life savings. It's still the
biggest bank failure in the history of the world. Thousands of people
were wiped out. And did any of those bank managers responsible
go to the Big House like Willie did? No they did not. They sat
around their country clubs laughing it up. Banks gamed the system,
fucked society, caused the crash of 1929, drove the world into the
abyss and paved the way for the rise of fascism—Stalin, Hitler—and
they got despicably, disgustingly rich in the process. Banks. Banks
did all that. So Willie only wanted to hurt banks, not people, which
is why he became a folk hero. Am I right, Willie?*

Antihero, Sutton mutters.

Is he right? Reporter asks Sutton.

Well now, Sutton says, it seems to me the Bank of United States actually stole $200 million of everybody's money.

No. I mean: Did you feel you were at war with banks? With society?

Which is it?

Either one. Pick.

Everybody's at war with society kid. Everybody's at war with everybody else. In every job you have to get over on someone, beat somebody out of something. Taking stuff that doesn't belong to you—no other way to survive. That's how the whole thing works, everybody robbing everybody else.

I don't rob anybody, Reporter says.

You don't, huh? You take people's stories away from them. Half the time they don't want to give up their stories, am I right? So you have to charm them, cajole them, con them. Or else make a deal with their lawyers.

Photographer laughs. What about me, Willie? You going to tell me I rob people?

Nah, you don't rob anybody. You just shoot them.

Photographer burrows into his buckskin jacket. Willie, brother, you make it hard to be a fan.

You're not the first to tell me that kid.

Reporter runs his finger along the map. So our next stop is Fiftieth and Broadway—did you rob a bank there, Mr. Sutton?

Nah. That's where I pulled a big jewel heist. A warm-up for banks. Banks were the regular season, jewelry stores were spring training. Or so I thought. This jewel heist wound up being the most fateful job of my career.

Marcus and Willie walk down Broadway. Marcus wears a gray flannel suit, Willie wears an indigo blue mailman uniform. Tuesday, October 28, 1930. Early morning.

They stop at Fiftieth Street, stand on the corner, pretend to be talking about the weather. Marcus flips a quarter in the air, catches it. A Negro man in blue pants, a pale blue work shirt, comes up Broadway. He stops, unlocks the door to Rosenthal and Sons, enters.

Marcus looks up and down the street. That the porter?

Willie nods.

They give the porter five minutes to cut the alarms, start the coffeepot. Then Willie moves in.

He knocks. The door opens. Porter—fortyish, graying at the temples, freshly shaved. Willie smells his bay rum.

Yes?

Telegram.

Who for?

Mr. Rosenthal.

He's not here.

You can sign.

They stare at each other. One one-thousand, two one-thousand.

Wait, Porter says.

He slams the door.

Willie looks up the block. He sees Marcus leaning against the streetlamp, flipping his quarter. He tells himself there's still time to walk away.

The door opens. So where do I sign?

Willie hands him a short clipboard. Here.

As Porter takes the clipboard, as both his hands are occupied, Willie pulls a .22 from his breast pocket.

Back in, Willie says. Nice and easy.

Porter steps backs. Willie jumps inside, shuts the door. He and Porter are inches apart, Porter staring at Willie, not the gun. Willie waves the gun, gestures to an empty showcase. Over there—go.

Porter backs behind the showcase.

Marcus comes through the door, his face covered with a

bandanna, which somehow accentuates its triangular shape. And magnifies his waterbug eyes. He walks up to Porter. Give me your leg, he says.

My what.

What're you deaf.

I can't hear you through your kerchief.

Marcus turns up a corner of the bandanna. Your *leg*.

Porter lifts his leg. From his breast pocket Marcus pulls a roll of picture wire. He ties one end to Porter's ankle, holds the other end like a leash. All the while Porter is glaring at Willie.

What's your name, Porter?

Charlie Lewis.

You ever been in a holdup before?

No.

You sure are cool about it.

No other way *to* be.

How many employees coming in today?

Three more.

When?

Soon.

Who has the combination to the safe in the back room?

Mr. Fox. Head salesman.

Willie gestures for Porter to stand at the door facing Broadway. The door has a shade in the window and Willie pulls the shade halfway down. Marcus stands to one side of the door, holding the wire attached to Porter, and Willie crouches on the other side, holding the gun.

A cop walks by.

Porter looks at Willie. What if a police officer tries the door?

Let him in, Willie says. We'll take care of him.

Ten minutes pass. Sweat is pouring down Marcus's forehead. His bandanna is sopping. Porter's face, Willie notices, is dry.

Just before nine, a knock.

It's Mr. Hayes, Porter says. One of our salesmen.

Open it.

A young man about Willie's age saunters in, removes his hat, throws it on one of the showcases. Hiya Charlie, he says to Porter, how come the door's still locked?

Willie sticks his gun in the man's back. Good question. Be real quiet and do as you're told.

He hands First Salesman off to Marcus, who wires his wrists to his ankles and sets him on the floor.

A minute later, another knock.

That'll be Mr. Woods, Porter says. Salesman.

Porter opens the door. This time Sutton does the tying while Marcus holds the gun. Second Salesman makes a sound, a wince or a cry.

Don't hurt him, Porter says, he's an old man.

I'm not hurting anybody, Willie says, annoyed.

Another knock. That's Mr. Fox, Porter says.

Willie pulls Third Salesman aside as he walks through the door, jams the gun in his ribs. Good morning. We've been waiting for you. Come with me, we're going to open the safe.

Can I hang up my hat and coat first?

Drop them.

Willie marches Third Salesman to the back room and stands him before the safe. Open it, he says.

Third Salesman fumbles with the dial. I can't remember the combination.

That's a stall, Willie says. Come on, open it   or I'll give you the works.

Are you really a letter carrier?

I'll ask the questions.

Third Salesman turns back to the safe. He's cursing, sighing, and he's sweatier than Marcus. I can't remember the combination, he says.

You're lying.

I tell you I can't remember. I'd open it if I *could*. Don't you think my life means something to me?

I don't know what the hell your life means. All I know is you're stalling.

Willie hears Porter calling from the showroom:

You must have scared the numbers clean out of him. Let me phone Mr. Rosenthal, I'll get you the combination.

Willie walks out to the showroom. He eyes Porter. Let him use the phone, he says to Marcus.

Porter dials while Marcus presses his ear against the receiver. Willie watches from ten feet away.

Yes, hello, Mr. Rosenthal? Charlie here. Mr. Fox has forgotten the combination to the safe, would you give it to me please? No sir. Mr. Fox has forgotten it. Yes sir. The store's not open yet. No sir. Nine-fifteen. I know sir.

Porter writes down the combination. Willie unties the wire attached to his leg and walks him to the back room. Porter spins the dial. It takes him three tries. Finally the safe door swings open to reveal an inner door—also locked.

I'll need *my* keys for this door, Porter says.

He walks back to the showroom. Slowly. He takes a set of keys from under the front showcase, walks to the back room. Even more slowly. He doesn't hand the keys to Willie. He dangles them before Willie's face.

You sure you've never been in a holdup before?

Nope.

You ever *done* a holdup?

I don't break the law.

You knew the combination this whole time, didn't you? You were trying to stall. And you were trying to tip the owner—weren't you? Weren't you, Porter?

Porter doesn't answer.

Willie grabs the keys from him. He turns to Third Salesman. Which drawers have the good stuff?

Three, five, and seven.

Willie opens them. Costume jewelry. Willie glares at Third Salesman. If he were a different man he'd shoot Third Salesman and Porter where they stand. How do they know he's not a different man?

From the showroom Marcus calls out to Willie: Hey. Nine twenty-eight. Better move.

Willie pulls out the other drawers. Jackpot. Diamond bracelets, diamond watches, diamond rings, ruby bracelets, platinum watches with diamonds around the faces—and one enormous diamond brooch that looks as if it came from an old pirate chest. Willie throws it all in a silk bag. Some of it spills on the floor.

He marches Third Salesman and Porter back into the show-room, ties them to a showcase. Marcus hands him a green topcoat to cover his costume. Willie addresses the employees.

Okay, you four. This concludes our business. Don't make a move until we're gone a full five minutes.

If you're gone, Porter says, how will you know if we've moved?

Willie stares hard at Porter. Porter doesn't look away. Willie squeezes the checkered grip on his gun, takes a half step toward Porter. Marcus touches Willie on the elbow. Don't.

They walk out, saunter casually down Broadway, duck into the first subway station and catch the first uptown train. Willie feels as if his heart is holding a gun against his ribs. But he's also smiling. He's going to have a steak for dinner tonight. His first meat in months. And it looks as if he won't need to worry for a while about sleeping on the street. He turns to Marcus. I can't remember the combination, he says, imitating Third Salesman's puling tone.

That's a stall, Marcus says, aping Willie's tough-guy voice. Come on, open it—or I'll give you the works.

Everyone in the subway car turns and looks. It's rare to hear men laughing at the start of the Great Depression.

Photographer cruises along Fiftieth, stops at Broadway. Sutton climbs out, followed by Reporter, then Photographer, who leaves the keys in the Polara, the motor running.

Aren't you worried about someone stealing your car? Sutton says.

In midtown? On Christmas Day?

Sutton shrugs. What do I know?

They walk down Broadway. Sutton stops before a black glass office tower. Beside the tower is a construction site girdled by a plywood fence, with holes for people to watch. Sutton looks up and down Broadway. The Big Stem, he says. That's what they called Broadway in the thirties. That's why they call New York the Big Apple.

Where was the store?

Willie points to the office tower. Right next to the old Capitol Theatre.

How much did you get?

Two hundred grand. Diamonds mostly.

Photographer whistles. In 1930?

Yeah, Sutton says. We fenced it for sixty. So my nick was thirty thou for about two hours' work. We were rolling in it.

Did you fence it through Dutch Schultz again? Reporter asks.

Yeah. Dutch was so impressed with this haul, he asked me to work for him. I told him I liked being my own boss. He begged me. The one time in my life someone begs me to take a job, it's a psychotic killer.

Willie and Marcus buy better guns, better costumes, a fast new Ford. No more riding the subway to their jobs. Then they go on a spree. That's what the papers call it, a spree, and Willie and

Marcus like this word. They say it to crack each other up. In just the first month of 1931 they take down three First Nationals, one National City, two Corn Exchanges, one Curb Exchange, and a Bowery Savings and Loan. Days of careful planning, discussion, precision timing go into each job, and yet there are so many banks, the names and lobbies and tellers all begin to run together in Willie's mind.

Their average haul is twenty thousand. Willie stuffs his nick into airtight jars, which he buries in parks throughout Manhattan and Brooklyn. He goes late at night with a spade he stole from Funck and Sons—a different kind of landescaping.

Cops are baffled by Willie's uniforms. They think a band of laid-off mailmen is on a rampage. Then they think it's a crew of disaffected Western Union boys. Then, after Willie pulls a job as a carpenter, another as a window washer, cops suspect a wave of rogue craftsmen.

Willie enjoys wearing a cop's uniform best of all. Never mind the irony, he just likes the way it feels. He's always had a swinging gait, a natural strut, but putting on that blue greatcoat, with that golden badge, Willie finds himself striding with a new sense of authority and prowess. Officer Sutton—checking door handles, parking meters.

By the opening day of baseball season, 1931, Willie's expanding his repertoire, experimenting with hair and makeup. He uses a pencil to give himself thicker eyebrows, applies Pan-Cake makeup to the sides of his nose to make it look thinner. On his chin he sometimes glues a fake wart, which mesmerizes bank employees. He sees them making a mental note to tell cops about it. As a result, he feels sure, they'll forget everything else.

He wears fake beards, eyebrows, sideburns. On one job he wears muttonchops and a mustache like Mr. Untermyer's. On another he wears a handlebar like a nineteenth-century prize-fighter. He haunts the theater district, befriends clerks at musty old costume shops. He buys a tackle box and fills it with every tool of the costumer's trade. For the second Corn Exchange job he wears an enormous set of false teeth. Driving to the bank that morning, Marcus looks over just as Willie inserts them. Marcus nearly drives into a hydrant.

Willie wishes he'd thought of the facial disguises sooner. He pleads with Marcus to wear one. And a costume. But Marcus says he'll stick with his bandanna and a fedora pulled low over his eyes. I'd feel silly in a getup, Marcus says. You'll feel sillier, Willie says, if the cops get a solid description of you.

Willie has one hard-and-fast prerequisite for every bank they hit. It has to be clearly visible from a good coffee shop. In the days before each job Willie buys a spiral notebook and sits in the coffee shop for hours, watching, taking notes. He records when the bank employees arrive, which ones look smart, which ones look as if they might get chesty. He uses draftsman's rulers and colored pencils to make detailed pictures, sketches, maps. Now and then he waits for the bank to close, follows the employees to whichever coffee shop or speak they use as their hangout. He eavesdrops, learns their names, the names of their spouses. During a job he'll refer to them by name, or casually drop the name of a wife. Do as I say, Mr. Myers, or you'll never see Harriet again.

It's so shocking, so unexpected, it immobilizes them.

Mr. Sutton, how many bank jobs did you pull in 1931?
   Ah kid, I don't know.
   Ballpark.
   Ballpark? Thirty-seven.
   Reporter looks up from his notebook. Thirty? Seven? Banks?
   I don't like to brag. But yeah.
   Photographer stomps out a half-smoked Newport. Hard for me to believe, Willie, that you can rob thirty-seven banks and not have a vendetta against banks. Against society.

Honestly, kid, I hate to disillusion you, but for me it was more about Bess.

Can a man really rob thirty-seven banks to win one woman?

Better question kid: Is thirty-seven banks enough for some women?

Willie and Marcus use the Automat in Times Square as their office. They meet every few mornings and the agenda is always the same. First they review the last job. Then they go over Willie's notes for the next job. Then they discuss what they'll do if they get caught. As repeat offenders they can expect twenty-five years.

One morning Willie lights a Chesterfield, does a double-take at the waitress. She looks like Mother.

I can't do that kind of bit, Marcus.

Me neither, Willie.

So it's simple then. We get pinched, we don't talk. If we tell the cops nothing, they can't make a case.

Marcus holds up his hand. On my kid.

You don't have a kid.

Dahlia's pregnant.

Oh.

Marcus beams. Yeah. I'm robbing for three now.

Days later, in their regular booth at the Automat, Marcus slides a glass vial across the table. Inside the vial are three small purple-pink pills. Willie scoops it off the table, into his lap.

Early birthday present, Marcus says.

What is it?

Instant death.

Willie squints. Huh?

We were talking about what to do if we get pinched. That's strychnine.

Willie closes his fist around the vial. He thinks of several moments in his life when he could have used these cuties.

Make sure you got no other options, Marcus says. It's not a good death.

Not good how?

Ever see an animal dosed with strychnine?

No.

They get stiff. Their necks arch. Foam gushes out their mouths.

How do you know all this, Marcus?

I tried it on some cats in my neighborhood.

From what I read, Mr. Sutton, it was with Marcus that you started using costumes? And makeup?

Yeah.

And apparently you had some kind of patter? To entertain the bank employees? Jokes? Poems? One employee told the FBI that being robbed by you was like being at a movie. Except the usher is holding a gun on you the whole time.

If we kept the employees happy, they were easier to control. Unhappy people are much harder to control. Ask any politician.

But you always used a gun?

Sure.

Loaded?

What good's an unloaded gun?

Willie rents a five-room apartment on Riverside Drive. He has no furniture. He doesn't want any. After prison, after the flop, he just wants space. And peace. He likes the apartment well enough, but it doesn't feel like home until he learns that John D. Rockefeller Jr. lives in the same building.

As spring turns to summer Willie begins to form a grand plan. He's going to amass enough money to find Bess and persuade her to run off with him. Ireland, he thinks. Maybe Scotland. He passes several pleasant evenings in the library, reading about remote coastal islands, where hermits used to hide from invading

Romans and Vikings. No one will ever find him and Bess there. They'll live in a thatch-roofed cottage on a grassy hillside with a dozen chickens and a few sheep and a sweeping view of the sea. Bess's kid will be better off with Willie than that bruiser she's married to. And if the bruiser and Bess's father do appear, and try to make trouble, Willie will have more than enough jack to outbid them for crooked cops, judges, customs officials.

Willie sits on the floor of his new apartment, mentally totting up the money he's got in buried jars. At least half a million. The grand plan doesn't seem all that far-fetched.

Marcus also takes a new apartment. Park Avenue. He buys a sleek new desk, a new Underwood, a box of new typewriter ribbons. The words are flowing again, he tells Willie. Everything's coming up roses.

A phrase I try to avoid, Willie mutters.

Marcus invites Willie to his new digs for a celebratory dinner. Willie brings a bassinet for the baby, a box of candy for Dahlia. Thanks, she says, downcast.

You okay, Dahlia?

She mumbles something about morning sickness.

Willie wonders how much Dahlia knows about his work with Marcus. He's always assumed that Marcus had enough sense not to tell her anything. But now he realizes that he doesn't know Marcus. And he sure as hell doesn't know Dahlia—who's giving him a bad feeling.

Marcus claps his hands, says he's been saving a bottle of top-notch bootleg gin for a special occasion. He's going to whip up a batch of martinis. He just needs some olives. He runs down to the market.

Dahlia tells Willie to sit, make himself comfortable. Pulling out a chair at the kitchen table, Willie lights a Chesterfield, gazes at Dahlia. She stands at the kitchen window, watching the traffic down below, distractedly rubbing her stomach. Willie thinks of Bess.

All at once Dahlia starts to cry.

Dahlia, honey. What's wrong?

I know, Willie.

Know what?

I *know*.

She turns from the window. About Marcus, she says.

Ah fuck, he thinks. What about Marcus? he says.

Tears roll down her cheeks, undulating over her moles. Please, Willie. When a girl looks like me, she can't afford to be stupid.

Willie says nothing. For the moment silence is the smartest play he can think of.

You're going to pretend you don't know, Dahlia says, sobbing. That Marcus, that Marcus, that Marcus is *seeing* someone.

Willie sighs with relief. Ah Dahlia, that's ridiculous.

Then why is Marcus, a dyed-in-the-wool mope, all of a sudden so confident?

Willie thinks back. He's lectured Marcus many times at the Automat about confidence. Whatever you do, do it from your nuts. Apparently Willie has created a monster.

Dahlia, he says, I'm sure Marcus is acting confident because he's writing again. He told me so himself. The words are flowing. He's not having an affair. Marcus loves you. He's thrilled about being a new father. He's just feeling—good. About his life. His work. You.

Dahlia wipes her eyes, looks at her belly. Really?

Yeah. Sure.

I want to believe you.

You can, you can. I never lie about love. I never even kid about it. It's much too important.

She laughs through her tears. All right, Willie. All right. Thanks. Hearing that makes me feel better.

He goes to her, puts his hands on her shoulders. He gives her his new phone number, tells her to call him if she has any troubles or doubts. Day or night.

Marcus returns. He mixes the martinis and Willie drinks two. Then Dahlia serves the dinner. Roast pork. Dry, burnt. Willie's glad when it's time to go. He wants a glass of bicarbonate and his bed. He tells Marcus to walk him out, he needs a word.

At the corner he asks Marcus how much Dahlia knows about their work. Marcus looks hangdog.

Christ, Marcus. Everything?

She's my wife, Willie.

Willie nods. Then tells Marcus about his conversation with Dahlia.

She thinks you're cheating, Marcus. So you need to be better to her. Pay more attention to her. Especially since she knows everything about our—thing. You mustn't give her any reason to seek revenge.

I am.

You are what?

Cheating on her.

Willie covers his eyes. Holy Mother of God.

I've met the love of my life, Willie. She's from St. Louis. A true midwestern gal. Wholesome. But kind of naughty too. She likes me to spank her. Can you imagine, Willie? Spank her. She had a falling-out with her family, I guess, and she moved to the East Coast, and she was selling dances to stay afloat. Until she met me.

Willie takes off his fedora, wipes his brow.

The things she says in bed, Willie, you can't imagine. She's from the Soulard neighborhood. That's one of the oldest parts of St. Louis.

Has Marcus lost his mind? Lighting a cigarette, taking the deepest possible drag, Willie stares at the tip. It looks brighter than normal, like a drop of blood.

We met at Roseland, Marcus is saying. I'll never forget our first dance. *I'm Good For Nothing But Love.*

Again, stunningly irrelevant information. Willie and Marcus keep walking, and Marcus keeps talking. They stop under a streetlight on Seventy-Ninth. Willie feels as if he can't take one more step. He reaches into his breast pocket, fondles the strychnine. This is all very bad news, Marcus.

Relax, Willie, I've got it under control.

Sure you do. Sure. Control. Look, Marcus, I don't care who you love, or who you bed, but Dahlia must be kept happy, do you understand? Dahlia's happiness comes first. Dahlia's happiness is essential to our happiness. My happiness.

Marcus nods.

Keep your taxi dancer well out of sight, Willie says.

Millicent.

What?

Her name's Millicent. I can't wait for you to meet her.

Willie glares, flicks his cigarette into the gutter, walks off.

Days later Willie gets a call. Dahlia. She's hyperventilating. She found a batch of letters written on Marcus's new Underwood.

Letters? To who?

Marcus's *whore*.

If they're to her, how did you find them?

They're *carbons*.

Willie puts his palm over his mouth. Carbons.

Willie, you said you never lie about love. But you did. You *lied*. You and Marcus *both* need to be in jail.

Jail? Dahlia, honey, what're you saying? You're jumping to conclusions. Let's talk this over. I can explain.

So explain.

Not on the phone. Meet me at the Childs restaurant in the Ansonia. Believe me, things are not what they seem. One hour. Childs. Please?

She hangs up without answering.

He arrives early. Dahlia is already there. She's sitting at a small table in the back, next to the kitchen, wearing a dreadful dress and a felt skullcap that looks like a leather football helmet. Willie kisses her on the cheek, drops his hat on the table. He orders a slice of pie and a cup of coffee for each of them, sits directly across from her.

How you feeling, Dahlia?

Baby's kicking like crazy this morning. Like he's trying to get out.

Know just how he feels, Willie thinks. Now, Dahlia, he says, those letters.

The waitress brings their pie and coffee. He waits for her to go away.

Yes? Dahlia says.

It's so simple, Dahlia. The novel, Dahlia. Marcus's novel.

The novel.

Sure. Those letters are from Marcus's novel. Obviously it's a novel in the form of letters. They call it an epistolary novel.

Oh *please*.

Sure, sure, those letters are nothing more than passages from a work in progress. It's laughable, really. I can understand why you thought—

But he *signed* them, Willie. With his own name.

Well, fine, Marcus has probably taken some true incidents from his romantic past, old affairs and so forth, and twisted them into a mix of fact and fiction. Writers do it all the time.

You're saying there's no taxi dancer named Millicent? From Soulard?

Willie eats a forkful of pie. Of course there's a Millicent, he says. But she doesn't come from Soulard. She comes from the fevered mind of Marcus Bassett. Your husband. Father of your unborn child.

He goes on at length about Marcus's literary aspirations, about how much words and books mean to Marcus, to both of them.

He talks about bumping into Marcus on the steps of the library, about how they both took refuge there in bad times. The more credible he sounds, the more despicable he feels. He was telling the truth the other night when he said that he never lies about love. He feels something in his throat, his gut, something he hasn't felt in a long time. Conscience, remorse, guilt, he doesn't have a word for it.

You swear, Dahlia says. You swear to me that those letters are fiction.

I swear.

Because if you're lying—a second time—after swearing you never would—I'd actually enjoy turning you in.

Turning me—what are you saying, Dahlia?

I know what you and Marcus have been up to.

Honey, please, keep your voice down.

Your—spree!

Sssh.

Willie is wearing a high stiff collar and a flowered necktie and he feels them both getting tighter. He looks nervously around the restaurant. People are staring. He leans across the table. My hand to almighty God, he whispers, Marcus is not cheating on you.

Dahlia fishes a tissue from her purse. She touches the tissue to her nose, then wads it into a ball, as if she wants to throw it at Willie. From his breast pocket Willie removes his linen handkerchief, extends it to her. She takes it, dabs her eyes. Her face softens. I'm sorry for that outburst, she says.

They sit in silence for several minutes. Abruptly she stands. Her chair scrapes, almost tips over. Thanks for meeting me, Willie.

Don't go. Finish your pie.

No. Thank you. I've taken up too much of your time already. I know you don't have much—time.

Willie hesitates, stands. Dahlia kisses him on the cheek, walks out. Willie sits back down, asks for the check. He eats another forkful of pie and the restaurant goes sideways. Four, six, eight cops come banging out of the kitchen, knocking Willie out of his chair. They pin him to the linoleum floor, cuff him. There isn't time to go for the strychnine. He hopes poor Marcus has time to go for his.

Photographer aims a finger gun at Sutton. What a trip, Willie. It just hit me, I think. You, about our age, packing heat, knocking over banks, jewelry stores. What a trip.

Shit, Reporter says.

What?

Over there. Channel 11.

A camera truck slams to a stop across the street. A young man with a tall Afro leaps out and sprints toward them, a TV camera on his shoulder. Reporter pushes Sutton into the backseat of the Polara and he and Photographer jump into the front seat. As they roar away Sutton looks out the back window: The young man is standing where they were standing, holding his camera like a suitcase, cursing and huffing like a man who just missed a train.

Photographer and Reporter howl, slap palms. That was close, Reporter says.

How the hell did Channel 11 find us?

I'm sure they were just driving along. Crime of opportunity.

If my editor sees Willie Sutton on TV—

Relax. The guy didn't get off a shot. He never even turned on his light.

Reporter glances over his shoulder. I hope I didn't hurt you back there, Mr. Sutton.

Nah kid. Nah. Felt like we were dancing. And it was a good lid-lifter for our next stop.

FIFTEEN

WILLIE LIES ON THE BACKSEAT, HANDS CUFFED BEHIND HIS
back. Two enormous cops fill up the front seat. The big one at
the wheel chews an unlit cigar, the bigger one riding shotgun
crams four sticks of Juicy Fruit into a freakishly small mouth.
We got your partner, Bigger Cop says over his shoulder. Case
you was wonderin.

I don't have any partner, Willie says.

You don't know John Marcus Bassett? Big Cop says.

Never heard of him.

His wife's the homely gal you was just havin pie and coffee
with.

You don't say.

And Bassett sure as hell knows you. He's givin detectives your
autobiography right this minute.

Then he's deranged. I tell you we've never met.

That's why you was with his wife.

She told me she was single.

You mean to say you were *makin* that broad.

That a crime?

Could be. Did you get a look atter?

She's a good person.

She looks like Lon Chaney. And she's in a family way.

That mean she's off the market?

Big Cop laughs, removes his unlit cigar, turns to Bigger Cop.
This guy's a riot.

They pull up to 240 Centre Street, a French Baroque palace

with statues and columns and a great big dome on top. Like some kind of Cop Vatican, Willie thinks, looking over the building. Popes and cops—they certainly think a lot of themselves.

On either side of the front door is a white stone lion. Ah the library—what Willie wouldn't give to be there right now. Just inside the front door a dozen cops in blue greatcoats stand around a high wooden desk. They greet Big Cop and Bigger Cop and congratulate them on the nice collar. One eyes Willie. Hope you enjoy your stay at the Centre Street Arms, he says—you probably won't need a wake-up call. They all roar with laughter, the fattest one haw-hawing so hard that he gets winded.

Big Cop and Bigger Cop drag Sutton into a blindingly bright room and stand him on a stage along with six other men. Heistmen, petermen, yeggs—Willie's colleagues. A group of civilians walks in. Bank employees. Willie recognizes them. They stand downstage, squinting up at him. He slouches, averts his eyes.

Sorry, they tell Big Cop and Bigger Cop. None of these men looks familiar.

Willie's costumes, his makeup and mustaches, it all worked.

Now in walks Porter.

Recognize any of these men? Bigger Cop says, inserting another stick of Juicy Fruit.

Porter scans the group, left to right. Yes.

Go on up and place your hand on the shoulder of any man you recognize.

Porter walks onstage, stands before each man. Making a little show of it. At last he comes to Willie. He stands with his nose inches from Willie's. Willie can smell his bay rum. Also the Stroganoff he had for lunch. Porter looks straight into Willie's eyes, three seconds. Four. He sets his hand on Willie's shoulder, turns to the cops. This man, he says. Then he turns away from the cops and cracks a smile only Willie can see. Name's Charlie, he says. Robber.

Big Cop and Bigger Cop take Willie into a side room with one metal table, one metal chair. Bigger Cop cuffs Willie's wrists behind his back. Big Cop pushes Willie into the chair. They stand on either side of him.

Bassett sang, Bigger Cop says.

I keep telling you, Willie says, I don't know who that is.

Bassett confessed to everythin, Big Cop says. He'd confess to working with Sacco and Vanzetti if we lettim, so it's over, Sutton, help yourself.

Bigger Cop rattles off details only Marcus could know. Banks, costumes, exact dollar amounts. Also, a complete inventory of Rosenthal and Sons. Willie shudders. Poor Marcus. They must have given him some beating.

Big Cop mentions the sixty thousand Willie got for Rosenthal and Sons, but he doesn't mention Dutch, because Willie never told Marcus about Dutch. Thank God. It's Dutch the cops want, Willie can tell. They have a suspicion. There aren't too many off men in New York who could handle that size haul. They scent big game, and they think Willie can lead them to it.

Sorry fellas, Willie says. There must be some confusion. Marcus is a writer. He must have told you the plot of the novel he's working on.

Big Cop and Bigger Cop look at each other. Believe this guy? Big Cop says.

Some bad novel, Bigger Cop says to Willie.

Yeah, Big Cop says. See, in the plot of this novel, an ex-con named William Francis Sutton, age thirty, dresses up as a New York City police officer and goes waltzin and traipsin into banks, tra-la-la, and sticks em up, which we frown upon novels about yeggs impersonatin cops, see? We take exception. That badge means somethin to us, see?

Big Cop lumbers around, stands before Sutton. He finally lights the cigar from the squad car. What's not in this *novel*, he says, what Bassett don't seem to know, and what you're goin to tell us right now, you Irish Town piece of shit, is where you hid the bank money and who helped you fence them jewels.

I want a lawyer.

These are the last words, the last intelligible words, Willie will speak for several days. A board or plank or two-by-four hits him at the base of the skull. His face smacks the table, his mind goes dark. Then—he's a boy again, leaping off an abandoned pier on the river. High into the air he flies, so high that he's diving into the sky. Gradually he tumbles backward and downward and then knifes through the cold black water. He hits something hard. Now someone is dragging him to the surface, back to the pier. It's Happy. And Eddie. Hey fellas what did I hit? And how the hell am I going to get away from these apes? Eddie reaches out, touches the base of Willie's skull. Sutty, you're bleedin. No, it's Willie reaching, touching. His fingers come away bright red, wet. He blinks, trying to clear his head.

Grab him, Mike.

Big Cop grabs Willie's ankles. Bigger Cop grabs Willie under the arms. They hoist him into the air, effortlessly, flop him onto the table, faceup, like a turkey they plan to carve. Then more cops rush into the room. There are shouts, curses, as they pin Willie's shoulders and hold down his feet and someone starts to whip Willie's stomach with a rubber tube or car hose. Willie shuts his eyes and screams. *I got rights.* They cram some kind of gag which isn't a gag into his mouth. They beat his legs, thighs, shins. He feels, then hears, one of his kneecaps shatter. He sees the women of Irish Town, the first warm days of May, draping rugs over fire escapes, whacking, whacking, and he feels something impossibly hot on his bare forearm, where his veins bulge. He tries to yank his arm away, but he can't, they've got him too tight. He smells his skin burning, and he knows, he just knows, it's Big Cop's cigar.

They hit him in the groin. Some kind of bowling pin or Indian club. Right on his dick. Ah fellas not that. He's out cold. He's gone. He's back—the burning flesh smell is now mixed with cop sweat. A voice asks if he's ready to talk. Damn right he's ready. He'll tell them anything. He's about to spill his guts, turn rat, which scares him more than whatever they might do next. Ratting scares him more than dying, so he bites down on this rag or sock or whatever it is they've shoved into his mouth and shakes his head back and forth, no no no.

Silence. Willie thinks maybe it's over. Maybe they realize he can't be cracked. Breathing hard, drizzling sweat, he keeps his eyes shut, feels the blood running down his face. Maybe.

He hears new voices in the room, knuckles being cracked. The new voices ask the old voices what seems to be the trouble. Then they start in. Fists. Big ones. Pummeling his ribs. The precinct boxing champs, Willie guesses. Middleweights, from the sound of them, and the feel. At least one light heavyweight. They're getting a good workout on Willie's torso. Jabs, hooks, rabbit punches. Each time one of Willie's ribs snaps it sounds like canvas being torn. The pain. It consumes him, obliterates him. His body feels as if it's made of fine spun glass and the cops keep smashing it over and over into smaller and smaller pieces, shards—how can there be anything left to smash? But they keep finding a new, pristine piece, smashing it. He's never felt such pain, and yet there's something familiar about the pain too. When has he been this anguished, forsaken, alone?

He remembers. Not in a conscious way, because he's only half conscious, but with a thin slice of his mind he remembers Bess. Being banished from her house. Meeting her father. Hearing she'd left the country. Watching her become the wife of another man. Learning that another man's baby was inside her. After all that pain, he tells himself between gulps of air, this pain won't kill him, and if it does, so be it. He screams at the middleweights.

G'head, g'head—do your fuckin worst! But he's delirious and he has a cop's underpants stuffed in his mouth. They can't understand.

Then he smiles. *That* they understand.

The blows stop.

They stand Willie up, tie a cord around his ankles. They blindfold him and take him from the room and drag him down the hall to the edge of a precipice. He feels an uprush of cool air. He must be at the top of a long staircase, which must lead to some kind of subbasement. He tries to back away.

Last chance, Sutton. Ready to talk?

He says nothing.

Bombs away, asshole.

He goes head over feet over head, lands on his broken ribs, on his shoulder, on his nose. His poor nose. Broken again. The cops scramble down the stairs. Resisting arrest, eh? Trying to escape, is it?

They all laugh and Willie hears one of them laughing so hard, haw haw, that he becomes winded.

Then they do it again.

Photographer turns down Centre Street.

Slow, Willie says. Slow.

There's a row of squad cars parked diagonally. They look just like the Polara, but they're black and white, with lights on top. Sutton points beyond the cars to the front steps, the two stone lions.

That building, he says. That's where they took me after they caught me and Marcus.

Photographer parks fifty yards away. I think this is as close as I can get, brother.

Sutton steps out, moves tentatively toward the building. He stops across the street, glowers at the officers and detectives who come and go between the stone lions. The old lion perisheth, he mutters. Lack of fuckin prey.

Reporter and Photographer come up behind him. What did they do when they brought you here? Photographer says.

What didn't they do?

Could you be more specific?

Put me in a lineup. Asked me a bunch of questions.

Did you talk?

Yeah, I talked. I told them to go fuck themselves.

Then what?

Then they gave me the beating to end all beatings.

Pigs, Photographer says under his breath. They love to bash skulls.

They do kid. It's true.

What was it like, brother? What was it like?

Sutton reaches into his breast pocket, takes out the fur-lined handcuffs. You want to know what it was like?

Yeah.

Put these on.

Photographer laughs.

That's what I thought, Sutton says. You're all about experience. Until experience comes knocking.

Photographer looks hurt. He hands his camera to Reporter, holds out his wrists. Sutton twirls a finger. Nah kid, turn around. Hands behind your back.

Photographer turns and Sutton cuffs his wrists. Three police officers slow their walk, watching the old man in the fur-collared trench coat slapping fur-lined handcuffs on the hippie in the buckskin jacket. And doesn't that old man look a lot like—Willie Sutton?

Cuffed, Photographer turns again. Sutton throws a crisp right at his midsection, stopping his fist an inch from Photographer's belt buckle. Photographer flinches, jumps back. Sutton smiles.

Now kid imagine that punch landed. Imagine another one

landing, and another, and fifty more. You can't breathe. You're
coughing blood. After a hundred punches to the breadbasket you're
ready to rat out your mom and dad and all the angels in heaven.

He throws a flurry of shadow punches, jab, feint, jab, each one
stopping just short of Photographer's belt buckle or face.
Photographer flinches at each one. Then Sutton steps off the curb,
into the street, bent into a fighter's crouch. He throws bigger shadow
punches at police headquarters. Right cross. Left. Uppercut.
Uppercut. Right hook.

I DIDN'T CRACK, DID I, YOU MOTHERFUCKERS?

Oh no, Reporter says.

I TOOK YOUR BEST SHOT, DIDN'T I, COPPERS?

Reporter puts his arms around Sutton, but Sutton wriggles loose,
keeps shouting. AND NOW HERE I AM! I'M BACK. I'M STILL
STANDING. AND WHERE THE FUCK ARE ALL OF YOU?
HUH? WHERE?

For the love of God, Mr. Sutton, please.

Willie opens one eye. He's lying on the floor of a holding cell.
He sees, just inside the cell door, a tin cup of water. It smells
like piss but he doesn't care. He takes a sip, or tries to. His throat
is closed, his Adam's apple is bruised, enlarged. There's also a
loud ringing in his ears. His eardrum is shattered. Now, above
the ringing he hears—sobbing? He peers around the cell, through
the bars, into a hall lit by one bare bulb. Across the hall, leaning
against the door of another cell, is Marcus. Poor Marcus. Willie
crawls to his cell door, presses his face against the bars. Marcus,
he whispers. Hey kid what'd they do to you? You okay? Hey
Marcus—the worst is over, I think.

Willie sees Marcus's waterbug eyes. They look different.
They've stopped—moving? And they're locked on Willie. Now
Willie notices that Marcus isn't bloody. Marcus isn't bruised.
Marcus doesn't have a mark on him. Through the pain, through

the ringing in Willie's ears, comes the revelation: Marcus did all that talking without suffering a single blow.

And he's still talking.

Willie I didn't know I didn't know if I'd known what they were going to do I wouldn't have said a word but they said they wouldn't hurt you they said it was the only way out Willie I'm so sorry I just couldn't face it they told me what they were going to do to me and I just couldn't—

Willie tests the hinges of his jaw. He spits up a bloody clump of something, which looks like an internal organ, and drags himself away from the door to the far corner of the cell. Curling into a ball he speaks three words, the last he'll ever speak to John Marcus Bassett.

You fuckin rat.

Now there are five cops outside police headquarters, watching a Boy Scout in a Brooks Brothers suit drag the old man who looks like Willie Sutton up the street as the handcuffed and buckskinned hippie follows.

You boys don't know, Sutton says, breathing hard. You just don't know. Until you're in that room, at the mercy of a half dozen sluggers with badges, you can't know. I've done a lot of things I'm not proud of. But the way I held up under that—I'm still proud. It might have been my finest hour.

He turns, gets in one more shout at the building. SEE YOU ROUND, RAT BASTARDS.

Mr. Sutton, I'm begging you.

They reach the Polara. Reporter guides Sutton into the backseat, as if placing him under arrest. He slams the door. Let's get out of here, he says to Photographer.

Get these cuffs off me, Photographer says.

I don't have the key.

Get it from Willie.

Let's get out of here first.

How am I supposed to drive? Photographer says.

I'll drive, Reporter says. Give me the keys.

They're in my pocket.

Reporter fishes the keys out of the buckskin jacket. He helps Photographer into the passenger seat, then runs around and gets in on the driver's side.

As they speed away Photographer wriggles his body to face Sutton in the backseat. Willie, man, unlock these handcuffs— they're cutting off my circulation.

Sutton, still breathing hard, stares out the window, not answering.

Willie, brother, come on. I'm starting to feel—panicky.

Is that a fact kid?

Willie.

How you enjoying the Willie Sutton Experience so far?

Photographer turns to Reporter. Tell him to uncuff me.

Right, because he does everything I say.

My trial was a joke, Sutton is saying. How do you not let in pictures of my caved-in face, my broken bones? My lawyer was all set to appeal, but after I was sentenced he got pinched himself.

What? Your lawyer was arrested, Mr. Sutton?

Albert Vitale. He was a former judge—it came out that he took a bribe while he was on the bench. From Arnold Rothstein.

The guy who fixed the 1919 World Series?

The same. They were tight. Guess who Rothstein's brother was married to? Mr. Untermyer's brother's granddaughter.

Willie, the cuffs. Please, brother.

What happened to Marcus, Mr. Sutton? Did they beat him too?

Nah. He was too busy talking for them to beat him. He thought if he ratted me out they'd go easy on him, but they still sent him away for twenty-five years. They turned him loose in '51 and he died a few months later. The Times *said he had two dollars and eighty-one cents to his name. He was found in a flop. Slumped over a typewriter. Fuckin rat.*

Willie on the bus to Sing Sing. February 1932. He can still hear the words of the judge, echoing off the marble pillars and the moon-pale walls of the courtroom.

Sutton, you are a type of criminal whose misdeeds have shocked the American people. You are regarded by the police of New York as one of the most dangerous men ever to prowl our streets. In point of daring, defiance of law, absolute disregard of property and life, your crimes are among the most brazen ever committed in this city. When we read about holdups of this kind in the Old West, we marvel. We say such crimes could no longer exist. But you are the equal of those bygone desperadoes. It is extremely hard for a New York judge to see before him a New York boy, raised in an environment that should have made you good rather than bad. But my duty is clear. Though you are only thirty, I must sentence you to a period of time greater than you are years of age.

Fifty years.

The bus pulls through the front gate of Sing Sing. Sutton looks over the grounds. The first thing he notices is the rose gardens. They're gone. And that's just one of fifty changes. Lawes has rebuilt the prison from bottom to top. He's turned it into a small city, with new industrial workshops, a new five-story cellblock, a new twenty-five-foot wall.

Of course some things are the same. As guards lead Willie into his office, Lawes beams. Welcome back, asshole.

Willie asks about the gardens.

We installed new plumbing. The flowers had to go.

Must have killed Chapin to see his roses bulldozed.

It did. We planted *him* last year.

Several more things are just as Willie remembers. The food,

for instance. Cornmeal for breakfast, beans for lunch, a gristly disc of pork for dinner. It's not just the same menu, Willie suspects it might be the same actual food from seven years ago.

Lawes assigns Willie to the shoe shop, mending soles. Fifty years, he thinks. Marching up and down the hill from the shoe shop to the dining room, marching back to his cell at the end of another long dismal day, Willie says over and over and over: Fifty years. With no Chapin, no gardens, no Eddie, no end point, it's more than he can fathom. More than he can do.

He studies the new layout of the prison, making a mental map. Eight portals stand between him and the outside. His cell door is one. Then a flight of stairs and a locked wooden door. Then a long hall and a padlocked metal gate. Then another hall and another locked wooden door. Then another padlocked gate. Then the dining room and another locked wooden door. Then a final padlocked gate. Then the cellar, on the far side of which is a giant locked steel door leading to the yard.

Even if Willie could somehow get through all eight portals, he'd then be at the outer wall. How do you climb a twenty-five-foot wall with guards standing along the top holding Thompsons?

Two months pass as Willie wrestles with this question.

One day a trusty lets slip to Willie that a single guard tower is unmanned overnight. This makes no sense to Willie. Until it makes perfect sense. The papers are filled with stories about Lawes's lavish remodeling. Now, the Great Depression worsening by the day, Lawes must need to cut costs. Why pay guards to sit in each tower, all night, when you've spent millions to build an escape-proof cellblock?

So Willie now thinks he knows the weakest point in the wall. But he's still faced with the problem of how to scale it. And he still hasn't solved the problem of how to get there from his cell. The eight portals. Another four months pass as he struggles with these problems.

In the late summer of 1932, sitting in the yard and mourning the absent roses, Willie looks up and sees Johnny Egan coming from the machine shop. Dark, handsome, Egan looks a bit like Happy, though he acts a bit like Marcus. Willie doesn't let himself dwell on this, however, because Egan's a trusty, meaning he's free to roam the prison grounds, free to flit in and out of the machine shops, which Willie now realizes are stocked with tools.

During yardout Egan likes to play handball. So Willie sets about learning the game. He becomes good enough to team up with Egan in prison tourneys. He gains Egan's respect, loyalty, plays doubles with him in the 1932 Sing Sing Championships. After one come-from-behind victory Willie wraps a sweaty arm around Egan's neck and says he might need a few things one day. He whispers a possible shopping list.

You crashing out? Egan whispers.

Willie doesn't answer.

Count me in, Egan says.

I work alone kid.

I'm in—or no help.

There's no sense arguing. Even if Egan could get the items on Willie's shopping list, the tools needed to get through the eight portals, Willie still can't imagine how to scale that wall.

It's Egan who finds a way. In November 1932, making his rounds, Egan passes through the cellar below the dining room and sees two wooden ladders behind some pallets. Each ladder is twelve feet long, he tells Willie. Not long enough to reach the top of the wall.

Unless taped together, Willie says.

So there it is. The plan is clear, and the time is now. Who knows how long those ladders will be there? Willie gives Egan his shopping list. For the doors and gates he'll need a torque wrench, hook pick, shim. For the bars of his cell door he'll need a small hacksaw.

I'm in, Egan says. Right?

Willie shakes his head.

I'm in, Egan says, or no dice.

Willie sighs. Fine.

The next day, as Willie and Egan practice their forehands, Egan slips Willie the picklocks and hacksaw and shim. Willie tucks them under his shirt, inside his waistband. Playing handball with tools inside his waistband—not easy. The hacksaw in particular cuts up Willie's back.

Later, after lights-out, he runs the hacksaw along a lower bar of his cell door. It cuts the bar as easily as it cut his back. He saws clean through, knocks the bar out, and props the bar back in place with chewing gum. The next morning at breakfast he tells Egan to get himself a hacksaw, do the same thing to one bar of his cell, then wait.

Willie knows he can pick the locks on all eight portals. He's that good. Except the last one. That big steel door in the cellar, leading to the yard, is beyond his talents, beyond anything Doc taught him. For that one he'll need a key. He gets a lifer to slip the master key off the head keeper's chain, while the keeper is in the showers, and make a wax impression. In exchange Willie promises that, when he's out, he'll drop a wad of cash on the lifer's family. Willie still has jars of money buried all over the city.

Using the wax impression Egan is able to sneak into a machine shop and cut a crude copy.

At the start of December Willie and Egan stand on the handball court, pretending to play, but in fact discussing what day would be best for a crash-out. Willie wants to go Tuesday, December 13, but Egan shakes his head. Thirteen is his unlucky number. All the bad things in Egan's life, including most of his arrests, have happened on the thirteenth of the month.

Fine, Willie says. The twelfth.

Egan smiles, serves a bullet into the wall. Willie dives to return the serve, falls, reopens the cuts on his back.

When the chosen day comes, Willie and Egan sit side by side at lunch, going over the plan one last time. Willie whispers that they'll have to split up soon after the crash-out. Egan says that won't be a problem. He has a brother on the West Side of Manhattan who can hide him.

They exchange a look. Egan nods. Willie nods. See you tonight kid.

The day passes like a decade. Willie can't focus on his work. He almost sews a sole to his finger. At last, after dinner, back in his cell, he lies down on his cot and tries to slow his heart. It's punching him in the throat. His heart knows—if he and Egan make one mistake, catch one bad break, the guards will mow them down, with pleasure. He pictures the newspaper headlines, writes the stories in his mind. From under his pillow he pulls out a letter from Eddie, who's finally been released from Dannemora. *Looking for jobs, Sutty. None to be had. People are still talking about you and Marcus. Good for you kid.*

The keeper on Willie's tier passes the cell door. He stops. You feelin okay, Sutton?

Yes sir.

You're sweatin.

Touch of the grippe. I guess. Sir.

Hm.

They study each other.

What's that on your shirt?

My shirt sir?

Those red marks.

Where sir?

There. On your side. And back. Looks like blood.

Oh. Cut myself playing handball sir.

Handball?

Yeah. Sir.

Hm.

Three seconds. Five. Eternity.

G'night, Sutton.

Night sir.

Five minutes. Ten.

Willie creeps to the cell door, kicks out the bar. Sucking in his gut and hunching his shoulders he somehow squeezes through the hole. He can't believe—*he's standing outside his cell. Unsupervised.* One portal down, seven to go.

He runs down to Egan's cell just as Egan is sliding through his own hole. They stand as they used to stand on the handball court, waiting for serve. Crouched, tensed, they can hear the keepers on the tier below.

Now what the hell do you think Roosevelt's goin to do that Hoover couldn't?

I'll tell you what he won't do. He won't gun down Army vets in the street.

Well now that's a point, that's a point.

Willie and Egan tiptoe to the end of the tier, down three flights of stairs to the ground floor. The second portal, a wooden door, has a standard six-pin Corbin lock. Every other house in America has a Corbin. Willie has picked dozens of Corbins and this one takes all of three minutes. Egan laughs like a loon. Willie claps a hand over Egan's mouth.

The third portal is a padlocked gate. Willie takes out his shim, pops it.

He and Egan creep down a hall to the fourth portal, another wooden door, another Corbin. His fingers warmed up, Willie picks this one in a minute flat.

The fifth portal, another padlocked gate, is also no match for the shim.

They're in the dining room. Willie's breathing is so loud, he can't believe it's not waking the cellblock. He and Egan slip among the empty tables, down another stairway, to the sixth portal, the last wooden door, a Yale lock, even easier than a Corbin.

The seventh portal is a padlocked gate. Willie shims the lock, but the shim breaks. Shit, he whispers. Then he remembers—there are no more padlocks.

They enter the cellar. There. The ladders. They tape them together and carry the makeshift ladder to the steel door. Willie holds his breath as he slides the duplicate key into the lock. It doesn't fit.

So that's how it ends. With a faulty fake key. Son of a—

Egan tries the handle. Unlocked. Slowly the eighth portal falls open. The yard is eerie, quiet. A frosty night. The stars look like a child's silver jacks. They sprint to the wall, staying between the beams of the searchlights, and set the ladder. Egan goes first. Then Willie. At the top is a catwalk. Willie braces for the twenty-five-foot drop. He can already feel his ankle breaking. But the grass is surprisingly soft. Other than a twisted knee he comes through the jump fine. Egan too. They dash up a dirt incline to the road, where their getaway car is waiting. A familiar face behind the wheel.

Photographer leans against his window. Are we almost there?

Almost, Sutton says.

Where are we going again?

The Sundowner Hotel, Sutton says. My first stop after I crashed out of Sing Sing. Forty-Seventh and Eighth.

Back to Times Square. Uh-huh. Great. We're officially driving in circles.

Life goes in circles kid. Why shouldn't we?

The radio squawks. Reporter turns it down. Mr. Sutton, exactly how did you crash out of Sing Sing? There's very little in the files.

Sutton puts a Chesterfield between his lips. Everything you ever saw in a prison movie, it started with me. Before me, you never heard about guys using hacksaws. After me, it was all the rage.

What I wouldn't give, Photographer says, for a hacksaw right now.

I made a friend, Sutton says. Johnny Egan. He got me some saws, picks. Then it was just a matter of arranging for someone to be waiting outside the prison.

Who did you get?

Bess.

Reporter hits the brakes. Photographer sits up. You're shitting us, Willie.

She read about my trial, of course. She came to see me my first month in the joint. Back then the visiting room at Sing Sing was pretty lax. No partitions, no guards monitoring conversations. So I told her straight, I was going crazy, I was crashing out, and I needed her help. I said I'd write her the exact date in a letter. Our mail was censored, so I promised to put it in code. Few weeks later, middle of a long rambling letter, I wrote: Do you remember that time we went walking at Coney Island, the stroke of midnight, December 12? She told her husband she had a bridge game with some girlfriends, snuck up to Sing Sing, picked us up outside the wall. She drove me and Egan down to Times Square, dropped us at the Sundowner—even brought us a change of clothes and some cash. And she was back home in four hours.

What was it like, Mr. Sutton? Seeing her again?

They stop at a red light. Sutton looks across the street. A coffee shop with a neon sign flashing in the window. COCKTAILS. COCK-TAILS. COCKTAILS. Outside the coffee shop sits a double-parked Dodge, no one in the driver's seat, a woman in the passenger seat. Sutton can tell. He can see it in her eyes. The woman is waiting for a man. A man that she loves.

Mr. Sutton?

Willie?

It felt like a dream, boys.

SIXTEEN

WILLIE SIGNS THE REGISTER MR. JOSEPH LAMB. HE TELLS
Egan to sign as Edward Garfield. Then he walks Egan up to his
room.

That was a real nice lady who picked us up, Egan says.

Yeah.

Awful pretty. How do you know her again?

Look, Egan, just go in your room and stay there. Don't come
out for anything. I'll come get you in the morning.

What if I want to go for a walk?

Absolutely not.

What if I need some air?

Open a window.

I get claustrophobic, Willie.

You were just in prison, Egan.

Willie looks hard at Egan, realizing how little he knows about
this kid. Most of their time together has been spent playing
handball. They've barely spoken fifty words. Willie doesn't even
know what crime landed Egan in Sing Sing. A sick feeling comes
over Willie. He remembers the first time he saw Egan, how he
was reminded of Marcus.

Closing Egan's door Willie staggers down to his room, falls
onto the bed, blacks out. Sunlight streaming through the dirty
muslin curtains wakes him three hours later. He bolts upright,
trying to remember. It all seems unreal. Egan, the portals, the
ladders. Bess. He runs out to a coffee stand and buys two cups
of coffee, four rolls heavy with butter, a carton of Chesterfields,

and all the newspapers. Now it seems real. He and Egan are on every front page. Lawes tells the papers that the three keepers on duty during the crash-out—Wilfred Brennan, Samuel Rubin, and Philip Dengler—are fired.

Willie lights a Chesterfield. Good luck finding new jobs, fellas. There's a Depression on, you know.

Willie pads down to Egan's room, knocks.

No answer.

He knocks again. Egan, he whispers. Time to go.

Nothing.

He knocks harder.

Silence.

The front desk clerk, who's just come on duty, says Mr. Garfield's room key isn't in its cubbyhole. He must be out.

Out?

Willie sits in the lobby, watching the front door. One hour. He goes back upstairs to his room, watches the street from his window. Two hours. He can actually feel his nerve endings fraying. What if Egan doesn't come back? What if the cops have already caught him? How long can Egan hold out before he tells them where to find Willie? How long should Willie wait before bolting the Sundowner? He doesn't want to abandon his partner, and he doesn't want to leave behind a loose end, especially a loose end that knows so much. But Egan might be talking to the cops right now. The cops might already be on their way.

Just before noon Willie looks out his window and sees Egan staggering up to the hotel. He runs downstairs and bull-rushes the kid.

I *told* you not to leave the room.

Hadda leave, Willie, I was gawin stir-crazy.

You stink of gin.

Thass a durry lie. I wiss dringin scotch.

Egan, do you realize the chance you took?

Din take nuttin. Needed a dring, Willie, my nerfs was shot. Thurz a cute lil joint rouna corner, come on ahl showya.

Willie leads Egan upstairs, pours him onto his bed. Pulls up a chair and watches Egan snore. The ninth portal.

Sutton, Reporter and Photographer stand before the Sundowner, a narrow four-story building wedged between two buildings that lean like palm trees. I can't believe it's still here, Sutton says.

He peers up the steep staircase that leads to a razor-scratched, finger-smudged glass door. The same glass door he steered Egan through thirty-seven years ago.

Back in 1932, Sutton says, a bed in this rattrap cost a dollar. Imagine? Clean sheets were an extra twenty cents. But that first night, as far as I was concerned, this was the fuckin Plaza. I never slept so sound. Then Egan gave me a scare. Went on a bender. After he came back, after I put him to bed, I heard sirens. I thought for sure he'd been made. But it was some poor girl down the hall—she slashed her wrists. So there we were, two escaped cons in a flophouse crawling with cops. It was touch and go for a few hours.

Willie?

Sutton turns to face Photographer. Yeah kid?

Can you please, please take off these handcuffs?

Oh, say, I completely forgot.

Sutton reaches into his pocket, comes out with the key. He uncuffs Photographer.

Hallelujah, Photographer says, rubbing his wrists.

Yeah. Hallelujah. That's what Willie used to say when they took off the bracelets.

Reporter pulls the map from his breast pocket. Our next stop isn't far from here, he says. West Fifty-Fourth.

Former home of Chateau Madrid, Sutton says. Headquarters of Dutch Schultz—who helped me solve my Egan problem.

* * *

After the cops carry the girl with the slashed wrists out of the Sundowner, Willie slips into her room. Just as he'd hoped, there's makeup all over the dresser. And a bottle of hydrogen peroxide. And some bloody razors. He holds out the tail of his shirt, scoops everything into it, hurries back to his room. He sits before a mirror, using the dead girl's peroxide to make himself blond. Next he uses her eyebrow pencil, her Pan-Cake makeup. Finally he goes down to Egan's room and, while Egan's passed out, shaves his head.

Later that night Willie and Egan slip into Central Park. Egan keeps lookout while Willie digs up one of his jars. Ten grand. Willie is amazed by how much better, safer, he feels with money in his pocket. They ride the subway to the Lower East Side. At an all-night speak on Avenue A they eat their first proper meal in two days. Willie lets Egan have two shots of whiskey, to steady his nerves, but no more.

Why are we in this part of town? Egan says.

I read once that cops don't like to come down here. Too many gypsies. So it's the ideal place for what we need to do.

After dinner they roam the dark streets and back alleys, looking in the windows of parked cars. At last they find a Chrysler with keys in the ignition. A fat woman in a quilted housecoat, sitting on a fire escape, smokes a clay pipe and eyes them. When she goes inside they jump into the Chevy and speed away.

Shifting into third gear, flying up East River Drive, Willie tells Egan it's time for them to go their separate ways. Where's that brother of yours?

Egan gives Willie an address in Hell's Kitchen. Willie zooms over to Tenth, weaving in and out of traffic, swings a right, spots the number on a mailbox. A two-family house, a Christmas wreath on the left door. He parks, almost knocking over a trash can.

Stay out of sight, he tells Egan. Stay off the sauce. I'll be in touch.

Willie keeps the motor running while Egan walks to the front door, the door without a wreath, and knocks. A ginger-haired man opens. He and Egan exchange a few calm words. The ginger-haired man then pushes Egan aside and comes running down the walk, yelling at Willie: Would you mind telling me what you think you're doing?

Keep your voice down, mister. I'm dropping off your brother.

The hell you are. I'd sooner you took a shit on my doorstep.

Egan comes down the walk, hands on his head. My own brother, he wails.

Shut up, the brother and Willie both tell Egan.

The brother bends at the waist, squints through the car window at Willie. Mr. Sutton I assume? Nice to meet you. I've followed your exploits with some admiration. Fecking banks. But you may not leave this sot on my hands. Off you go.

Willie stares straight ahead. Sorry, friend. I've gone as far as I can with him.

I'm afraid you've got a little farther to go, friend. Or else I'll give the cops your license plate and whereabouts, and I'll do it with a clear conscience, I can promise you that.

Willie, still staring straight ahead, thinks. Then nods. Egan gets back in the car.

Willie speeds away.

Guess you're stuck with me, Egan says.

You must have other family, Egan. How about your parents?

Ma died giving birth to me.

Uh-huh. Dad?

Whoever he was, he ran off years ago.

Any more siblings?

Five brothers.

Any of them local?

Let's see. There's Charlie. He's a bum, but he'll take me in. Bang a right at the corner.

Charlie the Bum meets them at the curb. Clearly he's had a phone call from the previous brother. He holds out his hand like a traffic cop. He's not accepting delivery either. He turns the hand over, palm to the sky. He's a little short of cash and he's hoping Willie Sutton, the famous bank robber, can float him a loan. Or else he'll be forced to call the cops. Now. Willie gives him five hundred bucks, speeds away.

Egan cradles his head. Willie considers slowing the car, kicking Egan out. But he can't help feeling for a guy shunned by his brothers. Name another brother, Willie says.

Egan thinks. Sean, he says. Yeah. Sean. He's probably forgiven me for that thing that time.

Sean lives on the other side of town. Willie cuts through Central Park, past a large Hooverville. More than a tent city, it's a tent metropolis, with streets, neighborhoods, dogs, cats. And it's not just hoboes living in this Hooverville. There are whole families. Good families. Willie brakes. He and Egan both stare. Fuckin Hoover, Willie says.

Yeah, Egan says.

Pig-face. Pawn of Rockefeller. Lackey to all those Wall Street boys. Did you know old Herbert was a millionaire before he was thirty?

Really? Is that a fact? Herbert Who?

They come at last to Sean's house, a handsome brownstone. Sparkling clean front stoop, trim red window boxes with orange geraniums surviving the winter. Sean, apparently, is the most successful of the Egans. This time Willie and Egan are met at the curb by Sean's wife. She says she'd sooner take in a wild dog, oozing with rabies, before she'd take in this sorry excuse for a brother-in-law.

She screams at Willie: He was *fine* where he was. We had a shindig the night he got convicted. Why did you help him break out?

He helped me.

And why is he bald?

It's a long story.

Well you're stuck with him. May God have mercy on you.

Sutton stands outside the former location of Chateau Madrid, now an Indian restaurant. What's that smell? he says.

Curry, Photographer says, rummaging in his cloth purse. And vomit.

Amazing, Sutton says, how certain parts of New York smell just like prison.

And what's the significance of this little corner of heaven, Willie?

Let's go in that bar and I'll tell you.

Reporter and Photographer look. A bar they hadn't noticed.

Jimmy's? Oh, Mr. Sutton, that place looks—awful.

It's seen better days. But I told you, Willie needs a hair of the dog and this joint meets my number one requirement for a bar.

What's that?

It's open.

Willie pulls into the alley behind Chateau Madrid. He and Egan slip through a side door, through the kitchen, into a dark barroom. A hanging lamp glows above the bar, where a bartender in a white shirt, with green sleeve garters, leans over a newspaper.

Willie clears his throat. The bartender looks up.

I'd like to see Dutch Schultz, Willie says.

He's out.

Bo Weinberg then?

Bo know you?

No.

Then he's out too.

I'm Willie Sutton.

Yeah right.

Willie steps into the light, pulling Egan by the elbow. The bartender looks at them, then at the front page. Then again at them. His eyes grow wide—a blond Willie Sutton and a bald Johnny Egan. Well if that don't beat all, he says.

Bartender slips through a hidden door in the bar back and returns moments later with Bo. Willie has never met Bo, but he's seen his mug shot in the papers many times and he knows the man's reputation. The most feared killer in New York. Bo took out Legs Diamond just last year.

What mug shots and reputation don't convey, can't convey, is Bo's size. Every bit of Bo is big. His head, his hands, his lips— even his chin is an overgrown bulb of flesh. Willie can't imagine how he shaves that thing. Bo motions for Willie to come back to the office. Willie feels his feet moving involuntarily. He tells Egan to stay.

The office is the size of a corner booth at the Silver Slipper. A large English desk barely leaves room for a hat rack and filing cabinet. Bo now sits behind the desk. You take a big chance, he says. Coming here. Heart of midtown. Some balls.

Dutch once said I should look him up if I'm ever in trouble. I'm in trouble.

So I hear. What do you need? Money?

No.

What then?

I need you to take something off my hands. Something that's slowing me down.

Willie jerks his head toward the barroom. Bo's eyebrows rise. You're joking.

I wish I was. He's a drunkard and possibly a mental case. His family wants no part of him and I'm starting to understand why.

This is your sales pitch?

I can't take him with me, but I can't leave him on the street. I need to deposit him with someone I can trust, someone who'll keep an eye on him, give him a job, a meal, maybe a smack when he needs it.

Why not ask for the moon?

I don't need the moon. I need this.

Bo turns in his chair, stares at a wall calendar. The last page of 1932. It's curled up at the corner.

Dutch has friends on the police force, you know.

I've heard.

Some of these friends—they work at 240 Centre.

Oh?

One night Dutch and I were making our monthly payoffs, and these friends mentioned that they happened to be at Centre Street when none other than Willie Sutton was brought in. What a pounding this Sutton took, these friends tell us—anyone else would have ratted out Dutch. Now these friends are no fans of Willie Sutton. These friends are on the job and do not like people impersonating cops. Still, after witnessing this beating, and briefly participating in it, these friends spoke of Sutton with what can only be called *respect*.

Willie's eyes water with pride. He worries that his makeup will run.

Bo takes a deep breath, lets it out fast as if blowing out a candle. Leave the kid, he says. Be on your way. Debts are debts and Dutch always pays his.

Willie nods, turns to go.

But Sutton.

Willie stops.

Let this be hello and goodbye.

Sutton looks down the barroom. Ten stools with red leatherette tops, two of them occupied by bearded men, their arms folded on the bar, their heads on their arms. They look as if they're playing hide-and-seek. The bartender, apparently, is It. He hides at the far end of the bar, reading the newspaper. He looks up, sees Sutton and Reporter and Photographer, frowns. He slides down the bar, past the sleeping regulars, sets out three napkins. What'll you have?

Jameson, Sutton says. Neat.

Nothing for me, Reporter says.

I'd love a Jameson, says Photographer, still rubbing his wrists. He sets his cloth purse on the bar.

Sutton looks down the bar at the sleeping men. I remember, he says, in the Depression of '14, thousands of men with no jobs, no homes, moved into saloons. The saloon owners begged the cops to roust them, but the cops wouldn't. Better the saloons, cops figured, than the streets.

Reporter opens his notebook, uncaps his pen. Um, Mr. Sutton, back to the escape. You and Egan went to the Sundowner, then came here—or near here. Why?

I had to get clear of Egan. He was dead weight, slowing me down. So I dropped him with Bo Weinberg, right-hand man of Dutch.

Bartender stops pouring the Jameson, looks up. Say now. Are you Willie Sutton?

I am.

Holy shit. Willie the Actor?

Yeah.

Put her there pal.

Sutton shakes Bartender's hand. This your place?

Sure. O'Keefe's the name. James O'Keefe. At your service. What brings you in, friend?

I'm giving these boys the nickel tour. Meet Good Cop and Bad Cop.

Reporter and Photographer wave limply.

Merry Christmas, Bartender says. Now how does my gin mill feature in the life and times of Willie the Actor?

I used to frequent a place next door.

Chateau Madrid. The Dutchman's place. Of course. Willie the Goddamn Actor. What an honor. This round's on the house.

In that case, friend, start pouring the second round. And won't you join us?

Twist my arm.

Reporter rubs his eyes wearily, flips through his files. Mr. Sutton? You were saying? Egan?

Sutton clinks glasses with Photographer and Bartender. To freedom, Sutton says. Fáilte abhaile, Bartender says. They throw down the whiskey. Photographer smacks his palm on the bar. Holy shit, he says. Who drinks this stuff?

Half of Brooklyn, Sutton says. All of Ireland—including newborns.

Mr. Sutton? Reporter says.

Yeah, kid, yeah.

Egan? Bo Weinberg?

Right. So I dropped Egan with Bo, hereabouts, and then I skipped town.

And what happened to Egan?

Two months later he was dead.

Dead?

Shot in a speak not far from here. Strange. The Times *said he had a coat check in his pocket—the number thirteen on it. Egan told me once that thirteen was his unlucky number. I guess he wasn't kidding. Come to think of it, I dropped him off on this block—the thirteenth of December.*

Who shot him?

The cops never made an arrest.

Reporter closes his notebook, narrows his eyes. That sure worked out well for you, Mr. Sutton. Your dead weight suddenly turns up—dead.

Kid you are sounding more like a cop every minute.

It just seems very convenient.

What can I say? I was the kiss of death in 1932. Bo Weinberg
also died not long after he met me.
Who killed Bo?
Bugsy Siegel, Bartender says.
Sutton nods. Dutch put out the contract, but Bugsy did the hit.
How come?
Dutch got wind that Bo was a rat.

Willie drives to Philadelphia, parks the stolen Chrysler under a
bridge. He takes off the license plates, sets the car ablaze, then
walks. And walks. He stops at a sign: TO LET. He asks for a room,
tells the landlady his name is James Clayton. The address is 4039
Chestnut Street.

At a corner market he stocks up. Canned tuna, chocolate bars,
cigarettes, coffee. He swings by the local bookstore, buys a few
bestsellers, a few Russian novels. Bolts the door to his room and
waits.

After three days, a soft knock. He slides back the Judas hole.
He throws open the door. What the hell kept you, he says.

Came as soon as I got your message.

Eddie drops a heavy duffel and stands before Willie, arms
outstretched. They hug, clap each other hard on the back. Willie
pulls Eddie into his room, locks the door. Let me look at you,
he says.

The years of prison and unemployment have chipped away at
Eddie. His face is leaner, harder. His blue eyes are washed out,
his blond hair is going thin. He notices changes in Willie too,
of course. He points at Willie's blond locks. What the?

You know I always wanted to be just like you, Ed.

Eddie laughs, punches Willie's shoulder. Then he rummages
in his duffel, pulls out a bottle of Jameson. Uncorking it, he takes
a swig. To freedom, he says, passing the bottle to Willie, who
takes a double swig and laughs for the first time in a year.

They sit up all night, drinking whiskey, filling each other in on the last five years. Things they couldn't say in letters.

Dannemora got bad after you left, Sutty. I was in some of the worse battles of my life. Kill-or-be-killed battles. When they cut me loose I made myself a promise: I'd never go back. I got a job moppin floors, cleanin bathrooms at a luncheonette. I showed up early, stayed late, took all the shit my boss could dish out. I saved my pennies, even met a girl. I was actually kind of happy. Then one day this fella walks in, starts harassin this woman. I don't know if he's her boyfriend, husband, what. I don't much care. He grabs her by the neck, starts draggin her out the door. What am I supposed to do? I knocked him cold. My boss sacked me on the spot. It was all I could do not to coldcock him too as I walked out. That was three months ago. I aint been able to find another job.

Willie waves the newspaper. You're not alone.

Thirteen million out of work, Eddie says. People hoardin gold. Fifty banks goin bust every week.

Food riots, Sutton says. I never thought I'd see the day.

Every man for himself, Sutty. Same as ever, only more so. We need to get ours while there's anythin to be got.

I made myself a promise too, Ed. I'm not going back to the joint either.

Then we'll just have to make sure we don't get caught.

Eddie unzips his duffel again. He pulls out a cop uniform. He stands, holds the uniform against his body. Still a forty regular?

Bartender wipes the bar top with a filthy rag. Another round, Willie?

Sure. A quick one though. Good Cop and Bad Cop look like they're ready to blow. What do we owe you?

Photographer jumps forward. We've got this, Willie.

Yes, Reporter says, put your money away, Mr. Sutton.

Photographer reaches into his cloth purse, takes out his billfold, opens it—stares. Wait, he says. What the. I could have sworn I had twenty bucks in here.

Reporter turns. Sutton turns.

When I paid for the handcuffs, Photographer says, I'm sure I saw two tens in here.

Don't worry about it, Sutton says. My treat.

Sutton reaches into his breast pocket, pulls out a ten.

I thought you only had checks, Reporter says.

My friend Donald must have slipped me some cash when I wasn't looking. Sweet guy.

Sutton slaps the ten on the bar.

Willie, Bartender says, I'll only take your money on one condition. You sign it, so I can hang it over the till.

Deal, Sutton says.

Bartender hands Sutton a pen.

What should I write?

Write: To the boys at Jimmy's. That's NOT where the money is.

Willie signs, puts the pen in his breast pocket. He feels the white envelope. He takes it out, stares at it.

What's in the envelope? Reporter asks.

My release papers.

Photographer holds his billfold upside down, shakes it. I know I had twenty bucks in here.

In their first month together Willie and Eddie take down eleven banks and make off with three hundred thousand dollars. If Willie and Marcus went on a spree, this is a frenzy.

Willie's disguises don't fool the cops this time. His style has become his signature. The cops even give him a nickname, which the newspapers find irresistible. Willie the Actor. Sometimes newspapers shorten it to the Actor. As in—THE ACTOR STRIKES AGAIN.

Willie doesn't care for the nickname. It's trivial, he thinks. Not to mention inaccurate. An actor is someone who plays at make-believe. An actor is someone who says lines that aren't real, because they aren't his. When Willie walks into a bank he's not playing, he's dead serious. He means, and owns, every word.

Between jobs he haunts secondhand bookstores around Philadelphia, buys up all kinds of books about acting. Some of what he reads eases his mind. He learns that the greatest actor-playwright ever was a thief—and a Willie. Arrested in Stratford for poaching, Shakespeare had to lam it to London. That's when he got into the theater. Willie reads that acting isn't about what you say, it's about what you don't say, what you vividly withhold. The audience doesn't want to know you, they want to feel that *desire* to know you. Since you never fully satisfy that desire, never come clean, acting is the opposite of confessing. Willie underlines this passage in pen.

In March 1933 Willie sits with one of his acting books in his lap and a new Philco console radio beside his chair. Eddie lies on the sofa smoking. The new president, Franklin D. Roosevelt, a month after an attempt on his life, has declared a nationwide bank *holiday*. To quell the panic in the streets, to stem the tide of people storming overextended banks and demanding their money, Roosevelt has ordered every bank in the country shut for four days. He's also scheduled a fireside chat to explain the bank holiday and what comes next. Willie and Eddie, like forty million others, listen.

Turn it up, Willie says.

My friends. I want to talk for a few minutes with the people of the United States about banking. To talk with the comparatively few who understand the mechanics of banking, but more particularly with the overwhelming majority of you.

In other words, Eddie says, all you idiots.

It is safer to keep your money in a reopened bank than it is to keep it under the mattress.

Except the ones we hit—eh, Sutty?

You people must have faith. We do not want and will not have another epidemic of bank failures.

Yeah right, Eddie scoffs.

Let me make it clear to you that the banks will take care of all needs, except of course for the hysterical demands of hoarders.

Eddie cackles, aims a finger gun at the radio. Hysterical demands—like, say, open the vault or I'll blow your fuckin head off.

The national bank holiday is followed by many state bank holidays. It seems a good time for Willie and Eddie to take their own holiday. Tweak their script, streamline their routine. Make their work more efficient. In particular they discuss how to deal with heroes. Nothing concerns Willie more.

It comes up about every fourth job. Some manager or teller or guard refuses to cooperate. Because Willie doesn't want to hurt anyone, these moments fill him with dread. Anything can happen, and sooner or later something will. Willie and Eddie talk it over and decide that bank employees, like people in the old neighborhood, are clannish. When an employee acts up, they agree, it's no use threatening him. Better to threaten his fellow employees.

Eddie suggests another adjustment. Deadlier force. People aren't afraid of pocket guns anymore. They've seen too many movies. But there's something about a Thompson—that fat drum, that skinny barrel. And nothing shuts people up faster than a sawed-off shotgun.

Finally Willie and Eddie decide that jobs will run smoother if they bring in a third man. It's too much for Eddie, helping Willie control the employees, collecting the money, *and* driving.

I got just the guy, Eddie says. Joey Perlango. We were in the same cellblock at Dannemora.

Perlango? *You* recommending a *Dago*?

What can I say? He's a right guy.

October 1933. In a roadside diner Willie and Eddie have their first meet with Perlango. A few years older than them, he has droopy eyelids and a nose that looks as if it's been ironed, clearly the work of dozens of boxing gloves. His teeth are large, white, even, but separated by wide spaces. When he smiles Willie thinks of the laces on a football. From the side pocket of his metallic gray suit, which shines like the fenders of a new car, Perlango removes a fingernail clipper and uses it while Willie talks.

So, Joey, what we have in mind—

Snap. A fingernail flies across the table, hangs in midair like a little crescent moon, lands in the sugar bowl. Call me Plank.

Sorry? Willie says.

Everyone calls me Plank. Even my folks.

How come?

Cause one time I hit a guy. *Snap.* With a plank.

Another fingernail goes flying, lands on Willie's sleeve. He picks it off, looks at Eddie.

The waitress appears. Willie orders three coffees.

I'll have *tea*, Plank says.

Willie looks away. Tea. Jesus.

The waitress brings their order, goes away. Willie leans across the table. We're planning to hit the Corn Exchange, Plank. Right here in Philly.

They give a fountain pen.

Huh?

With every new account. They give a fountain pen.

Uh-huh. Fine. If you say so.

Willie unfolds a map. With a red pen he marks it with x's, numbers. He puts an x where Plank will park.

I go in first, Willie says. Dressed as a cop. Minutes later I let in Eddie, also dressed as a cop. Ten minutes later, Plank, you start the car and drive here. We hop in, you drive away, along this route. The whole job shouldn't take fifteen minutes.

Plank pours his tea into his saucer, blows on it. What do I wear?

What do you—what?

What costume.

You don't wear any costume.

Plank looks into his saucer. Oh.

Something wrong?

Well. I thought I was goin to be a letter carrier, a fireman, somethin. It sounded like fun when Eddie told me.

No. You drive. That's all. But that's a lot. That's a very important job, Plank.

Plank nods. No one says anything for a minute. Plank lifts his saucer to his lips, slurps. How about a chauffeur costume? he says. You know. Cause I'm drivin.

I think you're missing the point, Willie says. No one's going to see you but us.

Plank nods. But he looks crushed.

Later Willie tells Eddie that they can do better than Plank.

If we picked some guy out of a soup line, Ed, he'd be better than Plank.

Eddie unwraps a stick of Juicy Fruit, bends it into his mouth. Willie thinks of Centre Street, remembers Big Cop and Bigger Cop. Flinches.

I'll admit, Eddie says, Plank doesn't make the best first impression. But he's a right guy, Sutty. You'll see.

Bartender puts his elbows on the bar, motions for Sutton to lean in. What I always liked about you, Willie, is the way you stuck it to those fuckin banks.

Sutton smiles vaguely.

Kids today, Bartender says, they don't understand how evil banks were back then. And everyone back then agreed they were evil, am I right? Editorials, cartoons, sermons, everywhere you looked someone was making the point that banks were bloodsuckers, that we needed to protect people from them. You remember, right?

Sure, sure.

And they're still bloodsuckers, Bartender says, but nowadays bankers are respected. The fuck happened?

One of the men asleep at the bar raises his head. He looks angrily at Sutton, Bartender. My brother, he says, is a banker.

Oh, Sutton says. Sorry friend.

My brother is a cunt.

Go back to sleep, Bartender says. We'll wake you when we decide to take a survey of morons.

They meet Plank at a neutral location. Stash Willie's car, pile into Plank's. Eddie rides shotgun, Willie sits in the backseat. They change into their cop uniforms while Plank drives. Willie looks at Plank's reflection in the rearview. He looks at his own reflection in Plank's suit. Another metallic suit—does the man buy them in bulk?

How you feeling, Plank?

Good, Willie. Good.

Willie studies the back of Plank's neck. A wad of fat surges over his collar. He stares hard at the back of Plank's head, wonders what goes on in there, what led Plank down so many wrong roads that he ended up a cabdriver for bank robbers. Willie sighs, looks out the window at the gray Philadelphia morning.

Course, Plank adds, I see you fellas in your costumes and I just wish—

Don't, Eddie says. Don't start.

Plank frowns at the speedometer. I just don't see the harm, he says.

Eddie buffs his police badge. We've been over this a hundred times.

Plank grunts.

No one's going to see you, Plank. Don't you get that?

That's my point, Plank says.

What is?

No one's goin to see me, so what harm is there in me wearin a costume?

I've known Sutty all my life, Eddie says, I told him you're a right guy. Don't make me sorry.

You can't be a right guy and wear a costume? You hear the illogic, Ed?

Illogic?

Plank smiles. My wife bought me a book on buildin vocabulary.

Lose the book. No one wants a wheelman with a vocabulary.

Willie rubs his forehead. Quiet. Both of you. Please. The bank is five blocks up on the right.

Plank parks. They sit in silence, the motor purring. At eight-thirty Willie steps out, walks to the bank, knocks. Routine check, he tells the guard, what with the recent rash of robberies and all.

Sure, sure, the guard says, throwing open the door—would you like a cup of coffee, Officer?

That'd be nice, Willie says, stepping in, lithe as a dancer, pulling his Tommy from under his greatcoat. Right behind him comes Eddie, sawed-off shotgun shoulder-high. Eddie pulls the guard's gun from its holster, ties him up. Then he and Willie tie up the employees as they arrive. There are twelve in all.

The manager, as always, is the last. The touch of the Tommy against his belly makes him tremble. He looks into Willie's blue eyes. You're—the Actor.

Never mind. The safe. Move.

275

The manager takes a step, stops. He looks sheepish. I need to iron my shoelaces, he says.

What?

Make water.

Safe first. Water second.

I'm not going to make it, Mr. Actor. I had an extra cup of joe at the house. I should've, you know, before I left. But I was running late, and now the sight of your Tommy there has—well. Sped things up.

Open the safe, Eddie says, his voice rising, or we start shooting your employees.

You're going to kill my employees because I need to make water?

Willie sighs. Eddie sighs. That does seem harsh, Sutty.

Willie walks the manager to the bathroom. He waits with the door open. The old boy sounds like a garden hose.

He goes and goes. And goes.

Jesus, Eddie mutters. Now I gotta go.

At last the manager emerges. He takes Willie to the safe, turns the dial, jerks the door. Suddenly it's Willie who needs to make water. Most safes are only partially full. This one is packed. There isn't room to slide a flick knife between all the green stacks.

Later, back at Willie's room, Willie and Eddie and Plank sit before the coffee table, the haul piled into a pyramid. They've counted it three times. Each time it comes to a quarter of a million dollars. Again and again Plank asks, Did you fellas know? Willie and Eddie don't answer. It's got to be one of the biggest hauls ever in this city, Plank says. Still they don't answer. This calls for a party, Plank says. Willie nods dumbly. Can I invite my wife? Plank says. Again Willie nods without thinking.

Mrs. Plank comes by train from East New York. A bookkeeper for a butcher, she looks the way Willie expected her to look—the only way Plank's wife could look. White blond hair, large sensuous mouth, no-one-home stare.

Eddie invites his girlfriend, Nina, a fashion model. She was on the cover of *McCall's* last summer. She dated Max Baer, the heavyweight heartthrob, Eddie says, and Clark Gable once made a play for her in a Schrafft's. She wears a tight sweater and a silk scarf knotted around her neck and a hat that slopes up and then sharply down and then up again, like a golf course. Willie can't take his eyes off her. He tries. He can't.

Everyone drinks too much. Plank and his wife drink much too much. Soon the girls begin shedding their clothes. In their garters and brassieres they dance around the coffee table. Mrs. Plank grabs a fistful of hundreds, throws it at Nina, who grabs two fistfuls and throws them in the air.

Willie sees Eddie laughing, slapping his thigh. He goes to him, wraps an arm around his shoulders. Hey, partner.

Hiya, Sutty.

Willie leers at Nina. How about letting me have a turn, he says.

Eddie stiff-arms Willie, looks at him with confusion. What?

Willie lowers his head, trying to think. He looks up. Sorry, Ed. I don't know where that came from. I'm drunk.

Forget it, Eddie says. He walks away.

Willie sits heavily on the floor, lies back. He puts a pillow under his head, tries to balance his glass of whiskey on his chest, spills half of it. His eyelids. He can't keep them open. Moments before letting them close he sees Eddie maneuvering Nina over to the window. Silhouetted against the fading daylight they look like Gable and Lombard on the big screen. Willie tries to stay awake, to read their lips. Out of the corner of his eye he sees Plank chasing Mrs. Plank toward the bedroom. He sees Mrs. Plank's ass, big and round, her bright purple garters, her disheveled white blond hair waterfalling down her back. A split second before passing out Willie sees something else.

In the morning he won't know if he actually saw it or dreamt it.

Plank—wearing Willie's cop uniform.

Bartender: The other thing I always admired about you, Willie, was the nonviolence part. If only more crooks were like you the world would be a better place. These days they think nothing of grabbing an old lady on the subway, hitting her on the head, taking her pocketbook.

Sutton: You're telling me. The kids I saw coming into Attica the last few years. You wouldn't believe. Violent, hooked on drugs. And lazy? They'd seek me out, ask me to teach them the secret of bank robbing. I'd tell them, The secret is hard fuckin work.

Bartender: Now you got these radicals running around, planting bombs outside banks, government buildings. They say they're protesting—they're just hurting innocent people.

Sutton: I used to get up at five, fill a thermos with hot coffee, walk down to the bank, freeze my ass off. I'd take reams of notes. I'd memorize them. I planned every job to the T so no one would get hurt.

Bartender: When I got back from Europe in '19, shrapnel in my hip, I couldn't find a job for two solid years. I got so angry, I had to fight to keep from putting my hands around someone's throat. I kept asking, What was the point? I might've thrown in with a guy like you. I almost did, to be honest. But I never could've thrown in with punks like we've got running around today.

Reporter: Mr. Sutton?

Sutton: Yeah?

Reporter: I'm just looking at this file here, and it says you and Eddie, while robbing a bank, fired off machine guns? And tear gas? Then led cops on a high-speed chase through the heart of midtown? That doesn't sound so—nonviolent.

Bartender: What's with this kid?

Sutton: I wish I knew.

Reporter: But I just—it's in the files.

Sutton: Have you never known newspapers to get anything wrong?

Bartender: What's the next stop on the nickel tour, Willie?

Sutton: Broadway and One Hundred Seventy-Eighth.

Photographer: Uptown again. Right by the stadium. I can't help mentioning that we just came from there.

Sutton: Patience and Fortitude here are miffed that I'm taking them through my story in chronological order.

Bartender: How else would you tell a story? What happened there, Willie?

Sutton: That's where they shot poor Eddie.

The soda jerk from the corner drugstore comes to Willie's door, says Willie has a phone call. Willie bundles up, walks down to the drugstore, slips into the phone booth.

Sutty, it's Eddie.

How's tricks?

I need to go to New York.

How come?

I need new license plates.

Seems awfully far to travel for new plates.

What choice do I have? I can't show residence here in Philly.

Mm. Okay. Call me when you get back?

Will do.

Be careful.

So long.

December 1933. One year since Willie escaped Sing Sing. He holes up in his apartment, drinking brandy, playing Christmas records on an old Victor. Feeling nostalgic. Thinking of Happy, Wingy, Daddo. And Mr. Untermyer. Willie wonders if Cicero has read about the exploits of his former gardener.

Now he thinks of Bess. He pours another brandy. What he wouldn't give to spend Christmas with her. Ah Bess. My heart's darling. The door blows off its hinges. Ten cops burst into the apartment. Willie jumps out of his chair just in time to catch a right cross from a detective with a flattop haircut, then a haymaker from another detective with a face like raw meat.

Willie, cuffed, comes to in the backseat of a cop car. Detective Flattop is driving, Detective Meatface is riding shotgun, doing all the talking.

Might never have found you but for your friend, Plank.

Plank? Who's Plank?

That's a hot one. He's only the dumbest guy in East New York. He aint got no job but he drives a brand-new Cadillac and wears hunnert-dollar suits, that's who Plank is. His neighbors noticed sump fishy, called us. We put a tap on his phone. Bingo bango, here we are.

Doesn't sound like the kind of moron I'd have anything to do with.

Your pal Eddie Buster Wilson aint winnin no brain contests neither. He got you and Plank on the blower this mornin, shot the breeze like it never occurred to him the line might be tapped. You he told he was goin to New York. Plank he told to meet him at Motor Vehicles. So—two and two together. Four. A little Welcome Wagon we ranged frim. He shoulda give up, but he chosed to lead us on a merry chase. Too bad frim.

What happened?

Shut up.

What'd you do to Eddie?

Shut up. You'll find out soon enough.

Sutton stands on the corner, the wind at his back. He looks at the George Washington Bridge a block away. It's swaying in the wind. Or maybe Sutton is swaying. A woman wrapped in two threadbare coats walks past him, guiding a little girl on a bike with training wheels. One training wheel is missing.

Bleak fuckin corner, Sutton says, huddling deep into Reporter's trench coat.

Reporter pulls out his notebook, waits for the little girl to pass. So Eddie died here, Mr. Sutton?

Better if he had. No, he was shot here, but he lived. One of the bullets cut his optic nerve. He spent the next twenty years groping around a cell at Dannemora. A judge set him free in '53. Eddie walked out of court with a cane, everything he owned wrapped in a sheet. They said he'd learned to read Braille. I saw that in the paper, I wept.

Reporter is writing, shivering. He shakes his pen. Ink's frozen, he mutters.

Sutton reaches into his breast pocket, pulls out Bartender's pen, hands it to Reporter.

Why did they shoot Eddie, Mr. Sutton?

The cops said he went for his gun.

Willie, Photographer says, your hands are shaking.

Sutton looks at his hands. He nods. He fumbles for his cigarettes, puts one in his mouth, pats his pockets. Either of you got a light?

Photographer hands him his Zippo.

Was anyone else in the car with Eddie, Mr. Sutton?

Sutton lights the Zippo, touches the flame to his Chesterfield. Eddie's girlfriend, he says. Nina. She threw herself across Eddie's body. That's love for you. She got a finger shot clean off. She wrote to me in the joint for years. Her letters were tough to read.

Emotional?

Illegible. She had four fingers.

What happened to Plank?

He told the cops everything. Which still might not have been a disaster. But he told them where I lived. He just never forgave me for not letting him play dress-up.

What?

I warned myself a hundred times not to let that numbwit know where I lived. I knew he wasn't a right guy. I knew. But Eddie kept vouching for him. Later I found out. At Dannemora some guys were trying to make Eddie their girlfriend. He was a great fighter, but he was slowing down, and he couldn't take on five guys at once. Plank stepped in, saved Eddie's ass. After that, in Eddie's book, Plank had a free pass. Eddie—loyal to a fault. I should have known. Ah what am I saying? I did know. I did. But I didn't act on it. Your gut kid. You remember Willie told you: In a tight corner your gut is the only real partner you've got.

PART THREE

But wherefore thou alone? Wherefore with thee
Came not all hell broke loose?

JOHN MILTON, *PARADISE LOST*

SEVENTEEN

TWO GUARDS DRAG HIM DOWN A LONG DIM CORRIDOR. THEY toss him into a box, four by six, with a stone floor, stone walls, an extra-low stone ceiling. And a wall-mounted shelf of rusted iron. The bed, he guesses.

They shut the door.

Darkness.

Total, seamless.

Their footsteps grow faint. The door at the end of the corridor creaks, slams.

He looks around. He can see nothing. But he can hear everything. His blood slugging through his veins, his lungs expanding and contracting, his heart. He never realized until now that ribs are nothing but bars made of bone, and the heart is just a scared prisoner pounding to get out.

Easy, boy.

He shuts his eyes, curls into a tight ball.

His leg jerks. Did he just fall asleep? He opens his eyes. Is he asleep now? The darkness is darker. Almost liquid.

He looks up, down. Where is he? With great effort he remembers. Eastern State Penitentiary. Downtown Philly. He's been here nine months, he thinks. Maybe a year. A few days ago the guards caught him making a papier-mâché bust of his head—with real hair saved from his haircuts. He'd planned to put the head on his bunk, to make the guards think he was sleeping, then hacksaw his way out.

They found his hacksaws too.

The warden, Hardboiled Smith, seemed personally insulted that Willie would try to leave Eastern State before his fifty years was up. Capone just did a bit at Eastern State, and even Scarface didn't have the nerve to try an early departure. So Hardboiled ordered Willie thrown into the punishment block, also known as Iso. Also known as a Dark Cell. Willie dimly remembers Hardboiled saying: You can rot there for all I give a shit.

How long ago was that? Two days? Two months?

He sits up, blinks. He wonders if this is the kind of darkness Daddo saw. The kind Eddie now sees. He wonders if the darkness of death can be any more complete. He prays that he'll know soon. His arm jerks. Another muscle spasm. Did he just fall asleep again? How long was he out? Ten minutes? Ten hours? The not-knowing gnaws at the edges of his mind.

There are only two breaks in the darkness each day. A Judas hole claps open, a hand with a tin plate of food comes through. Willie doesn't know what the food is, and tasting it doesn't solve the mystery. Cornmeal? Oatmeal? Farina? It doesn't matter. He scoops some into his mouth with his fingers, pushes the plate aside.

He's allowed no visitors, no letters, no radio. No books. He'd kill for a book, though it would be useless in this darkness. To simply hold a book, to imagine what it *might* say, would be comfort. He vows, if he ever gets out of this Dark Cell, he's going to memorize books, poems, so they'll always be in his head, just in case.

He imagines his cell crowded with all the people he's ever known, sitting, standing along the wall. They exhort him, joke with him. The nerve of this warden, they say, thinking he can break the likes of Willie Sutton. Yes, Willie tells them—it's funny isn't it? They laugh. He laughs. He screams with laughter. All the jokes in the world have been condensed into one joke that only Willie gets. Just as suddenly the joke isn't funny. It's tragic. He weeps.

In his third week of Iso he wakes to a voice. Hello, Willie.

At last they're letting him have a visitor. Ah but not just any visitor. He crawls to her, wraps his arms around her legs, rests his head on her lap. How did our lives get so crossways, Bess? I don't know, Willie. I thought we'd be together always, Bess. Me too, Willie.

It should be the simplest thing, Willie tells her, you love someone, they love you back. You said love was simple. But it's not. Not for us. We must be cursed. I must be cursed.

Oh Willie.

Nothing has panned out for me. As a kid I thought I'd grow up to be happy. And good—I thought I'd be a good person, Bess. But I'm as bad as they come. The judge said.

No no no. You're a good man who's done bad things.

What's the difference?

There's a difference.

Are you still married, Bess?

She doesn't answer.

Did you have the baby?

No answer.

Bess, are you happy? I need to know. If you're happy, that would be enough.

He clutches her legs. He hears the guard laughing through the Judas hole.

They're telling me our time is up, she says.

Don't go, Bess.

She stands, passes through the wall. I'll be back, Willie.

He crawls to the door, curls against the Judas hole, falls asleep.

They pile into the Polara. Photographer cranks the heat, grabs the radio. City Desk, come in, City Desk.

Garble static, where are you guys?

Uptown.

Uptown again? Can you guys garble swing by Rockefeller static Center? Get a garble shot of Sutton static standing in front of the garble Christmas tree? Special request from the powers that be. Static.

Ten four. Willie—you mind if we pause the nickel tour?

Sutton presses his face against the window. Nah. I'd love to see the tree.

So, Reporter says, Mr. Sutton. After you got arrested in Philadelphia, they put you in Eastern State?

Yeah. World's first penitentiary. Built in the early 1800s by some seriously fucked-up Quakers. Terrible place. Naturally I tried to escape right away. They caught me, threw me in a Dark Cell. Which they also called Iso. I almost shattered. Then they tossed me into Semi Iso. Which meant I had a skylight. There was a long pole to push the skylight open, and pull it shut, and the pole never worked, so the skylight would always get stuck in the open position. Rats would scurry along the roof of the cellblock and fall through the skylight. But that was a small price to pay for having the sun and the moon. Then, finally, a guard tossed a Bible into my cell. That saved me.

So you believe in God, Mr. Sutton?

I was just set free on Christmas Eve kid. What do you think?

Have you always?

More or less. It's people I have trouble believing in.

Would you call yourself—religious?

Nah. But in prison I found a lot of comfort in the fact that God makes mistakes. And that He regrets them.

It says that in the Bible?

Exodus: And the Lord repented of the evil which He thought to do unto His people. *You can't repent of something unless it's a mistake, right? Unless you'd do it differently if you had it to do over again? Jeremiah:* The Lord will repent Him of the evil which he had pronounced against them. *God feels so guilty at one point*

He says: I am weary of repenting. *Boy does Willie know that feeling.*

After eighteen months in Semi Iso, Willie is released into general population. It's not liberating. It's terrifying. He jumps at all the different voices, shies from the sudden whirl of faces. He knows he should work at resocializing himself, reacclimate himself to humanity, but during yardouts he prefers to sit alone, having a staring contest with the sky.

Every prisoner in general population must have a job. Hardboiled makes Willie a messenger. Six days a week Willie jogs back and forth across the prison grounds, carrying messages, documents, packages, from guards to administrators and back again. He also runs slop buckets up and down the towers. There are no toilets in the towers and guards can't leave their posts. Thus, when Nature calls—buckets. Several times a day Willie stands at attention, waiting, while a guard groans and strains over a bucket. Then Willie carries the sloshing bucket down the steep tower stairs and out to the nearest toilet. Not the best way, he thinks, to reacclimate to humanity.

After a year of good behavior Willie is rewarded with a better job. Hardboiled makes him secretary to the prison psychiatrist. Willie types up the chapters of a textbook Shrink is writing, and notes from Shrink's therapy sessions. Reading the harrowing confessions of his fellow prisoners, their gruesome autobiographies, Willie begins to think about his own. While typing Shrink's transcripts he begins to type up notes for the narrative of Willie Sutton—a memoir, a novel, he isn't sure.

Sometimes, at the end of a workday, Willie will sit and chat with Shrink, mainly because he doesn't want to leave the book-filled office, the best-smelling place in the prison. It's redolent of glue and paper and pencil shavings. Willie has no interest in being psychoanalyzed, and Shrink seems relieved to be off duty, so the chats are always strictly informal.

Shrink is roughly Willie's age, mid-thirties, but looks much older. Anyone would think that Shrink is the one who's done the hard time. His hair is sparse, his cheeks hollowed out, his eyes plump with fatigue. He always wears the same green tweed blazer, which doesn't flatter him. It makes his chest and shoulders look twice as concave. One day Shrink brushes some ashes off the green blazer and interrupts Willie in the middle of a story about Marcus. Don't you think it's remarkable, Willie, that you've never made a mistake?

What now?

Whenever you're caught, it's always someone else's fault. You always describe yourself as a sort of lone knight, on a solitary crusade, forced to work with others—and it's always they who trip you up.

Well, I'm just telling you what happened.

On the other hand, don't you think it odd that you speak so well of your quote unquote *clan*? When they haven't done right by you at all?

I don't know if I'd say that either.

But you have said it, Willie. I'm only saying it back to you. Your brothers were monsters. Your sister was invisible. Your parents were cold.

Well. Now. Um.

Tell me more about your father. What did he do?

I told you. He was a blacksmith.

But what did he *do*?

Shod horses.

And?

Made tools.

Such as?

Hammers, axes, nails.

Don't blacksmiths make locks?

Sure, all kinds of locks.

Shrink lights a cigarette. He uses a black holder like President Roosevelt and smokes a foreign brand that smells like an electrical short.

So your father, who never spoke to you, made locks. And you are now locked up—in part for *picking* locks. You think that's all coincidental.

Isn't it?

Shrink smokes, shrugs. Tell me more about Bess.

Willie would rather not. But he picks a story at random, tells Shrink about their first night at Coney Island, then summarizes the robbery of her father.

It's commendable, Shrink says. In a way.

What is?

You remain devoted to this girl, even though she used you, destroyed your future, without so much as a by-your-leave.

I didn't *say* that.

But it goes *without* saying, Willie. She led you into a life of crime, then ran off, got married, and left you holding the bag.

Willie feels his cheeks growing hot. Her father forced her, he says.

She doesn't sound like the sort of girl whose father can force her to do anything. In fact, wasn't it her rebellion against her father that was the start of all your troubles? Forced her? Willie, come now, you know better than that.

Willie asks if he can bum a cigarette. Maybe these chats with Shrink aren't so informal after all.

Later Willie researches Shrink, as he once did Mr. Untermyer. This time he doesn't have the resources of a great library at his disposal, so he ransacks the doctor's office files. Once again he's shocked by what he learns. Besides being the world's leading expert on the criminal mind, Shrink is an authority on hypnosis.

So there it is. Shrink is somehow putting Willie under. Why else would Willie be spilling his guts? How else would Shrink know so much? Many of the stories Willie tells Shrink are lies, but Shrink still manages to find the seeds and kernels of truth within. How else but through hypnosis?

In early 1936 Shrink sits in his leather chair, smoking, reading a book by Bertrand Russell, while Willie types up his most recent Jungian session with a murderer. Willie has played chess many times with this murderer—he never knew. He makes a mental note: from now on let the man win. As he stacks the typed pages, and slides them into a folder, Willie thinks about the way Shrink spoke to the murderer. Gently, without judgment. Willie slots the folder into the filing cabinet, eases into the chair across from Shrink.

Excuse me sir.

Shrink looks up from his book. Yes, Willie?

Can I ask you something?

Of course.

Willie purses his lips. Can I ask you to be totally honest sir?

Yes.

Do you think I belong here?

Oh Willie, I don't know.

No. Really. Do you think I should spend the next fifty years of my life in this stinking tomb?

Shrink shuts Bertrand Russell, sets the book on his lap. He watches the smoke curl up from the tip of his cigarette. Willie the Actor, he says under his breath. The Actor who doesn't like the roles in which he's cast himself.

Willie already regrets asking the question.

The Actor who has a conscience, Shrink says—or thinks he has. Okay, Willie. Why not. Since you asked. But remember, you're not my patient. This isn't a diagnosis. Just an opinion.

Right.

So then. The alienation from the mother and father, the sibling abuse, the grim poverty of your early years, the simultaneity of your life span with a series of the most violent economic convulsions in history, it all created an uncommonly dangerous and potent witches' brew. By the time you came of age you were very likely to go down the wrong path, to have a great deal of trouble controlling your impulses, but my God, Willie, add to all that the convergence of your first crime with this overpowering first love—that sealed it. We don't know if criminal natures are born or made, but you were certainly shaped to some extent, to a large extent, by external events, and by an environment that rendered criminality all but inevitable. Now, what makes you different, what makes you more dangerous than other men in this institution, is your first-rate intelligence. Thoughtful, sensitive, articulate, empathetic, an inspired storyteller and a determined self-mythologizer, you're also alarmingly—what's the word? *Cunning*. All of which makes you highly appealing, seductive, charismatic, to accomplices, to casual observers, to newspapers, even to some of your victims. I've heard you say that you've never hurt anyone, a point of pride with you, but look at the people with whom you've crossed paths. How have they fared? They're all in jail, or blind, or dead. A likable criminal can be more lethal than a snarling ax murderer, because people don't take the necessary precautions. People think a *gentleman bandit* is cute, cuddly, and so he is, like a newborn lion cub. But take him into your home and one day you'll discover how cute and cuddly he is. People will always want to embrace you, Willie, to follow you, to imitate you, to throw in with you, to write about you—to *diagnose* you—and they'll often pay a dear price. But no one will ever pay more dearly than you, Willie, you, because *you* still don't think *yourself* a criminal. You see yourself, or portray yourself, which amounts to the same thing, as an honest person who happens to have committed crimes. And yet your dedication to crime, your great skill—well, I believe you're every bit a criminal, in your marrow, drawn ineluctably to the life because you're so *good* at it, and because every time you rob a bank or open a safe I believe you feel what you must have felt that first time with Bess. That thrill of first love and that arousal of complicity and illicitness and danger. And sex, of course. Sex, Willie. Sex and parents—I can't think of a single neurotic complex that doesn't originate with one or the other. Imagine the human psyche as a skein of different color yarns. We spend our lives trying to understand and organize all the colors. Let's say sex is blue yarn, Mom is red yarn, Dad is white yarn. In you, Willie, in your skein, I see these three colors being extremely tangled. When you rob a bank, I believe, that blue yarn becomes a bit less tangled, a bit looser, for a brief while, and this must provide a tremendous, though temporary, relief. That's why—I'm sorry to say, Willie, but you asked—yes, I do, yes, I think, yes you belong exactly where you are. Yes.

When they let you out of Semi Iso, Mr. Sutton, did they give you anything to do? A job?

I was secretary to the prison psychiatrist. He was one of the leading authorities on criminology in the country. He wrote the textbook that's still used in colleges.

Did you read it?

I typed it.

Did he ever try to analyze you?

Nah. I was too complex for him.

EIGHTEEN

BASEBALL IS EVERYTHING AT EASTERN STATE. IT'S THE BEST way of killing time, of forgetting time, and one of the few sources of triumph and manly pride. The six prison teams, therefore, play to win. Murderers pitch inside. Mob bosses crowd the plate. Arsonists steal home every chance they get. Things can get out of hand quickly.

And yet every game also features a moment or two of pure calm. With each home run comes a tranquil pause, not just for the batter to round the bases, but for everyone else to stare in envy and wistfulness at the spot where the ball went over the wall.

Throughout the 1930s, home-run balls from Eastern State become coveted souvenirs in downtown Philadelphia. Then they become vessels. Instead of hitting them over, players toss them over, with letters attached. Prison mail is censored, but no one can censor a horsehide. *Whoever finds this please deliver to Mickey Whalen, 143 Spruce Street, Phila, PA. Reward!*

In time balls start flying *into* the yard, stuffed with drugs, money, razors. One ball contains a midget stick of dynamite.

Willie is a star in the Eastern State League, an agile second baseman with a quick bat, who rarely strikes out and always hustles. Baseball helps him reacclimate, finally, rejoin the community of prisoners. Then his knee gives out. June 1936. Done for the season, he's consigned to the stands with the other middle-aged players. Between innings he trades newspapers, cigarettes, rumors.

Most of the men at Eastern State are inspired liars, so Willie tends to ignore all rumors. But one keeps cropping up. Again and again Willie hears that somewhere below the baseball diamond is a sewer pipe, which snakes all the way to the wall and beyond. Then, while watching the Eastern State Pirates whip the Eastern State Yankees, Willie hears a new twist on the familiar rumor, hears it from Tick Tock, an old con who seems to know everything except the time. He's forever asking Willie for the correct time of day even though Willie is forever pointing at his watchless wrist. Tick Tock says he recently found a loose floorboard in the basement under Cellblock 10, and far beneath the floorboard was the unmistakable sound of rushing water: It's gotta be the sewer, Tick Tock says, and if the sound is that loud, there must be a hole in it—and if a few guys could pry up that board, and if a guy with a slight build could maybe slip down into that sewer, then maybe, just maybe.

Willie nods.

Nasty down there though, Tick Tock says.

Nasty in here, Willie says.

They make a deal. In exchange for help writing a love letter to his girl—How do you spell *twat*, Willie?—Tick Tock agrees to help Willie sneak into the basement.

Christmas 1936. While Shrink is seeing patients Willie hurries across the yard. With him are three lifers, friends of Tick Tock. Willie barely knows them, but Tick Tock says they're right guys.

One nice thing about Eastern State—it operates like a small village, with dozens of shops and guilds humming all day long. Even the cells are left open during the day, so prisoners can come and go to their jobs. Guards don't think twice, therefore, about Willie and three lifers walking briskly, at midday, toward Cellblock 10.

Tick Tock, as promised, has left a window unlatched. Willie slips in first, then the three lifers. They run down to the basement, find the loose floorboard. They pry it up. They kick off their shoes and socks and strip to their underwear. One by one they drop through the hole in the floor. They land on the sewer pipe, in which, sure enough, there's a man-size hole.

The last one through the hole in the pipe is Willie. He lands with a loud splash. Warm water comes to his shins. Not water exactly. More like East River muck mixed with apple chutney. It squishes between his toes, slides between his calves. His thighs. He carries an electric torch stolen from a supply room. He clicks it on. Bugs the width of field mice slither away, up and down the sides of the pipe. The beam of light barely pierces the darkness. It picks out a mound of waste here, a bigger mound there, an iceberg of gauze and bandages from the prison infirmary. Willie remembers that the prison was built a hundred years ago. He whips the beam back and forth and thinks: a century worth of human—

He feels the three lifers staring at him. He faces them. All three are big, tough, heartless, but a childlike terror fills their eyes. Willie creeps forward. The three lifers follow. After twenty feet the pipe abruptly slopes down. The muck rises to their hips.

Don't think about it, he tells the lifers.

But he's really telling himself.

He tries to think of Chapin's garden, and the grounds of Greystone, and Bess's delicate perfume, but it's not easy when the muck turns to custard. And rises to his belly. Now his nipples. Shoulders. He recalls the guards in their towers squatting over the buckets. He wonders which guard is responsible for this particular scoop of custard now bobbing against his chin.

At last, as the custard reaches his bottom lip, Willie decides they must be near the end of the pipe, meaning they must be at the wall. Beyond, there's supposed to be a basin, then a manhole, then the street. He motions for the lifers to follow. They shake their heads—nothing doing.

Alone, Willie steels himself, presses forward. As the lifers watch in horror he shuts his eyes, pinches his nose, dives.

He wriggles ahead. No basin.

He reaches out with his right hand. No basin.

He swims and slithers another few feet. Still no basin.

Running out of air, he starts to panic and loses his bearings. He's suddenly not sure which way is forward, which way is back. He turns, swims a few feet, reaches, prays that his hand will touch the knee or thigh of a lifer.

Nothing.

He turns the other direction, reaches—nothing.

His lungs are begging him to inhale. But if he opens his mouth, he knows what will fill it and rush up his nose and down his throat. He reaches, *reaches*, and at last feels something hard. A lifer. He grabs hold, pulls, breaks the surface with a violent gasp. He smears a path on his face so that he can open his eyes. The lifers are staring. He can't tell if it's horror or pity in their expressions. His head, hair, eyes are covered, slathered with this, *this*—he can't avoid the word anymore. Shit. His mouth is full of it. He coughs. He spits and spits. Shit, shit, shit. *Shit.*

Now they all turn, peer back down the pipe at the darkness into which Willie just ventured. That way lies freedom. Beyond a solid sea of shit.

They trudge back to the hole in the pipe, climb up and through, then up through the floorboard. They have one rag. They take turns wiping themselves, but it's hopeless. They dress, pull baseball caps over their slimed hair and march double-time to the showers.

Willie wishes he could stand under the hot spray all day. But he has to hurry back to Shrink. He spends the rest of the afternoon typing, trying not to think about where he's just been. He can still feel that scoop of custard against his lip. He'll always feel it.

Days later, in the middle of the night, Willie and the lifers are rousted from their cots. Their clothes and shoes are confiscated and lab tests find that dirt from their shoes matches dirt from the basement. Willie is national news again. The arch bank robber is also a wily, relentless escape artist. Newspapers give him another nickname, Slick Willie, which he likes less than the Actor. Hardboiled throws him and the lifers into Dark Cells for a month, then Semi Iso for another year. Once again Willie reads the Bible. Front to back. Back to front.

Photographer speeds to the heart of midtown. Sutton stares out the window, seeing nothing but a blur of new buildings, until he spots St. Patrick's Cathedral. He remembers, decades ago, anarchists setting off bombs inside St. Patrick's. The anarchists were furious that the church had refused sanctuary to hundreds of unemployed workers. A priest was killed. The same anarchists tried to blow up Rockefeller's mansion. The bomb didn't go off. Willie never noticed before how much eucharist *and* anarchist *sound alike.*

He's going to die today.

Photographer double-parks on Fifth. They all pile out, march single file into Rockefeller Plaza. Everywhere you go in this city, Sutton grumbles, you run into that name. Rockefeller.

Photographer shoots a few frames, advances the film. Okay, Willie, first let me get a couple of you in front of that gift shop window. With that Nutcracker guy.

Sutton looks. A wooden soldier, taller than a grown man, stands guard beside an artificial tree and fake fireplace. Sutton walks over, leans against the window, eyes the wooden soldier.

Perfect, Photographer says. Just like that, Willie. Wait—camera's jammed. Shit. Fucking Leicas. Hold on.

While Photographer examines his camera, Reporter steps forward, stands beside Sutton, admiring the wooden soldier.

Did you know that I swam through shit kid?

Pardon?

Shit.

Metaphorically, you mean.

Do I seem like a guy who speaks in metaphors? Christmas 1936, I did the Australian crawl through human feces. Literally.

I'm sorry, I'm not following.

There was this sewer underneath Eastern State.

Okay.

The rumor was, it led to freedom. But I found that it led to shit and more shit and that shit then led to deeper realms of shit. When they caught me, they threw me back in a Dark Cell, then back in Semi Iso. They almost broke me that time. I was so desperate for human contact, any contact, I drained the water from the toilet and spoke through the pipes to the man in the next cell. At least I think he was in the next cell. We could barely hear each other, but we'd speak for hours—one of the strongest bonds I've ever had with another person. Then one day the voice was gone. Got released, died, I never did find out. A year or so later, when they let me out of Semi Iso, I was a good boy. I took correspondence classes, got a degree in creative writing, became a model prisoner. Swimming through shit—it changes a person.

I would think.

Shit. People use that word too casually. They say shit *when the littlest thing goes wrong. They'd never say it so freely if they actually had to swim through it. In fact, people would think different about everything they want in life if they asked themselves: Am I willing to swim through shit for it?*

Sutton faces Reporter, throws back his shoulders like the wooden soldier. Is there anything right now, kid, that you'd be willing to swim through shit for?

Let's see. You, standing at the site of the Schuster murder, telling me who killed Arnold Schuster.

Sutton pulls Reporter's trench coat tighter around himself. Shoves his hands deep in the pockets. You really missed your calling kid. You should have been a cop.

The seats in the prison movie theater are boards set on cinder blocks. They wobble like seesaws every time a new man sits down.

Willie is watching newsreels. *The bloodiest fighting so far for our brave GIs!* He wobbles as someone sits heavily on his right. Freddie Tenuto, a hothead from South Philly. Black eyes, sideways nose, bad skin—real bad. Angry skin for an angry man. A mob assassin, Freddie was known on the streets as the Angel of Death. Willie wobbles again. Someone sits heavily on his left. Botchy Van Sant. Another Philly guy. Hatchet face, smile like a wince.

Spring 1944. Operation Gardening is under way. Under the boom-boom of Allied bombers bombing the Danube, Botchy and Freddie tell Willie that they're digging a tunnel. They have nine guys working round the clock. They've already gone twenty feet down, through solid rock, and now they need to dig a hundred feet straight ahead and they'll be under the lawn along Fairmount Avenue. Then all they need to do is dig straight up, thirty feet.

Where's the tunnel start? Willie asks.

Under Kliney's cell, Botchy says.

Willie nods. Kliney is a scavenger, a pack rat, and a nut. It makes sense that he'd be involved in a scheme like this.

Big job, Willie says.

The Angel of Death whispers in his ear: That's why we need you, Willie. We need a place to put the dirt.

They think the best place would be the sewer, and Willie is the local sewer expert. They want Willie to tell them where their tunnel is likely to intersect with the sewer pipe. But Willie isn't eager to go underground again. It's been seven years since his sewer excursion, *seven years*, and still he has nightmares. He still wakes up spitting shit. Also, he gets a bad vibe, a Marcusy, Plankish vibe from the Angel of Death and Botchy. One is ruthless, the other is hopelessly dumb. The Angel of Death got his nickname not because he kills, but because he kills for pleasure, and Botchy got his nickname because he botched so many holdups. Willie keeps staring at the screen. Now it's a newsreel about the journalists waiting to cover D-Day. *Say hello to the brave cameramen preparing to record the Allied invasion of Europe!* Who else is in? he asks.

Botchy rattles off nine names. Willie recognizes one. Akins. An imbecile, a nervous Nellie. Not exactly the 101st Airborne, this crew. But what choice does Willie have? It's the tunnel or nothing.

Part of him is resolved to stay forever in Eastern State, to die here, to be buried here, or reburied, as he thinks of it. In the last six years he's found contentment, even some happiness, in books. Books are all he has to live for, but some days they're enough. He's getting an education, finally, the education he never got as a boy, the education that might have made everything different. Even the name of the damn prison—Eastern State—sounds like a fucked-up college.

His dean is E. Haldeman-Julius. People call Julius the Henry Ford of literature, because he's created an assembly line of professors, scientists, eggheads, who churn out crisp, simple booklets on every subject under the sun, from Hamlet to farming, mythology to physics, U.S. presidents to Roman emperors. Everyone in America has read at least a couple of Little Blue Books—Admiral Byrd took a bunch to the South Pole—and Willie has read hundreds. His cell is filled with them. This year alone he's read *A Guide to Aristotle*; *How to Write Telegrams Properly*; *Hints on Writing One-Act Plays*; *Evolution Made Plain*; *A Short History of the Civil War*; *Tolstoy: His Life and Writings*; *The Best Yankee Jokes*; *The Art of Happiness*; *Poems of William Wordsworth*; *Irish Poems of Love and Sentiment*; *A Book of Broadway Wisecracks*; *The Weather: What Makes It and Why*; *Essays on Rousseau, Balzac, and Victor Hugo*; *A Voyage to the Moon*; and *How to Build Your Own Greenhouse*.

Once he's surveyed a subject with a Little Blue Book, he knocks down the seminal works within that subject. Currently he's tackling the classics of philosophy—Plato, Aristotle, Lucretius. And psychology. He's read half of Freud, most of Jung, chunks of Adler.

When weary of his studies he simply rereads *Wuthering Heights*.

There are nights when he's satisfied with a hot meal and a few hours of reading before lights-out. He was fascinated recently to learn that the saints led similar lives. He read a Little Blue Book about them. They slept in cells, read all the time, did without women. So Eastern State isn't just his college, it's his hermitage. Or so he thought. Until right now. Listening to Freddie and Botchy, watching GIs muscle up for the biggest street fight in history, Willie feels ashamed. He realizes that he's grown soft. He's been betrayed yet again by that small voice in the back of his mind, always urging him to quit. Books are *not* all he has to live for. He has other things. The one thing. The same thing.

He's recently connected with Morley Rathbun, an accomplished sculptor and watercolorist on the outside, feted and celebrated until he stabbed his girlfriend-model in the neck. Rathbun now spends his days keep-locked, separated from other prisoners, doing oil portraits of people from his past. But sometimes he takes commissions, smuggled to him by corrupt guards. Months ago Willie sent the solitary artist three cartoons and a detailed description. Rathbun's Bess now hangs in Willie's cell, its golden-flecked blue eyes looking hauntingly down on Willie while he studies, and sometimes while he writes long letters to the real Bess. Letters he never sends.

I'm in, he says.

The Angel of Death claps him on the back.

Photographer, his camera unjammed, snaps a dozen more shots of Willie and the wooden soldier, then moves Willie to the Christmas tree. Willie delights at the glittering, twinkling lights, and Photographer shoots him delighting. Now Photographer moves Willie to the railing overlooking the ice-skating rink. Willie looks down at the forty or fifty children gliding in slow ovals.

Nice, Photographer says. Yeah, yeah, that's a cool shot, Willie.

Yeah. You look like you're thinking deep thoughts. Hold it. Shit. I'm out of film.

Photographer rummages in the pockets of his buckskin. I left the film in the car, he says. Be right back.

He runs across Rockefeller Plaza in the direction of the Polara.

Sutton lights a Chesterfield. He looks across the rink at an enormous golden statue. He calls back to Reporter: Who's that statue of kid?

Reporter steps forward. Prometheus.

Very good. You know your mythology. What'd he do?

Stole fire from the gods, gave it to mortals.

He get away with it?

Not exactly. He was chained to a rock and birds pecked at his liver for eternity.

He must've had one of my lawyers. In the joint I read a booklet about religion. Alfred North Whitehead, brilliant guy. He said every religion at heart is the story of a man, totally alone, forsaken by God.

Do you think that's true?

It's all just theories kid. Theories and stories.

So, after the sewer debacle, Mr. Sutton—what then?

We dug a tunnel. Everything I went through in prison was a life lesson, but none quite like that tunnel. It seemed so hopeless at first. Every day we'd chip chip chip away, and every night we'd have almost nothing to show for it. We'd encourage each other, tell each other—little by little. Keep on. I still get letters from all around the world, people saying that my tunnel inspired them. People battling illnesses, people faced with all kinds of crises, write to me and say if Willie Sutton can tunnel out of a hellhole like Eastern State, they can tunnel out of their problem, whatever it is.

How long was this tunnel?

Hundred feet.

You dug a hundred feet underneath the prison—with just your hands? That seems impossible.

We had a few spades, spoons. Kliney was a scavenger.

How did the guards not know?

The entrance to the tunnel was in the wall just inside the door to Kliney's cell. Kliney was a trusty, so he got into the woodshop and fashioned a fake panel to cover the entrance.

It still seems impossible.

It was.

Weren't you afraid of a cave-in? Of being buried alive?

I was already buried alive.

But a hundred-foot tunnel. How did the walls not collapse?

We propped them up with boards.

Where did you get boards?

If you gave Kliney two weeks he could get you Ava Gardner.

Through the summer of 1944 the tunnel crew works in two-man teams, in brief shifts of no more than thirty minutes, so that none will be noticed missing from his job. Willie spends half his time digging, half his time trying to manage the mood swings of his teammate, Freddie, whose rage to be out of Eastern State is psychotic. This only makes sense, since Willie recalls Shrink concluding in his notes that Freddie was borderline psychotic.

Freddie often reminds Willie of Eddie. The anger is similar, though the root cause is different. With Freddie it all starts with his height. He's painfully self-conscious about being five foot three. Botchy, who knew Freddie on the outside, says Freddie always, *always* wore lifts. Freddie's all-consuming need to get out of Eastern State feels somehow related. He can't bear people knowing how short he is. He needs those lifts. Size six.

Freddie also suffers from an unspeakable skin disease. Every few months his face and arms and chest erupt in hives and pus-filled sores. The prison doctors don't know the cause. The best they can do is send Freddie to local hospitals for whole blood transfusions, which only help sometimes. Freddie tells Willie during their time in the tunnel that it all started in his childhood. The youngest of twelve, he was sent to a foster home when his mother died, and he suffered his first skin attack after one of his foster siblings abused him. Some days Freddie wakes with his face so swollen, he can't open his eyes. But he still insists on going down into that tunnel. He makes Willie think of a mole. A psychotic mole.

Though not much taller than Hughie McLoon, Freddie is an astonishing physical specimen. He often takes off his shirt when he works in the tunnel, and his tattooed chest, arms and stomach ripple and swell with hard bulging muscles. Willie and Botchy joke that if they could only find a way to leave Freddie alone in the tunnel for a week, he could claw his way to downtown Philly.

Despite Freddie's anger, despite the constant air of violence that hovers about him, he's a lamb with Willie. He asks in worshipful tones about Willie's bank jobs, escape attempts, famous associates. He can't believe Willie met Capone, Legs, Dutch. He wants to know all about Willie, and Willie answers his questions truthfully. It takes too much energy in the tunnel to lie. And somehow the truth takes less air.

Above all Freddie is awed that Willie has never betrayed a partner. Besides Eddie, Willie has never met anyone who hated a rat more than Freddie.

Some days, kid, we'd go down in the tunnel and it would be filled with rats. We'd stab them with our spades. They were big, plump—you had to stab them half a dozen times. My digging partner kind of enjoyed it.

The Angel of Death?

How'd you know that?

It's one of the thickest folders in the Sutton files.

By the end of 1944 they're almost at the wall. But they're so far from Kliney's cell, they're running out of air. Willie and Freddie go down to relieve a team and find them panting, minutes from passing out. Kliney calls a meeting of the tunnel crew and warns everyone against pushing too hard. If someone becomes incapacitated down there, or dies, Hardboiled will throw them all in Iso for the rest of their lives.

Darkness is a factor too. Drop your spade or sharpened spoon, it might take you twenty minutes to find it. Kliney hooks a thin wire into his cell's electric socket and strings the wire all the way down the tunnel, to power a half dozen bulbs. Now there is light. And air. He also hooks up a rotary fan stolen from the warden's office.

How long exactly did it take to tunnel out?

Almost a year. Things started going faster when we finally intersected with the sewer, so we could throw loose dirt in there. Before that we had to bring the dirt out in our pockets, scatter it in the yard.

Sutton watches a group of children skating backwards, figure-eighting, spinning. Look, he says. They're so graceful. So innocent. Was I ever that innocent?

Reporter spots a pay phone next to the snack bar. Mr. Sutton, I need to call my girlfriend.

Go ahead. Free country.

Um. Well.

I'm not going to take a run-out powder on you kid. I'll be here when you get back.

Maybe you could come with me?

I'm not sitting with you in a phone booth while you call your ball and chain. Besides, better you don't call her. Ever.

Mr. Sutton.

You don't love her.

Because I hesitated when you asked me?

You're wasting your time. A thing you should never waste. And you're playing with fire. You're putting yourself in a position where you might have to leave hot. Never leave hot.

What does that mean?

When I started running my own crew, taking down banks, I had a rule. Never leave a bank hot. I always made double sure we'd walk out nice and easy, our wits about us. Before the alarms went off, before the cops showed up—before there was any gunplay.

This relates to my girlfriend how?

Banks, broads—always leave on your terms, before you can't. With a girl, that means before she's seeing someone else and you marry her out of jealousy. Or before the rabbit dies and you're trapped. Never leave a bank hot, never leave a broad hot.

Sutton glowers at Prometheus. Bottom line, kid, choose your partner carefully. The most important decision you make in life is your partner.

And what should one look for in a partner?

Someone who won't rat.

I mean a life partner.

So do I.

Sutton looks down, sees a young girl, five or six, wearing thick blue ski pants, a hat with a furry red ball on top. She's inching around the rink, held by her father. As if feeling the weight of Sutton's gaze, she looks up. Sutton waves. She waves back—nearly falls. Sutton flinches, turns away. He looks at Reporter for several long seconds. I have a daughter, he says.

Really? I didn't see anything about that in the files.

When I first walked out of Dannemora, in '27, I bumped into a girl from the old neighborhood. I was fresh out of the joint, angry, lonely, living in a flop, and this girl was crowding twenty-five, which was old maid territory back then. It was like when I bumped into Marcus. The fuse meeting the flame.

Reporter jots a note.

My daughter, Sutton says—then stops himself. I don't let myself start too many sentences with those words. I've got a long list of regrets, God knows, but she's near the top. Early on, her mother would bring her to see me in Sing Sing. You know what smells the opposite of a prison? A three-year-old girl. Those visits were torture. They say a child makes you want to be a better person, but if you're already a lost cause, if you're facing a fifty-year bit, a child just makes you want to dry up and blow away. Hard as they were on me, the visits were harder on the kid. And her mother. So they stopped coming. Her mom filed for divorce. Disappeared. I didn't blame her.

I wonder why there's nothing in the files about that, Mr. Sutton.

Sutton shrugs, points at his head. I pulled all the files on that subject from my own mental filing cabinet—long ago.

He rubs his leg, grimaces. People who say they have no regrets, that's the bunk, that's a grift. Like living in the present. There is no present. There's the past and the future. You live in the present? You're homeless. You're a bum.

Sutton takes one last look at the skaters. My daughter, he says. She must be about forty now kid. She probably wouldn't know me if she walked past us right now.

Sutton turns, looks at Reporter, winks: But I'll bet you all the money I ever stole—I'd know her.

Willie and Freddie are the first ones who spot roots. April 1945. Willie sees Freddie's face light up, then Freddie frantically pointing. Roots mean grass, and grass means they're directly under the strip of lawn that runs along Fairmount Avenue. At the same moment they both understand—technically they're *free*.

Freddie starts clawing upward. Willie holds him back.

We have to wait for the others, Freddie.

But Freddie won't stop. Six feet from the surface, four feet, he's clawing up, up. Willie grabs Freddie around the neck, pulls him back down into the tunnel. Freddie pushes Willie away. Willie grabs Freddie by the collar. By the hair. Freddie turns, swings, hits Willie in the nose, grabs a fistful of Willie's shirt and punches him again in the nose, and again. The nose would be broken if there were anything left to break.

Freddie resumes clawing. He's nearly at the surface. Willie, his nose streaming blood, yells at him: You can't do this, Freddie. You're betraying the others. We're all in this together. If you do this, you're no better than a rat.

Freddie stops. He slides down, slumps against the muddy wall of the tunnel. Heaving, gasping, his rash-covered face bright pink, he says: You're right, Willie. I lost my fuckin head. The idea of bein out. I got crazy.

They crawl on all fours back down the tunnel and spread the word among the tunnel crew. It's time.

The next morning everyone gathers in Kliney's cell. They've always planned for the escape to take place right after breakfast, when the greatest number of prisoners are moving about. Now, with no discussion, no need for discussion, they line up and jump through the hole, one by one, like paratroopers over the target. Kliney takes the lead, then Freddie, then Botchy, then Akins, then seven other guys, then Willie. One by one they slide down the shaft, into the tunnel, crawling crab-like toward freedom.

Nearing the hole, seeing the sudden shaft of white daylight, Willie is overcome. A kind of religious ecstasy floods his heart. He erupts in a prayer of thanks. Oh God I know that I'm a sinner and I know that I've led a sorry life but this moment is clearly a gift from you and this shaft of light and this fresh air is your blessing and I can't help but believe it means you haven't given up on me yet.

He climbs up up up, through mud, roots, grass, pokes his head out of the hole. It's one of the first warm days of spring. He smells the moist earth, the new flowers, the warm sweet syrupy sunshine. He pushes his shoulders through the hole, then his hips, his chest, and flops onto the ground, covered with blades of grass and mud. A second birth. *He wasn't born, he escaped.*

He lies on his side and blinks up at the black walls of the century-old prison. Hand-cut stone, jagged battlements, long narrow slits for windows. He's been inside this place for more than a decade and he never knew how hideous it was.

He gets to his knees, looks up the street, catches a glimpse of Freddie and Botchy rounding a corner. He looks across Fairmount and sees a truck driver, mouth agape, who chose this moment to pull over and open his thermos and check his map. He hears heavy footsteps behind him. He turns. Two cops. He jumps to his feet and runs.

Bullets spark along the pavement beside him. He dashes around a car, across a lawn, leaps a child's tricycle, sprints down an alley, bursts through a door that leads into some kind of warehouse. He shuts the door, crouches in a corner. Maybe they didn't see him.

Come out or we'll shoot you through this fuckin door.

He walks out, drenched, filthy, inconsolable. All that work, all those months of chipping, scraping, digging, for a three-minute jog in the spring sunshine.

Along with Willie, eight of the others are captured right away. One manages to stay free for a week, then knocks at the front gate of the prison. Tired, hungry, he asks to be let back in. That leaves just Freddie and Botchy still at large.

Each member of the tunnel crew is brought in chains before Hardboiled. The crash-out is front-page news across the country, around the world, and Hardboiled sees that this will be his legacy. He'll forever be the laughingstock who let twelve prisoners dig a hundred-foot tunnel under his nose. He's not the sort of man who can shrug off being laughed at. Someone must pay.

There are ancient punishment cells at Eastern State. Prisoners call them Klondikes. They're belowground, barely larger than sarcophagi, and they haven't been used in decades. Hardboiled orders each member of the tunnel crew stripped and dropped into a Klondike.

They will stay there, he decrees, until the last two are recaptured.

It takes eight weeks. Cops in New York City finally catch Freddie and Botchy in a nightclub. Botchy is wearing a tuxedo. Freddie is wearing lifts. Hardboiled removes the tunnel crew from the Klondikes. They're all near death. He has them clothed, scrubbed, fed, then ships four of them, the worst of them, to Holmesburg, a maximum-security prison ten miles up the road.

Sutton looks around. Where's your partner?

Reloading.

He's reloading all right.

Yeah.

Is he a good—what did you call him? Shooter?

The best.

You like working with him?

That's a different question.

Mm.

Talent aside, he's like all the other shooters at the paper. No more, no less.

Faint praise. Listen kid, I left my smokes in the car. Why don't you walk me back, leave me with Bad Cop, then you can run and call your girlfriend.

Sounds good.

They walk through Rockefeller Plaza to Fifth Avenue. The Polara isn't where they left it. They look up and down the street. There it is—fifty feet away, in the shadow of the statue of Hercules. Windows up, Photographer talking on the radio. Why did Photographer move it? They approach warily. Reporter opens the passenger door. The cloying, giddy odor of marijuana wafts out.

Photographer lowers the radio. Cop made me move the car, he says.

Uh-huh, Reporter says.

I'm talking to the City Desk. They want us to shoot Willie at some bank a few blocks from here.

Fine. I need to leave him with you for two minutes.

Cool.

Sutton climbs into the passenger seat. Reporter runs back across the Plaza to the pay phone.

We'll head there in a few, Photographer says into the radio. Yeah. Manufacturers. I got the address. Yeah. Ten four.

He sets the radio on the dash, looks at Sutton. Sutton looks at him. Life Saver eyes again. You look—happy, Sutton says.

Happy?

Peaceful. Almost.

Photographer laughs nervously. If you say so.

You been smoking that shit a long time?

What shit?

Kid. Please.

Photographer sighs. Actually, no.

What made you start?

Photographer unwinds his barber pole scarf, rewinds it slowly around his neck. Once upon a time, he says, I was pretty good at not letting this job get to me. I was bulletproof. I was known for it. I took pictures of the most horrible shit you can imagine, and none of it stayed with me. But a couple years ago the paper sent me up to Harlem. A young mother with too many kids to feed, not right in the head, threw her baby daughter out a sixth-floor window. The reporter and I got there before the cops did and we found the girl, this beautiful one-year-old girl, lying in the street. Eyes open. Arms spread wide. I did my job, fired off a roll of film, same as always, but when I got home I couldn't sit still, couldn't stop shaking. So I went out, asked the guys on the corner for something, anything, to get me through the night. They sold me a few tabs of acid. I dropped one, and instead of getting better, I got worse. A whole lot worse. I had what they call a death trip.

What's that?

I won't describe it. It wouldn't be fair to you. And besides, I honestly can't. Let's just say I went to a very messed-up place. I felt like I was in the land of the dead. I felt like, for the first time, I really and truly understood death, understood how awful, how bottomless, death is. Which was about the last thing I wanted to feel at that moment. I started freaking out, started screaming, crying. My old lady wanted to call an ambulance. I wouldn't let her. I thought it might cost me my job. She went back down to the corner, bought some weed, and that mellowed me out. Stopped the sweats, the horrors. Weed brought me back, got me over the memory of that little girl. So I started turning on every night. Right after work. Then before. Then during the day. Weed is still the only thing that works.

They sit quietly for a minute.

There used to be a guy, Sutton says. At Attica. He grew a little weed in his cell.

No kidding.

The hacks thought it was some kind of fern.

Photographer laughs.

The guy told me weed made him feel like he wasn't in Attica. Like he was floating above Attica.

Yeah. That sounds about right.

Sutton looks at his Chesterfields, looks at Photographer. I may have misjudged you kid.

Thanks, Willie. Me too.

So—you got any of that shit left?

Really?

Sutton stares.

Photographer looks down Fifth Avenue, looks back at Sutton. They both look at Hercules, ready to hurl the world down on them. Photographer opens his cloth purse and Sutton shuts the Polara door.

NINETEEN

WILLIE IS KEEP-LOCKED. FREDDIE TOO. MEANING THEY'RE kept in their cells all day, all night, even during meals. Their only break is a half hour every morning, when guards let them into a small yard for exercise. And mockery.

Welcome to Holmesburg, ladies. Welcome to the Burg.

Welcome to the Jungle, dumbfucks.

Willie and Freddie stand in a windy corner of the yard, hands jammed under their armpits. Willie thinks of the animals in the Hudson slaughterhouse, the way they huddled in the pens.

Where are the others? he asks.

D Block, Freddie says.

Fuckin tunnel, Willie mutters.

Wasn't worth this, Freddie says.

Nothing's worth this, Willie says.

One day, at the end of their yard time, as guards herd them back to the cellblock, a feeling sweeps over Willie. He doesn't want to go back. Of course no prisoner wants to go back to his cell, but Willie *really* doesn't want to. He considers pleading with the guards: *Please don't make me go back, I can't take it. Please!* This strikes him as both the most insane and the most sane thought he's ever had. Instead, when he walks back into his cell, when they shut the door, he throws himself against the wall, hurls his body against it again and again until he falls in a crumpled heap on the floor. His shoulder is dislocated. Days later, with his release from the hospital, his yard privileges are revoked.

He gives up. He lets himself sink into that soft void between apathy and insanity which claims so many prisoners. He hears them at night, the broken ones, his brothers, berating the moon. He joins them. For much of 1946 he's as broken as they come.

When he's not screaming, he's sleeping. He sleeps fourteen, sixteen hours a day. In dreams he can be with Bess, walking the beach at Coney Island, driving through virgin forest. Waking from such dreams is agony. Being returned to the real world is worse than being returned to his cell. And yet it's a trade he's willing to make. He sleeps more, and more, and ever deeper.

But slowly, inexorably, he gathers himself. He starts by rebuilding his body. Push-ups, sit-ups, he does hundreds each day. Then his mind. He's permitted two books each week from the prison library, and he devours them, learns them by heart. He revisits old favorites. *Come into the garden, Maud, I am here at the gate alone.* He recites them, sings them to the walls. *Now you will come out of a confusion of people!* Let the others berate the moon, he romances it. *Out of a turmoil of speech about you.*

Reporter returns to the Polara. Okay, he says, let's roll.

Sutton gets out, climbs into the backseat. How's the girlfriend? he asks Reporter.

Fine, Reporter says.

Sutton laughs. But it's not his typical craggy laugh. More a squeaky giggle.

Reporter notices. How's everyone in here? he asks.

Good, Sutton says. Never better.

Photographer starts up the Polara, swings onto Fifth, eases into traffic. Reporter opens his notebook. Mr. Sutton, before our next stop—you never finished telling me how the tunnel escape turned out.

Not well. I was only free a few minutes.

And when they recaptured you, they sent you to Holmesburg?

Silence.

Mr. Sutton?

Reporter turns. Sutton is staring into space.

Mr. Sutton?

Still staring.

Mr. Sutton.

What? Oh. Yeah kid. Holmesburg. They called it the Burg. And I was in C Block, where they kept the worst of the worst. The crazies, the incorrigibles. They called C Block the Jungle. It was a jungle but with more bugs and shittier air. They did medical experiments on us without our knowing. Doctors at the Burg were bagmen for the drug companies. If you wanted to stay alive, you had to stay out of the infirmary. But that wasn't so easy for me. A third of my life behind bars—it was starting to tell. Acid stomach, bad back, sore knees. And talk about constipated. I'd have shanked you both for a prune. The docs were more than happy to give me a pill or a shot. Sometimes they said it was medicine, sometimes vitamins. But it was poison. I always felt weird afterward. Weird. I felt—weeeird.

Reporter glares at Photographer. Don't tell me, he says.

Tell you what?

A trusty comes into Willie's cell each morning to deliver his mail, his books, the latest poisons from the doctors. Twenty-three years old, the trusty talks slowly, walks slowly, and wears his blond hair long and low over his brow, covering one eye. Maybe it's the hours spent with Shrink, or maybe it's all the Freud and Jung he's read, but Willie sees right through this trusty, knows instinctively that the trusty craves an older man's approval. Knows he'd swim through shit for it.

Willie turns on the charm. How's tricks kid? How you feeling?

Good, the trusty says, thanks for asking. None of the other fellas ask.

The other fellas don't ask because the trusty is a rat. He was in a smash-and-grab crew, in North Philly, and when he got pinched he gave up his buddies. It makes Willie sick to befriend such a rat, to stroke his ego, but he's Willie's only contact with the outside world. Which means he's Willie's only hope.

Willie spends months working Rat, mapping his circuits and buttons, learning his favorite teams, songs, actors, listening to his bullshit stories, all of which end with Rat as the triumphant hero. He laughs at every one of Rat's inane jokes, frowns dramatically when he leaves Willie's cell to go finish his rounds.

Gradually, subtly, Willie plies him with questions. Kid did you have a trade on the outside?

I was a house painter.

Is that so? I always thought that seemed like interesting work.

I was good too. That's why the warden lets me leave the joint on day jobs.

You don't say. Into the city?

Why sure. Hours at a time. I can even visit friends. Which is good, since I don't got none in here. All these guys think I'm a rat. But I'm a right guy, Willie.

I can tell kid. I can always tell a right guy.

Anything I told the cops, it was only because they beat me.

You're lucky they didn't kill you. Cops.

Man. You really get me, Willie.

I do kid. I do. But you're dead wrong about one thing.

What's that?

You've got one friend in here kid.

On New Year's Eve, 1947, Willie and Rat sit together, listening to the radio. A new song. *What Are You Doing New Year's Eve?* Margaret Whiting is wondering, asking repeatedly whom Willie will be kissing at the stroke of midnight. Fuck her. Willie tunes in the news. A snowstorm hammers the Northeast—nearly one hundred people are dead. A verdict comes down in the first

Auschwitz trial—twenty-three people are set to be hanged. Ancient Bible scrolls are found in a cave—somewhere near the Dead Sea. Willie turns down the volume.

Listen kid. On your next trip to the city, I need you to get me something.

Sure thing, Willie.

I need a gun kid.

He says it casually, as if he wants an extra pinch of salt on his Salisbury steak. Rat reacts just as casually. He puckers his lips. Nods.

Some saws too.

Another nod.

Willie drops his voice. And when the time's right I'm going to need to know if there are any ladders around this joint.

Rat gives a microscopic nod. Slow-motion cameras wouldn't detect it.

Days later, delivering Willie's mail, Rat hands him a small package. Wrapped in tight plastic. Covered in paint. Because it was smuggled in a paint can.

Cookies from home, Willie. Make sure they stay fresh.

Willie has no home. He stuffs the package under his mattress. Between bed checks he rips off the plastic.

A loaded .38.

And two shiny new hacksaws.

Photographer stops at Forty-Third, points. There it is, Willie.

Sutton wipes the fog from the window to his left. Now that's what I call a bank, he says.

It's a giant glass box. In the center is a massive safe, round, seven feet tall, with a door nearly two feet thick. It looks like the kind of safe in which the formula for the atomic bomb might be kept. Photographer does a U-turn, double-parks, slaps the PRESS card on the dash. He turns to Willie.

City Desk says this bank was built because of you, brother.

How so?

*Apparently you'd just knocked off some Manufacturers Trust?
In 1950?*

Allegedly.

And Manufacturers Trust wanted to reassure jittery customers.

Reasonable.

*So they built this completely transparent branch. The idea was,
customers could always see if Willie Sutton was there. Ergo, Willie
Sutton would never be there.*

I'll be a son of a bitch.

*The world's first Sutton-proof bank. City Desk wants a shot of
you in front of it, beaming at it, like you built it.*

Apparently I did.

*Sutton steps from the car, limps up to the bank. He puts both
palms against the glass. Photographer fires off a dozen shots. A
little to the left, Willie. Good, good. Okay, that's enough. We're all
set.*

*Take a few more, Sutton says. I'll use them for my Christmas
cards next year.*

Photographer laughs, fires off a few more.

*Sutton laughs and laughs, still doesn't move, doesn't take his
palms from the glass. Reporter comes forward. Mr. Sutton?*

They went to all this trouble kid.

Who?

*They. Because of me. A punk from Irish Town. They went to
all this effort.*

It is—impressive.

My legacy.

*Sutton stands back, tilts his head. He considers the safe from
different angles. Puts on his glasses. Strokes his chin. Huh, he says.
How do you like that? It's a Mosler.*

How can you tell?

How can the doctor tell your tonsils need to come out?

He takes another step back, looks up and down the street. You know something kid?

What?

A good crew, a pot of black coffee, a lookout I can trust—I could still take down this fuckin bank.

Willie peers through his cell window. Snow. The storm he's been waiting for. February 10, 1947. Why is it always February, this sawed-off month, this Hughie McLoon of months, when all the big things in his life go down?

At lunchtime the cell door clatters open. Here's that book you wanted, Willie.

Thanks kid. How's tricks?

Can't complain and if I did who'd listen?

I would kid. I would.

Willie drops his voice: Pass the word to Freddie. Tonight.

Rat nods. Then lingers. Not staying exactly, not leaving. He brushes away his forelock, out of his eye, takes a step forward.

I'll miss you, Willie. A lot.

Willie looks down, clenches his teeth, curses himself for not catching the signs. While he's been working Rat, Rat has been working him. And now, if Willie doesn't handle this moment just right, the kid will go straight to the warden. Once a rat. Willie looks up. Yeah. Uh. I'll miss you too kid.

Rat takes another step. I love you, Willie.

Oh. Yeah. I love you too kid.

Willie embraces Rat in a fatherly way, but Rat isn't having that. Taking Willie's face between his palms, Rat pulls him closer. Kisses him. Willie tells himself not to pull away, not to cringe. It's either kiss Rat back or spend the rest of his life here in this cell. He has to do more than endure this, he has to act as if he likes it. No. He has to like it. When he feels Rat's tongue, he touches it lightly with his, pushes his own tongue deep into Rat's mouth. Rat moans, runs his fingers through Willie's hair, and Willie lets him, then does the same to Rat.

Rat tries for more. Willie wheels. Ah kid, he says. Please. Go. Before I don't *let you* go.

He waits. He hears Rat's labored breathing. He hears Rat's labored thinking. At last he hears the cell door clatter shut.

Heart pounding, Willie lies on his bunk. Our best performances in life, he tells the wall, are delivered with no audience.

He lies there all afternoon. He doesn't touch his food. Doesn't read, doesn't write. After the midnight inspection he counts to nine hundred, slides the .38 from under his mattress, into his waistband, and crawls to the door. He kicks out the loose bar, wriggles through the hole. He runs down the tier and finds Freddie doing the same. Freddie leaps at Willie, hugs him, thanks him for hatching this plan. They creep back to the main door of the cellblock, crouch behind it.

Willie hands the gun to Freddie.

At the stroke of midnight they hear two voices on the other side of the door. Keys tinkling. This is it, Freddie whispers.

The door swings toward them. They lunge. The guards are quicker than Willie expected. They nearly manage to pull the door back. But Freddie hits the opening like a fullback crossing the goal line. With all his anger, all his muscle, he whams through, grabs the first guard by the throat, knocks him to the ground and shoves the .38 into his mouth.

The guards at the command center, six feet away, leap for the rack that holds their shotguns.

Willie barks: One fuckin move and your buddy's dead.

They freeze.

Willie orders them to take off their clothes. They undo their belts, drop their pants. Keep going, he says. When they're down to only their underpants, they lie on their sides. Willie hog-ties them.

Now Willie puts on one of the guard's uniforms, slips the master key off the hip of the guard captain, runs down to D Block. Kliney and Akins let out a cheer. Willie unlocks their cells, leads them back to the command center. Freddie and Kliney and Akins all put on guard uniforms. Frantic, the four rumble down to the cellar.

The ladder is right where Rat said it would be. Each man grabs a rung and like four firemen they burst through the cellar door, into the yard.

The snow is still falling. Heavy flakes the size of index cards. Willie sets the ladder against the wall and Freddie scrambles up first. The beam of a searchlight swings wildly back and forth across the snow.

You there! Stop!

Willie hears boots stomping, guards scattering in the towers above. One guard squeezes off a round. Bullets cut up the snow, splinter the ladder. Two rungs blow away like dust.

Willie yells to the tower. Hold your fire—can't you see we're guards?

The guards peer down. They see the uniforms but can't make out the faces. The snow is too heavy and the snowflakes are reflecting the searchlights. In that one moment of indecision Willie and Akins dash up the ladder and do a swan dive from the top of the wall. This is why Willie waited for the biggest snowstorm of the year: not only do the snowflakes provide cover, the deep snowdrift at the bottom of the wall makes for a soft landing.

Kliney is last. He's at the top of the wall. The guards blast away. Jump, Kliney! He lets go, free-falls, lands headfirst. Willie and Akins try to pull him out of the snow but he won't move. He's hurt, Freddie says.

I think I broke my fuckin neck, Kliney moans.

So long as it's not your legs, Willie says, dragging him to his feet.

They run. Holmesburg is surrounded by open land, parks. Willie feels strong. He feels every push-up and sit-up of the last few months. He gulps the crisp air—he's *free*, which gives him even more strength, a second burst. They cross train tracks, come to a stream, splash across, tearing off the guard uniforms. Their prison uniforms underneath aren't too conspicuous. Black pants, blue work shirts. At least they're not wearing grays or stripes. As they come to the main road the prison siren starts to wail.

Willie looks up and down the road. No cars.

They jog half a mile. Still no cars.

They have a minute left, maybe two, before the guards and dogs are on them. Why are there no fuckin cars?

Freddie points. Headlights.

Some kind of truck, Kliney says, kneading his neck.

Willie stands in the road, waving his arms. The driver of the truck forgets he's near a prison and stops. Freddie reminds him. He jams the .38 under the driver's chin.

They all leap into the truck. The driver is sobbing. Don't hurt me, please don't hurt me.

Drive, Freddie says.

Where?

Drive, you mutt.

The driver hits the gas. Willie hears a loud clanking and jingling. He looks around. It's a milk truck. His burst of strength is suddenly gone. He remembers he hasn't eaten all day. He's so weak, he can barely turn the cap on a bottle. He takes a long drink, wipes his mouth on his sleeve, passes the bottle to Kliney, opens another. He samples a buttermilk, a cream, a skim. The finest wines, the rarest champagnes have never tasted this good. He closes his eyes. Thank you again, God. You must be pulling for me—you must. Why else would you keep sending me these gifts, blessings, every time I crash out?

For the rest of Willie's life the taste of milk will bring back memories of this moment. The milk running down his chin, the snow-packed roads, the drifting snowflakes. And all the memories will be bathed in radiant white. The color of innocence.

Reporter checks his watch. We should go, he says.

They get back in the car, quickly, as if the bank alarm is going off, and peel away.

After the tunnel didn't work out, Mr. Sutton, I'm amazed that you were able to work up the will to attempt another escape. Not to mention that officials at Holmesburg must have been keeping a close eye on you. It seems impossible.

It was.

So how did you manage it?

The main reason no one escapes from prison is they think they can't. They're told they can't, every day, by the guards and the warden and their fellow prisoners. And by all the outward signs—the bars and walls. Step One in every escape is believing you can do it.

And Step Two?

There was this pip-squeak trusty rat. I worked him, charmed him, got him to sneak me a gun and some saws.

Like Egan.

Yes and no.

Someone tell me where I'm going, Photographer says.

Staten Island Ferry Terminal, Sutton says.

Why?

You'll see.

Reporter opens his briefcase, removes some files. Mr. Sutton, I have to say, the clips give a different account of that breakout.

Do they.

According to several newspapers from that time, it was Freddie who got the gun smuggled to him in prison. It was Freddie who broke the lock on his cell. With a chisel. Then Freddie freed you

and the others, and someone used a pair of scissors to stab a guard,
William Skelton, and then you all used Skelton as a human shield
when the guards started firing.

That's not how I remember it.

When they reach the edge of town they debate killing the driver.
They put it to a vote. Watching them raise their hands, one by
one, the driver wets his pants. Three to one, the Let Him Lives
win.

Before jumping out of the truck Freddie grabs the driver by
the collar. Go straight home, Freddie tells him. Take the phone
off the hook. Say nothin to nobody or I will come find you.

The driver swears, he'll never tell a soul.

I still say we kill him, Freddie says as the others pull him
away from the driver and down the road.

They split up. Freddie and Willie go one direction, Akins and
Kliney go another. Willie feels lucky to be with Freddie, who
still has the gun, who grew up in Philly and knows places they
can hide. They walk through the snowstorm, side by side,
hunching their shoulders against the wind. A dozen blocks. Two
dozen. Then, from behind them, sirens. They duck behind a
house. Cop cars skid up to the curb. Red lights strobe the snow.
Willie runs straight up the backyard fence, like a man in a
cartoon. Freddie is right behind him. Shotgun blast—the fence
explodes. Freddie cries out. Willie lands awkwardly but bounces
back up, sprints down a snow-packed alley. Somehow managing
to stay on his feet, he hits his stride, tells himself not to look
back, not to think about the guards taking steady aim, the bullets
hurtling toward a spot exactly halfway between his shoulder
blades. The darkness that's about to swallow him.

His lungs burning, his legs about to give, he cuts right, darts
into a side yard. A cellar door—he grabs the handle. Locked. He
pulls harder, breaks the lock, dives. The floor is cement, frozen.

He lands on his face. His nose gushes blood. He scrambles to his feet, pulls the cellar door shut.

Sirens go wailing past. Then. Slowly. Fade.

He waits. He hums under his breath, trying to hold himself together. *I don't wanna play in your yard. I don't like you anymore.* He paces. After two hours he climbs out the cellar door. *You'll be sorry when you see me. Sliding down our cellar door.* He runs and runs through snow up to his knees. The snow is coming down harder and the wind is gusting. Flakes blow into his eyes, mouth. His shoes are full of snow, he can't feel his toes. Where the fuck is the highway?

There. Through those trees—blurry headlights. Now he hears the sizzle of Goodyears on macadam. He stations himself on the shoulder, thumb out. A black Nash stops, a man in a flashy gray suit at the wheel. You look clear froze, chum.

I am, Willie says. Car broke down. Damn Chevys.

That's why I'm a Nash man.

How far you going?

Princeton. That help?

And how. I got a sister there.

Hop in.

Turns out it's not simple kindness that made the man stop. He stopped because he needed to tell someone about his sex life. The different girls he's laying, exactly how he's laying them, unbeknownst to his wife. And his girlfriend—unbeknownst to her too. He likes this word, *unbeknownst*, shoves it into every sentence, rams it in there, hard, whether or not it fits. He tells Willie that he owns rental properties all over Long Island, New Jersey, Queens, and when he goes around to collect rent, that's when he scores.

Just the other day, he says, I collected on this family, just the mom and three kids, Dad died overseas, you know how that goes, and well so Mom tells me she can't pay the rent, she lost her job, boo hoo, she pleads with me not to put her and the kiddies out, and she's a real looker, let me tell you, so I say sure you can stay, no problem, hot stuff, so long as you bend over that chair right there and let me ball you, because I aint about to give somethin for nothin. She says please no my kids are in the next room, so I say fine then you're out on your keister, but well just then out of the bedroom comes the daughter, I mean what a doll, fifteen going on twenty-five if you get me, and friskier than the mom, and well I guess I don't have to tell you what happened next.

No, Willie says. You don't. Please.

Willie longs to let his head fall against the seat and shut his eyes, but Sex Maniac won't stop. Worse, Sex Maniac is now sulking, offended that Willie's not contributing to the conversation, which is apparently the hidden cost of a ride to Princeton. If you want to ride with Sex Maniac, Willie realizes, you better put out. So Willie regales Sex Maniac with a series of fake carnal exploits, which takes all his talents as a storyteller, because he's only been with a few women in his life and the last person he kissed was a man. The effort of fabricating conquests, inventing perversions, makes him break out in a cold sweat. Overpowering guards and outrunning shotguns was easier.

But it seems to be working. Sex Maniac is guffawing, slamming his palm on the Nash's steering wheel. You showed her, Sex Maniac shouts. You gave her what for, didn't you, chum? I'll say you did! Then what?

Willie points. Princeton Junction—next exit.

Sex Maniac pulls over. Willie steps out. His third narrow escape of the night. Sex Maniac tells him to wait. He writes his phone number on a book of matches, hands it to Willie.

Now, chum, I live just on the other side of that hill, you call me next time you're in Princeton. Me and my gal, you and yorn, we'll have dinner.

328

Sure, Willie says. Say, speaking of dinner, I haven't eaten since last night, and I just remembered, I left my dang billfold back in the Chevy. It's a long walk to my sister's.

Sex Maniac holds up his hand. He's only too happy to lend Willie two bucks.

Willie walks until he comes to an all-night diner.

Cup of coffee, please. Buttered roll.

A *Star-Ledger* lies on the counter. He flips through it. Nothing about the escape. Too soon. And yet the waitress looks at him funny. Maybe it's been on the radio in the kitchen. New York, he thinks. He needs to get to New York. Where he'll blend in. Where people don't notice anything, because everyone's a fugitive from something.

The waitress keeps eyeing him.

Willie wets a finger, runs it around his plate, picking up the crumbs. He's starved, but he doesn't want to spend the last of Sex Maniac's money. He stands, smiles at the waitress. Well. Better be shoving off.

He can feel her watching him all the way out the door.

He sets out for the highway, but soon comes to the Princeton campus. He stops, takes it all in. Ah to be a student here. To sit in that beautiful library and just read books. To know as sure as you know anything that you have a future and that it's bright. How are some people so lucky? He circles the library once, his soul clotted with envy, then trudges off again in search of the highway. He wanders back roads, dirt roads, loses the road altogether. The snow in some places comes to his knees. His waist. Better than shit, he says aloud.

A stray dog growls, charges him. Teeth white as the snow. Willie doesn't care. His total indifference scares off the dog.

He would cry, but his tear ducts are frozen. His ears too. He cups his hands over them. They feel as if they might crack and fall off his head. Climbing a hill he loses his footing, falls backwards, hits a tree with the base of his spine. He climbs again, up and over, trudges through woods so thick that there's scarcely room for him to pass between the trees.

His clothes are starting to freeze. They feel like a suit of armor. He hears a voice. He turns in a circle. Who's there? Why did he let Freddie keep that .38? Show yourself, he growls.

Above him. He shields his face, looks up. A barn owl, the size of a toddler, sits on a low branch and looks directly at Willie with mustard yellow eyes. Now it furrows its brow and slowly spreads its wings. Avenging angel. Willie wonders if Freddie's been caught yet.

He walks farther, loses all sense of direction. Never mind the highway, he needs to find shelter, right now, or he's done for. He wants to fall down, curl up, quit. A little farther, he tells himself. Little by little. Keep on. He comes to a clearing, a farm, an old red lopsided barn. He knocks at the rotted door, gives it a kick.

Rakes, scythes, saddles, tractor. He climbs into the hayloft, burrows into a corner. Wind comes singing and whistling through the walls, freezing his eyelashes, the hairs inside his nose. He remembers reading an article about hypothermia. Sleep precedes death. Or was it death precedes sleep? Either way. He stands, does jumping jacks. He talks to God, proposes a pact, a covenant. I know you're pulling for me, God. You can't fool me. The tunnel. The milk truck. Of course you root for prisoners. You were a prisoner yourself. You spent your last night on this earth in jail. I know you're on my side, God, so please save me again, get me out of this one, God, and I will change.

And while you're at it, God? A smoke?

He remembers Sex Maniac's matches. He manages to get one lit. In the corner of the abandoned barn, with some hay and scrap wood, he starts a small fire, which is his salvation.

At dawn he sets out again, finds the highway. Within minutes a truck pulls over.

Car broke down, Willie says, wringing wet, teeth chattering. Damn Ch-ch-chevys.

The trucker doesn't notice anything unusual about Willie's appearance or demeanor. He doesn't notice anything about anything. He's hauling oak tables to the Bronx and he's mad for company. Tables make damn poor company, he says.

But what he's really mad for is sleep. They've only gone a few miles when Willie sees the trucker's face drifting down down down to the steering wheel. Willie taps Trucker's knee. Trucker jerks awake, looks at his knee, looks at Willie, eyes narrowed, as if Willie is a pervert. Then Trucker realizes that he almost killed them both. Sorry, Trucker grumbles, aint been sleeping much lately, trouble at home.

He fumbles in the breast pocket of his work shirt for a cigarette. He comes out with a crumpled pack, offers one to Willie. Even before he looks, Willie knows. Chesterfield. He takes the cigarette, puts it between his lips. Trucker lights it with a silver Zippo. Willie thought the cold milk was delicious, but that was nothing compared to this Chesterfield. The first puff tastes sweet, like the first bite of cotton candy at Coney Island. The second puff tastes spicy, peppery, nutritious, like the steaks Eddie and Happy bought him when he was down on his luck. Smoke fills his lungs and quickens his blood and instantly restores his vitality, his will to live. He takes another drag, and another and another, and tells Trucker stories, riveting stories, fantastic stories, wildly untrue stories, which keep them both awake. If life has been nothing more than a build-up to this moment, this ethereal high, this bonding with a stranger, then it hasn't been in vain.

He watches the snow-filled woods fly by, and the highway signs, and he speaks again to God, who feels closer than the gearshift. Dear Lord, I don't know what I've wanted from you all my life. Communion? Amnesty? A sign? But with this Chesterfield I finally know what *you* want from *me*. You're agreeing to the covenant I proposed. I hear you. And I will *show you* that I hear. I will change.

He smokes the Chesterfield to the nub, to nothing, until it burns his fingertips. Even the burning feels good.

Trucker drops him right at the turnoff where the cops shot Eddie. Willie doesn't let himself think about that, doesn't think about anything as he waves to the George Washington Bridge and walks and walks all the way downtown. He focuses on his footsteps in the snow, and on the fact that it's a beautiful winter morning and he's not in C Block. He's in New York, New York.

He's in Times Fuckin Square.

He stops, looks up. Hello, Wrigley sign.

Neon fish, pink and green and blue, swim through the blizzard. Above the fish, in blinking green neon: WRIGLEY SETTLES THE NERVES. And above the neon letters the Wrigley mermaid welcomes Willie home.

He ducks into the Automat, hands his last dollar to the nickel thrower, who hands him twenty nickels. He buys a fish cake and a cup of piping hot coffee and takes it to a table by the window. He eats slowly, watching the people, but there aren't many people—it's early yet. When his food is gone he drinks the hot coffee, every drop. He runs a finger around the inside of the empty cup and runs the finger inside his mouth. He stares at the steam table, imagines piling a plate with beefsteaks, creamed potatoes, creamed spinach, poppy rolls, apple tartlets, jelly cookies, pumpkin pie. He holds his last twenty cents in his fist and closes his eyes and feasts on the smells. Not just the food smells, but the New York smells. Cigars, peppermint, aftershave, plastic, leather, gabardine, urine, hair spray, sweat, silk, wool, talc, semen, subway funk and floor wax. Ah New York. You stink. Please let me stay.

At the stroke of nine Willie steps into the phone booth and dials the first employment agency listed in the yellow book. The woman asks his name.

Joseph Lynch mam.

He hears her typing a form.

I'm new to town, mam, and I need a position, anything, just till I can get on my feet.

She doesn't have much.

Anything, he says again.

The only thing I can think of—no, wait, Sandy filled that one yesterday. Hum-dee-dum, let's see. Where did I put that gosh-darned card?

Willie squeezes the phone. *Anything*.

Ta-da, she says. Porter.

Mam?

The Farm Colony out in Richmond. That's Staten Island. Ten dollars a week, plus room and board, Joseph.

I'll take it.

It's on Brielle Road.

She tells him the name of the head nurse, but it doesn't register. She says she'll phone the head nurse to say Joseph is on his way.

Porter, he tells himself, walking to the ferry. Porter? He thinks of Porter from Rosenthal and Sons. How the mighty have fallen. Except the mighty were never mighty. And the fallen were never fallen. With one of his last three nickels he buys a ticket on the ferry. At the gangplank is a newsstand and on every front page is his face. He tries to read the articles from a distance, but he can't. His eyes are getting bad. In four months he'll be forty-six years old.

The whistle blows. All aboard.

He flows with the crowd onto the ferry, eases onto a wooden bench and turns his face to the window, pretending to sleep. Half the passengers are reading papers, staring at his photo. At last, when the boat pulls away, Willie jumps up, runs onto the deck. No one else is out there, it's too cold. He leans against the wooden rail, leans into the wind, watches the city grow fainter.

The ferry churns up a wake of thick white foam. He puts a hand on his empty stomach, wishes he'd thought to save one bottle of milk.

A seagull appears. It hovers beside the boat, only needing to flap its long gray wings once every five seconds to keep pace. Willie would give anything to be that seagull. He thinks about reincarnation. He hopes it exists. He hopes this stray thought won't anger the Catholic God who's gotten him this far. Who now holds his marker.

As Manhattan disappears behind a wall of mist, Willie drops into a fog. He grips the wooden railing and imagines falling over. Maybe it's the only thing that makes sense—end all this running. He can feel the first shock of the white foam, then the bitter cold water. He can taste the salty brine, see the murky green darkness, followed by that different darkness. Waiting for that different darkness—a minute? five minutes?—would be the hard part.

The ferry enters deeper waters. It's a hundred feet down out here, he read that once. He knows what a hundred feet of darkness will feel like. The tunnel beneath Eastern State. And Meadowport Arch. He feels himself floating down, down. His body might never be found. There will be a victory in that.

He starts to climb the railing. Now he looks up. The Statue of Liberty. So beautiful. He looks at her feet. He never noticed before that she's stepping out of leg-irons. How has he never noticed this until now? He looks and looks and suddenly shoots out his arm and raises his hand to the statue. I get it, he shouts, smiling. I get it, honey.

He climbs down, pushes himself away from the wooden rail. I get it.

Photographer drives onto the ferry. As soon as the Polara comes to a stop Sutton steps out, limps to the rail, looks eagerly at the water. He points. Look, he says. There she is. Jesus, isn't she beautiful?

Photographer wipes the mist off his lens, shoots Sutton pointing at the statue.

Did you know, boys, that island where she stands used to be a prison?

Is that true? Photographer says. That can't be true.

The morning after I broke out, I got to this point and I was on the verge of despair. No, not the verge. I despaired. Right here. I tell you, I was two seconds from jumping. But she told me not to.

She? Told?

Sutton faces Reporter. She talks kid. She's the patron saint of prisoners and she ordered me to keep going. I know it's cornball and square these days to love the Statue of Liberty. It's like loving U.S. Steel or Bing Crosby. But we don't choose who we love. Or what. And that morning I fell for her. No other way to say it. I knew her, and she knew me. Inside out.

After fifteen minutes the ferry slows, floats toward the pier on Staten Island. A ferryman, wearing a Santa hat, emerges from the pilothouse. All ashore, all ashore.

Reporter and Photographer climb back into the Polara. They wait for Sutton, who reluctantly follows.

Photographer drives slowly off the ferry. A one-legged seagull stands in the way. Photographer honks. The bird scowls, hops off.

We're looking for Victory Boulevard, Reporter says. Mr. Sutton, you remember the way?

Silence.

Mr. Sutton?

Reporter turns. Sutton is grazing in the donut box, his mouth smeared with Bavarian cream and jelly. Jesus, Sutton says, these donuts are the best thing I've ever tasted. I never had such a sweet tooth in my life.

They pass block after block of tiny houses, identical, each one *with barred windows, an American flag, a lawn Santa or reindeer. Photographer looks at Sutton in the rearview. Willie, brother, you walked all this way? On no sleep, no food? Wearing a prison uniform? Seems impossible.*

I keep telling you boys, it was.

They turn up a hill, around a bend. They see a deep woods, then the faint outlines of massive brick buildings, dozens of them. Drawing closer they see that most of the buildings are covered with graffiti. Trees grow through their roofs and glassless windows.

Whoa, Photographer says. Ghost town.

A hurricane fence surrounds it all. Photographer pulls up to the fence.

This was the famous Farm Colony, Sutton says. Before Medicare, before Social Security, this was where New York put its sick and old and poor people. Thousands of them.

A landfill for humans, Photographer says.

A big one kid. Fifty buildings. A hundred acres. Not a happy place. But the perfect hiding place for me. And it had a kind of strange beauty. Twenty-four hours after I busted out of Holmesburg, I landed a job here. In the women's ward. As a porter. And for a while, shit. I was happy. I was actually happy. Because it wasn't me.

TWENTY

———

THE HEAD NURSE POINTS TO THE FLOOR. SHE'S CROWDING sixty, loveless, bloodless, squeezed into a white elastic nurse's uniform that seems to cut off her humanity along with her circulation. I want to see myself *right there*, she says.

Willie, wearing gray coveralls, JOSEPH stitched in red over the heart, squints. Mam?

The floor, Joseph. Your job is to make the floor shine like a mirror every night, so I can see myself in it every morning. The women in this ward have nothing. Less than nothing. The least we can do is provide them with a clean floor.

Willie nods, moves his mop a little faster. Yes mam.

Willie thinks Head Nurse might be insane. She goes on. And on. She talks and talks about the optimal shine and luster of the floor until Willie fantasizes about mopping it with her.

But in time he sees her point. There *is* a noticeable improvement in the overall mood of the women's ward when the floor is clean. He's always worked hard, taken pride in whatever he's put his hand to. Why shouldn't he be the best mopper he can be? As he did with robbing, he makes a study of mopping. He never knew there were so many wrong ways to mop, or that there was just one right way. Lots of hot soapy water, two cups of ammonia, a smooth semicircular motion when applying the vanilla-scented wax. Like frosting a cake. He stands back. Voilà. He recalls that most of the banks he robbed had dull floors. Figures.

About once a week people walk a bit more gingerly across

Willie's floors—a woman in the ward has died. Aside from mopping, the other part of Willie's job is loading the deceased onto a horse-drawn wagon and delivering her to the morgue. He dreads this task, but tries to perform it manfully, respectfully. Other porters call the morgue wagon the meat wagon. Willie never does.

This is the price of freedom, he tells himself as he lifts the lifeless woman into the wagon.

Better this than the Burg, he tells himself as he lifts the woman out.

Godspeed, he tells the woman as he drapes her onto one of the marble slabs.

On his day off Willie goes exploring. The Farm Colony sits in the center of Staten Island, a wilderness of thick, primeval woods. He can't get over the variety of trees—maples, sycamores, elms, oaks, peppers, apples. Some were here when George Washington was alive, and their longevity gives Willie an odd feeling of comfort. He lies at the base of an old elm, floating on his back in the pool of shade, and feels calm. He tries to think of the last time he felt calm. He can't.

One of the women in the ward tells Willie that Thoreau used to come to these woods. To get away.

Newspapers say that two of his fellow escapees—Kliney and Akins—have been recaptured. Only Willie and Freddie remain at large. So Freddie wasn't shot after all. Good for Freddie. Go Freddie go. Willie hopes he's wearing four-inch lifts, feeding papaya to some heart-stopping showgirl in Havana.

Then, gradually, newspapers move on. It's 1948. A new era. With Truman's bony finger on the Button, no one has time to worry about some Depression-era bank robber. Willie the Actor is dead, long live Joseph the Porter. In the Farm Colony library, Joseph reads several books on reincarnation.

The women of the Farm Colony adore Joseph, and he thinks

of them as he thinks of the trees. They provide a kind of comfort, a psychological shade. Willie spent much of his life in a world of men; Joseph dwells happily in a world of women. Of course many of the women talk as much as the trees. But several are chatterboxes. While waiting for his floors to dry, Joseph likes to sit with them, listen to their stories. They're alone, like him. They're trying not to think of tomorrow, like him. They're stuck here, like him. They despise banks. Many ended up at the Farm Colony because they lost their life savings to a failed bank or a crooked broker.

Sutton stands just inside the front entrance, Reporter and Photographer right behind him. The door is gone, the furniture is gone. Everything is gone but a few iron filing cabinets. A uniform hangs in a doorless closet.

He points. That was the head nurse's office.

They hear scuttling, fluttering. A pigeon flies past their heads. Photographer shoots a few photos through a large spiderweb.

Sutton backs out. He turns, stares at the surrounding woods. It wasn't just the Farm Colony, he says. Back then Staten Island was like a colony of broken people. No wonder I fit right in. Over that way was the biggest hospital on the East Coast for tubercular cases. Over there was the old seaman's home. Snug Harbor. Bunch of great old tars lived there. I used to play pinochle with them. They were always, but always, drunk. Couldn't tell a meld from a trick. No one drinks more than a retired Irish sailor. Nice bunch of fellas though. They introduced me to Melville. Still, if I had a night off, I preferred my ladies at the Farm Colony.

His favorite is Claire Adams. With her long wrinkled hand she often pats the chair beside her bed. Come, Joseph. Have a chat.

Yes, Mrs. Adams.

She insists that he call her Claire. He frowns, shakes his head.

She's too queenly, too beautiful, for him to be so familiar. She's at least twice Joseph's age but he tells her that he's in love with her.

Stop it, she says.

He puts his hand over the name patch on his shirtfront. Honest, he says. Ass over teakettle.

She laughs. If I thought you meant it, Joseph, I'd get out of this bed and dance you across the floor.

Mrs. Adams has traveled the world. She's dined with viscounts and generalissimos and Nobel laureates. She speaks four languages, has perfect pitch, and her gaze is so penetrating, so wise and free of condemnation, Joseph wants to tell her every one of his secrets. The compulsion to confess is so strong, he doesn't trust himself. He often sits, mouth shut, and lets Mrs. Adams do all the talking.

She tells him many times about the love of her life.

Oh Joseph—he had the most beautiful face. To look upon his face made me weak. His beauty *afflicted* me, can you understand?

Yes mam.

But my parents didn't approve. He was a Catholic, you see.

What happened?

They packed me off to Europe. The Grand Tour, they called it back then, but for me it was *l'exil à queue*. I was never so miserable. On the Seine, I wept. In the Sistine Chapel, I wept. On the Grand Canal, I wept and wept. All beauty saddened me, because it reminded me of my Harrison. That was his name. Harrison. Finally after ten months I defied my parents, sailed for New York. I flew to Harrison's side.

And?

He had married.

No.

She nods, looks off. It was so long ago, she says. How can it still have—such—?

Power, Joseph says.

Yes. That's the correct word, Joseph.

July 1949. With a coat of floor wax drying, Joseph sits with Mrs. Adams, looking through the Sunday newspapers scattered across her bed. An article in one of the papers mentions Picasso, which reminds Mrs. Adams of a famous portraitist who once begged her to sit for him.

At the very start of our session this young artist asked me to remove my hat. I did. He asked me to remove my top. I refused. He commanded me. I put my hat back on and stood to leave. He gnashed his teeth, pulled his hair, pleaded. He said he'd never be able to paint again unless he could see my body. I told him I'd never be able to face myself again if I showed him my body.

Joseph is laughing. Mrs. Adams is laughing. Now, Joseph, I must tell you, this artist was very—

She stops. She looks to the side, seeking the right word. Joseph smiles, waits. Temperamental? Talented? Minutes pass. His smile fades. He looks around for a nurse. He feels his palms growing clammy.

Then Mrs. Adams looks back at Joseph, blinks once, smiles. What was I saying?

Joseph can't tell if she knows that she's been gone. He doesn't ask.

It happens again days later. Mrs. Adams looks off midsentence and disappears, this time for ten minutes. This time her eyelids close. Joseph can see her eyes moving under the lids, like fish in a frozen pond. He tells her he'd better get back to his mopping. He stands, backs away from the bed.

In the weeks that follow it happens more and more, and each time she's gone a bit longer. He always stands, reluctantly, always leans over her bed, kisses her forehead. She's unaware of his kiss. His presence. She's far, far away. The Grand Tour.

In the late fall of 1949 Joseph is sitting by Mrs. Adams's bed, waiting. It's been almost two days since her last departure. Now, as if someone has thrown a switch, her eyelids quiver, open. She turns her head. Joseph smiles. She smiles. I came as soon as I could, Harrison.

Joseph's mouth falls open.

I thought of you every day in Italy. I went all to pieces.

Joseph looks around.

Harrison—did you wait for me?

Joseph rubs his neck.

Harrison, my darling, Father will not listen to reason. He's the most *stubborn* man.

Joseph folds and unfolds his hands in his lap.

Whatever will we do, Harrison?

Joseph tugs his earlobe.

Harrison?

We'll—*elope.*

Her face brightens. When?

Joseph clears his throat. Soon, he says.

Where shall we meet, Harrison?

You know.

She looks searchingly. Where?

Come into the garden, Maud.

At the place, Joseph says. Our special place.

I love you so, Harrison.

I love you, Mrs.— Claire.

When the time comes Joseph lifts her from the bed, carries her to the wagon. Draping her onto the marble slab, he holds her hand for a while. Then he goes and finds Head Nurse.

Mam?

What is it, Joseph? I'm busy.

I was just wondering, mam, what's to become of Mrs. Adams.

Head Nurse tugs at the elastic of her uniform. What happens to all of them, Joseph.

There's no family then?

None that wants to be found.

Where do they—where will they bury her?

Head Nurse stares at Joseph's floor. Potter's Field, I expect. That's typically the place.

Joseph waits until after midnight. A misty rain is falling. He walks to the ferry, sails to Manhattan, rides the subway to Brooklyn. He walks to Prospect Park, sits on a bench, making sure he hasn't been followed. Quickly he digs up a jar of his bank robbery money. A hundred yards from Meadowport.

He ducks behind a boulder, hidden from the street, pries open the jar. It's sealed tight, but not tight enough. Moisture has managed to get in. Mold has eaten away at the bills. All that planning, all that risk, all those years in prison—for this? *This?* Joseph stares at Ulysses Grant's mottled face. An awful chill comes over him as he wonders how airtight Mrs. Adams's container will be.

Out of sixty thousand dollars he's able to salvage about nine. He throws the rest in a trash can. Head down, collar up, he sets off for the ferry, but his feet take him a different direction. Within minutes he finds himself walking down President Street. He can feel his heart thudding as he comes close to the Endner house. It looks the same. The stained glass, the fancy balustrades, the iron fence. Someone has planted a small garden along the fence. Black-eyed susans, bittersweets, peonies. Several kinds of roses. There are no lights on. He creeps to the mailbox. No name. No telling who lives there, if anyone.

Hours later, back at the Farm Colony, Joseph sneaks into the morgue and sets a white envelope full of fifties on Mrs. Adams's chest. Wrapped around the money is a note. *Give her the works.*

A couple of women in this joint left a real mark on me. One was Mrs. Adams. She made me remember that we only go around once.

Gather ye rosebuds, Reporter says.

Gather whatever the fuck you need to gather. Just make the most of it.

Sutton reaches into the breast pocket of his suit, takes out the white envelope.

Mr. Sutton, why do you keep looking at your release papers?

No reason. Come on. I want to show you boys something.

Mrs. Adams is the first of many. Each time a woman dies, nurses at the Farm Colony find an envelope full of cash on her chest. Some say it's the Lord. Some say it's the Angel of the Farm Colony.

Joseph can't help himself. He knows he's taking a big risk, but it's the only joy he has. The only mischief.

Then, January 17, 1950. In the North End of Boston a crew hits the Brinks Building, making off with three million dollars, the biggest heist in American history. Cops say the crime is so bold, so stylish, it simply has to be the work of Willie Sutton, whose picture is on the front pages again.

Joseph keeps his head down, keeps mopping, hoping it will all go away. From down the hall he hears his name.

Joseph. Oh Joseph?

He turns. Head Nurse is marching across his wet floor. If Head Nurse is disregarding his Wet Floor signs, this can't be good.

She stops before him, looks at his face. Joseph, she says.

Mam.

That's not your name, is it? Joseph.

Mam?

You're Willie Sutton.

She hands him the newspaper. He looks at the photo. Looks at her. Yeah, he says with a sigh. Yeah. You got me.

I—what?

I'm Willie Sutton, he says. What a relief to finally say it out loud.

The color slowly drains from Head Nurse's face.

I knew this day was coming, he says. I guess I'm lucky, I've had a few good years.

But—what?

Joseph waits. And waits. That's a hot one, he says. Me—*Willie Sutton*. With all his money? A high-flyer like Willie the Actor wouldn't be caught dead mopping floors at the Farm Colony. No offense mam.

Head Nurse looks at Joseph, looks at the front page. She inhales sharply. Right, she says, suddenly laughing. I don't know what I was. Well. But he does look like you.

I guess. Around the eyes a little.

He turns back to his mopping.

Sutton leads Reporter and Photographer behind the women's ward, down a hill slick with mud and wet leaves. Reporter grabs Sutton just before he falls. Thanks kid. They push through a group of intertwined trees, into a clearing. A spear of sunlight pierces the trunk of an enormous apple tree. Sutton approaches cautiously. He puts on his glasses, examines the bark. He smiles. Curved into the bark is a rugged heart. Inside are three letters.

What is that, Mr. Sutton?

Photographer moves closer. S-E-E?

Boys, you are now standing in Willie's sacred grove.

Hold the phone. S-E-E? Sarah Elizabeth—Bess? She was here?

After the Brinks job the Feds put me on their Most Wanted list. Their first list ever. Kind of an honor. They listed all my aliases, all my women—starting with Sarah Elizabeth Endner. I knew she'd be in a state. I looked her up in the phone book—I remembered her married name. And why did I remember? It was Richmond. And I was living in Richmond. You think that's not a sign? Sure enough she was in Brooklyn. And just as I thought, she was beside herself. She was panicked. She didn't know what to do. Reporters were calling her, cops were calling her. A few hours later I met her at the dock. We got in her car, drove to these woods. We only had a few hours before she had to get back. But that's all you get in life. A few hours here, a few there. If you're lucky. Mrs. Adams taught me that. She's buried on the other side of this hill.

Photographer shoots Sutton, the tree. Was Bess still married, brother?

Yeah kid. She was.

Reporter looks at the sky. The sun is getting low, Mr. Sutton. I hate to take you away from your sacred grove, but we're officially pressed for time. I have to file my story in a little more than two hours. So. We need to get to Brooklyn.

We're taking the Verrazano back, Photographer says. It's faster.

Okay, Sutton says.

Just one more stop on your map, Mr. Sutton. Dean Street. Then—Schuster?

Mm.

Mr. Sutton.

Yeah kid. Yeah. Whatever you say.

TWENTY-ONE

WILLIE DOESN'T CATCH THE LANDLADY'S NAME. SOMETHING like Mrs. Influenza. She speaks no English and he speaks prison Spanish, so they have a hard time communicating. He tells her that he's a veteran, that he needs quiet, that his name is Julius Loring. She smiles, bewildered. He peels off two hundred dollars, six months' rent in advance. The language barrier crumbles.

The address is 340 Dean Street. It's a narrow three-story clapboard in the barrio. Landlady gives Willie her best room, third floor, overlooking the street. It's tiny, but furnished. Dresser, Hide-A-Bed, club chair. He doesn't need more. The club chair sits by a window that catches the afternoon light. He spends the first few days sitting there, watching the sunsets, thinking. The first order of business, he decides, is his face.

He prowls the docks, wharves, waterfront saloons, looking for guys he knew in the joint. He finds Dinky Smith, who sends him to Lefty MacGregor, who gives him an address for Rabbit Lonergan, who sends him to an old coffee warehouse, in the back room of which he finds Mad Dog Kling reading a newspaper by a gooseneck lamp. Well fuck a duck in Macy's front window, Mad Dog says, squinting up through the corona of light. If it aint America's most wanted.

The years since Sing Sing have not been kind to Mad Dog. The years have kicked Mad Dog's ass. Pursed mouth, goggle eyes, he has a bleary, defeated Book-of-Job air about him. He reminds Willie of those black-and-white photos: Dust Bowl Farmer. He wears a baggy brown suit with a frayed blue necktie, but looks as if he should be wearing denim coveralls and watching a cloud of locusts eat his crops.

Willie tells Mad Dog he needs help. Shrink once mentioned a network of disgraced doctors, guys who lost their licenses but still do back-alley stuff. Abortions, bullet removals, so forth. Willie asks Mad Dog if he has any connections in that network. Mad Dog relights a cigar stub.

I might, Willie. But those quacks don't come cheap.

I've got some—savings.

Mad Dog grins, mirthless. I bet you do, he says. I read the papers.

Not as much as you think, Willie says. Which brings me to my next question. What are you doing for dough these days, Mad Dog?

Odd jobs. Bits and snatches. For the waterfront boys.

Bits and snatches?

You know. Guy owes, guy can't pay, I drop by. Goodbye elbow.

What do you get for a thing like that?

Fifty bucks.

Willie looks away. He hates Mad Dog, and he's pretty sure the feeling is mutual. What kind of life is this, to seek out such people, to need such people? To ask such people for help?

Fifty bucks, Willie says. Not much.

Oh, elbows are easy, Mad Dog says, misunderstanding. It's just a hinge. You bend it the wrong way, snap.

Willie steps into the light of the gooseneck. What I'm saying, Mad Dog. How would you like to help me take down a few banks?

Mad Dog points his cigar stub at Willie. That's like Marciano asking if I want to spar.

Sutton stands before 340 Dean Street, pointing. I used to sit at that window right there. Afternoons, children would come running

out of that school up the block. They saw me one day, sitting there,
my face covered with bandages, they about-faced and ran in the
other direction.

Photographer does a back-stretching exercise against the hood
of the Polara. Bandages, Willie?

From the plastic surgery.

Reporter holds up his hand. Plastic what now?

He sees patients in the middle of the night, in the office of a
legit colleague who gets a kickback for every illegal procedure.
Mad Dog sets up the meet, and offers to drive Willie, but Willie
wants to do this alone.

A nervous receptionist shows Willie into a small examining
room. After half an hour the quack comes in through a second
door. The underside of his chin hangs like an udder, his cheeks
sag like bread dough. Willie wonders why Quack hasn't let one
of his colleagues, disgraced or legit, fix his own kisser.

Hello, Mr. Loring.

Willie hands him an envelope full of cash. Quack shoves the
envelope quickly into the pocket of his white coat, tells Willie
to sit on a paper-covered table. Holding up a sketch pad, he
draws a giant circle, marks the circle with x's, dotted lines. The
circle apparently is Willie's face.

First, Mr. Loring, I'm going to make a two-inch incision in the
columella. That's the tissue just between your nostrils. Then I'm
going to peel back the skin. Then I'm going to cut away any excess
cartilage and scar tissue and take a grindstone to any protruding
or asymmetrical bone. Essentially reshaping the nose God gave
you. I'll need to work faster than normal, because of the, ah, special
circumstances. And I won't have an assistant. So I must tell you,
this may not be perfect, and there will be more risks than typically
associated with such a procedure. Infection, so on, so forth.

What were you thinking to do for the pain?

You'll be completely under.

Nah. Give me a local.

Willie isn't letting anyone put him under. He has too many secrets, too many memories of Shrink, the slippery hypnotist. Quack opens his eyes wider. Whatever you say, Mr. Loring.

He sounds tickled that Willie will be awake. He also sounds a little too keen to get down to cutting. He asks if Willie would like him to do the eyes while he's at it. Give the lids a lift? Stay away from my eyes, Willie says. Willie looks again at the diagram of his face on the legal pad. He's troubled that Quack has misspelled the word *nasal*. Willie wishes he'd asked Mad Dog what Quack did to lose his medical license. Watching Quack fondle his blades, Willie thinks it might have been something bad.

Willie lies back. In goes the needle. The pain isn't much. It's the other sensations that make the operation traumatic. Willie can feel every cut, every chip, every grind. Such violent acts on such a delicate appendage. He thinks about sawing the bars of his cells, chipping the rock under Eastern State. He thinks about Father hammering an anvil. He passes out.

When he opens his eyes the lights are off. Quack is gone, the nervous receptionist is gone. Willie is still on the paper-covered table, still on his back. He feels as if his nose has been removed, the hole filled with a tent stake. He rolls off the table, staggers to a wall mirror. He has two black eyes and across the center of his face are two blood-soaked bandages in a large X.

His fedora pulled low, he walks home. Landlady happens to be coming down the stairs as he's going up. She shrieks, babbles. Thank God he's been brushing up on his Spanish with her grown daughter. *Estoy bien*, he says. *No es nada. Gracias. Me metí en una pelea con unos hombres en un bar.*

For weeks Willie hides in his room. Mad Dog brings him food and books—a bizarre assortment of titles. Willie told Mad Dog to ask the clerk for some great books. The clerk must have thought Mad Dog meant the Great Books. So while convalescing Willie encounters Dante, Woolf, and Proust for the first time.

Proust overpowers him. The sentences are so long they make his nose hurt. Either this Proust is bughouse or else Willie's having a bad reaction to Mad Dog's black-market painkillers. He can't make heads or tails of the plot. There is no plot. And yet sometimes an interminable sentence will end with an image that brings a lump to Willie's throat, or a turn of phrase will knock loose a piece of Willie's forgotten past. Something deep inside him responds to Proust's obsession with time, his defiance of time. Only a man at war with time would write a million-word book. Willie can't wait to get to the sixth volume—*The Fugitive*.

At Willie's request Mad Dog also brings him *Peace of Soul*, by Bishop Fulton J. Sheen. Willie read a review in the paper. He's been troubled about his soul, he longs for peace—it sounded interesting. In fact it rivets him. He sits up all night, reads the book cover to cover, goes back and rereads the parts about remorse. Whole passages seem addressed to him. Remorse, according to Sheen, is a sin. Remorse is prideful, self-centered. Judas felt remorse. Instead, Sheen says, we must emulate Peter— *who felt not remorse but God-centered regret.*

Willie has no remorse, and some days he feels nothing but regret, so he's comforted. According to Sheen, his account with God is square.

Then, however, Sheen says something that haunts Willie, that stays with him longer than the memory of Quack's blades. Along with regretting, Sheen says, a sinner must fully *confess*. Willie sets the book down, lights a Chesterfield. Regret *and* a full confession? Pretty steep price for eternal salvation. He looks at the ceiling. Being a fugitive has made him more acutely aware of the Eyes that always see. The One from whom we can never hide. He asks the ceiling of his tiny furnished room if Sheen is right. Confess? Really? And if he doesn't—what then?

He feels an answer coming. A judgment. He has a hunch it's going to hurt. Distracted, he blows smoke through his sutured nostrils, causing a tiny atom bomb of blinding pain.

A week after the surgery Willie is due to have Quack remove the stitches. He can't face that ghoul again. Mad Dog brings him a bottle of Jameson and a pair of needle-nose pliers. Willie gulps the whiskey, bites a rag, yanks the stitches himself. Mad Dog holds the mirror.

After, Willie apologizes to Mad Dog for all the screaming.

Mad Dog laughs. Please. I'm used to guys screaming.

Sutton takes one last look at his former window. When you're a kid, he says, wondering how your life is going to turn out, you never imagine you might end up living under an assumed name, in a furnished room, your face covered with bandages, scaring schoolchildren.

Reporter fetches his briefcase from the Polara. He puts it on the hood, clicks it open. I saw nothing in the files, he says, about plastic surgery. But now that you mention it, these old photos—there is a difference. They really don't look like you.

Maybe we do *have the wrong guy, Photographer says.*

Sutton touches his nose, gives it a squeeze, looks up the block. That quack was insane but he did nice work. Then one day I was walking back to my room and right here I met a girl. Right about where you boys are standing she gave me the big eye. I thought that meant my new nose was a hit. But of course she was a hooker. They can spot a lonely guy from a mile away. With just one look she knew who I was, what I needed. Turned out, though, I was what she needed too.

She has pale white skin, jet-black hair, large black eyes. One eye is slightly larger than the other. Willie tells her it's cute. She taps a finger below the larger eye.

This one, she says, was always the same size as its brother. But lately it keep getting bigger, I don't know why.

He tells her she should see a doctor. She says she doesn't like doctors. He insists, but she's stubborn. Half Irish, half Egyptian, she tells Willie.

That explains it, he says.

She was born and raised in Cairo. Her mother was from Dublin, her father was a Mizrahi Jew. During the war, she says, their life was hard. But peace was much harder. Peace unleashed a more localized chaos. Mobs surged into her neighborhood, carrying clubs, torches. They blew up buildings, set houses ablaze, pulled people from their beds. They dragged men through the streets and bludgeoned them in front of their families.

Why? Willie asks.

Israel, she says. Land. Religion. Why people do anything?

The last time she saw her father, he was standing at the front door of their house, waving a carving knife, keeping the mob at bay. He yelled to her mother, Run, run, I'll find you!

She and her mother bolted out the back door to a neighbor's house. In the morning her father lay in the street. Pieces of him, she says. She and her mother fled with the neighbor, overland on foot, then by boat to America. On the boat they had to fight off men, even boys. One night they had to fight off the neighbor.

Her mother died four days before the boat reached New York Harbor. Grief, shame, illness, maybe all three. When the boat docked she watched immigration officials carry her mother off like a bag of mail.

She tells Willie her name is Margaret. Willie tells her his name is Julius. They're in a coffee shop near his room on Dean Street.

Why you wear these dark glasses, Julius?

Some people are after me, Margaret.

Why they after you, Julius?

I'd rather not say, Margaret.

You did crimes, she says softly.

He lights a Chesterfield, looks at the tabletop. He straightens the cutlery. He takes a sip of black coffee. Nods.

Do you hurt anybody?

He doesn't answer.

She makes two fists, holds them before his face. Do you make harm on anybody?

I go out of my way not to.

You promise?

Yeah.

Fine, she says. Is all that matter to me.

Willie doesn't have a phone, and neither does Margaret, so they arrange their dates well in advance. They only go out late, very late, when there's less chance of Willie being spotted, which suits Margaret. She already lives in a nighttime world. She comes to Willie's room, or else he picks her up from her room at the other end of Brooklyn, and they hit an all-night diner, a jazz club, a movie theater.

They both love movies. Willie feels safest when slouched low in a dark theater, his face in a bag of popcorn, and Margaret feels safest when she can lose herself in a soaring love story. There are many to choose from in 1951. Together they see *A Streetcar Named Desire*, *An American in Paris*, *The African Queen*. Margaret adores *The African Queen*. As the music rises and the credits roll, as the men and women in the theater crush their cigarettes under their heels and hurry toward the exit, Margaret touches Willie's arm.

Please, she says.

He looks at her, smiles, eases back into his seat. Sure, he says. I guess I can take another trip down that river with Bogie and Kate.

After the second show they go for coffee. Margaret can't stop talking about the movie. We are like them, she says.

Who?

Humphrey Bogie and Kathy Hepburns.

Willie looks around the diner, to make sure no one is listening. She chides him. No one care my thoughts about Humphrey Bogie, she says.

Sorry, Willie says. Force of habit. You were saying.

They on their leaky boat, we on ours.

I see. Yeah.

Is them against the world. Is us too, Julius.

Which one of us is Bogie?

She laughs, reaches across the table, takes his hand. You *look* like Bogie.

Willie twitches his lips, rolls his cigarette. Here's looking at you kid.

Her eyes widen. Julius, you just like him. You should be an actor.

Nah.

What this means, she asks—here is looking at you?

Oh, he says. It's an expression.

But what it means?

It means—here's to you.

She squints.

It means cheers, Willie says. Sort of a toast. Like *L'chaim!*

And what it means when Bogie says, Let us go while the going is good.

Another expression. Figure of speech.

But what it means?

It means the bad guys are coming, the bad guys are about to kick in the door, let's get out of here.

But this expression—I don't understand.

It just means—now.

Then why he does not say *now*? It take less time to say *now*. If he want to go when the good is going—

Going is good.

—then why he waste time with all these words? While he is so busy saying let us go now, the bad guys can be coming.

Willie starts to laugh. A piece of pie goes down the wrong pipe. He coughs, laughs harder. His eyes fill with tears. Now Margaret laughs, and soon they're both pointing at each other, wiping their eyes with paper napkins.

Ah Margaret, I haven't laughed in I don't know how long.

The waitress behind the counter stares.

The waitress is looking, Willie whispers.

Here's looking at *her*, Margaret says.

They're going to ask us to leave.

While the going is *good*.

After their dates Margaret usually spends the night at Dean Street. She wakes before dawn, dresses quickly in the half-light, kisses Willie goodbye. One morning he tells her not to go. She has no choice, she says, she has to work. He tells her no, wait, he has something for her. While she perches on his club chair he gets out of bed and fumbles in his suit, which hangs neatly from the top drawer of the dresser. He pulls out a roll of cash wrapped in a rubber band. The nick from his last bank job with Mad Dog. He hands it to Margaret.

What this is?

Gift.

Why gift?

Why what?

Gift for who? For you or me?

What's *that* supposed to mean?

Are you giving me? Or buying me?

For Pete's sake, I just want you to take it easy, find another job.

Is no other jobs for me. You know this, Julius. Is no way out.

There's always a way out, Margaret.

Why you doing this?

I want you to be around more. Spend more time with me. Is that so bad?

Why?

Say, what kind of crazy third degree is this?

People do not just help other people for no reason.

Okay. You want a reason? I like you.

She holds up the roll of money. What this make us?

I don't think there's a word for us, Margaret.

She thinks. She wraps both hands around the money.

I just want you to be happy, Margaret.

Is very kind. Thank you, Julius.

At Willie's request, Mad Dog pays a visit to Margaret's boss and delivers her resignation, effective immediately. Now, while Willie is off planning the next bank job with Mad Dog, Margaret is arranging fresh flowers in his room, shopping for his books, combing the newspapers for jazz concerts and movies they might like.

Some nights, if Willie is too tired, if he has a job coming up, he and Margaret heat some soup, listen to the radio. She likes him to read to her. He teaches her Tennyson. *Come into the garden, Maud.* He replaces Maud with Margaret. He teaches her Pound. *Now you will come out of a confusion of people.* She loves this line, says it over and over, though she's not sure what it means.

Poetry doesn't have to mean anything, he says.

So poetry is like Humphrey Bogie.

Well—no. It's just that sometimes a line of poetry is beautiful, that's all. And the beauty is the meaning. Or it's all the meaning you need.

I like things that have meaning.

I think people care too much about meaning. Meaning is a pipe dream. A grift. I like things that are beautiful. That's why I like *you.*

She smiles, presses her cheek to his.

Best of all Margaret enjoys stretching out on Willie's bed and wrapping an arm across her eyes while he sits in his chair and reads the newspapers aloud. They have a similar slant on the world, a kindred sense of good guys and bad. She hisses when he reads about Joseph McCarthy, smiles when he reads about Gandhi.

Before they both get under the covers and turn out the lights she reads their horoscopes. Her mother was fascinated by astrology. What is your birth date, Julius?

June 30.

Uh-oh. Cancer.

That bad?

Same as me. We the only sign ruled by the moon.

What's that mean?

We moody, sensitive, emotional.

That's the bunk.

Is true. You do not know yourself.

What makes you say that?

No one do.

No one knows me, or no one knows themselves?

No one knows nothing about no one.

For Willie's fiftieth birthday Margaret buys him a new fedora. For Margaret's twenty-seventh birthday Willie buys her a charm bracelet, a silk scarf, a black-and-white bonnet. Though it cost the least—thirteen dollars at Saks—she likes the bonnet best.

You'd think I bought you a mink coat, he says.

I like this better. Nothing is hurt for this.

He thinks of the money he used to buy that hat, the bank he robbed to get it. One of the tellers sobbed with fear the whole time he and Mad Dog were cleaning out the safe. He puts the thought from his mind as Margaret sets the hat on her head like a diamond tiara. She glides around Willie's room wearing nothing else. He tells her that her body is remarkable.

I know.

He laughs. He calls her his Irish Cleopatra. Get it? he says. Clee *O'Patra*?

She doesn't get it, and he can't explain.

Late on the Fourth of July, very late, it's too hot to sit in the room on Dean Street. It's too hot to sit anywhere. Willie takes Margaret for a ride on the ferry. They stand on the deck, enjoying the breeze, smelling the water, listening to the last fireworks crackling onshore. Margaret is happy. Willie is content. Until the Statue of Liberty comes into view. The seven rays of the statue's crown, representing the seven continents, look exactly like the seven cellblocks of Eastern State and the Burg—he never noticed until now. How is it that every time he looks at this statue he sees something he didn't see before?

Margaret puts an arm around his shoulders. You are having unhappy thoughts, Julius.

I am.

I see in your face. The moon is ruling you again.

Yeah. Maybe.

I forbid you to have unhappy thoughts.

He turns, places a palm under her chin.

I like when you touch me like that, Julius.

She takes off her silk scarf and wraps it around his neck. Julius?

Yeah, Margaret.

I think you would like to touch *her* like that.

Who?

She points at the statue. Her. I do not like the way you looking at her.

You got me. Dead to rights. She means a great deal to me. I've been seeing her on the side for years.

Margaret makes a clucking sound. This statue make people crazy. I do not understand. She promise everyone is free. Is a lie.

Maybe so. But it's a beautiful lie.

She is a *liar*. If I have to be poor, if I have to earn a living on my back, fine, but this is not free. Do not tease me with this word—free. Where I come from we have a word for this kind of lady tease.

Everyone has that word, Margaret.

She is a *bitch*.

Willie pulls Margaret close. You make a valid point, he whispers, but maybe it's best not to shout it on the Fourth of July.

She looks around. Tourists along the railing are staring. I did not know I was shouting, she says.

As the summer winds down, Willie wishes he could take Margaret to Ebbets Field. Along with the rest of New York he's obsessed with the pennant race. His sainted Dodgers are trying to hold off the deathless Giants. What he wouldn't give to spend a few hours behind first base, cheering on Jackie Robinson. But an outdoor stadium, in broad daylight, surrounded by thirty-four thousand people? Impossible.

Then the season comes to its historic crescendo, one final game, and Willie has no choice. He has to see it. He walks Margaret down to Frank's Bar and Grill, one of the few bars in Brooklyn with a TV. It's also a cop hangout, so Willie wears extra-dark smoked glasses, fake sideburns, lots of Margaret's makeup.

Along the way she questions him. All summer your Dodgers could not lose?

Yeah.

And these Giant mens were dead.

Yeah.

And then these Giant mens come back from the dead?

They did.

How they do this?

They never quit.

I like these Giant mens.

No, no. Margaret, we're rooting for the Dodgers. Yes, the Giants never quit. But neither did the Dodgers. When the Giants came back, the Bums could have hung their heads, but they won the last game of the season—that's what forced a tie. That's why there was a three-game playoff. The Giants won the first game, and still the Dodgers didn't quit. They won the second. Now, today, is for all the marbles.

Why it matter so much to you?

You identify with Hepburn. I identify with the Dodgers. They're bums, they're losers, but if they could win just once, it would be a sign.

Margaret hooks her arm in Willie's. I will root with all my heart for your Dodgers.

She sits on a stool at the corner of the bar, wearing her birthday bonnet, while Willie paces up and down the bar, pleading with the TV mounted above the bottles. His pleading works. Brooklyn takes a 4–2 lead into the ninth.

Three outs to go, Margaret. Three little outs.

She blows him a kiss as if he's on the mound. Hooray, Julius.

The Giants quickly get two men on base. Then drive one in: 4–3. Thomson stalks to the plate. No, Willie says, please, not Thomson. Everything about Bobby Thomson frightens Willie, even his name. He thinks of all the prison guards who held Thompsons on him. Thomson even looks like a prison guard. That big round face. That ape-like grin.

Willie begs the Dodgers not to bring in Branca to pitch to Thomson. He begs the bartender not to let them bring in Branca. Thomson just hit a home run off Branca, he tells the bartender. In the first game of the playoff, remember? Doesn't anyone remember?

When the Dodgers bring in Branca, when Thomson swats a fat Branca fastball high beyond the left field wall, the bar goes silent. Willie has heard this kind of silence only once. A Dark Cell. The solitary confinement of the fan.

As Thomson rounds the bases, *the Giants win the pennant*, Willie is on his knees in the middle of the barroom. Margaret jumps off her stool, *the Giants win the pennant*, runs to him. She helps him stand, pays their tab, leads him out of the bar.

Is only a game, Julius. Is only a game.

It's not, Willie says. It's a sign. It's a judgment.

My head just wasn't screwed on straight, Sutton says, pacing up and down Dean Street. Five years on the run will do that to you. I got involved with this girl—Margaret. I got wrapped up in that fuckin pennant race. Fuckin Thomson.

The shot heard round the world, Photographer says, lighting a Newport.

Poor Branca, Reporter says.

Fuckin rat, Sutton says. A sportswriter back then said Ralph Branca was so hated, he should find Willie Sutton and take fugitive lessons. I'll admit, that gave me some solace.

Okay, Mr. Sutton. It's time.

Reporter opens the door of the Polara, waits for Sutton to get in.

Sutton doesn't move. Time for what kid?

You know.

Valentine's Day, 1952. Willie buys Margaret flowers, chocolates. He sings to her. *I don't wanna play in your yard, I don't like you anymore.* She claps, jumps up and down, hugs him. I want to play in your yard, Mr. Loring.

You may, Margaret.

What we doing for Valentine's Day?

A rare treat, he says. We're going on an outdoor excursion. In broad daylight.

She gasps. Where?

You'll see.

They ride the subway. Margaret is so excited she can't sit. She has to stand, hanging on to a strap. Willie is excited too. But as they get off in the Bronx, as she grows still more excited because she realizes they're going to the zoo, his mood slowly changes. Walking through the front gate, seeing the animals in their cages, he realizes this was a bad idea. He recalls his many different cells—even his room on Dean Street is just one more. He can't hide his sadness. He doesn't want to. He leads Margaret to a bench near the lions and begins to tell her who he really is, all he's done.

She puts her hands over her ears.

Margaret?

I do not want to hear. You promise you hurt no one, that is enough. The rest is not for me. I do not want to know, I do not want this burden.

But—

La la la la la.

He takes her hands away from her ears. You're afraid that you might think less of me if I tell you who I am?

I afraid to think less, I afraid to think more. I think of you just enough. You do not want to know everything I done to survive, I do not want to know everything you done.

Willie looks at the lions. They look away quick, as if ashamed to be caught eavesdropping. It occurs to him that though he cares about Margaret, though he wouldn't hesitate to jump into the lion cage to save her, she's a stranger. He knows only a story she told him, which he chose to believe. She might not actually be from Egypt. Her name might not be Margaret.

You're right, he says. Yeah. Sure. We know enough.

But later, lying in bed, Willie needs to know one thing. He asks Margaret if she's ever been in love.

Yes, of course.

A boy back home?

Yes.

Did you hurt him?

I never hurt nobody.

She rolls onto her back, kicks off the covers. In the glow of the streetlamp outside the window her body is breathtaking. She could be one of the nymphs in Mr. Untermyer's Temple. She sits up, sighs.

Everyone is loving someone else, Julius. No one is loving anyone they with. This is how is the world. I do not know what is God doing. He give us love, we so glad to be alive, and then He take it away. Why He do this? What He is *doing*? I still believe in Him. But He make it hard.

Willie sits up, lights a Chesterfield, hands it to Margaret. He lights one for himself. By the flame of his Zippo he notices that Margaret's eye is much larger than it was yesterday. And it's grown cloudy.

Margaret, dear. You need to see a doctor.

I do not like doctors.

No one does. But I'm taking you. Tomorrow. End of discussion.

He puts a hand on her cheek. She smiles. Yes, Julius. Whatever you say. Here is looking at you kid.

TWENTY-TWO

THEY HAVE A BANK JOB SCHEDULED TOMORROW MORNING. They go over the fine points, the details, the driver. Once again it will be Johnny Dee, an old friend of Mad Dog. Willie doesn't like Dee, who looks like one of the Marx Brothers, the unfunny one, but Willie can't kick. Though he and Mad Dog have a good working relationship, Willie wouldn't put it past Mad Dog, in the heat of a disagreement, to break his elbow.

Just after one o'clock Willie rides the subway from Mad Dog's apartment on the West Side of Manhattan back to Brooklyn. He checks his watch. Margaret's doctor appointment is at two-thirty. Cutting it close. He sits where he always sits on the subway, near the doors, his back to the wall. He opens his copy of Sheen. A quote from St. Augustine. *The penitent should ever grieve, and rejoice at his grief.* He reads the same line three times. Rejoice at his grief?

He feels someone watching him. He looks up from Sheen, then quickly down.

It's just some kid. Early twenties, baby face. A Boy Scout face.

Again Willie looks up, down. Dark wavy hair, sharp beak— the poor kid's got to be self-conscious about that nose. He's nicely dressed though. As if for a hot date or a party. Pearl gray suit, starched white shirt, flowered tie—and blue suede shoes. Why does a Boy Scout wear blue suede shoes?

Because he doesn't want to be a Boy Scout. And he's not going on a date, or to a party. He's going *nowhere*, in every sense. He's got a humdrum job and doesn't want to be humdrum. He wants to be hip, cool. Everybody does these days. Maybe he's staring because he thinks Willie's cool.

Willie runs a finger along the thin mustache he's recently grown, tries to refocus his mind on Sheen. He can't. A third time he looks up. This time he makes eye contact with the kid, one, two, before looking back at his book. *God's pardon in the Sacrament restores us to His friendship, but the debt to Divine Justice remains.*

Debt? To Divine Justice? He thinks of Mad Dog collecting debts. He wonders if God has his own Mad Dog.

The kid's eyes are uncommonly dark, soulful, and they're definitely locked on Willie. Now, letting his own eyes drift from the book to the blue suede shoes, Willie can tell, can feel—the kid has made him. The kid has seen through Willie's plastic surgery, through his makeup, past his mustache. But how? Most mornings Willie barely recognizes himself in the mirror. How can some random kid, on a crowded local, in the middle of a Monday afternoon, recognize him?

Now you will come out of a confusion of people.

Willie turns the page, pretending to be engrossed. A fourth time he looks up, down. How is it possible? One of the kid's eyes is larger than the other. Is something going around, some epidemic of uneven eyeballs?

The conductor announces Willie's stop. Pacific Avenue. Willie stands, shoves Sheen under his arm, lines up at the door. He can feel the kid's asymmetrical gaze following him. He pushes off the train, weaves through the crowd, hurries up the steps of the subway station, forcing himself not to look back.

On the street, a block away, he looks.

Pfew. No kid.

He walks three blocks, comes to his car. Again he looks.

Still no kid.

He gets behind the wheel, checks the rearview. No kid. He

sighs, strokes his mustache, dabs his makeup. He wishes he could phone Margaret, tell her he's running late. She doesn't have a phone. He turns the key.

Nothing.

No no no, he says. He turns the key again. The engine clicks but won't start. Son of a— He gets out, lifts the hood. It's got to be the battery. But how can it be? The car is new. He just bought it. He wonders how long it will take Sonny's Service Center, over on Third, to come give him a jump. He checks his watch. Margaret's doctor appointment is in forty minutes.

From behind him he hears someone. He turns. Two cops. The muscles in his legs twitch—he nearly runs. But then he notices the cops' relaxed posture, bored eyes. They're not after him.

The cop on the left pushes back his hat. You the owner of this car?

Yes, Officer.

License and registration.

Willie fishes in his breast pocket, hands his license and registration to the cop on the left. The cop on the right looks Willie up and down.

It's good, Left Cop says to Right Cop.

Left Cop folds the registration, tucks it under the license, hands it back. Sorry for the bother, he says. Have a good day, Mr. Loring.

No bother, fellas.

Their black-and-white is parked behind Willie's car. They get in, drive off.

Willie leans back under his hood. If he could hook his racing heart to this dead battery, he'd be on his way.

They leave Dean Street, cruise south on Fourth. At a red light Photographer sets his camera on his lap, pats it like a dog. He opens his camera bag, picks a lens, checks it for smudges—fixes it to his camera like a bayonet.

Locked and loaded, he says to Sutton's reflection in the rearview. Show time, brother.

The light is green, Reporter says.

Photographer hits the gas.

Reporter unwraps a candy bar, puts half in his mouth, opens a file. So—Mr. Sutton. February 18, 1952. According to this article you're living on Dean Street, dating Margaret, knocking off a bank every few weeks with two guys. Tommy Kling and Johnny DeVenuta?

Sutton loosens his tie. Mad Dog and Dee, he says. Yeah.

Walk us through that day.

I was supposed to take Margaret to the doctor to see about her eye.

What was wrong with her eye?

It kept getting bigger.

Bigger?

We didn't know why. And she was afraid of doctors. So I had to insist, and promise to go with her. I had coffee that morning with Mad Dog. Then I headed back to Brooklyn. I was late. As I walked down the steps of the subway station I heard the train coming. I ran. All out. Like Jackie Robinson stealing home. Imagine kid?

Imagine what?

How much would be different. If I hadn't run. If I hadn't jumped through those doors just as they were closing. If I hadn't had a dime in my pocket. If the fare had still been a nickel. You know who kept the subway fare a nickel all those years? Mr. Untermyer. He practically ran the transportation system in New York. But he died.

What would be different?

For openers? We wouldn't be sitting in this goddamn car right now.

The cops return minutes later.

Mr. Loring, Right Cop says. We're going to need you to come with us.

What's the trouble, Officer?

Left Cop hitches his pants. There's been a rash of car thefts in this neighborhood. Our sergeant wants us to check everything.

I showed you my license and registration.

Yes sir, Right Cop says. It's just routine.

Willie shrugs, drops the hood. He follows the cops to their squad car, climbs in the backseat.

Where are we going?

The Seven Eight. It's only a half mile away.

Willie tells them he's got to take his girlfriend to the doctor.

We'll have you back to your car in no time, Right Cop says.

You having some engine trouble? Left Cop says.

Dead battery, Willie says.

We can give you a jump when we get this all cleared up, Left Cop says.

At the precinct they lead him through a door with a pebbled glass panel. An interrogation room. All his old scars tingle.

Coffee, Mr. Loring?

Sure, thanks.

He sits at the table. They take his fingerprints. Procedure, Mr. Loring.

I understand, fellas. Doing your jobs. Mind if I smoke?

Go right ahead. Where you from, Mr. Loring?

Brooklyn. Born and raised.

You a Dodgers fan, Mr. Loring?

Och—don't remind me.

They talk about Branca. Sutton's got a .22 tucked into the breast pocket of his suit coat.

What line of work you in, Mr. Loring?

I'm a writer.

You don't say. That seems like a tough racket.

It is, it is.

What kinds of things you write?

Novels. Stories. I don't sell much, but my folks left me a little money, so I get by.

More coffee, Mr. Loring?

Sure. You fellas make it strong. That's how I make it at home.

Left Cop leaves, comes back. Right Cop leaves, comes back with a detective. They ask about the car, the battery, then they all leave. Then Right Cop and Left Cop come back and they make some more small talk about the Dodgers. From outside the room, far down the hall, a cheer. As if Thomson just hit another homer. Loud voices, hasty footsteps, the door with the pebbled glass rattles and bangs open. In walk three, five, ten cops, and half a dozen detectives, all grinning. No one speaks. No one is sure who should start. Finally one of the detectives steps forward. Hello, he says.

Hello, Willie says.

It's a real pleasure to meet you, Willie the Actor.

Laughter.

Someone tells Willie to stand. Someone else frisks him. When they discover the .22, the laughter abruptly ceases. Right Cop and Left Cop look at each other, then at the floor.

And so it ends.

And also begins again.

They book Willie, photograph him, interrogate him. They ask who he's working with, who's been hiding him, where he stashed all his money. They ask about his friends, girlfriends, partners.

He stares.

They ask again.

He stares, smokes.

Then they do something shocking. They sit back, smile. Willie's refusal to talk is part of his legend, and the cops are enjoying that he's being true to form. They accord him a grudging respect. They ask if he'd like another cup of coffee. They offer him a donut.

At dusk they politely ask him to stand, he's going to Queens. Why Queens? he asks.

We have witnesses who put you at the Manufacturers Trust job in Queens.

I don't see how, he says. Wasn't me.

He's already plotting his defense. He's thinking of how good a lawyer he might be able to afford. If the cops don't hate him, maybe a judge won't. Maybe the system will go easy on him. At the very least maybe he can stop them from sending him back to Holmesburg.

The hallway is full of reporters, photographers, gawkers. Two cops stop Willie at the front door, where the police commissioner takes him by the elbow and gives a speech. The commissioner must be running for something. He praises Left Cop and Right Cop, praises the entire force. Then, in a moment that feels both political and personal, he shouts: We've got him! We've caught the Babe Ruth of Bank Robbers!

Flashbulbs pop—a sound like carbonated beverages being uncapped. Willie grimaces, not at the lights, but the nickname, which will be splattered across tomorrow's front pages, and along the Times Square headline zipper. He likes Babe Ruth. But couldn't the commissioner have compared him to a Dodger? Would it have killed the commissioner to call Willie the Jackie Robinson of Bank Robbers?

In Queens they give Willie a private cell with a cop at the door around the clock. He lies on his bunk thinking of Margaret. Will she see the news? Will she be bold enough, foolish enough, to visit? He thinks of Bess—same question. At midnight the warden appears. Open it, he tells the cop at the door.

Willie stands. The warden gives him a look that's hard to read. Hello, Willie.

Hello, Warden.

Willie Sutton.

Yes sir.

In my jail. Willie the Actor.

Some call me that.

Born June 30, 1901.

I take people's word for that. I don't remember.

Anything you need, Willie?

Need?

Yes, Willie.

Now Willie sees: the white hair, the blue eyes, the face lined with red veins like a bus map of Belfast. Warden is Irish.

Gee, Warden, I'd love a book.

He can see that Warden wants to smile, to wink, but his position, his role, prevents it.

A book, Willie?

I'm a big reader.

You don't say, Willie. Me too. What book would you like?

Warden tells the dozens of reporters outside the jail that Willie the Actor has requested the epic historical novel by John Dos Passos—*1919*. The reporters breathlessly include this detail in their stories and none knows its significance. Despite the private cell, despite the cop at the door, Willie Sutton has escaped again. He's in 1919, with Bess. He's never really been anywhere else.

New York is enthralled by the story of Willie's capture. Left Cop and Right Cop, even though they didn't know at first whom they'd caught, get the hero treatment. They're pictured on every front page, shaking hands with the mayor, accepting a promotion from the commissioner. A red-letter day for two conscientious cops, outfoxing the slickest fox ever, that's how the story plays, until everything goes haywire. The kid from the subway comes forward and tells the newspapers it was *he* who spotted the Actor, *he* who followed the Actor off the subway—*he* who alerted the cops. The kid walked up to the nearest radio car and said, Don't think I'm crazy, but there goes Willie Sutton. Left Cop and Right Cop checked Willie's ID, decided the kid was indeed crazy. Then went back to the precinct. Luckily they told the story to the desk sergeant, who told them to go back and bring in this Julius Loring, just to be sure.

Naturally the kid wants the reward. For years banks have been touting a big payday for anyone with information leading to Sutton's arrest. The amount is said to be north of seventy thousand dollars. The kid just got out of the Coast Guard, that kind of money could set him up for life. He could get married, start a family. Also, he tells reporters and cameras pressing in around him at the Seven Eight, he'd like to help his parents fix up their house in Brooklyn. Maybe even buy them a better house.

Shy, earnest, the kid says these things with a thick Brooklyn accent, just like Willie's.

Reporters ask him how old he is.

Twenty-four, he says, as if it's an accomplishment.

In fact he celebrated a birthday just days before spotting Willie on the train. He was born in February, of course, the month of all momentous occurrences in Willie's life. Twenty-four years ago, just after Willie left Dannemora and returned to the world, the kid was entering the world. His parents, Max and Ethel Schuster, named him Arnold.

Arnie to his friends.

The cops stonewall for a day or two, but they can't win against Arnie's Boy Scout face. They're forced to admit that the first official version of events—vigilant beat cops, crackerjack police work—wasn't quite accurate. With gritted teeth they usher Left Cop and Right Cop offstage and embrace Arnie Schuster, the Good Samaritan. For the cameras anyway.

If Arnie has irritated the cops, he's infuriated parts of Brooklyn. To many he's the rat who squealed on a hero. He's the stoolie who put the finger on Willie the Actor. And he's Jewish. Many of the death threats he receives are addressed: Dear Judas.

People know where to write him because every newspaper prints his address: 941 Forty-Fifth Street.

Meanwhile, the cops continue to search for Willie's crew. They sift through the contents of his wallet, find his address, barrel into the boardinghouse on Dean Street. Landlady leads them upstairs to Willie's room, where they discover tens of thousands of dollars, a small arsenal, and a bookcase overflowing with books. What shocks them most are the books. Newspapers publish the list. The bank robber's syllabus.

Within a day bookstores sell out of Proust.

The room is also full of Willie's paperwork. Sketchbooks, notebooks, a draft of a novel—and one slim address book stashed under the mattress. The cops find and arrest Mad Dog and Dee. And Margaret. When they kick in her door she's lying in bed, a hand over her eyeball, now twice its normal size. Anguished, she pleads for a doctor. The cops won't let her have one until she gives them information. She swears she knows nothing.

Cops and reporters fan across the city, visiting all the banks mentioned in Willie's notes. They get a call from Head Nurse and race over to Staten Island, where they learn about Joseph the Porter, the Angel of the Farm Colony. Landlady helps fan the flames of Willie's growing myth, telling one reporter that Willie was always a perfect gentleman, that he gave her money for a doctor when her son was sick, that he bought her roses for her birthday. The cops want to question her daughter, who was tutoring Willie in Spanish. The daughter tells the cops to suck eggs, which makes her a heroine in the barrio.

A week after his arrest Willie is lying on his bunk. He lifts his head. He hears something. It sounds at first like the breakers at Coney Island.

Guard?

Yeah.

What is that?

Crowd.

Where?

Outside.

What are they doing?

Chanting?

What for?

You.

Me?

Willie cups his ear, trying to make it out.

WILL-ie, WILL-ie, WILL-ie.

The guard turns, eyes him through the bars. With heavy sarcasm he says, You're a hero.

Willie hears only the word, not the sarcasm.

Photographer turns left on Ninth. Reporter, rifling through files, speaks quickly:

Arnie Schuster's poor mailman. That guy was busy in February and March of '52. Death threats started pouring into the Schuster house. Crude, unpunctuated, misspelled. Here's a nice one. Mac—Your number is up. You stooled on Sutton. You know what happens to double-crossers. You're finished. Signed, One of the boys.

The newspapers printed the threats, Sutton says. Which encouraged more people to make threats.

Here's another one, Reporter says. A model of simplicity: Rat Rat Rat.

Photographer looks in the rearview. Hey—what happened to Margaret? Your girlfriend?

Sutton lights a Chesterfield, looks out the window.

Willie?

Her eye, Sutton says.

What about it?

It just— I don't know how to say it. Exploded.

It did what?

Margaret kept begging to see a doctor, and the cops kept refusing, and the tumor in her eye—that's what it turned out to be—just—exploded. An infection set in. She went blind. She sued New York for negligence. I don't know what became of the suit. I wrote to her many times, but I never heard back. She just disappeared.

Around midnight, when the chanting crowds have gone home, when the jail is quiet, Warden stops by Willie's cell. He confesses to Willie: he grew up in Irish Town. Not far from the corner of Nassau and Gold. He even went to St. Ann's. They talk about the old neighborhood. They talk about swimming the East River.

Most often they talk about books. They love all the same authors. The warden mentions Joyce.

Put two Irishmen in a cell, Willie says, sooner or later they'll talk about Joyce.

Warden laughs. I reread *Ulysses* once a year, he says. History is a nightmare from which I'm—you know.

I'm partial to the stories. I tried reading *Ulysses* during my last bit. I only made it as far as Episode 12.

The Cyclops! Sure. The scene in the pub—with the anti-Semite.

Tough sledding. This go around, I guess I'll have time to read it front to back.

Stately, plump, Warden offers Willie a smoke.

Chesterfield, Willie says. My brand.

I know, Willie. I know.

On March 8, 1952, around midnight, Willie is lying on his bunk, reading Dos Passos. Warden appears at the door. Willie sits up, slips in a bookmark. His mind is still with Eugene Debs and Henry Ford and William Hearst—he never knew that Hearst's friends called him Willie.

How's tricks, Warden?

He sees in Warden's face, in the set of his mouth, that books could not be farther from his mind. O Warden let me up out of this.

* * *

Photographer hits the brakes. The Polara almost rams the back fender of a Buick that's stopped for no apparent reason in the middle of the street. Photographer leans on the horn.

Go around, Reporter says to Photographer.

This asshole won't move, Photographer says. Move, asshole!

Reporter, shouting to be heard over the horn, tells Sutton: Here's an interesting story in the files. After spotting you on the subway Arnie went home and found his mother at the kitchen sink. He told her, Guess what—I just saw a thief. Arnie's mother said, Go away with you, who'd you see? And Arnie said, I saw Willie Sutton. His mother said, Who's that? And Arnie said, He's a man police want, I pointed him out, I played detective today. Arnie's mother recounted this conversation word for word to investigators. After—you know.

Poor Arnie, Photographer says.

He held up like a champ under the pressure, Reporter says. He wrote a pretty stiff-necked letter to one of his best friends, who'd just joined the Army. Want to hear it, Mr. Sutton?

No.

It's dated March 4, 1952. Dear Herb—How are you, boy? How does the Texas weather agree with you? I'm sorry I didn't write any sooner but as you know I've had plenty of excitement these past two, three weeks and I've been pretty busy. Now things are getting back to normal and I'm getting back to the same old grind. But let me tell you—it was murder.

Ah God, Sutton says.

It's funny how your life can change from one day to the next. One day I'm just plain Arnie Schuster and the next I'm THE Mr. Schuster and now I'm back to just plain Arnie again. Oh well maybe I can realize something out of it. But even if I don't I won't be sorry. Right now I'll just be happy to have the whole thing blow over. Arnie.

The banks fucked him, Sutton says.

The banks?

The banks didn't pay him the reward. The banks said they never promised any reward. They said the newspapers made it all up about the reward. Arnie got nothing.

Fucking banks, Photographer says.

Interesting how many things you had in common, Mr. Sutton.

Who?

You and Arnie Schuster.

How do you figure?

Both sons of Brooklyn. Both Dodgers fans. Both folk heroes—and also public enemies. Both unpopular with cops.

Sutton closes his eyes. Out of a turmoil of speech about you.

Sorry?

I didn't say anything.

Anyway, Reporter says, Arnie had a cold. He'd been in bed all week, and March 8 was his first day back on the job. He worked all day at his father's clothing shop. About eight-thirty that night he phoned Eileen Reiter, sister of his best friend, Jay. Arnie and Jay belonged to a Brooklyn basement club—the Knaves.

Knaves? Sutton says.

Yeah. They'd get together once a week, plan social events, talk about girls. They'd fine each other a quarter for bad language.

Boy Scout, Sutton says.

Arnie and Eileen made a plan to meet up later that night. A party. First Arnie was going to head home, take a shower, change clothes. He locked the door to the shop, walked three blocks, boarded a bus on Fifth Avenue, rode to Ninth Avenue and Fiftieth, walked down five blocks to Forty-Fifth. He might've been thinking about the party. Or the reward. He might even have been thinking about you, Mr. Sutton. He had sixty seconds to live.

Photographer turns on Forty-Fifth. Cars are bunched tight along both sides of the street, but there's one space along the right. Photographer pulls in. Sutton looks up and down the street. Narrow brick apartment buildings, brick stoops, barred windows. Some of the bars are painted white to make them look less like prisons.

Arnie's street, Reporter says. He turned right where we just turned, and crossed the street immediately. He walked the same route he'd walked a thousand, ten thousand times, which took him to that sidewalk over there.

Reporter points directly across the street. Sutton wipes the fogged window with his hand.

Arnie got about eighty feet, Reporter says, and then right there—someone stepped out of that alley. You can see how dark it is. There are still no streetlights. Whoever it was, Arnie wouldn't have seen him until they were inches apart. If Arnie ever saw him.

Perfect spot for an ambush, Photographer says. He lights a Newport, shoots a picture of the alley through the smoke and his window.

The trajectory of the bullets was sharply downward, Reporter says. Which means the shooter shot Arnie once and then stood over him and fired and fired as Arnie fell to the ground or lay on the ground writhing. It was reported that Arnie was shot in both eyes and once in the—you know, groin.

Fuck, Photographer says.

But it's not exactly true, Reporter says. There's a story about the autopsy in this file—wait a sec. Here it is. Arnie was shot once in his stomach, below the navel—that bullet didn't exit. Then once in the face, just to the left of his nose—that bullet exited below his right eye. Then once in the top of his scalp—that bullet exited and burned the back of his scalp. Then once above the back of his left ear—that bullet went through his brain and exited the back of his head below his left ear. The photos, Mr. Sutton, make it look like Arnie was shot in the eyes, and maybe the shooter was aiming for the eyes, since that was a mob thing—sending a message. But there's no way to know.

No one heard the shots, Sutton whispers.

Right. It was so fast, bang bang, bang bang, if anyone did hear they thought it was a bus backfiring. But also—there was loud music playing in that synagogue right there. They were celebrating Purim.

Sutton turns and looks at the synagogue on the corner.

Reporter flips open a new file, reads: Often called the Jewish Halloween, Purim is the Jewish celebration of Esther, whose heroics saved her people from mass slaughter. Jewish children wear masks, go door to door, pretending to be characters from the biblical story.

Photographer opens his door, flicks out his Newport. Old Testament trick-or-treaters? Not in my neighborhood.

Then you don't live in a Jewish neighborhood. And they're not trick-or-treaters, per se. They ask for money, not candy. And they smoke cigarettes.

Why?

Because it's forbidden. Purim is a holiday when the forbidden is—bidden.

Photographer laughs. Little hoodlums. I'd like to shoot that.

Around nine-fifteen, Reporter says, a woman walking down this street, Mrs. Muriel Galler, tripped over Arnie. He was lying across the sidewalk. It was so dark she didn't know what she'd fallen over. A rug. A log. She got to her feet, saw it was a body, and ran to—let's see—that house.

Reporter points to the brick building beside the alley: Dr. Solomon Fialka rushed outside, checked Arnie's pulse, determined that he was dead—but didn't recognize Arnie. Dr. Fialka didn't recognize his own neighbor, that's what the bullets had done to Arnie's face, eyes. Mr. Sutton, did you know that Arnie had one eye larger than the other? According to the autopsy.

I remember.

Photographer looks at Sutton in the rearview. Everyone who had anything to do with you, brother.

What?

Eddie. Margaret. Arnie.

Sutton stares at the rearview. Please, he says. No more.

Dr. Fialka went through Arnie's billfold, Reporter says. Arnie still had fifty-seven bucks on him. So clearly this was no robbery.

Then Dr. Fialka found Arnie's ID and someone screamed, Oh God it's Arnold Schuster.

No more, Sutton says. Let's get out of here, boys.

Moments later Arnie's family heard the news on TV. A bulletin. Good Samaritan Arnie Schuster has been gunned down outside his Brooklyn home. All the Schusters ran outside and found Arnie a hundred feet away—on his back, blood running into the gutter. Arnie's mother, inconsolable. Arnie's kid brother, wailing. Arnie's father, running up and down the sidewalk, that sidewalk right there, screaming: They took my son, I don't want to live. *Here's a picture. Look at the anguish in those faces. And if the whole scene wasn't strange enough, according to this clip—the joyful music of Purim wafted over all.*

Willie. Arnold Schuster is dead.

Willie blinks. Schuster?

He stares at Warden, who stares back in disbelief.

Schuster? Schuster, Schuster. Then Willie remembers. The kid from the subway. The Boy Scout. Dead? How?

Shot.

Willie's mind goes reeling. Why would anyone shoot *Schuster*? Mother of God, because Willie is a hero and someone in that chanting crowd outside the jail, or someone in sympathy with that crowd, thought they were striking a blow on Willie's behalf. In fact it's a blow against Willie, a heavy blow, because it will surely turn public opinion. All these thoughts quickly dawn on him, and lead him to one terrifying and inescapable conclusion, which he blurts out like a cry for help, causing Warden to recoil with horror, with disapproval, with shame for his race.

That *sinks* me.

Photographer and Reporter step out of the car. Sutton doesn't follow. Please, Sutton says. No.

Mr. Sutton, we've gone everywhere you wanted to go. We've held up our end of the bargain. It's your turn.

Sutton nods. He steps out. He walks between them across the street. They stop at the alley. Photographer tries to shoot Sutton but can't get a good angle. Also, Sutton refuses to look at the alley. He looks at the sky, trying to find the moon.

Reporter opens his briefcase, pulls out a stack of crime scene photos. He hands them to Sutton, who puts on his glasses, shuffles through them quickly. Arnie on the sidewalk. Cops standing over Arnie. Arnie's blood-soaked suit. Arnie's blue suede shoes.

I remember these, Sutton says. From the papers.

Reporter hands him a sheaf of front pages. The headlines are enormous. One catches Sutton's eye. He adjusts his glasses. DEATH OF A SALESMAN.

I remember this one, he says. The headline writer earned his money that day.

How so?

Because Death of a Salesman *was still in the theaters. Margaret and I had just seen it. And because Willie Sutton sounds like Willy Loman. And because Schuster was a salesman.*

He was, Reporter says. But did you know, Mr. Sutton, that when he wasn't selling clothes, Arnie was in the back of his dad's shop, running the presser. Above it he'd tacked the FBI Most Wanted list. That's how he recognized you. The FBI made sure to hand out that list to every clothing store in Brooklyn, Mr. Sutton, because you were known to be a sharp dresser. Like Arnie. Another thing you two had in common. Did you know that Arnie was engaged?

He was?

He met his fiancée, Leatrice, on the Boardwalk in Coney Island?

Mermaid Avenue.

Pardon?

Nothing.

Of course, many people suspected you were involved in Arnie's murder.

Reporter and Photographer freeze, waiting. Sutton says nothing.

The search for Arnie's killer, Reporter continues, is the largest investigation in the history of the New York Police Department.

The largest?

No manhunt has been larger.

I'm not feeling well, boys.

The commissioner called this case the department's top priority: We have nineteen thousand cops in this city, and all nineteen thousand know what their Number One job is today—to trap the rats involved in this outrage. *But they never did solve it.*

How crazy is that, Photographer says, catching a shot of Sutton glancing quickly at the alley. That the commissioner would use that word—rats? And how crazy is it that they never solved it? Okay, Willie, let's walk up the street, get a shot outside the Schuster house, and we're done.

Sutton walks, Reporter and Photographer on either side.

Mr. Sutton, Reporter says, public opinion really turned on you after Arnie's death.

Yeah.

New York did a one-eighty. People reconsidered everything they ever thought about heroes, rats, crime. You.

I remember kid, I remember.

An enormous crowd gathered at Arnold's funeral. Look at this picture.

I wrote his parents. Maybe that was a mistake.

This is it, Photographer says. Nine four one. Arnie's house.

They stop. A narrow brick row house, it's exactly like the ones on either side and up and down the street. A small front stoop, a white door. There's no sign that it was once the most talked about address in the city, in the nation.

The lights are off. Either no one lives here, Photographer says, or no one's home.

As the hearse carrying Arnie pulled away from the cemetery, Reporter says, the cantor asked, Why? And the mourners took up a baleful chant: Why? Why? Why?

Sutton murmurs: That's what I want to know.

Through several anonymous tips, and a few clues from the scene, the cops decide that Arnie Schuster's killer was most likely the Angel of Death, Freddie Tenuto, which makes Freddie the most wanted man in America. His mug shot appears in every newspaper and magazine, gets posted in every airport and train station and bus depot. Soon there are Freddie sightings all over New York. Someone sees him with a gorgeous redhead at a prizefight in Madison Square Garden. Cops stop the fight, search the crowd. Someone sees him on the Long Island Rail Road. Cops stop the train, check every passenger. Someone sees him at a steakhouse in Williamsburg. Cops burst into the joint, line everyone against the wall. The city feels under siege. People clamor for the Angel of Death to be caught.

No matter who shot Arnie, however, the public has already concluded that Willie is the real culprit. Willie's misspent life led to Arnie's death. Willie might not have pulled the trigger, or sent the triggerman, or even known the triggerman, but in the public's mind he's responsible. The fickle city: for weeks New York celebrated Willie, shunned Arnie; now it shuns Willie, makes Arnie a martyr.

Against this backcloth Willie is speedily tried for the Manufacturers Trust job. Dee cuts a deal, takes the stand, tells all, and the jury is quick at their work. Willie, wearing a chalk-striped suit, his hair slicked back, stares at the enormous American flag over the judge's head, barely listening as the judge sentences him to spend the rest of his days in Attica: *I only regret that the law prevents me from sentencing you to death.*

The cops grab Willie roughly from his chair and cuff him and drag him away. Gone is the grudging respect.

Over the next few years at Attica, Willie hears all kinds of stories about Arnie. Every guy gives the story a different twist, but the essential facts are always the same. It was Freddie who killed the kid, and it was Albert Anastasia, the lunatic Brooklyn crime boss, who ordered the hit. Anastasia, often called the Mad Hatter, paid Freddie to kill Arnie, then paid someone else to kill Freddie, to grind up his body and feed it to some livestock on an upstate farm. Covering the trail, tying up loose ends—standard mob procedure.

But why? Why would Anastasia get mixed up in something that didn't concern him? Because he was Brooklyn born, Brooklyn raised, and there was nothing he despised more than a rat. When he saw Arnie on TV, getting the hero treatment, he exploded. *This Boy Scout stands to collect a reward? For ratting out a right guy like Willie Sutton?* Willie was a hero to many different New Yorks—Irish New York, Immigrant New York, Poor New York—but he was a god to Underworld New York. So Anastasia sent the Angel of Death to wrestle with Arnie. That's the story Willie hears in Attica.

The guy who tells Willie the most compelling version of this story is Crazy Joey Gallo, who's serving a seven-year bit for extortion. And Crazy Joe adds a hellacious coda. Five years after the murder of Arnie, Crazy Joe killed Anastasia in a midtown barbershop. As Anastasia lay in a chair under a piping hot towel, Crazy Joe and his brothers walked in and hosed the place with bullets. Crazy Joe claims the hit was ordered by one of the other crime bosses, who had no use for Anastasia, hated the way Anastasia did business, including his targeting of Arnie, an innocent civilian. So much carnage, so much confusion, all because Willie and Arnie caught the same subway one February afternoon.

Willie and Crazy Joe spend much of the sixties sitting together in the yard, trading stories and cigarettes and books. They become good friends, because they come from the same place, because they've traveled similar roads. They both grew up in Brooklyn, both had two brothers, both started as small-time hoods and ended up folk heroes. But Crazy Joe is aptly named—he wears a straw van Gogh hat, sets up an easel in the yard and does portraits of the hacks—so when he tells Willie the story of Arnie and Anastasia, Willie doesn't know which parts are true, which parts are Crazy Joe being crazy. Ultimately Willie decides it doesn't matter. It all has the ring of truth, and it closes a loop in Willie's mind. Willie decides that's all any story needs to do.

Willie, Photographer says, please, I just need this one shot, you with the Schuster house in the background, and then we can all go have dinner. Please, for the love of God, stand still.

Sutton pats his pockets, looks back at the Polara. I've got to have a smoke first. This whole thing—this whole day—I'm shaking like a leaf.

No, Photographer says. Shoot first. Then smoke.

If I don't have a smoke I'll pass out. If I pass out you won't get your shot.

Photographer sighs, lowers his camera. Okay.

I left my cigarettes in the car.

Have one of mine.

I can only smoke Chesterfield.

Sutton hobbles back up the street. On his right is the alley. He tells himself not to look, but he looks. The blue suede shoes, the eyes streaming blood. He isn't remembering the photographs, or the front pages, he's seeing Arnie. The kid is right there. At Sutton's feet. Sutton sees.

He crosses the street, slumps against the Polara. He sees his Chesterfields on the backseat. He sees the keys in the ignition. He sees that Photographer has left the motor running again.

He doesn't hesitate. He gets behind the wheel, peels away.

TWENTY-THREE

HIS NERVES. CHRIST, HIS NERVES. HE NEEDS DISTRACTION.
He clicks on the AM radio. News. He turns the dial. Jagger. *Rape!*
Murder! He turns the dial. Sinatra. *Have Yourself a Merry Little*
Christmas. Eddie used to say Sinatra couldn't be all Dago. He's
too smooth, Sutty, he must have *some* Irish in him. Poor Eddie.
Sutton's eyes fill with tears. He can't see the streetlights.

He wipes his eyes, pulls the white envelope from his breast
pocket, opens it with his teeth. Removes the piece of loose-leaf.
Tries to read Donald's drunken, childlike handwriting.

Left on Thirty-Ninth? No. That must say Thirty-Seventh.

Right on—Furth? No. That must say Fifth.

To think Reporter complained about *Sutton's* handwriting. He
pounds the steering wheel. Donald, you crazy sot. You can fence
anything, you can pick any lock, you can find anyone living or dead
within one hour—how is it possible that you can't read or write?

Up ahead he sees Prospect Avenue. He turns left. Now, he
reads aloud: Look for Hamilton.

There. Hamilton.

He squints again at Donald's writing. One mole mill? No. That
must be *one more mile.* Then Hicks Street. Then: Look for—
Middagh.

Sounds like a word from the Old Country. A good sign maybe.

The windshield is fogged. Willie wipes it with the sleeve of
Reporter's trench coat, leans forward, tries to read the numbers
on the houses. He sees an old house the color of newsprint, then
a bright yellow house that looks as if it might be the first ever

built in Brooklyn. Funck once said that Brooklyn, in Dutch, means Broken Land. True enough. Funck—long gone. Food for flowers. He's well and truly landescaped.

Now. There. Sutton sees Middagh. He turns, sees a quaint old Colonial-style house, and on the door is the number on Donald's sheet.

The windows shine with buttery yellow light.

He parks a block away, under a sign: NO STANDING. He leaves the engine running, walks slowly back to the house. Stands before it on the icy sidewalk. Limps up the steps. Makes a fist to knock. Can't. Limps down the steps, back toward the Polara. Stops. Marches back up the block. Creeps to the windows, as he used to do with banks. Twenty people, well dressed, gathered around a baby grand. Someone sure knows how to play.

He limps away, slowly, back again to the Polara.

From behind him he hears a door open, a knocker rattling. Can I help you?

He pivots. A young woman. Eighteen, maybe nineteen. She stands on the top step clutching a man's overcoat around her shoulders. In the dim light from a sconce Sutton can't make out her features, but he can see that she has ash blonde hair—and blue eyes?

Oh, he says. I was looking for an old friend. There's no chance that this might be the Endner residence, is there?

Endner?

Or maybe—Richmond?

Richmond, she says. Did you say Richmond?

Ah no. My mistake then. Sorry to have bothered you.

Are you looking for Sarah Richmond?

Sarah? Well. Yes. Sarah. I guess I am.

I'm sorry. She passed. Three years ago.

Passed. I see.

She was my grandmother.

Your grand—of course.

Are you by any chance. Willie Sutton?

But how could you have?

You're all over the television.

Right. Sure.

And I've heard the stories. From my grandmother. And my mother. Family legend.

Legend.

A heaviness comes over Sutton, a disappointment so crushing that he wants to lie down on the ice-caked sidewalk.

I'm sorry to bother you, young lady. It was a long shot. I just thought.

How in the world did you find this address?

I have a friend. He has friends. Department of Motor Vehicles. Voter registration. Newspaper subscription records. They can find anyone these days. Was this your grandmother's house?

She bought it years ago. With her second husband.

Second.

We were just having Christmas dinner.

I feel terrible for intruding. I would've called first. I couldn't find a pay phone.

You're not intruding. Would you care to come in? Have a glass of wine?

No. Thank you. I couldn't impose.

You wouldn't be imposing. My name's Kate, by the way.

Kate. I'm—well you know who I am.

Yes. It's a pleasure. Kind of a trip, actually.

Trip. Yeah. That seems to be the word of the day.

Sutton takes a halting step toward her. More like a lunge. I've come so far, he says.

He scolds himself—what a foolish thing to say. That sinks me. His leg nearly buckles. He grabs it. The pain is suffocating. That shit Photographer gave him made the pain disappear, for a while, but now it's back. Worse is the fatigue. All those years lying on a cot, in a cell, doing nothing, he should be rested. Instead he feels the exhaustion of the laborer, the athlete, the soldier. He remembers: he's going to die today. Maybe the moment is now.

I'm sorry kid, he says. I didn't mean to be so dramatic. It's just that there's so much I wanted to say. So many things I never got to say, things I dreamed of saying, and now it's too late. If only someone had told me back when I was your age that you need to *say* what's in your heart, right away, because once the moment is gone—well, kid, it's gone.

She smiles uncertainly. Her eyes are blue, yes, they are, but this damn street is so dark, it's impossible to see if— He wishes he could get closer, have a better look, but he doesn't want to scare her. She's the picture of youth, of innocence, and he's an ancient bank robber roaming the city on Christmas. He almost scares himself.

You know what kid? I'm babbling. I'm an old fool. Thank you for being so kind.

He flips up the fur collar of Reporter's trench coat, waves, starts to walk off.

She calls after him. But—wait.

He stops, turns, sees her coming quickly down the steps.

If there's something you wanted to say, Mr. Sutton. Maybe you can still.

What? Oh. I don't think.

But why not?

No. I just couldn't. No.

She walks toward him, stops thirty feet away. It seems a shame to come so far and then leave without saying what you wanted to say. Like you said. When something is in your heart. And of course I'm curious.

Well. But I don't.

I loved my grandmother very much, Mr. Sutton. And she told me everything. Everything. We had no secrets between us. She always said I was the best listener in the family. And I do love the old stories. I'm sort of the keeper of the family history.

Keeper.

She moves closer. Twenty feet away. She stops. The sidewalk between them glistens, as if paved with crushed diamonds. Besides, she adds, it's Christmas and I just have this funny *feeling* that my grandmother would want me to—I don't know. Lend an ear? Stand in for her?

You have a voice like hers kid.

I do?

Takes me back.

It does?

Come into the garden, Maud.

Pardon?

Your grandmother had the most beautiful voice I ever heard. Especially when she read one of her favorite poems aloud.

She did, Mr. Sutton, it's true. I hear her in my head all the time. When I'm scared, when I'm in trouble: Take a chance, Kate. Try it, Kate, what have you got to lose? She was so—fearless.

Fearless. That she was. I can still see her, a snowy day in 1919, half of New York City looking for us—she wasn't the least bit afraid. She had more guts than me and Happy combined.

Oh she loved to tell that story.

Did she?

Happy, I gather, was a handsome devil.

Sutton stands up straighter. He heaves a sigh. The thing is, he says. I just wanted.

Yes?

To say.

Uh-huh?

His eyes fill with tears. It's just that I never. What I mean is, I can't. Ah Bess. Bess. Bess. I just *miss you* so *much.*

Silence. He waits. In the distance an ambulance wails. Then it passes and silence descends again. He can't see anything through his tears, but he knows he's miscalculated, misread the situation. Ashamed, he bows his head, slumps forward.

Then: I miss you too, Willie.

He stops breathing. He takes a half step, sideways, like a stagger.

Bess, he says. Ah Christ. I know I've lived a sorry life. But not for the reasons people think. The crimes, the prison time, all that stuff isn't what I regret. My deepest regret is that you and I—that we never.

I told my granddaughter so many times that I hoped you'd—move on.

You certainly did. You got *married*.

Yes.

I died that day.

I know.

Watching you walk down that aisle.

I was so—startled—to see you there. That's another story I told my granddaughter many times.

If only we'd gotten married right away, Bess. Like we planned.

Like we. If only *we'd* gotten married? I'm not sure I understand.

Being with you, those few days, on the run, that was the high point of my life, Bess.

But, I'm sorry, I'm just not following. I was going to—that is, my grandmother, she was going to marry Happy. She was *eloping* with Happy.

Everything would be different if that sheriff hadn't barged in.

Okay, now, I heard about the sheriff, but I know my grandmother said he barged in while she and Happy—

No one would have gotten hurt.

Who got hurt?

That guard from Eastern State. All that blood running down his face.

Oh dear.

And Eddie. And Margaret.

Who?

And Arnie Schuster.

Schuster. Yes. They were just talking about him on the—

I admit I thought he was a Judas. But you know who's the real Judas? The lover who spurns you. Judas was a lover after all. Before ratting out Jesus, what did he do? He gave Jesus a kiss. That's why you're the real Judas, Bess, and that's why you're to blame for everything.

Maybe this was a bad idea.

I BLAME YOU, BESS.

Sutton's voice chokes. He puts his hands on his knees, leans over, sobbing.

Bad idea, she says. Definitely.

I'm sorry, Bess. I didn't mean that. It's just been—a really really long day. I love you, Bess. And I always will. It's cost me everything, absolutely *everything*, but maybe it's not love if it doesn't cost us everything. I love you, and I always will, and that—that is what I came here to say.

He straightens, puts a trembling hand over his eyes.

Um. Okay. Gosh, Mr. Sut—

Sutton drops his hand, looks at her, pleading.

Right, she says—Willie. I told my granddaughter, many times, that you were very special to me. Very dear. Those were my exact words. Very. *Dear*. I'll always be grateful to you for coming to see me on Coney Island when I was in trouble with my first husband—remember?

Sutton nods.

I told my granddaughter: You were always so sweet, Willie. So devoted. So loyal. The way you'd look at me, saucer-eyed, it was touching. But I was with Happy. I was in love with Happy, desperately in love. I wanted to marry him. My father wouldn't allow it, of course, because Happy was so poor and we were both so young, and then one night, at Finn McCool's, Happy got the idea that we should elope. Happy asked you to help us break into my father's office, because you and Eddie had been doing things like that for a while. Remember? Of course I knew it was hard on you, being a third wheel. I knew you'd give anything to trade places with Happy. You told me as much several times. But I told you that we just weren't meant to be. Didn't I? For so many reasons, Willie, we just weren't meant to be. Surely you remember me telling you that, Willie.

Sutton looks up the street. He doesn't answer.

Willie?

People tell us all kinds of things in this life, Bess.

He reaches into his breast pocket. He doesn't know what for. The envelope? A cigarette? A gun? Force of habit? There's nothing there.

If I could just hear you say it once more I could move on.

It?

What I wouldn't give.

I don't.

Oh Willie.

Excuse me?

The thing you always said. *Oh Willie.* No one ever said it like you. I thought if I could hear it one more time, I could stop running. I could maybe—I don't know. Find some happiness of my own. Before the end. But. Like you said. It wasn't meant to be.

He waves, turns, walks a few steps. His head is swimming, he feels faint. He might hit the sidewalk face-first. He surely won't make it to the Polara. But then he hears something. He stops, looks back. Oh, she says, as if starting to sing the national anthem. Oh—Willie. *Oh Willie. Oh.*

He tugs his earlobe. Shakes his head. Cracks a half smile.

It's not exactly like your grandmother, he says. But it'll do. It *will* do, Kate. Godspeed kid.

Merry Christmas, Mr. Sutton.

TWENTY-FOUR

THE CLERK AT THE FRONT DESK GIVES HIM A GOOFY SMILE.
What brings you down to Florida?

I'm a reporter. Writing about Willie Sutton.

Oh right. I heard. Sad.

The clerk hands Reporter the room key and explains about
the free breakfast.

Reporter finds his room, just off the pool, throws his suitcase
and briefcase on the bed. He turns up the AC, closes the drapes,
clicks open the briefcase. The old files spill out. Nothing brings
back that Christmas Day eleven years ago like the old files.
Somehow they still smell of Chesterfields.

Sutton's memoirs fall out too, both of them. Highlighted,
underlined, filled with Reporter's Post-its. The first, *Smooth and
Deadly*, was published in 1953. Reporter didn't even know of its
existence until 1976, when the second one appeared. *Where the
Money Was*. Sutton decided to write that one after publishers
rejected the novel he wrote in prison.

Reporter teased Sutton often about the title. Mr. Sutton, he
said—that's a total sellout.

Sutton chuckled. Kid I'm now going to say something to you
I've never said before in my life. Guilty.

Reporter sits on the hotel bed. He thinks about the front desk
clerk. *Oh right. I heard. Sad.* Yes, sad, except that Sutton lived
eleven years longer than anyone expected, eleven years longer
than he led doctors and reporters and the parole board—and
himself—to think he had left. Sutton's final elusiveness, his

395

crowning trickery—to live and live and live. In fact his will to live was one of the primary reasons that, despite everything, despite professional instincts and personal wariness, Reporter became fond of Sutton through the years.

Before they could become friends, Reporter had to forgive Sutton for stealing the newspaper's Polara that first Christmas. Upon filing his story, dictating it from a coffee shop near Schuster's house, Reporter tracked Sutton and the Polara back to the Plaza. Sutton, sitting at the hotel bar, nursing a Jameson, apologized profusely, telling Reporter that he just couldn't face his guilt over Schuster. Reporter accepted this explanation and they shook hands.

How's Bad Cop doing? Sutton asked.

I won't lie to you, Mr. Sutton. You shouldn't expect a Christmas card next year.

They both had a laugh about that.

In the eleven years that followed, Reporter and Sutton spoke every now and then on the phone, and they always got together for dinner when Sutton came through Manhattan. After dinner they would retire to P. J. Clarke's for a nightcap. Reporter enjoyed installing Sutton, America's most prolific bank robber, among the bankers and Wall Streeters along the bar at Clarke's. It was there, one autumn night in 1970, that Sutton, full of Jameson, loudly mused: I think America is the way it is, kid, because it's the only country ever founded over a beef about money. It strikes Reporter now, cranking up the AC, that Sutton at the end was a walking embodiment of America. Underneath all the delusion, all the bluster, all the wrongdoing, admitted and denied, there was something intractably good. Eternally salvageable.

And resolutely optimistic. Though filled with regret, Sutton always emphasized the positive, always expressed a touching gratitude that he was living out his final years in freedom and peace. Still, Reporter now recalls one dark phone conversation.

September 1971, the night of the bloody riots at Attica. Sutton knew many of the forty-three people killed, and he claimed to have known the riots were coming. I saw it kid, he kept saying, I knew it was going to happen. And if fuckin Rockefeller hadn't let me out when he did, I'd have died with those men, facedown in D Yard. I just know it.

How do you know it?

The way I always know things. In my gut.

After they hung up Reporter couldn't sleep. There was something odd in Sutton's voice. He wasn't merely shaken by his close brush with death, or sad for the men who died in D Yard. He was also deeply troubled to owe a debt of gratitude to a Rockefeller.

TWO YEARS BEFORE SUTTON DIED, REPORTER MET HIM AT A midtown TV studio, where he was taping a segment of *The Dick Cavett Show*. Sutton wore a beautiful gray suit with a red tie knotted in a full Windsor. Standing behind him in the dressing room, watching the makeup artist powder his nose, Reporter noted how relaxed Sutton seemed, as if he'd done this all his life. Reporter then stood backstage and watched the interview. Sutton was witty, eloquent, remarkably cool. More than once Reporter thought: he's dressed like a banker, but he's every bit the actor.

After the show Reporter and Sutton got on the elevator with Zsa Zsa Gabor, who'd also been a guest. Gabor wore a necklace of chestnut-size diamonds. She made a point of nervously covering the necklace with her hands and darting glances at Sutton. When the elevator reached the lobby Sutton held the door for Gabor. Ever the gentleman. But as she walked past he said, Honey you can take your hands off your jewels. I'm retired.

As Sutton's celebrity grew, so did his audacity. Reporter thinks about the first time he saw Sutton's face materialize on the TV screen during a Yankees game. A commercial for, of all things, the New Britain Bank and Trust Company of New Britain, Connecticut. It was funny, of course, but also strangely disillusioning to see Sutton endorsing a new kind of charge card, with the cardholder's photo embossed on the front. A new weapon against identity theft.

Cut to Sutton smiling for the camera.

Now, when I say I'm Willie Sutton, people believe me!

Cue announcer urging folks to bring their money down to the bank.

Tell them Willie Sutton sent you.

The commercial made Reporter almost angry. Not that Reporter wanted to see Sutton robbing banks again. But he hated like hell to see Sutton shilling for them.

Sutton insisted to Reporter that he had no compunction about shooting that commercial. Willie's got expenses kid—you know what a pack of Chesterfields costs these days? He wouldn't even admit to feeling the slightest pang of guilt in 1979 when the housing market collapsed and the stock market crashed and the Fed warned about bank failures. Thousands of people wiped out by unchecked greed. Again. *That's where the money was*—the apocryphal Suttonism is now invoked every day by some journalist or economist, professor or politician, not to explain the motive of a Depression-era bank robber, but to explain generic human avarice. People do things, all kinds of things, because that's where the money is.

The financial crisis is the only reason Reporter's editor agreed to send him to Florida now, late December 1980, seven weeks after Sutton died from emphysema. Reporter's editor is several years younger than Reporter, and he doesn't remember Willie Sutton. But the economy is on everyone's mind and he liked Reporter's pitch. An old bank robber who once spent Christmas with our paper? It's kitschy, the editor said. Give me two thousand words.

* * *

REPORTER EATS DINNER AT A STEAK HOUSE IN THE LITTLE town where Sutton spent his last days, Spring Hill, a pleasant nowhere nestled in a notch along Florida's west coast. The waitress is blond, sun-burnished, squeezed into skintight bellbottoms. Reporter is no longer with the woman he was dating when he met Sutton. Or the woman who came after her, or the woman who came after her. When the waitress brings his salmon Reporter asks if Willie Sutton used to come here.

Willie? Sure. He was a regular. Sweet old dude. Always ordered the porterhouse. With a glass of milk—always.

Reporter is about to ask if Sutton was a big tipper, if any tips ever went missing. He can't get the words out before the waitress is called away.

He phones Sutton's sister, hoping to see a copy of Sutton's letters or journals. Or the novel. It was called *The Statue in the Park*, Sutton once said. The hero was a banker whose life is a lie. Reporter asked to see a copy, many times, but Sutton always demurred. Now the sister won't return Reporter's calls. And he can't locate Sutton's daughter. Elusiveness—it runs in the family.

After two days in Florida, two days visiting the local libraries and the local banks and the local bars, Reporter is due to leave tomorrow. But he's not ready. He can't shake the sense that he's missed something, that he's failed to find the thing he came down here to find, though he can't say exactly what that thing is. Some clue, some sign. Surely a man who escaped three maximum-security prisons would be unable to resist the challenge of sending word from the Other Side. A kind of hello. A posthumous wink.

Reporter admits to himself, driving from the steak house back to the hotel, that it's a ridiculous hope. But no more ridiculous than being fond of a hardened, unrepentant felon. Then he corrects himself. He wasn't fond in the usual sense of the word. He wouldn't want to live in a world full of Willie Suttons. He's simply not sure that he'd want to live in a world with *no* Willie Suttons.

Reporter lies on the hotel bed, rereads a few pages of Sutton's second memoir. He laughs. Sutton must be the only person ever in the history of literature to write two memoirs that directly contradict each other, even on basic biographical facts. In one memoir, for instance, Sutton says that before breaking out of Sing Sing with Egan, he'd arranged to have an empty getaway car waiting outside the prison. In the other memoir Sutton says the mother of his daughter drove the getaway car. And yet Reporter can still hear Sutton, more than once, describing the way Bess looked at the wheel as he and Egan came running up the hill.

In one memoir Sutton meticulously describes robbing the Manufacturers Trust of Queens. In the other memoir he swears he didn't do it. And so on.

How many of the contradictions in Sutton's memoirs, or in his mind, were willful, and how many were dementia, Reporter doesn't know. His current theory is that Sutton lived three separate lives. The one he remembered, the one he told people about, the one that really happened. Where those lives over-lapped, no one can say, and God help anyone who tries. More than likely, Sutton himself didn't know.

Reporter has looked everywhere for Bess Endner, but she's vanished. He's searched high and low for Margaret—again, no trace. He's obtained hundreds of documents from the FBI, pored through scores of old newspapers and magazines and court transcripts, rooted through long-lost police files on Arnold Schuster, files he found rotting in the attic of a retired police sergeant. It all leads nowhere. FBI files contradict newspaper clips, newspaper clips contradict police files, and Sutton's two self-negating memoirs refute everything. The more Reporter digs, the less he knows, until it seems that he spent Christmas eleven years ago with a shadow of a phantom.

Among the hundreds of FBI documents is one hea‍
Interesting Narrative. A summary of Sutton's psyche, it v.
written by an agent in 1950, when Sutton was the nation's mos‍
wanted fugitive:

*Religion: Sutton was a Roman Catholic but his belief was
destroyed through reading.*

*Leisure habits: Spent most of his time reading, attended
movies once in two weeks, dramas once in six months, attended
football games, took long auto rides for pleasure, and smoked.
Read classics.*

*Personality and temperament: Introverted temperament, chronic
but benign; depression with occasional suicidal moods; emotional
instability with suggestion of sensory petit mal; tendency to worry
and anxiety; general neurotic failure to achieve happiness.*

Except for the business about reading, and smoking, Reporter
doesn't recognize in this Interesting Narrative the Sutton he
knew. Which doesn't mean it's inaccurate. All we can have of
Sutton, of each other, is Interesting Narratives.

Last week Reporter visited the Farm Colony, and Attica, and
Sing Sing, and Eastern State, where he suffered an attack of
claustrophobia in a cell exactly like Sutton's. Eastern State is now
a national historic landmark, and though the curator didn't know
exactly which cell was Willie's, they were all alike, all equally
squalid and inhuman. Reporter left with a new appreciation of
Sutton's grit, and more questions than ever about why Sutton
wasn't able to put his good qualities to better use.

Reporter didn't set out to become such a hard-core
Suttonologist. He doesn't know why he feels compelled to accu-
mulate all this information, enough for fifty articles. Last night
on the phone his editor, losing patience, called it jerkoffery.
Reporter answered coolly, in a tone Sutton would have
commended, that at least it wasn't clusterfuckery.

Reporter tells himself that he wants to know all he can about on because he's a reporter, driven by curiosity, and because s an American, titillated by crime. But mainly he wants to know ecause of Bess. She's only part of Sutton's story, but for Reporter she's the central part. It doesn't matter if the old clips seem to suggest that Sutton's love for her was delusional. All love is delusional. What matters is that the love endured. Near the end of Sutton's life he was still talking about Bess, still describing her to his ghostwriter. There were other women in Sutton's past—he married at least twice—but he wrote about them with detachment, in contrast to the delicacy and melancholy with which he recalled Bess. Whether or not Bess returned Sutton's love, in any portion, she's the key to Sutton's identity. And maybe to Reporter's. As a writer, as a man, Reporter has spent much of his life in two vaguely related quests—storytelling and love. Sutton never gave up on either. Through all his confinements and wanderings, he was a storyteller and a lover to the end. Reporter finds this inspiring. He finds it sad. Maybe Reporter is only projecting his psyche onto a dead bank robber, but so what? Storytelling, like love, requires some degree of projection. And if someone, someday, wants to project their psyche onto Reporter, so be it.

Closing Sutton's memoir, Reporter clicks on the TV. The news. A story about John Lennon's murder two weeks ago in New York. A story about President-elect Ronald Reagan promising to deregulate banks. A story about rising unemployment, and another about global population nearing five billion. A confusion of people. Finally, a feature about Christmas celebrations at a local roadside park, the oldest roadside park in Florida, called Weeki Wachee. A bizarre little rabbit hole, it's a glass dome built on an underwater spring, with pretty girls in mermaid costumes performing underwater acrobatics.

It sits just five miles down the road from where Sutton died.

Reporter jumps off the bed.

* * *

turns right on Cortez, left on U.S. 19, follows the signs unt. sees plastic flags along a wall. Then a tall turquoise statue o mermaid. It looks like the Statue of Liberty. Reporter never realized how much the Statue of Liberty looks like a mermaid.

Reporter buys a ticket and a program, which says one hundred million gallons of water bubble up daily from vast underground caverns beneath the park. Just fifty feet down the water surges up so violently, it will rip the face mask off a diver. Which is why no one knows just how far down the caverns go. No one, the program says, has ever gotten to the bottom of it.

Reporter enters a small theater. Instead of a stage there's an enormous glass wall. Music starts up, a sheer curtain rises, revealing an enormous canyon of blue-purple water. Suddenly on the other side of the glass are two mermaids. They wave at Reporter, and he forgets that they're pretending to be mermaids. They're too beautiful to be pretending. They swim backwards, sideways, upside down, their long blond hair twirling in their wake. They twist, tumble, waggle their fins, exult in the absence of gravity. Every few minutes they swim to the side of the tank and take a long suck on an air hose. The only break in the vivid dream.

After the show Reporter runs backstage, finds the dressing room. A sign on the door reads: Mermaids Only. He approaches the first mermaid who emerges. He introduces himself, says he's a reporter writing about Willie Sutton. The mermaid, now wearing her walking-around fin, made of shimmering aquamarine skintight fabric, like a pencil skirt that goes a foot past her feet, gives him a blank look.

You know, Reporter says, Willie Sutton? The bank robber? He died last month?

Blank.

Anyway, Reporter says, I just have this hunch that Sutton

have spent a lot of time here—at the end. That he might ＿ stopped by this dressing room. Maybe spoke to you or one ＿ the other mermaids?

She runs her fingers through her long wet hair, trying to untangle it. Guys come back here all the time, she says.

Right, Reporter says. But this guy would have referred to himself in the third person. Willie thinks you're beautiful. Willie thinks you look like a girl he knew in Poughkeepsie. That kind of thing.

The mermaid adjusts the waistband of her fin. I don't know what to tell you, mister. The name doesn't ring a bell.

Maybe you could ask some of your fellow mermaids?

She takes a deep breath, as if sucking on the air hose. Hold on.

She pivots—not easy in her fabric fin—and waddles back into the dressing room.

Reporter leans against the wall. A minute passes. Two. He's never smoked in his life, but he has the strangest craving for a Chesterfield.

The dressing room door opens. A different mermaid emerges. She's not quite as pretty as the other mermaid. But—blond hair, blue eyes—her beauty seems more wholesome. More old-fashioned. Willie's type, Reporter thinks.

She too is wearing a fabric fin. Skin-tight. Gold-specked. She sashays toward Reporter, smiling.

Reporter knows, he sees it in her blue eyes, she's got an envelope containing a letter from Willie. Or else the manuscript of *The Statue in the Park*. She'll say Reporter's name, and Reporter will ask how she knows his name, and she'll say: Willie—he had a hunch you'd be stopping by. Then she and Reporter will go for coffee, and discover a thousand things in common, and eventually fall in love, and get married, and have babies, and their life together will be Willie's everlasting gift to Reporter. He can see it all. He reaches out his hand, starts to speak, but the mermaid sidles around him, past him, into the arms of a young man just behind him.

You look beautiful, the young man tells her.

Uck, she whispers, I can't wait to go home and get out of this stupid costume.

Reporter walks slowly out to his car. He drives to the airport. Along the way he turns on the radio. A story about the first-ever space shuttle, which is due to blast off in six months, directly east of Spring Hill. Reporter looks out over the black swamps and the dense woods and pictures the launch. He knows Sutton would give anything to see it. He suddenly remembers something Sutton said. Though it was eleven years ago, almost to the day, he hears that craggy voice, that smoke-cured Brooklyn accent, filling the car, clearer than the radio, and it makes Reporter smile.

Hey kid—did you know that when the astronauts got back to earth, Collins was a mess. He couldn't eat, he couldn't sleep. He'd drift off in the middle of a sentence. The man could not function. Finally he told the docs at NASA that after gazing at the moon all that time, after orbiting it again and again and never actually touching it, he'd fallen hopelessly in love. His words, not mine. In love with the moon—imagine kid? Imagine how fuckin lonely you have to be to fall in love with the moon?

ACKNOWLEDGMENTS

Deepest thanks to Andre Agassi, Hildy Linn Angius, Ellen Archer, Spencer Barnett, Violet Barnett, Lyle Barnett, Aimee Bell, Elisabeth Dyssegaard, Fred Favero, Gary Fisketjon, Rich Gold, Paul Hurley, Bill Husted, Mort Janklow, Ginger Martin, Eric Mercado, McGraw Milhaven, Dorothy Moehringer, Sam O'Brien, J. P. Parenti, Joni Parenti, Kit Rachlis, Derk Richardson, Jaimee Rose, Jack La Torre, and Peternelle van Arsdale.